• BOOKS BY LOREN D. ESTLEMAN •

Kill Zone

Roses Are Dead

Any Man's Death

Motor City Blue

Angel Eyes

The Midnight Man

The Glass Highway

Sugartown

Every Brilliant Eye

Lady Yesterday

Downriver

Silent Thunder

Sweet Women Lie

Never Street

The Witchfinder

The Hours of the Virgin

A Smile on the Face of the
 Tiger

City of Widows*

The High Rocks*

Billy Gashade*

Stamping Ground*

Aces & Eights*

Journey of the Dead*

Jitterbug*

Thunder City*

The Rocky Mountain Mov-
 ing Picture Association*

The Master Executioner*

Black Powder, White Smoke*

White Desert*

Sinister Heights

Something Borrowed,
 Something Black*

Port Hazard*

Poison Blonde*

Retro*

Little Black Dress*

Nicotine Kiss*

The Undertaker's Wife*

The Adventures of Johnny
 Vermillion*

American Detective*

Gas City*

Frames*

The Branch and the
 Scaffold*

Alone*

The Book of Murdock*

Roy & Lillie: A Love Story*

The Left-Handed Dollar*

Infernal Angels*

Burning Midnight*

Alive!*

The Confessions of Al
 Capone*

Don't Look for Me*

Ragtime Cowboys*

You Know Who Killed Me*

The Long High Noon*

*A Forge Book

The
Long High
Noon

⫷ **AND** ⫸

The Adventures of
Johnny
Vermillion

· **Loren D. Estleman** ·

A Tom Doherty Associates Book / New York

THE LONG HIGH NOON AND THE ADVENTURES OF
JOHNNY VERMILLION

The Long High Noon copyright © 2015 by Loren D. Estleman

The Adventures of Johnny Vermillion copyright © 2006 by Loren D. Estleman

All rights reserved.

A Forge Book
Published by Tom Doherty Associates, LLC
175 Fifth Avenue
New York, NY 10010

www.tor-forge.com

Forge® is a registered trademark of Tom Doherty Associates, LLC.

ISBN 978-0-7653-8801-8

Our books may be purchased in bulk for promotional, educational, or business use. Please contact your local bookseller or the Macmillan Corporate and Premium Sales Department at 1-800-221-7945, extension 5442, or by e-mail at MacmillanSpecialMarkets@macmillan.com.

First Edition: June 2016

Printed in the United States of America

0 9 8 7 6 5 4 3 2

Contents

The
Long High
Noon

To the memory of Jory Sherman;
a force of nature, now
inexplicably stilled

Love is a kind of warfare.

—OVID

1

You never get a second chance to make a good first impression.

No one but Randy Locke and Frank Farmer knew just what it was that had blackened the blood between them, but it didn't lose its kick with time.

That it had to do with a woman suggested itself right away, and when fifteen years after their first run-in Abraham Cripplehorn christened her Mississippi Belle, the legend was complete. The fact that the writer/promoter had named her after the boat he kept in Gulfport was universally overlooked: Romance is everyone's weakness.

Money was the inevitable second suggestion; but ranch hands didn't covet it, only the fun that comes with it, and the effects didn't last long enough to justify violence.

If either remembered the actual cause, it rode drag behind the standing strategy, which was to annihilate the other man whenever the pair wandered onto the same plot of real property. It was the one fixed thing in a changing West, and it was in place so long, and was so thoroughly a part of their alchemical makeup, I really think they got so they could smell each other across a slaughteryard.

Most likely whatever set them on the prod happened when both were working for the old Circle X in south Texas just after the end of the Rebellion, potting and being potted at by Don Alvarado's vaqueros across the border over cattle of indistinct claim. Randy and Frank were a close match with pistols, although Frank had the edge with a carbine after years of sniping Confederates from trees. He saw it as a point of honor not to use that advantage over Randy, because he didn't want suspicions of imparity to take the shine off dancing a jig on his enemy's grave.

Physically, the two were indistinguishable from the lot that flocked to the big ranches looking for work in those heady early years of the North American cattle trade. Randy was short and thick, and had the distracting habit of blinking constantly, his eyes being sensitive to sun and dust, which were the principal exports of the desert Southwest after stringy beef and chili peppers that burned like fire ants going down and like molten iron coming out. He favored Mexican sombreros with umbrella brims to cut some of the glare, and which some of his less-sensitive colleagues said made him resemble a roofing nail. Randy is generally reckoned to have been about twenty-two at the time of that first confrontation. Frank was lean, looked taller than he was because of his long legs, but when he sat a horse his hat came level with Randy's when he rode alongside. Both men sported whiskers, Randy's on the slovenly side, Frank's trimmed into neat imperials whenever a barber was handy. The entry of his birth in the family Bible in Pennsylvania put him at twenty-four in that year of 1868. He was tidy in his dress and grooming, whether he was wearing wool worsted or faded dungarees. His fellow hands said he could roll in cowflop on Saturday afternoon and take a duchess to a dance Saturday night. They called him Lord Percival when he was out of earshot: He was too good with a long gun, and his fists when it wasn't inside reach, to chance it otherwise. He told Shuck Ballard he spent half his wages on boots and tailoring.

"What about the other half?" Shuck asked.

"Frittered away on fool things."

Curiously, Randy, round-faced and not given overmuch to hygiene, seldom wanted for female company of his own. It wasn't unusual for him to enter a saloon with one on his arm, and sometimes both.

"I treat 'em like ladies, that's the secret," he said. "I always take off my socks. Sometimes they don't even charge."

When that got back to Frank, he curled his lip. "That little stump'd have to pay a sheep."

The first time they turned their pistols away from Mexicans and on each other was in the Bluebottle Saloon in El Paso, from either end of the fifty-foot bar the owner touted as the longest west of St. Louis. Both missed, being of an alcoholic temperament at the time, but stout Randy corrected that the next morning when he rousted lanky Frank out of a tub of bathwater in the Cathay Gardens on Mesa Street and broke one of his short ribs with a .44 slug when Frank lunged for his Colt in its holster hanging on the back of a chair.

He recovered, of course, or our story would end here, and he went looking for Randy, who'd been turned out of the outfit for shorthanding it just before the drive to Kansas, when every man jack was worth twice the price of his string. (The Circle X foreman, George Purdy, was infamous for solutions that doubled the original problems. He wound up a state senator in Indiana.) Frank caught up with Randy in a stiff Wyoming winter in the middle of wolfing season and shot his horse out from under him—a result of windage, which is easier to miscalculate when you're using a short gun at a distance. The horse rolled over on Randy, dumping fifty dollars in bounty pelts lashed behind the cantle and shattering his leg.

This a little more than evened the account, because while Frank's wound had healed, leaving him with nothing worse than a throbbing misery when it snowed or rained, Randy's injury left him with a limp and not much prospect of ranch employment unless he put in for cook, and prolonged exposure to greasy fumes gave him the Tucson Two-Step, and an unfortunate nickname among the hands. He reckoned that as one more charge against Frank's side of the ledger.

As it happened, though, Randy's fortunes improved as a direct result.

The buffalo harvest was coming to its summit, with the Industrial Revolution going full tilt back East and in perpetual need of leather to make the belts to drive the gears of its manufactories, lap robes selling like tortillas among the carriage trade, and the army offering to redeem empty cartridge shells for cash in order to offset hunting expenses and encourage the starvation of the pestiferous Indian. If the winter was long enough and the thermometer stuck on zero, the big shaggies grew coats that dragged the ground and made an enterprising man's fortune in a season.

Randy oiled his good Ballard rifle, bought an elm-wood wagon and four months' worth of tinned sardines and peaches, and set off for the prairie with an experienced skinner and a half-breed guide. They prospered. Notwithstanding the inconvenience of a three-month head cold and one frostbitten cheek that never did heal completely, Randy's share when they sold their first load of hides came to more than he'd seen roping and branding semi-tame bovines the previous four years.

The breed guide, who for unexplained reasons went by the name of Prince Robert, asked him how he intended to invest his share.

"Now I know how to hunt buffler, I'm fixing to spend every last dime tracking down Frank Farmer, putting a slug in his brain pan, and curing his hide in the hottest sun I can find this side of Pharaoh—and the other side, too, comes to that."

Prince Robert didn't pursue the point. He'd spent months

of nights hearing his charge muttering Frank's name in his sleep, modifying it in terms that would shame a Virginia City bullwhacker. In the language of his Pawnee father, the guide referred to him in his thoughts as Snake-Who-Drinks-His-Own-Venom. He got his fill of it after one season, turned down the offer of another at twice the percentage, and signed on with the Seventh Cavalry, with whom he spilled out his life's blood on the field the Sioux and Cheyenne called the Greasy Grass; no doubt thanking the Man Above with his last breath he didn't have to listen to Randy Locke consigning Frank Farmer to Hell Everlasting any more.

Needless to say, Randy's happier financial condition hadn't made him grateful to his nemesis. He knew that game leg was not the result of an altruistic act. If anything, prosperity gave him the luxury of turning his attention from the humdrum concern of survival to refining the details of his vengeance. Over open fires he chewed on buffalo tongue, pretending it was Frank's liver, and whenever he rode into a town to pick up supplies and provisions, he circulated a description of the man he hated among all the locals.

They weren't much help, being locals and not inclined to travel and gather news in those brief few years when railroad construction was progressing at a crawl against natural obstructions and hostile tribes determined to eject the white man from their ancestral hunting grounds. If anything, his zeal for information made some of them suspect him of being a bounty-killer, one of those flightless raptors the war had spewed out into the frontier, or worse, a lawman, and the rare drifter who might have been persuaded to part with a valuable morsel of intelligence took it on the scout because there was paper out on him offering a reward over some little misunderstanding in some other territory. The winter went by with no response to

Randy's queries beyond blank faces and shrugs and the occasional fast exit aboard a lathered mount.

This made him poor company even among the women, who had reason enough to hate their own and sense enough to chalk it up to circumstances beyond their control. There followed a long dry spell between feminine comforts.

Frank meanwhile was working for the Kansas Pacific Railroad, grading track and keeping his Winchester handy to pick off Sioux raiding parties through that same buffalo country. It's quite possible that he and Randy spied each other at a distance without realizing it; since the great brutes had grown too wary of man to venture within a thousand yards of a rowdy construction gang, the man who hunted them altered his course wide upon spotting one at work.

True, there were times when these men paused in the midst of reloading or spitting out coffee grounds, turned their faces to the wind, listening—sniffing?—for something familiar and despised, then shook their heads and returned to the necessity of the moment; both were still too new to the sensation of blind hatred to trust their instincts completely. And so once again their reunion depended upon fate.

2

Should auld acquaintance be forgot?

At this point you may be wondering who I am.

It's my fault, for slipping into first-person a while back, violating every journalist's rule about not making yourself a part of the story; but try as I will I can't figure a way to strike out the reference.

Well, we know what's the oldest profession, but story-telling surely comes next. The guy had to tell *some*one, and he wasn't about to tell it as if it happened to someone else.

I'm a writer, or I've tried to be. I joined the Circle X a few months after Randy Locke and Frank Farmer pulled out, leaving behind their legend. I was just off two semesters with the Columbia School of Creative Writing, and eager to glean firsthand experience to fuel my work; but my superabundant vocabulary made me a suspicious character in the bunkhouse, and my time there ruined my grammar for anything but sensational fiction. My bedroom is papered with rejections from *Frank Leslie's Illustrated Newspaper* and *The New England Journal,* among a dozen others, and sometime or other it dawned on me that I wasn't the next Mark Twain. I labored with Buffalo Bill's Wild West, grinding out fanciful tales of William F. Cody's adventures under the house names of Prentiss Ingraham and Ned Buntline for the gift shop, and a generation later scenarios for Thomas Ince and—for six delirious days—D.W. Griffith.

In between I waited tables in railroad hotels, tended bar in Denver and Las Vegas, New Mexico, battled bedbugs the size of lobsters in the county jail in Nebraska City, and sweated out six months in a laundry in San Francisco—cheek-by-jowl with the great Jack London, although I didn't find that out until much later, when Jack was too famous for me to approach with a humble request for a reference—and in all that time I could count the number of times I actually laid eyes on Randy Locke and Frank Farmer on the toes of Long John Silver's foot. Well, that's more than anyone else you could name. I guess you could call me a pilot fish, sucking the saltwater sweat off a couple of sharks who are all but forgotten in the great current of history's ever-rolling ocean.

My name? Forget it. You would anyway, five minutes

after I told it. But I can make one unique claim: I'm the only soul living who can tell you anything you want to know about the longest gunfight in the history of the American West.

Not that you'd want to hear it. Their names don't resound with the thunder of a Wild Bill Hickok or a Wyatt Earp or even a Neanderthal like Clay Allison, who had the good grace to end his murderous bullying ways under the wheels of his own wagon when he was too drunk to hold his seat at the reins. As a result, my name wouldn't ring any farther than a lead nickel bouncing across shifting sand.

But I was there, and where were you?

When the K.P.R. spur reached Abilene, Frank put in for provisions—not before stopping in the establishment of a German tailor to order a Prince Albert coat, three linen shirts, and two pairs of striped trousers—and was emerging from the mercantile with a double armload of bacon, coffee, and one hundred rounds of ammunition, when he heard a familiar voice.

"Farmer! Palm your piece!"

Randy was smoking a cigar he'd just purchased from the profit of his latest delivery of hides. It was smoldering in the corner of his mouth when he dropped his hand to leather. Frank let go of his packages, meat, beans, and ordnance spilling into the gutter, and went for his hardware. Both men drew simultaneously; their reports sounded as one.

Frank's slug grazed Randy's collarbone, missing the big artery on the side of his neck by a quarter inch, and exiting out the back, taking along a measure of flesh and muscle. Randy's aim was higher still in his haste, and sliced off the top of Frank's left ear.

Both men required medical attention, but because

Randy's condition was more serious he was still recovering on a cot in the room behind the doctor's office, a place of yellow oak, square bottles of laudanum and horse liniment on shelves, with a reek of alcohol as solid as any of the furnishings, when he opened his eyes to see what appeared to be a two-headed demon coming through the door with a pistol.

This doctor was a great proponent of preventing infection by enveloping fresh wounds in yards of gauze and white cotton; a toe severed in a wood-cutting accident was good for a rod, and the victim of a serious miscalculation by a barber had tottered out of the office looking like a giraffe with a cut throat. Another inch or two of wrap and Frank Farmer wouldn't have gotten his injured ear through the doorway.

Randy, fogged up as he was with tincture of opium, had sense enough to know that devil or mortal enemy, the intruder was cause for swift action. He rolled off the edge of the cot an instant before his pillow exploded. With the air filled with feathers, disinfectant, and the stink of spent powder, he managed to grasp the lip of his white-enamel chamber pot and skim it in the general direction of his assailant.

He was lucky in the trajectory. Frank yelped.

The cry woke the doctor, an addict to his own painkillers who had passed out in his horsehair leather desk chair from the effects of self-treatment. He lurched to his feet and after some groping found the door to the back room, then managed to manhandle Frank back into the office. This and the action of disarming him took place somewhat more easily than it might have under most circumstances, because the chamber pot had struck Frank's mangled ear as surely as if it had been aimed with precision rather than hurled in blind panic. The fiery pain distracted him, making him easier to manipulate.

A summons to the law in the persons of a marshal freshly retired from buffalo skinning and two deputies who'd served with the Army of the Potomac deposited Frank in jail. There inside bars made from flat steel strips held fast by rivets, the doctor opened his bag and amputated the rest of the ear with one snip of his scissors, the heavy projectile having nearly finished the job.

Frank, remember, was vain of his appearance. He kept his teeth clean with baking powder when he could get it, yellow soap when powder was unavailable, and took a bath every other week when he was in town. When the flesh healed, he borrowed the use of a catalogue belonging to the doctor and ordered a prosthesis from a medical supply firm in San Francisco. It arrived three weeks later, a shell-shaped object molded from pink gutta-percha in a small box with the firm's name stamped on it in gold with instructions for its care and application. These required fixing it in place with a daily dosage of sealing wax, which had a demoralizing habit of softening and letting go in the heat, usually at inopportune times. He fell to keeping it in his pocket when he wasn't in civilization or among strangers. The inconvenience and its humiliating nature put Randy's account deep in the red, to Frank's estimation.

"An eye for an ear," he told the man in the cell adjoining his.

"That ain't exactly what the Book says," replied the other, who was in for lascivious conduct in broad daylight with a Rumanian woman.

"Randy Locke ain't exactly in the Book."

But payment was delayed.

By the time Frank was released from jail, Randy had returned to the buffalo hunt, conscious of the fact that his shooting arm needed time to recover before he took on anyone more challenging than a dumb brute. He was off to

Nebraska, with a new skinner who wasn't nearly as stimulating company as the old, but the other man had found work with another outfit while Randy was down. This time Randy didn't hire a guide, the plains all being pretty much alike, down to the yellow-ocher grass and the same clapboard saloon, livery, and mercantile everywhere there was water enough to breed mosquitoes. He carried neither maps nor a compass. A man who couldn't identify the North Star when he saw it might as well wear a stiff collar and live in town.

Frank's fine for disturbing the public peace emptied his poke, so he rode back to the railhead to shoot Indians and grade track. The first gandy dancer who kidded him about getting his ear bit off by a Texas Street whore got a slug in his foot for his joke; the foreman who bound the wound, a former medical orderly with the Fifth Mississippi Volunteers, told him he was fortunate that Frank was saving his homicidal impulses for Randy Locke. Their relationship, with some healthy encouragement from bored newspaper publishers, was by this time entering the country of frontier legend.

The buffalo meanwhile were entering the country of the extinct.

The bottom didn't fall out of the market so much as it fell out from under the buffalo. Where the great herds had darkened the plains only a few years before, spilling over the nearest rise like thunderclouds rolling down from the Divide, little now remained but scattered bones. Soon even they were gone, scoured by pickers to sell by the ton to manufacturers to pulverize and run sugar through to remove impurities and to press and bake into fine china. Few easterners realized they owed their sweet pies and Christmas table dressings to a tick-ridden beast. Overnight, it seemed, the stacks of stiff green hides vanished from pole barns put up by buyers, and the buyers themselves disappeared into other enterprises, usually on one or the other coast by way of the new Transcontinental Railroad.

Randy drank up half his profits in a succession of establishments given to that practice, gambled the other half away on games of chance, and took his meals and shelter serving time in various jails for drunk and disorderly. One early morning he woke up in an alley in Omaha with his boots missing, his pockets turned inside out, and a hangover the size of Texas.

"Never too late to make a fresh start," he said, fumbling for his watch and finding the silver chain snapped in half and the timepiece gone.

But the ranches he applied to all had cooks they were satisfied with, and the work he picked up loading grainsacks into wagons and swamping vomit and sawdust off saloon floors staled after a week or so. For a time he panhandled for money for drinks, food, and lodging, in that order, but after a couple of months his clothes looked like livery rubdown rags held together by rotten thread, dirt crusted his face and hands, and he stank like spoiled potatoes. There were no women in his life to bail him out when he was pressed into a work gang for vagrancy, shoveling horseshit out of a stable in which the county sheriff had a half-interest and cutting the throats of steers for a butcher whose brother-in-law sat on the bench of the circuit court. It was a lot of sweat and time, and none of it brought him an inch closer to Frank Farmer and the end of their transactions. He reckoned at that point he'd hit stony bottom.

Frank wasn't finding life any easier.

After the buffalo ran out, the Indians returned to reservations to subsist on government rations, when they weren't being embezzled by unscrupulous traders and Indian agents from Washington. The raids on survey parties and track-layers fell off, and with it the demand for sharpshooters to defend against them, particularly with the army taking up the slack, rounding up strays from the reservations and providing the same protection on the taxpayers' ticket that Frank had supplied for wages. The Great Undertaking having been completed at Promontory Point, the railroads laid off men in hordes, including part-time graders like Frank.

When he was offered work by the Santa Fe line as a common guard, dozing in some stuffy strong-car hoping for an assault by a gang of highwaymen just to break up the monotony, he demanded the time he had coming and rode to the nearest poker game. In a mining camp in Colorado he shot and killed a man over one pat hand too many and barely escaped a lynch mob when the deputy who'd arrested him, a naïve New Hampshire native lured West by dime novels, changed clothes with him and took his place in the cell while Frank left by a back door. (The mob, which had come there to lynch *some*one, strung up the deputy.)

Frank got away on a wind-broken bay he'd managed to steal from a corral, without a firearm or a cartwheel dollar to his name, just the clothes on his back and his Saturday-night ear in his pocket. He camped out under the stars, avoiding towns where the Thunder Creek Committee of Public Vigilance might have shinplasters out on him offering a reward for his hide, and stoned jackrabbits to survive.

His skill with a piece of shale did not measure up to his marksmanship with a carbine. In the wee hours of a frosty Colorado morning he started awake, convinced Randy Locke was standing over him aiming his Colt between his eyes, and in his panic kicked dust at a scrubby jack pine. When he recovered his senses he knew the vision for a hallucination caused by hunger, aided by a dose of Rocky

Mountain Spotted Fever. Wasting away, his belt buckle scraping a gall in his spine, burning hot when his teeth weren't chattering, skin bleeding where he'd scratched it raw, didn't distress him so much as the prospect of squandering his last hours fighting ghosts instead of Randy.

He calculated he was as low as low got.

Then God opened a window.

3

A houseguest should never arrive empty-handed, nor should a host point out the fact.

Two windows, actually.

Frank's sabbatical in the wilderness turned out to be a stroke of luck. A team of young prospectors found him close to death and brought him to their camp, where the old witch woman who ran the laundry nursed him back to strength with some remedies she'd learned in Albania. During his recuperation she told him, in broken English, of a drifter she'd treated for a fractured skull that had remained undiagnosed since he left Utah Territory weeks earlier. It seemed it had been laid open by a wolfer named Locke with a bottle in Salt Lake City over some difference of opinion the patient couldn't remember. The description he'd given her matched Randy.

The old woman let Frank repay his debt working the washboard, and when he was well enough to travel gave him a bear's-claw necklace she'd made as a hex against bad luck. From there, walking and accepting rides from passersby, he went to Pueblo, where he traded the necklace to a greenhorn for a toothless roan, which got him as far as Grand Junction before it keeled over and died. He stockclerked in a general merchandise store for a month, bought a decent mount and a Remington revolver with a cracked grip but not too much play in the action, and lit a shuck for Mormon country.

While the buzzards were still sizing Frank up in Colorado, Randy Locke was fattening his bankroll in Wyoming. He had what happened to the buffalo to thank for it.

Its population swollen by the easy life of gorging on millions of skinned carcasses left to rot, the Great Plains Wolf crunched down the last overlooked bone and turned its attention to cattle. The ranchers objected, and offered hefty bounties for fresh pelts.

Randy, who was no stranger to wolfing, approved, and in the case of some white-muzzled veterans shrewd enough to avoid traps and poison, cashed them in for rewards worthy of a gang of human desperadoes. Soon he could afford to dine in the best restaurants in Laramie and Cheyenne and sleep between clean hotel sheets every night he wasn't working.

He could afford to, but he didn't.

The improvement in his finances didn't extend to the habits he'd acquired as a piteous drunk. Waiters served him only at back doors, where the stink of old guts on his rags wouldn't offend fellow diners, and hotel clerks refused him accommodation entirely. He slept in stables and out in the weather and practiced his draw for hours, wearing down the scar tissue that slowed his right arm. In his impatience he shifted back and forth until he could clear leather and hit his mark with either hand as well as most men did with the one they favored.

It wasn't the wolves he was practicing for. The local species was dying so fast it was getting so all a man had to do was give one of them a mean look and it would roll over and kick itself still. It had taken the white man a century to kill off the buffalo, but only two years to send the Great Plains Wolf to extinction.

Poisoning was the cause more than hunting. With meat herds falling prey to the packs, it was considered a breach of good manners to venture out on any sort of errand without including a bottle of strychnine crystals in one's gear. If a man came upon a carcass that still had meat on its bones, he tainted it. A single crystal killed more scavenging grays than an experienced hunter with a repeater.

People, too. A fellow down on his luck found out his fortunes hadn't changed when he fed his family a loin of windfall venison and watched them contort and die. The frontier was a hard place, harder still with the arrival of Man.

A great shift was taking place. The Indian problem was all but settled: President Grant had authorized the plan of General Terry, Captain Benteen, and Colonel Custer to bottle up the Sioux and Cheyenne nations in an obscure valley in Montana Territory, the wild beeves had been cleared to make room for domestic cattle, and predators were reduced to roving independent operators named Hardin, James, and Younger, with bounties on their heads like the wolves themselves. Homesteaders were fencing in the open range, building schools and churches on grounds formerly reserved for pagan worship. Soon the frontier would be as much a part of dead history as tricorne hats and powdered wigs. If a man stood still and pointed his ears toward the East, he could hear the earth turning.

But two men refused to stand still. When they had food in their bellies and full pokes on their hips, each had the other in his craw.

When Wyoming Territory ran scarce of lobos, Randy crossed into Utah, where he busted a jug of Old Pepper over a fellow's head for commenting on his odor and when the law came looking for him withdrew above the treeline to trap and shoot wolves. He gave his victim a month either to die or to get better and the tin stars to lose interest, then returned to the city on the big lake to sell his pelts, celebrate his prosperity, and ponder where to start looking for Frank Farmer.

Who was looking for him.

The Latter-Day Saints were close-mouthed in the presence of strangers, particularly when they were asking about other strangers: The whole population seemed to deny any knowledge of English when Frank pleaded for help finding his long-lost brother, who couldn't be reached to be told of their mother's death, and kept its hands at its sides when he offered money.

Mormons weren't supposed to partake of hard liquor, but he found that not to be universal his first night in Salt Lake City when he lifted flat-brimmed hats off men sleeping in alleys, looking for a familiar round face with a squint. All he got was tangled beards, fermented breath, and best wishes on his salvation.

"Save the saving for yourself," he said, dropping their hats back onto their faces.

He was about to give it up as a cold trail when a druggist he bribed with a double eagle, a skinny gentile with ears like a ewer and an Adam's apple that stuck out like a third elbow, told him he sold two bottles of snakebite medicine nightly to a tramp who answered Randy's description.

"As a rule I'd offer him a snake just in case," said the pill salesman, "but he stinks up the alley. The cats are starting to complain."

"Where's he hang his hat?"

"Don't know and don't care, just as long as it's downwind."

The sun was sinking toward the flats, painting purple fingers on the brine.

"He been in yet tonight?"

"Never by daylight. He got into some kind of trouble a while back, but why he bothers to wait for dark I can't say. You can smell him before you see him."

"Wolfers stink and no mistake."

"Not like this one. He smells like his heart's corrupted clear to the center."

"That's my man."

"Why you'd want him is the question. I'd refuse him, even if the accounts wouldn't balance at the end of the week, but that blink of his gives me the fantods. He's crazier'n a foaming dog."

Frank flipped another double eagle—his last—and held it out. "I'll have two bottles and your apron."

"That all? You can have the skullbender for a half-dollar and my apron for free. I change 'em by the week, on account of the strychnine."

"That and a seat by the back door for an hour or two."

The druggist looked at the cracked butt of the Remington sticking out of Frank's belt. "I don't want no trouble."

"This buys plenty."

The jug-eared man worked his Adam's apple, then agreed to the bargain.

Frank smoked what was left of his tobacco sitting on a three-legged chair inside the door to the alley while the proprietor ground prescriptions and entered numbers into his big ledger up front. His boy came in from a delivery and he told him to go home.

"What about that case of codeine you wanted me to unpack?"

"I unpacked it. Things are slow."

"Well, I left my schoolbag in back."

"It'll keep. Tomorrow's Saturday."

When the druggist came back to make sure his visitor wasn't stuffing his pockets with tablets and tongue depressors, he saw the bottles were still unopened.

"Ain't you going to take even a swig?"

Frank shook his head. "You don't mess with your bait."

"It's getting late. Maybe he ain't coming."

"You said he came every night."

"I told you he's crazy."

"Who told you I ain't?"

"You can have your double eagle back, and you're welcome to the liquor. I'm commencing to think that coin's jinxed."

"Suit yourself, but I'm sticking." Frank stretched his arms above his head, bringing the butt of the Remington into view.

"My mama told me I'd catch my death in Utah. I was just too full of piss and vinegar to listen."

"A man should listen to his mother, then shut up about it when he didn't."

The jug-eared man returned to his accounts and prescriptions.

It had been full dark three-quarters of an hour, and the druggist kept hauling out his turnip watch and looking at it, then at the front door, which was two doors down from the marshal's office, when someone knocked on the alley side.

Frank got up so quickly the chair tipped and almost fell, but he caught it before it could make a noise that might spook his quarry and set it carefully back on its legs. He bent, picked up the bottles, and cradling them in his left arm, used that hand to turn the knob while with the other he drew the secondhand pistol from under his apron.

He put it away in haste.

A young woman stood in the alley wearing a red wrap over tarnished sequins and feathers in her hair. Her face was painted and she smelled as if she'd fallen into a rain barrel filled with lavender and toweled off with verbena leaves. It wasn't the rank odor Frank had expected, nor the form and features to go with it, and when she smiled at him, showing a gold tooth, and thrust out a handful of coins, he reached for them automatically; he was broke, after all.

The woman stepped to the side then, revealing the leering, filth-smeared visage of Randy Locke with its leprous patch of frostbitten cheek, crouched behind her stinking to high heaven and fisting his Colt. Fire flew from the muzzle.

4

A gentleman never sees his name in a newspaper.

The impact of the shot slung Frank on his back. Miraculously, the bottles were spared, rolling harmlessly across the pinewood floor to a stop at the base of a crate filled with headache powders, where the druggist rescued them and placed them back in inventory, snakebite apparently being very common on the shore of the Great Salt Lake and the source of a large percentage of his income. It was a cinch the customer who'd paid for them wouldn't have any more use for spirits where he was headed.

The doctor, a respected elder in the Church of All Saints, a Godlike fellow with snowy hair and beard and eyes as blue as the lake, despaired several times of his patient's recovery, from the moment a pair of solid citizens carried him in, with a fly crawling undisturbed on his face, through several relapses just when it looked like he might be turning the bend. At the finish he thought about submitting a paper on the case to the *American Medical Journal* in Boston, but on reflection he reckoned it smacked of pride.

The slug lay close to the heart, too deep to reach through the chest, and had to be extracted through the back with a sure and steady hand. Dr. Elgar was sure of his hand, but not of the network of nerves that propelled the fingers; he eschewed strong drink, being a man of deep faith and conviction, but he'd reached his threescore and ten and the copper bracelet he wore on each wrist didn't appear to have made much headway against creeping rheumatism.

Many hours of surgery were required. Fatigue and self-doubt on top of his swollen joints led to tremors and many breaks for rest were necessary. Much blood was lost, and although some discoveries had been made in the science of transfusion, blood types remained a mystery. Many a rabbit and white rat had sacrificed itself to no progress at all.

When at great length the bullet was free with no damage to the heart or spine, infection set in, complicated by pneumonia. This doctor had served with the Prussian Army in Jena, and knew rather more about enteric fever, and not enough about its treatment, than he cared to admit. Frank's temperature soared. The sheets he lay on were as hot to the touch as boiled linen, and poultices were applied and removed with no sign of success. Telegrams went out to leaders in the medical field. One suggested leeches; another suggested the leader who'd suggested them should be burned at the stake as a reverse heretic. A Viennese physician who was turning his attention to the health of the mind wired in favor of cocaine, then sent another cable canceling the first. During this exchange, Frank's fever broke; but whether the poultices and soaking his sheets in ice water had anything to do with this reversal of fortunes no one could say.

"Ach!" pronounced the doctor. "Perhaps there is a God after all, and He is less judgmental than advertised."

During his long recuperation, in a makeshift hospital established in a back room of the ornate Mormon Temple, with a ponderous crucifix leaning out from the wall above his bed like the Sword of Damascus, the patient learned that Randy had caught wind of Frank's search, anticipated the trap he'd lain, and bought the services of a woman of dubious occupation to confuse him and slow his hand. Randy had ridden out of town directly his mission was accomplished, long before a citizens' commission could be appointed to pursue him.

In all likelihood, he thought his enemy was dead.

Upon regaining his strength, Frank worked off his obligation to the doctor by sweeping his office and scrubbing his medical instruments. It occurred to him that he'd spent most of his working hours paying out the expenses of his recovery from ailments related directly to Randy. This scarcely softened his opinion of the central fixation of his life.

By the time Frank's debt was dismissed, Randy's trail might as well have led across an icepack. He struck out in search of employment and a place to bide his time until news surfaced of the whereabouts of his ancient antagonist.

Seasons passed before Randy discovered that he'd failed to lift the burden of Frank Farmer from the world.

In Carson City, Nevada, he celebrated his victory with a long, blistering soak in a bath house, got a shave and haircut, bought himself a complete new wardrobe and a valise to pack it in, and secured first-class passage in a Pullman coach to San Francisco, that sinkhole of pleasure. He'd saved enough by eating simple fare and staying out of hotels to keep his wolfing profits largely intact, and there was no better place to burn money than the Barbary Coast. He leaned back against the plush headrest and dreamt about good whiskey, friendly cards, and accommodating women. It was his first holiday since Appomattox.

Unnoticed by the pair in their relentless determination to destroy each other, the West had begun to extract a deep fascination from the East: The faster it barreled toward past history, the keener the curiosity among those in a position to monitor it from a safe distance.

Custer's spectacular finish, gun battles in the gold camps and cattle towns, and the expertly managed exploits of a saddle tramp who called himself Buffalo Bill, had kindled a blaze of interest that demanded fresh fuel by the week. It was only a question of time before a running gunfight that had involved the same two men for more than a decade aroused journalistic notice.

Randy had made the rounds of San Francisco's saloons, music halls, opium dens, and bordellos for weeks. It was like attaching a hose to his pockets and reversing the pressure, sucking out coins and paper currency with marvelous speed. His capital was so low it had to stand on tiptoe to peer over the gutter. He'd moved his baggage to a hotel far less lavish than he'd grown accustomed to, with roaches the size of cigar butts, rooms separated from their neighbors by two sheets of wallpaper, and a woman's false eyelash cemented to the basin in the dry-sink. He stretched his funds by rescuing yesterday's *Examiner* from a trash barrel and came upon the following paragraph in the local section:

It has come to our editors' attention that Mr. Randolph Locke, the notorious Texas pistoleer, is visiting our city and at last word was stopping at the Eldorado Hotel. Readers familiar with our telegraph columns will recall that Mr. Locke and Mr. Frank Farmer, also originally of Texas, have been taking target practice upon each other across the map of the western states and territories since the spring of 1868. Mr. Farmer was last reported in Salt Lake City, U.T., taking the salt air and recovering from the most recent mortal attack upon his person by Mr. Locke.

The maid assigned to Randy's room—the widow of a forty-niner, Henrietta by name—complained to the hotel manager that she'd been forced to pick up hundreds of torn fragments of newspaper that had been flung about the premises before she could begin dusting.

The manager yanked a bale of hair from a nostril and examined it against the sunlight coming through the painted glass in the lobby door. "That's your job, if I recollect correctly."

"Sure, and I wouldn't mind it so much if I didn't hear the man that done it taking the Lord's name in vain all the way down the stairs."

Randy's chagrin upon learning that he'd failed to finish the job in the drugstore was exacerbated by the army of newspaper reporters who tracked him to his current lodgings, each crying for an exclusive interview. Wearing their trademark bowlers and ripe unwashed linen, they laid ambush for him in the lobby, loped at his heels as he climbed the stairs, and bribed hotel personnel to let them wait for him in his private room. He ran them out at pistol point and directed the house detective to prevent any more such visits if he preferred walking without bullets in his kneecaps. That fellow nodded eager assent; and so Randy was greatly annoyed when within hours of their conversation a fresh knock came to his door.

The small man who greeted him when he tore it open was dressed better than the shabby gentlemen of the press, in a printed yellow waistcoat, striped trousers, velvet lapels, fine boots with tall heels, and a pearl-gray Stetson. His left eye was varnished ivory, with the painted-on iris a shade darker brown than its living mate. He introduced himself as Abraham Cripplehorn, originally of Atlantic City, New Jersey, and in lieu of a calling card presented him with a volume slightly larger than a banker's wallet, bound in scarlet and goldenrod pasteboard and titled:

BRIMSTONE BOB'S REVENGE,
or
GUN JUSTICE IN ABILENE
Being a True and Authentic Account of
Robert Turnstile's Quest for Bloody Vengeance
on the Chisholm Trail.
as told by
JACK DODGER,
an Eye-Witness

"Who's this Jack Dodger, at all?" asked Randy.

"He is I, sir: a *nom de plume,* to spare typesetters the chore of constructing my born appellation. The original Dodger made good on his surname by departing his hotel room in St. Louis, by way of the fire escape, leaving behind an unpaid bill and twenty-five copies of *Petticoat Betsy, the Bandit Princess,* by Jack Dodger. I sold them to a local lending library, which was eager to have them, as Buffalo Bill was appearing locally, and thus financed the rest of my North American tour."

"Which one of these is you?" He pointed to a pen-and-ink drawing on the paper cover of two men in range gear firing pistols at each other at point-blank range, their weapons held out at shoulder length.

"Neither. The fellow on the left is a reasonably accurate likeness of Brimstone Bob Turnstile. His opposing number traveled under the name Creek Morgan until that slug put him six feet under in Kansas. A reputable journalist never places himself in the story."

"I had my fill of writers this day." He started to close the door. A highly polished toe held it open three inches; wide enough for Randy to poke the Colt's muzzle through the space.

Cripplehorn's reaction was to smile under his brush moustache.

"I'm not interested in penning merely another dime novel commemorating a long-standing feud between dangerous men; that would be an expenditure of valuable resources toward too small a reward."

"That's a lot of big words. Which one you want to be your last?" He drew back the hammer.

The visitor was cool in the face of a threat; the reasons behind it I'll go into later and at length. His mission, he explained, was to produce an extravaganza that would pit Randy Locke and Frank Farmer against each other before a paying audience.

"Firing blanks and gibbering like a couple of monkeys in the circus. I ain't interested, and unless Frank's changed since I put a bullet through his chest wall, neither is he."

"I'm not suggesting a Punch-and-Judy show. The arenas are filled with those. This will be a unique exhibition. A duel to the death."

"The law won't stand for it." But Randy held his fire.

"Allow me to worry about that. There are ways and ways; which is why you need me, and why I am not hesitating to share a valuable idea as this free gratis with a man I've just met. I propose to charge two dollars a head for the privilege of witnessing two genuine frontiersmen engaged in mortal combat; the take to be divided equally between myself and the survivor—or his designated heirs in the event he expires soon after."

"Compared to cash in hand, money in the mouth's worth less than a penny on the dollar."

The man's smile remained as fixed as his ivory eye.

"I'll stand the expense of advertising and promotion. Your only obligation will be to show up on the day, loaded and sober."

"Look around you, Mr. Dodger."

"In informal conversation I prefer Cripplehorn."

"Whatever your name is, look around. This ain't exactly the honeymoon suite in the Bella Union. I'm bust. Gunsmiths don't trade ammunition for tickets to a show."

"I read of your arrival in San Francisco in the telegraph column of *The Chicago Herald*. The fare and accommodations were princely, and I am still awaiting a bank draft from New York City for delivery of my most recent manuscript. I can have a hundred dollars for you in a month."

"I got enough for but two more days, and there ain't no fire escape. A month from now I'll be back in Wyoming, skinning wolves to eat. You can reach me in Sheridan, care of Western Union. Wire me fifty and we'll talk."

"That's a gamble."

"You saying I can't be trusted?"

"If these past ten years have proven anything, it's that you're a man of your word, Mr. Farmer too. But what if he decides not to cooperate?"

"He will, if it's a chance to get at me."

"The only obstacle," Cripplehorn said, "is the difficulty of locating him."

"If that piece in the paper went out on the wire, he'll come here under his own steam."

"What if one of you kills the other before I can raise the money?"

"It's a fair possibility. Risk like that, I wouldn't want to be in your shoes."

5

Good businessmen are invariably polite, patient, and in step with their customers' best interests.

The intriguing thing about the man who walks in the footsteps of the adventurous is he exposes himself to the same adventures, except in his case with his eyes wide open. Which one is the more courageous and determined, the one who stumbles into hazard or the one who knows of it based on the other's experience and goes on anyway?

Abraham Cripplehorn would hardly have held himself a man of courage. Like any successful salesman, he never bought his own merchandise.

He lost his left eye trying to stay out of the army. Intending to deal himself out of Mr. Lincoln's draft, he took aim at his off foot with an old Paterson, but loaded it with the wrong size ball and it blew up in his face. For a time he wore a piratical patch, but it was anathema to his chosen line of work, which depended on the illusion of comfortable reliability. Blown-glass eyes fell outside the budget of a twenty-year-old entrepreneurial hopeful, but after alighting from a freight in Baltimore he won ten dollars in a game of euchre with a yardman named Tingley, who was short on funds but had an uncle who made pianos. This uncle fashioned an eye from the ivory he used to manufacture keys. It was an improvement over the patch, but the blank white orb still made people feel uncomfortable. With the profits from selling two gold bricks to a naïve postal clerk in Boston, he hired a woman who painted miniatures to add an iris. It didn't fool many people, the color being off a shade, but it made them feel more at ease, and when he told them he'd received the injury at Cold Harbor, it actually worked to his benefit.

"People want to believe a good lie," he said to a companion under the relaxing influence of a bottle of peach brandy, his spirit of choice. "They'll meet you halfway if you show effort in it."

He never repeated the remark. The young man he told it to did, cocking up an enterprise he'd invested a month in preparation, and turned up in a rubbish bin in Pittsburgh with his throat cut. His father, who owned part interest in a coal mine, decided that he'd fallen in with gypsies. Two days later a group of miners attacked a bunch of them in a local camp with pickaxes and burned their tents and wagons. Cripplehorn read about it in a week-old copy of the *Picayune* in a train station in Buffalo, and shook his head.

"Poor rag-headed bastards."

He himself was the son of an Atlantic City plumbing salesman who lived on the road, raised by a succession of aunts who were always coming and going and never seemed to run out of reinforcements. One, who claimed to be a Creole from Louisiana (although he was fairly certain she was Greek, and not the classic variety with a long straight nose and intelligent forehead but a woman with big red hands and a moustache), took his virginity when he was twelve. He thought it was their private secret—illicit lovers sharing a special bond—but after she told his father, describing the cute face little Abie made when he came, the plumbing salesman broke his cheekstrap with a pipe wrench and threw him out of the house.

A neighbor who went to the door to investigate what sounded like a wounded animal moaning on his front porch found him and took him to a doctor, who set the broken bone and put him to rest on a cot in the room behind his office. When the bone had knitted sufficiently for the patient to speak, he said he'd fallen down the back steps of his house, and since his father was on the road with his samples he was on his own. While the doctor was away delivering a baby, Abraham got his clothes from a cupboard, found cash in a tin behind a row of medical journals on a shelf, and crawled into an empty cattle car in the railroad yards, where he fell asleep. When he woke, the world swayed beneath him. He had no idea which way he was headed until the train slowed down approaching the station in Wilmington, Delaware.

Years later, when Abraham had made his way in the world, he traveled back a thousand miles looking for his father with a Stevens shotgun, only to find a granite-and-marble bank sprung up where the house had stood. None of the neighbors remembered anyone of that name. He placed an advertisement in several newspapers, offering a reward for information on the whereabouts of Noah Cripplehorn, with a description. He received nothing but the odd rambling answer from people patently hoping to collect on vagary alone. He gave it up when his money ran out, but he refused to abandon its purpose. As many cities as he visited throughout the years, and as often as he crisscrossed the continent, he never stopped asking after the man, and he kept the scattergun clean and lubricated.

Abraham Cripplehorn never forgot an insult or an injury no matter how slight, and had the patience to wait months or years to even a score.

Stopping in St. Louis in 1872, he got into a scrap with a store clerk over the coloring of a twenty-dollar banknote and cut the man's arm to the bone with a clasp-knife, his preferred weapon of self-defense; he was saving the Stevens for his father. A policeman happened to be present. Cripplehorn came to in a cell with a crusty bump on his head from the officer's nightstick, pleaded guilty to the reduced charge of aggravated assault, and spent six months in the state penitentiary in Jefferson City. His cellmate, an elderly confidence man named Mike Hurly, told him he was wasting his time unloading gold bricks on the gullible and trying to pass counterfeit currency. A young man of his obvious intelligence ought to try his hand at selling trust.

Cripplehorn smiled. "Trust, what's that?"

"Only the difference between going to the customer instead of having him come to you."

"I don't just have the capital right now to rent a storefront."

"I'm talking about personal transactions, not real estate. You can sell pomade to a bald man if you know what you're about."

"That the sound policy that put you in here?"

Hurly's smile was beaming; as opposite to his cell mate's as blue sky to overcast. He was a redheaded Irishman with a nose full of shot veins and ruddy skin pulled all out of shape by a lifetime of beaming. He was thirty-two at the time of their meeting.

"I got drunk celebrating a score and stole a horse and buggy that happened to belong to the mayor of Springfield. It don't count against what I'm telling you."

"Telling or selling?"

"Just now I'm fresh out of merchandise, so you can believe what I'm saying. Under other circumstances I'd be fleecing you out of that Dutch eye. I don't like to see a young man squandering his potential on store clerks without a pot to piss in. How much time you got left?"

"Five months, sixteen days, eleven hours, and change."

"I got another four beyond, on account of I bust that mayor's yellow-wheeled wagon against a telegraph pole misjudging a turn. That's plenty of time to turn you out from Hurly University."

"Does it come with a key I can hang from my watch chain?"

Hurly tapped the other man's chest. "You wear it in there,

and it'll open every door this side of St. Peter. Where you go from there depends on what you learn after you leave here."

It was in that cell that Cripplehorn learned the best way to sell a man something he didn't want was to refuse to offer it to him.

He learned also to dress consistently and with dash; nothing so tawdry as a gold tooth, but an article of clothing that set him apart from the bowler-hatted drummer and the sharp in the straw boater. In Jefferson City after his release, he picked a pocket hanging on a peg in a barber shop, bought a readymade suit, and booked a coach to St. Louis. On the platform, a fellow in a cloth cap and mackinaw smoking a cigarette thrust a flyer into his hands, printed in square-serif letters on coarse stock:

OPERA HOUSE!
Friday & Saturday, November 17 & 18
Civilization v. Savagery!
Border Perils! Indian Fights!
Performed Right On Stage Before Your Eyes!
BUFFALO BILL!
(W. F. Cody)
TEXAS JACK!
(O. B. Omohundro)
PRINCESS DOVE EYE!
(Mme. G. Morlacchi)
CALE DURG!
(E. Z. C. Judson: "Ned" Buntline)
in
Scouts of The Plains

After a glance he crumpled and threw it into a trash barrel, but was accosted three times on his way to a hotel by similarly attired ruffians bearing identical leaflets, and shook his head at a street peddler offering *cartes de visite* bearing the photographic likenesses of Cody, Omohundro, Morlacchi, et al; others were not so difficult to persuade, as a small group had gathered on the sidewalk to consider the man's wares.

The hotel was a rattrap, the best he could afford while he considered the business of acquiring *dash*. There he made the acquaintance, by proxy, of one Jack Dodger.

He read *Brimstone Bob's Revenge* in one sitting. When he stood at his window and craned his neck, he could just read the gaslit legend on the marquee of the St. Louis Opera House:

SCOUTS OF THE PLAINS

With what a lending library gave him for the twenty-five copies of Dodger's opus—and it was glad to get it with the Wild West in residence—he bought a better suit and a fine Stetson hat. He hadn't enough to buy a new pair of boots, but at a bootmaker's he procured a pair in glossy black glove leather for the price of resoling, as they'd gone unclaimed by the customer who had brought them in. They pinched his toes, but when he stood before a trifold mirror he decided he could bear them until he could afford a replacement.

By the end of the week, for the small expenditure of a printer's bill, he'd sold enough rolls of tickets at wholesale price to *Scouts of the Plains* to order a pair in his size.

He resisted the temptation, however.

Custom bootmaking takes time, and he had to clear out before the exasperated manager of the opera house set the police looking for the man responsible for two hundred enraged customers who had to be turned away at the door.

When *Scouts of the Plains* closed in San Francisco after a wildly successful tour, William Frederick Cody had become famous. On a smaller scale, it made Abraham Cripplehorn's reputation for disgruntled theater operators all along the circuit, and the only fiction he ever wrote was the names he signed in various hotel registers when Cripplehorn and Dodger were too dangerous to use.

Chicago was always his destination of choice when his pockets sagged with cash. Its pleasures were many and its expectations few. There, in the fall of 1877, he was sitting up in bed in his suite in the Palmer House, eating a princely breakfast and reading the *Sun,* when he first read the names of the Messrs. Locke and Farmer, and saw his way toward a lifetime of the same.

6

A man of patience is always content, whereas an impatient man is always suffering from thirst, even when up to his neck in fresh water.

Randy waited for Frank to find him in San Francisco until his money ran out. That process was accelerated by the incentives he'd left among desk clerks in all the likely hotels and porters at the train station to report the arrival of strangers whose ears didn't quite match.

Ten days after his meeting with Abraham Cripplehorn, the situation became untenable. He collected his gear and lit out for wolf country. He wondered if Frank had come to grief; wondered it with a touch of concern, as if he'd lost someone close.

* * *

Frank, however, had lost nothing but his touch with current affairs.

He was back in Colorado, working for the territorial stock-growers' association, armed with a Remington rolling-block rifle his employers had charged against his first month's wages, riding fence for all the big ranches and discouraging rustlers; which was a term loose enough to cover a variety of pests, most often small-time ranchers who represented an obstacle to progress.

The small-fry countered the pressure by forming an association of their own and sending delegates to Denver, but the courts there and eventually the governor ruled against them on the grounds that nearly all of the complainants had paid a fine or served time for cattle theft.

Neither the members of the bench nor the governor had worked in the trade. They could not be made to see that every spread, the large ones included, had begun with someone swinging a wide loop. The big fish had just gotten there first, before there was a badge to intervene or a capital to try the case.

Although Frank was not offered a badge, he and his fellow designates upheld the law as set forth in the Denver decisions, and assumed the added responsibilities of judge and jury, pronouncing and carrying out sentences of death on the spot. It was a question of arithmetic, and of simple economics: a citizen's arrest, followed by a trek of a week or more to the nearest district court, with at least three men to guard the prisoners and two to give testimony. With cases already backed up into next year, months went by with the ranches short-handed. A rifle in the right hands served the same purpose in less than a second.

"What we fixing to call these fellows?" asked one beef baron, smoking a cigar in a silver holder to keep from staining his white beard with tobacco.

A short silence followed among those gathered in the

association's club room. A baron with an ear trumpet broke it.

"Regulators. Seeing as how we're paying top-hand wages to return things to regular."

The pay was good, no question, but it might have been Confederate scrip for all it was useful four months out of the year, apart from stuffing his shirt and waistcoat to keep out the infernal cold. Frank spent his first winter in a dugout line shack built into a foothill in the San Miguels, bark logs in front and the rest dirt. When he wasn't snowed in, he patrolled a region the size of a European duchy, going weeks without seeing a white man. The only newspapers he saw were months old, left behind by the shack's previous occupant to start fires, and the circumstances of his employment prevented him from pumping drifters for information about the world outside. Those he came across were where they shouldn't be; he shot them out from under their hats when he could, or else kicked up a clump of snow at their feet that sent them over the nearest ridge lickety-split.

The Indians he saw—stragglers off the reservation— were too wily to come within rifle range, much less offer conversation; in any case, they were unlikely to be abreast of what was going on in California, or for that matter the moon.

It was a bad winter, and spring was worse. He could hear the ice breaking up above the treeline, the noise like dynamiters blasting tunnels for the railroad, and the rumble of avalanches. When after one ten-day circuit he couldn't find the shack, he knew it was gone, pounded flat as a griddle under tons of snow and rock. He reckoned then it was time to return to civilization.

Two days' ride from ranch headquarters he spotted Juan Valiente, a fellow Regulator, cutting west from the Animas.

He recognized his deep-chested dun first, then the man himself by the elaborate moustaches he wore in a hammock when he slept to keep them tame. Frank didn't like him, having lost friends and a good horse to men who looked like him near the Rio Grande, but he saved his strongest emotions for someone else. They drew alongside each other, the dun facing north, Frank's gray pointed south, the mounts' breath mingling in a cloud thick as custard.

"Any?" asked Valiente.

"One. Three more still running, I reckon. You?"

"I shot a boy."

"How old?"

The Mexican shrugged, the elegance of the gesture inherited from conquerors in brass hats.

"*Diez y tres,* maybe. Maybe fourteen. That skinning knife it made him older."

"Sure he had it on him when you shot him?"

Valiente shrugged again.

"Got paper for rolling?"

"Just the newspaper. Warmer than longjohns." Valiente reached inside his bearskin and pulled out a thick fold of newsprint.

Apparently the Mexican burned as he read, having smoked his way through all the pieces about schoolteachers running off with their students and illustrated advertisements for ladies' foundation garments, leaving only telegraph columns and optimistic predictions for the wheat harvest. Frank was tearing out a square when an item caught his eye:

San Francisco, Mar. 16—It has come to our editors' attention that Mr. Randolph Locke, the Notorious Texas pistoleer, is visiting our city, and at last word was stopping at the Eldorado Hotel. . . .

The range manager's wife, a tall woman who dipped snuff, kept the books. She worked for wages same as Frank, but she gave up every company penny like she was passing a kidney stone.

"Rebuilding a line shack takes time. I ought to take it out of yours."

"You already did. I lost some gear when the mountain fell on top of it."

"A man should know better than to shoot during a thaw. It brings landslides."

"It's what you pay me for, only I'm still waiting."

"I sometimes wonder who is costing us more, you gun men or the dirty cattle thieves."

He was gone an hour when a rider caught up with him. The sheriff, a German named Dierdorf, said he had to take him in for threatening the range manager's wife with a revolver.

"I just showed it to her, asking where I could get the grips replaced."

"That is too thin for me."

"First they hire me to stop the stealing, then they try stealing from me. What do you do when a man goes to robbing you—or a woman, comes to that?"

"*Verdammt!* I had a dog mean as her I'd feed it to a grizzly, but I work for the association same as you. I got to take you to town."

"I'm late as it is, by about three months. Tell her you missed me."

Dierdorf sighed and laid the muzzle of his horse pistol alongside Frank's temple.

Sixty days, said the judge in Denver.

The shinplasters called the wolf White Ike, but the only thing white about him was his muzzle, and as to Ike, whoever put up the bounty had probably had an uncle by that name nobody liked. Anyway it looked good with a five-hundred-dollar bounty printed under the description and a woodcut illustration that looked as if it had been done by a child.

Randy had come all the way to the top of Montana Territory to answer the flyer he'd seen in Billings; what with tracking a trail that doubled back and crossed itself like a crazy man on a bicycle, and blizzards wiping out even that, he wasn't sure but that he was in Canada.

White Ike was one of those aged loners, cast out of the pack by some young whelp with faster reflexes and the itch to lead, who'd gotten shrewd in order to survive on his own. He sprang traps by kicking dirt and snow on them, gobbled the bait, and picked off stray calves not yet learned in the ways of self-preservation, at a rate that had placed his likeness in store windows and on barn walls alongside wanted murderers. The men who gathered in saloons in broad daylight claimed he'd developed a taste for babies and came down from the mountains to climb through windows and snatch them from their cradles, but those were stories told to tenderheels for the price of a shot of Old Gideon. Nothing he'd heard about wolves attacking humans had stood up under close questioning.

On the other hand, creatures left on their own took on ways no man could predict. This he knew from personal experience.

Anyhow, it was all the same to him, and better, if it hiked the bounty. Wolfing was going the way of buffalo running; all Randy had to show for the season was a couple of moth-eaten pelts he'd peeled off starved carcasses and some coyote skins he'd tried to pass off as the real thing and gotten himself run out of Helena for the trouble. He was down to his last half-pound of bacon and an elk quarter that had commenced to spoil. He'd carved off what he could for jerking before the stink made his eyes water, but he was loath to shoot another. Crossing the Missouri near Fort Benton, his horse had spooked when a hawser snapped in two, capsized the ferry, and dumped them both into the water. The ferryman had swum to shore and Randy, too, but his horse was last seen treading water on the way to Great Falls with his pack aboard. He was down to the cartridges on his belt, and he wasn't too sure of all of them after that soaking. After he shot Ike, he'd take his chances on the rest for meat. Then he'd shoot the mule he'd traded for at a ranch. It was hardy enough, but it had to be beaten with a rope-end to get started.

He was carrying his Colt and his old Circle X Ballard rifle, its stock scratched many times over with pawnbrokers' identifying marks. He wasn't the hand with a long gun Frank was, but if you got close enough to an animal like Ike to shoot it with a revolver, you might as well sprinkle its tail with salt.

He was close now, he could tell. The wolf kept climbing, headed for the treeline, where prey was scarce. It knew it was being followed. Its best hope was to draw him far enough from his own kind to even the odds.

Randy smiled at that. Even a smart wolf was too dumb to count, and too ignorant of his pursuer's situation to know he lived his life far from his own kind.

He was thinking these thoughts, when what he ought to be thinking about was wolf only, when snow squeaked and he turned and looked up in time to see two rows of fangs and a red mouth surrounded by a halo of pale muzzle and two sets of claws streaking his way, the whole foreshortened against blue sky, as if it had dropped from a hot-air balloon: the drop a good sixty feet straight down from a rocky outcrop square above Randy's head. He could feel the heat of the animal's desperate breath when he stuck the Ballard straight up and fired.

* * *

A Cheyenne dog soldier named Bending Bough found them, so tangled together he thought at first he'd discovered one of the half-men-half-beasts of tribal legend. After he sorted them out he treated the man's frightening wounds with mud and dried herbs, fed him soup made from White Ike's liver, and brought him across the back of the mule to the nearest settlement.

It was a place of clapboard and canvas, hanging by its fingernails to the side of a mountain the settlers were systematically hollowing out in search of a vein of silver that came and went like a broken line on a map. Everything appeared to be held together by soot, including the miners. The rigorous toil and inescapable filth had made them surly and suspicious of strangers, particularly those who came in strange colors.

Bending Bough tried to pass as the wounded man's guide and sell the dead wolf's pelt, but the Indian had gotten himself as confused as Randy, thinking himself in Canada: It was Montana, and the locals considered any red men coming from the north to be fugitives from justice following the Little Big Horn massacre. The mercantile owner to whom he'd offered the pelt sent word to the citizens' committee, who hanged the Indian in the livery stable. For a time, Randy was kept under guard in a back room of the assayer's office as a suspected turncoat, his wounds tended by a barber who was the closest thing the town had to a medical man, but when he was well enough to give an account of himself they argued over the matter, then decided one hanging would hold them for a while. They loaded him aboard his mule, aimed it south, and gave it a hard smack. White Ike's pelt stayed behind, to be sold and the five hundred divided among the miners.

7

In order to speak to a lady for the first time, an introduction is required, either by a relative or by a mutual acquaintance if no relative is available.

After he was voted out of office on account of age and deafness and he was left all on his own, Gunter Dierdorf didn't blame his widowed state for his loneliness, nor his daughter's desertion, nor even Frank Farmer, who had probably hastened his wife's death and certainly had deprived him of his only child. If there was one mortal soul in this world he hated—hated as much as Frank and Randy hated each other—it was Morris Fassbinder, professor emeritus from the Utica College of Engineering. If the old gentleman was still living and wandered inside range of the sawed-off Greener the sheriff had carried throughout his tenure and which now hung above the stone fireplace in his retirement shack, the burial service would need Mason jars.

If a man had to be incarcerated, he could have done worse than the jailhouse in the county seat where Frank served out his two months for persuading the range manager's wife to pay him what he'd earned as a Regulator. The cells were clean, the sheets laundered and placed on a real bed (iron thing, might have been built from a cemetery fence, with a ditch down the middle of the mattress, but a bed just the same), and a lamp provided for reading the week-old newspapers from Denver after the sheriff was through with them. The meals were bland—Mrs. Dierdorf skimped on salt, which was not included in the official budget—but they were hot and never undercooked, and best of all they came in a picnic basket covered with a checked cloth hung on the slender arm of Evangeline Dierdorf.

The sheriff's daughter had attended a presentation by Doctor the Professor Morris Fassbinder in the Masonic Hall, a major stop on the Chautauqua lecture circuit originating in New York State. The elderly scholar, a scarecrow in a clawhammer coat, stiff collar, hard black hat, pinch-nose spectacles, long white hair, and dandruff, had served on the parole board in Elmira, and circumnavigated the country pressing for prison reform.

"Contrary to conventional belief," he told his audiences, "unfortunates placed under lock and key for their offenses against the statutes are not there to be punished or re-formed, but rather for storage. Society simply does not know what to do with them, and so when the offense is not of a capital nature it shelves them out of sight, and too fre-quently out of mind. When they have paid their debt, what course is left to them but to return to old habits? They of-fend, they are captured, tried, and placed once again on that remote shelf, to begin the process all over again when they are released.

"Surely a Christian nation can do better. . . ."

The Fassbinder System (as it was advertised in playbills and on a large pasteboard sign propped on an easel down-stage) involved humane treatment for these overlooked individuals. It was based upon the parable of the Good Samaritan, and although it offered no guarantee that he who was done unto as others would have done unto them would pass along the favor, the present system of penalty through neglect was a virtual promise that the cycle would repeat itself "*ad infinitum, ad absurdum,* world without end."

The lecture came with statistics demonstrating the sad percentage of recidivism as it stood, and projected figures based on the professor's exhaustive studies of the behavior of certain wild animals kept in captivity and the docility of those that were provided with a healthy diet, their cages cleaned regularly, and treated overall with patience and kindness, as opposed to those that were not. (This part of the programme was the only one wherein the speaker referred to notes printed in his neat hand on three-by-five cards; the fact that the projected figures were his own invention did not impose itself upon the mesmeric rhythms of his sentences or the melodiousness of his voice.)

"Surely"—his favorite adverb—"a man built in God's image and a woman fashioned from the First Man's costal cartilage, whatever his or her transgressions, is worthy of the same gentle treatment as a bear or a lion."

Evangeline was impressed, as much by the presenter's erect bearing and sonorous tenor as by his central theme, and returned to her parents' home from the evening with her handsome head filled with ideas about reading lamps, clean sheets, and good food delivered with a charitable word and a sweet smile. The sheriff and his wife doted on their daughter, whose three siblings had died in infancy. The elder Dierdorfs never stood a chance: The reforms were put into effect.

Moreover, she was a graceful creature, long-necked, with a high intelligent brow, a straight nose, agreeably curved lips, and a waist a man's two hands could encompass without effort. Her eyes were brown, clear, and required no spectacles to see that the prisoner was a man pleasingly formed (his artificial ear brought sympathy for his unfortunate past rather than revulsion), clean in his habits, and sufficiently well-bred to rise when a lady approached his cell.

Evangeline Dierdorf was twenty-two when Frank Farmer walked out of that cell a free man and ran away with her to Denver.

* * *

The couple did not remain long in that town.

Although Frank considered that the sheriff would not be long in tracing them (he arrived a week later), that eventuality didn't bother him so much as the time that had elapsed since the last news of Randy. He was still carrying around the piece he'd torn out of the newspaper in Colorado, worn gossamer thin and the print nearly rubbed away from taking out and rereading. It was too much to hope his enemy was still in San Francisco, but that was the place to start looking. Randy's new notoriety would certainly leave a trail in the memories of those who had encountered him.

Evangeline was thrilled. The delights of Denver, piled atop the discovery of her body, were sufficient to spin the head of a sheltered young lady; the City on the Bay had always seemed as far away and as drenched in romance as Mecca.

With Evangeline's life savings, together with what he got from selling his horse and the long-range rifle, Frank booked a coach to the coast. But long before the train rolled into the station he grew weary of the company, and slipped away in the confusion of people on the platform. Evangeline spent the rest of the money she'd brought on hotels she got little good from, wandering the streets most of the time hoping to glimpse Frank, then dropped out of the lives of all who knew her. Scant months later, a woman answering her description was found in a rented flat overlooking the railroad tracks in Carson City, Nevada, dead of an overdose of laudanum, and buried in an unmarked grave in a potter's field. The local marshal was a former deputy of Gunter Dierdorf's. The Colorado sheriff, wearing a mourning band for his recently deceased wife, came in person to arrange for the disinterment, identification, and transportation home.

* * *

On the day Frank had arrived, a loafer holding up the porch over the platform with his shoulders saw a man threading his way through the crowd, moving on the double. He passed close enough for the loafer to spot his gutta-percha ear.

He hadn't seen the man who'd promised him a reward for that information in months; but if it was worth something to him, the fact that he was interested in that ear might be worth something to the man who wore it. He pushed his dirty hat determinedly forward to his eyebrows and followed on the man's heels. On the way he passed a pretty young woman with a parasol, anxiously peering around herself in the middle of the throng. He hesitated, sensing an errand there, and pocket money in it, then resumed his pursuit of the man with the ear, shaking his head. It was either drought or downpour in his work.

Frank went first to the Eldorado Hotel, but the desk clerk couldn't find Randy Locke in the current register. Further inquiries led finally to his last-known stop in town, in a hotel not reputed for its elegance, equipped with roaches the size of cigar butts, two sheets of wallpaper separating each room from its neighbor, and a woman's false eyelash stuck to the basin in the dry-sink. He thought he could smell Randy on the sheets; which may not have been pure fancy on his part. For three days he lay on the bed his old acquaintance had slept on, hoping to draw intelligence from the contact; but apart from the attention of bedbugs he drew nothing from the experience.

"I was glad to see the last of him," said the manager, contemplating a bale of hair he'd plucked from a nostril. "He was starting to attract reporters."

"Any other visitors?"

The manager dislodged the hair from his fingers onto his lapel, staring at Frank. Frank stuck a banknote across the desk.

"One-eyed jasper in a ten-gallon hat."

Frank got out another banknote. The manager looked at it regretfully and said he never got the man's name. His guest checked out.

"Frank Farmer?"

He spun, dropping his valise and dragging the worn revolver from its holster.

"Steady, feller!" A man wearing a dirty coat and dirtier plug hat stood on the boardwalk with his hands in the air.

"How'd you know my name?"

"When somebody says there's money in it, I ain't likely to forget it, nor the name of the one offering."

"Well?"

"Feller called Locke."

"When?"

"A spell back. Last fall it was."

"That's no good to me."

"Maybe no, maybe yes; but it was right there in that hotel I talked to him. There's generally always somebody needs some sort of favor in places like it. I make it a point to keep it on my rounds."

"I already know he stayed there."

"What you don't know's the name of the man I seen coming down from his room before that. Had him on good boots and a pretty hat. I asked him if he needed any errands run. He gave me a dollar and told me to bring him a bottle of peach brandy at the Palace. This here's what he gave me instead of cash when I showed up with it," he said bitterly. "I been carrying it since I seen you at the station. You lost me, but I reckoned you'd turn up here sooner than later."

Frank looked at the scuffed cover of the book the loafer had pulled from his hip pocket:

BRIMSTONE BOB'S REVENGE,
or
GUN JUSTICE IN ABILENE
Being a True and Authentic Account
of Robert Turnstile's Quest for Bloody Vengeance
on the Chisholm Trail
as told by
JACK DODGER,
an Eye-Witness

"Who's this Turnstile?"

"Never heard of 'em, nor Dodger neither. He said it wasn't even his name."

"What was?"

The loafer grinned at him. Frank grunted and fished out another banknote.

8

A firm handshake and a pleasant way of speaking are the working capital of the successful businessman.

Abraham Cripplehorn was suffering the longest string of bad luck of his career.

He laid it to Jack Dodger.

The elusive Jack had always been his rabbit's foot: Those copies of *Petticoat Betsy, the Bandit Princess* he'd found in his hotel room had brought direction to an aimless life, but the association had not been so rosy for The Mercury

Press of Cincinnati, Ohio, which had declared bankruptcy in 1876, leaving five hundred copies of *Brimstone Bob's Revenge* unclaimed at its printer's. Cripplehorn had happened upon this information while visiting that city, and had obtained them by settling the bill. When he gave the last one to a St. Louis theater manager he'd hoped to persuade to advance him money against a public duel to the death between Randy Locke and Frank Farmer, his fortunes turned sour.

The manager, who'd demanded time to think over his proposition, turned him down the next day, and he was ejected from his hotel at the end of the week for nonpayment, minus his luggage. In due course he found himself in an establishment not unlike the one where he'd met Locke, and after he pawned his silver pocket watch to finance his stay there, he faced the fact that the street would be his next place of lodging if something didn't happen soon to reverse his situation.

Walking around the block to consider the matter, he stopped on a corner to wait for a brewer's dray to pass and read an engraved brass plaque attached to the four-story brick building at his elbow:

REDEMPTION HOUSE

Not being one to fail to recognize an opportunity or an omen, he climbed the front steps and rang the bell. A woman in black bombazine with her hair in a bun answered, frowning at his gaudy waistcoat, high-heeled boots, and dramatic hat brim.

"Pray, madam, what is the nature of this establishment?"

The woman adjusted her rimless spectacles. "We are a charitable institution affiliated with the First Unitarian Church. Our ambition is to reform the drunkard and close the temple of blue ruin for good and all."

He let fall his crest. "I took it for a pawnshop. Do you know of one in this neighborhood?"

"Certainly not." She began to close the door.

He plucked out his ivory eye and held it up. "I intended to barter this for the price of that blue ruin you mentioned; but perhaps it was the Lord, and not my infernal thirst, that led me to your door."

Which thereupon opened wide.

For an incentive, the desk clerk at the Palace Hotel brought out an old registration book from the back room and found a forwarding address for Abraham Cripplehorn: The Palmer House, Chicago. Frank cursed his luck, and while he was at it Sheriff Gunter Dierdorf and the range manager's wife in Colorado. His money wouldn't cover the cost of a wire to ask if the man was registered there, much less a trip that far east; and even if it would, he'd sooner spend it looking for Randy direct.

In any case, the fellow might be just a chance acquaintance. There was no surety he knew something Frank didn't.

The desk clerk said, "You might try your luck around November. Mr. Cripplehorn often spends the winter in San Francisco, and he always stays here."

Frank thanked him for the information. November was three months off; but what was that against the years he'd put in already? It wasn't as if he hadn't another pursuit to occupy him in the meantime.

Cripplehorn was a gifted speaker. He'd discovered the fact in Deadwood, where a run of cards no one quite accepted as accidental had forced him to talk his way out of a short rope and a long drop. Not long after in St. Paul, Minnesota, when his capital was almost as low as at present, he'd stepped in at the last moment for a lecturer on personal hygiene who'd been detained for lewd and lascivious conduct. He'd sent the male half of the audience in the Gaiety Theatre running for the nearest bathhouse with his tale of a Union infantryman whose masculine member had fallen off at Gettysburg for lack of attention to the foreskin.

The ladies of Redemption House, once they'd obtained his pledge never again to partake of strong drink, asked him to address the congregation at the First Unitarian Church, laying open his sordid story and assigning the credit for his reform to the efforts of the organization; for there is a little of the confidence man in us all, when everything's said and done. No remuneration was offered, but when some twenty of his listeners came forward after the final hymn to sign the Pledge, a charter member of the charitable society pressured her husband, a booking agent for Chautauqua, to send him on tour with a salary and all expenses paid. (Coincidentally, he shared his first bill, in Des Moines, Iowa, with Dr. Morris Fassbinder, that well-known advocate for a humane penal system.)

His narrative always started out gently, as if in private conversation. When he came to his sad, riveting story, his voice fell to a murmur, as if he hoped to obscure the shameful details. (His listeners, in fact, were forced to lean forward in their seats and strain their ears during this portion of the address, and therefore captured every word.) Finally he built to a proud and powerful annunciation of his faith in the Lord and the dramatically improved situation that had come of finding Him.

He used just enough of his own story—the spoliation of his innocence, his father's pipe wrench, the horrors of the road—to lend weight to the presentation; he left out evading Mr. Lincoln's draft as impolitic, assigning his injury to an alcohol-influenced incident during army training leading to a medical discharge. The rest of it he'd drawn from a slim volume he found in a bookshop in Cincinnati, purporting to be the privately published confessions of its author. The low point—his attempt to trade his artificial eye for temporary oblivion—was the most popular feature. In time it came to consume the greater part of his oratory. It was his *East Lynne.*

He had a rich tenor, pleasing to men and women both (although to a greater degree in the case of women), which he obtained by seasoning his vocal cords backstage with a pull at a flask filled with peach brandy. In lecture halls, tents, open-air arenas, and melodeons from the Ohio Valley to the High Sierras, the Hon. Abraham Titus Cripplehorn (he added the Titus halfway through the circuit, assuring himself two lines in the playbills), Deacon of the First Unitarian Church of Cincinnati, Ohio, and the Voice of Redemption House, railed against the devil in the bottle, shared in the box office proceeds, and put away a little each week to finance the extravaganza he regarded as the venture that would allow him to retire to a lifetime of presidential suites and champagne cocktails.

The tour finished in San Francisco, just in time for winter.

"Mr. Cripplehorn?"

He turned from the register in the onyx-and-marble lobby of the Palace Hotel, expecting a word of praise from an attendant of his lectures, and found himself facing a long-legged man in a town suit that despite recent brushing had absorbed more than its share of dust, sweat, and wood smoke, with a sunburn that looked as if it went all the way to the underside of his skin. He had a pink left ear and visible traces of wax where it had been attached.

9

Winter: when Mother Nature doffs her bright autumn fashions and dons soft white flannel.

"Cookie, your right name's Locke, ain't it?"

Randy was fishing for a fly that had dropped into his kettle of stew. "Who's asking?"

"Hell, it's me, Shorty. We been in the same bunkhouse near a year now."

"You're all Shorty or Slim or Stretch or Simp. All of you start with *S* and you all got the same jug ears and monkey face. I stopped trying to cut you out a long time ago."

He'd been working on the Lazy Y spread in Nebraska since last fall; his predecessor, also called Cookie, had confused loco weed with wild asparagus, took a taste, saw a thousand Sioux mounted on ten-foot ponies, and run smack-dab into the smokehouse stone wall, breaking his neck.

"It's a big outfit," said the foreman, a man as brown and wrinkled as a tobacco pouch made from buffalo scrotum. "Think you can feed it?"

"I already got a leg up over the last. I hate asparagus."

And now this.

"Well, is it Locke or ain't it?" Shorty pressed. "Rudolph, right?"

He cornered the fly against a floating piece of bacon fat, scooped it up with the wooden spoon, flung it back over his shoulder, and stirred the stew with the spoon. "Randolph. I'm Randy to foremen and better. Mr. Locke to you rannies."

"Sandy Ross bet me a cartwheel dollar you're the Locke shot a fellow named Farmer in Texas and again in Utah."

"He left out Kansas."

"You saying you're him?"

He said nothing, concentrating. One fly generally led to another.

"What'd he do to you, you wanted him in the ground all this time? He steal your girl or what?"

"Why steal 'em? You can't trade 'em later for a saddle."

"Well, then, what?"

"Don't like him."

"I don't much like Sandy, but we don't go gunning for each other."

"You never met Frank."

"You're fooling me. You're no pistolero. That leg of yours always gets into camp five minutes after the rest of you. Why is it all you cookies are stove up?"

"What whole man wants to shake out while the rooster's still snoring and get a fire going just to keep a bunch of worthless tramps from starving to death?"

"Aw, you're full of sheepdip. Do I get that buck out of Sandy or what? I—"

Before the stubble-face cowhand could react, Randy swept his Colt out from under his bloodstained apron, cocked it, and sped a slug past his left ear.

"You're lucky you ain't Frank. I took that same ear clean off with just a chamber pot."

Randy hadn't the born talents of a chef. He was a good enough man with a skillet or a kettle, and his coffee was strong without being bitter, but he could never find tracks in a biscuit. They always came out burned on the bottom and doughy inside, and as a hot biscuit smeared with lard was the first thing a man sank his teeth into on the range, the men of the Lazy Y began each day out of sorts. But when the story of what happened to Shorty Cochran got around, they stopped griping.

The world was turning still, faster west of St. Louis. The

Comanches had been whipped in Texas, Sitting Bull was a federal prisoner, and the only hostiles anyone had seen lately outside Apache country were the ones who had chased the last cookie into the smokehouse wall. Abilene was closed to cows and cowboys. People were roller-skating in Dodge City. When the Lazy Y sent its beef to market, the drive ended after two miles, where the bawling Herefords were loaded aboard the cars in Lincoln. If the tourists didn't waste their money on silver belt buckles shaped like longhorns, Randy might have forgotten what the flea-bitten bastards looked like. Homesteaders were fencing the open range into little-bitty squares where hogs rooted and sugar beets swoll up in the ground the buffalo had trod hard as iron, cutting off the cattle outfits from water. In the last year alone, the Bar 9 in Wyoming and the Double Diamond in New Mexico had broken up and sold all their equipment at auction; every time the wind blew east, it brought with it another dusty band of hands looking for work that wasn't there. A man got up in the dark to heat up his Dutch oven and when it got dark again he didn't know if there'd be a ranch still there in the morning.

Then came winter, and it was all gone in a season.

September and October were mild, more like spring than autumn. The grass stayed slick and green, and the syndicate based in Indiana that owned the Lazy Y was considering expanding next year and taking over acreage belonging to smaller competitors less equipped to weather the changes in the industry. Christmas was snowless, the sky scraped clean of clouds; Randy put on his mackinaw to start breakfast and by the time it was served had shucked it off, the lining sodden with sweat. On New Year's Eve, those hands who'd drawn the short straws and stayed home from Lincoln and its saloons sat outside around a fire, pouring whiskey into their tin cups and passing the bottle. At midnight, under a sky punched through with stars and a three-quarter moon as bright as a new Morgan dollar, one of them produced a firecracker from his shirt pocket; the explosion set the horses rustling in their stalls and left behind a stench of brimstone.

Around 1:00 A.M. someone drew a gray sheet overhead and wrung out a drizzle that rattled against the galvanized iron roof of the bunkhouse like bits of shattered crystal. An hour later the sleet became snow: big, downy, wet flakes at first, floating aimlessly and sizzling when they touched down, then turning to powder, coming faster, swept along by a mad coyote wind from the north whose howling drowned out the panes rattling in their frames. Standing at the windows, staring out between hammocks of white in the corners into the leaden dawn, the hands of the Lazy Y could not know how many others were doing the same at that moment, in a line of bunkhouses stretching from as far up as Dakota to as far down as southeast Texas, and from the bootjack of the Platte in northern Colorado to St. Louis. Somewhere in the heavens a massive flour sifter moved from west to east, dumping two feet of powder over drift fences and buffalo wallows, and behind it a bellows blew it into eight-foot drifts, obliterating sharp contrasts in the earth's surface and smoothing it all into a gently undulating mass dense as fresh-poured cement.

A peaceful sight, when the storm ran out of steam after three days and three nights; until a rider kicking his horse through chest-deep snow moved from solid earth to a hidden swale and found himself buried to the crown of his hat, or a herd of cattle bunched together tight for the heat and froze, to be found still standing in a stiff mass of a hundred when the snows receded in the tragic spring. The mercury dropped to twenty below and ran out of thermometer at the bottom. Cottonwoods burst from the relentless contraction. Locomotives and the string of cars behind them stood motionless, their wheels invisible so that they appeared to have been abandoned unfinished, only the smoke from their stacks showing any sign of activity as their firemen struggled to keep the boilers from cooling and cracking apart. Wood parties wrapped in bearskins and mackinaws trudged out in snowshoes and brought back frozen limbs that snapped and spat as they thawed in the flames and sometimes put out the fire with the sudden release of water. The mail could not go through and the telegraph wires were down, so the men of the Lazy Y couldn't know the situation was the same in Waco and Wichita, Rochester and Rapid City.

The cattle that didn't freeze died of starvation and thirst; thirst, with snow to their chins because the knot-headed beasts didn't know it was frozen water and could be eaten. A schoolgirl outside Omaha didn't return home from school and her body was located when someone spotted a green hair ribbon almost buried in snow, a hundred yards from her house. A Lazy Y cowboy named Shag, nineteen years old and in good health, burst his heart trying to get hay to a stranded herd across four miles of drift; his snow-blind horse was found helpless beside his body, the pallet of feed behind it, still tethered to its saddle. The ground was too hard to bury him, and so a rick of wood was moved in order to get to the insulated earth beneath.

Randy Locke kept his fire stoked all day and all night, feeding the hands as they straggled in to refuel, change horses, and then go back out, trying to contain the damage. No one complained about his biscuits.

Three hundred died, some homesteaders frozen in their shacks when firewood ran out and all the furniture had been broken up to feed the hearths. It was futile to attempt to count the cattle that had perished; the original inventories were based on speculation, much of it over-optimistic;

few had any idea of how many they had in the fall, but could guess at how many they had in the spring; they were that easy to count now. Teams of workhorses hauled tons of rotting carcasses into buffalo wallows and covered the common graves to prevent plague. Wolves, at least, found an advantage. With meat available for the picking in greater amounts than any since buffalo days, the packs swelled. An experienced wolfer could make a fortune—if only there were any big ranchers left to pay the bounty.

The blizzards of the 1880s ended the open range—without debate, and almost without complaint; those immediately affected had already shouted themselves hoarse against un-maternal Mother Nature. Fences were required to keep the herds from drifting before the blasting winds, away from ranch headquarters and moving with the storm rather than out of it. The annoyance of it was having to stop every couple of miles and open a gate. The tragedy of it was looking out on a land once untamed, now cut into squares like a pan of dowdy, and proud, sprawling feudal estates gone on the block.

"Where do you go from here, Cookie?" The foreman with the wrinkled brown skin of a scrotum tobacco pouch counted out his wages from the scratched green strongbox on the butcher-block table he used for a desk.

"Where do you?" He scooped the banknotes into his sweaty old hat and swept it onto his head swiftly, to avoid spilling; it was like flipping a flapjack.

"Hartford, Connecticut. My daughter's been after me to move in with her and her husband since I turned fifty. She's scared I'll fall off my horse and bust my hip. You got any kin?"

"I had a brother. He was born dead, with two heads. They got him in a jar of alcohol in a museum in Michigan. I don't allow as he's much company. I reckon I'll turn west and keep on riding till my bones thaw if ever."

"How old are you?"

"Thirty-six or -seven. Nobody ever wrote down the date that I know of. They probably thought I'd wind up in a jar myself."

The foreman chuckled, working the rheumatism out of his knuckles. "Your bones'll thaw, don't you worry about that. You figure Texas?"

"Nothing for me there. San Francisco. I got enough to put me up in something better than that bug hatchery I was in last time."

10

True friends are always close, no matter the distance that separates them.

The West was a big place, sure enough; but not yet settled. There was a relative handful of lively venues where a rootless man could find work or fun or both, so it was never a coincidence when two men who knew each other well kept crossing paths. While it was true a visitor to New York City, stacked twelve-deep as it was so that when someone came in from outside someone else was pushed out to make room for him, could spend a winter there without ever bumping into an old acquaintance, Tombstone and Fort Griffin and even a sprawl like St. Louis weren't any of them big enough to get lost in.

Randy Locke, however, had managed to step square off the face of the earth.

Wires to ranches in all the places he and Frank had worked came to nothing, beyond a tinhorn gambler going by the name of R. Lockwood, who'd been drug bare naked through mescal outside Las Vegas, New Mexico, from slipping up and dealing two queens of clubs during a friendly game in the Bloody Dog Saloon; but that hideless fellow didn't sound like Randy, who'd been known to cheat himself inadvertently in a game of Patience and invest his last ten dollars in the cowhands' Christmas fund as a self-imposed fine. Frank submitted that Randy was made out of honester clay than he himself.

It was as obvious as finding a trout in one's whiskey that he was out wolfing, which was solitary work and anonymous, encompassing a piece of North America roughly the size of western Europe, with parts as big as the Hebrides that no two could agree on as to their topographical nature. The rangy critters had got cagy of late, withdrawing higher into the mountains and deeper into the wilderness, where a man's footprint in the fallen pine needles was as rare as a whorehouse blush. Frank reckoned he'd have to wait for the thaw for the old thorn in his side to fester out.

(As it happened, Randy had come down from the mountains almost a year earlier, joining the Lazy Y in the middle of its last true trail drive after its cookie brained himself escaping phantom hostiles, relieving the boy who scrubbed his frying pans of his temporary promotion; such brevet appointments rarely reached the general record, and even the foreman scratched his head over Cookie's right name.)

Frank meanwhile took work as an officer for the local Committee of Public Vigilance, breaking up dens of vice and corruption in that part of San Francisco known as the Barbary Coast. The committee, headed up by clergy and the respected sons of forty-niners, was sworn to beat out the vermin like trod-down dirt from a very old rug, in the interest of saving the city from the whole reason their fathers had come to it in the first place. When an establishment known for entertaining certain pleasures came under special scrutiny—an heir dead of too much opium here, an old reprobate vanished through a trapdoor into the bay there—whereupon he metamorphosed into "an elderly gentleman fallen upon difficulties beyond bearing"—Frank went in with a squad of "reserve officers of the Metropolitan Police" and, armed with truncheons, brass knuckles, and bulldog pistols, cleaned the place out of everything fragile, portable, and potable. It was volunteer duty, paying only in the warmth of the Lord's work well-fulfilled and whatever collateral benefits resulted. Frank sold half a dozen cases of confiscated skullbender the day after his first raid, and paid off his bill outstanding at the Hotel de Paris with change to spare. The next week, he led a raid on the establishment that had bought it, reclaimed half what he'd sold along with a case of genuine French champagne (bottled in San Diego), and sold it next day to the Bella Union, with a tinge of regret; the proprietor was a large contributor to the vigilance committee, and enjoyed a clean bill as a consequence.

These were palmy days for Frank. A man could do the Lord's work, and be comfortable in the bargain. He only regretted he hadn't seen the light years earlier.

On his third week on duty came a revelation.

In a hovel built entirely from wrecked ships—ancient barnacles clinging to the timbers looking like dried-up onions—an old Chinaman, himself built entirely from burlap stretched over weathered canvas, a rusty black mandarin's cap pasted to his skull, looked up at the intruders with a butcher's cleaver clutched in one hand, stained with something that was not rust. A young Chinese woman whom it developed was his daughter lay at his slippered feet with her head nearly clean off her body. As Frank reconstructed the situation, she had taken up with a twenty-year-old white man, scion of a fortune struck in '49 or thereabouts, in direct rebellion to a match that had been agreed upon in Shanghai before her birth. Her father had acted from honor—"Good faith," in his broken English.

"Send my bones home, please, sir." Frank put a bullet in his skull, wrapped him in an old blanket reeking of opium and other filth, and dragged him over the nearest pier and into the greasy water in the harbor.

The local tong would go on looking for the white man in the pointed beard until the industry of the vigilance committee directed its efforts toward personal protection.

Frank made arrangements for the girl's burial in a Buddhist cemetery. During the religious ceremony, not a detail of which he followed, he thought of Evangeline Dierdorf.

"I didn't serve her well," he thought; "no, not at all." And began efforts to trace her movements from San Francisco. In time, with help from the Pinkerton National Detective Agency until his capital ran out, he received a clipping from a newspaper in Carson City, Nevada:

> Responding to a complaint from an unruly house in this city Thursday last, police removed the remains of a young woman known only as Angie, dead of an abuse of tincture of opium; associates reported that she'd sought relief from pain owing to an extraction of eight badly impacted teeth, misjudging the dosage. She had been a resident of the house for some weeks. Burial has taken place in the cemetery for indigents.

Frank "sought relief" from a contraband bottle he'd held out from the general lot, and was ejected from his hotel for vandalism. A number of furnishings were smashed beyond repair, including a basin with a woman's eyelash stuck to it.

He found a billet not demonstrably different from the one he'd just left, submitted his resignation to the committee, and inquired at the Palace, as he'd done on and off throughout the autumn, about Abraham Cripplehorn. The clerk, a fair-haired consumptive from Wisconsin, sighed—Frank's was a familiar face across that marble-topped desk—and consulted his registration.

"Not checked in yet, sir; but he sent a wire reserving a suite. We expect him Monday next."

"Mr. Cripplehorn?"

The man signing the register, small in stature but well set up in a silk waistcoat, gabardine suit of clothes, high-heeled boots, and a Stetson that had never held a horse's fill of water, regarded him with one working eye; the other was store-bought, like Frank's ear. Frank, sensitive about that feature, knew when it was spotted.

"Would your name by chance be Farmer?" asked the man.

"It would, and not by chance. I'm told you know a fellow name of Locke."

Cripplehorn picked up his valise. "We'll talk in my suite."

There was a sitting room connected to the bedroom, with fresh flowers in a copper vase, deep leather chairs, and a Gainsborough print leaning out from a wall. Through a half-open door gleamed a brass bed piled high with pillows in tasseled shams. From inside his valise the guest of the hotel withdrew a matching leather case that opened to reveal three cut-glass decanters held in place with leather straps. Brass tags hung from tiny chains around their necks were engraved BOURBON, RYE, and BRANDY. Frank asked for rye and watched him unstop one of the decanters and pour golden liquid into a hotel glass. He paused two inches from the top.

"Shall I ring for ice?"

"I didn't come here to skate."

Cripplehorn smiled and filled the glass the rest of the way. He poured brandy into another.

They sat. Frank's host watched with amusement as he flipped half his drink down his throat. "You're the authentic article, that I can see."

"You're partial to that word. I read your book."

"I sometimes forget the literacy rate out here. I know the owner of a highly successful manufactory back East who can barely write his name."

"It's either learn to read or bonk yourself on the head with a rock from boredom. Things ain't as various out here as it says in your book. I'm a mite surprised I never heard of this Turnstile. I counted eighty-two dead by his hand."

"Eyewitnesses will embellish. His mistake was to go on killing after all his grievances were addressed. The good people of Virginia City broke him out of jail while he was awaiting trial for killing a popular bartender and hanged him off a railroad trestle. Three wives showed up to claim the body."

"I'd of kissed the ones with the rope for pulling me out of that." Frank put down the rest of his drink. "About Randy."

"About Randy indeed." Cripplehorn sipped brandy and set his glass on a low table between them. "He gave me a general delivery address in Wyoming, but all my letters came back for inability to deliver."

Frank stood. "I won't be taking any more of your time."

"I'd be grateful if you'd let me take some of yours."

"Who's asking, Cripplehorn or Dodger? I get jumpy around fellows with more than one name. It's like carrying two sets of dice."

"The former. I find it easier to get around without dragging the burden of fame behind me. In certain places Jack Dodger is better known than Charles Dickens."

Frank didn't doubt that, not knowing who was this Dickens. He refilled his glass and sat back down.

Abraham Cripplehorn told him of his plan to charge admission to see Randy Locke and Frank Farmer settle their affairs in public.

"I don't see how far we'll get, seeing as how we'll all be in jail the minute what we're about gets around."

"I'm surprised you gentlemen are so concerned about the law, given your method of resolving your differences. However, dealing with such obstacles will be my contribution. I didn't just come up with this idea. I've had two years to think about it since I spoke with Locke."

"You talk a good game. What's the color of your money?"

From a pocket Cripplehorn produced a fold of banknotes in a spring clasp with an Indian head in copper and held it up. A fifty-dollar note was wrapped around the outside.

"I met a pump-organ drummer carried a roll like that in Rocky Fork. It was all singles inside."

"You're free to inspect it, once we come to an agreement."

"You seem mighty sure we will."

"Why would we not? Assuming you're still resolute."

"Don't you worry about that. What's to stop me from crawfishing once I take your money? I don't need no business arrangement to put Randy in the ground."

"As I told Mr. Locke, the record of your association is fee simple that your word is good. This fifty is a deposit. The rest will go to the survivor of the contest—or his heirs should he expire shortly after his opponent."

"What if we go together?"

"That, sir, would be a windfall."

Frank unbuttoned his coat, exposing the Remington's cracked grip. "You never know in a crowd like that where a stray bullet may come from."

Cripplehorn smiled.

"I understand the implication, and I don't resent it. I will state that I am no gun man—you may inspect me if you wish, I go unarmed—and would be taking my life in my hands against either one of you. And to employ a surrogate would be to share the reward, which would render the exercise pointless."

"I can see you worked this out."

"It has been my ambition for some time now, as I said."

"I don't have heirs. You can keep my share if Randy gets lucky. I won't need it where I've gone."

"Then we have an understanding?"

"I reckon so. We been running around going on fifteen years, trying to kill each other for free. I don't see any sin in making a buck off it."

Cripplehorn freed the fifty-dollar note from the clasp, letting him see a second one underneath, and put the first on the low table. Frank scooped it up, stretched it between his hands, and held it up to the window. "I ain't seen one of these in so long we're plumb shy around each other." He folded it in quarters and poked it into his watch pocket.

The other man picked up his glass, sipped, and made a face as if it contained alkali water. "Unfortunately, the situation is the same as when I spoke to Mr. Locke, although this time around he's the one who can't be reached."

"He'll do the reaching, soon as he hears I'm in town."

"That's just what he said about you."

"And here I sit."

"Two years later. This time we'll accelerate the process."

11

The press is an institution run by the inmates.

Major W. B. Updegraff (the W stood for Wisdom, but the men who accompanied him to sporting houses called him Dub) came out of Second Manassas with the rank of sergeant-major and a chunk of Yankee mortar in his right knee. He was Major to the staff of *The Barbary Spar*.

He hadn't set out to be a publisher. He won his first printing press, a lever-operated Columbian patented in 1813, playing poker in Tennessee. Before that he wasn't even a regular reader of newspapers, but it seemed everyone else was, especially the farther he moved West. The ten-cent price covered expenses, and advertising and jobbing (election leaflets, business cards, and letterheads) had kept his head above water during the Panic of '73.

He was forced to leave that first press in Yankton when a local manufacturer of fireworks came looking for him with a bullwhip. He bought another, a Prouty platen, when the Kansas Pacific Railroad left behind an end-of-track town in Colorado, cheap from a publisher who'd grown weary of transporting his equipment every time the railroad moved on. It now stood, an impressive arrangement of gears, rubber-covered rollers, and an enormous cast-iron flywheel with curved spokes, in a building constructed from packing cases within earshot of the splash whenever a drunk was robbed, slain, and flung into San Francisco Harbor. Its sign, printed in Olde English letters on a pine board, hung by chains from the spar of a ship that had run aground off Goat Rock, and for which the establishment was named.

The building was not much larger than a carriage house. This compact arrangement suited the Major, who in a trice could walk from the press to the lithograph stone with its polished slab of gunmetal-colored rock to the yellow-oak cabinet where lead type was stored in shallow drawers to his heaped rolltop desk with tubes of foolscap like piano-player rolls sticking out of the pigeonholes to the type-writer, a knee-high pile of ratchets, pulleys, and balance wheels mounted on casters with a treadle like a sewing ma-chine, without overtaxing his bunged-up leg.

He never used the type-writer himself. He called it the Contraption, preferring to confine his mechanical acumen to the platen press. But every modern office had to have at least one type-writer on display, and he was loath to sur-render any part of his tight quarters to anything purely dec-orative. He'd hired a male secretary away from a city superintendent to operate it, not to write copy but to bring an air of efficiency to his business correspondence. Young Greenfield took dictation as fast as the Major could give it—and he was a rapid speaker, brooking no interruption—and used all ten fingers on the keyboard; when the lad's pilot light was on, the noise sounded like an army of tim-berjacks clearing a stand of redwoods. On a truly produc-tive day, the chopping of the strikers and the clunkety-clunk of the press producing sheet after sheet of dense print drowned out the foghorns bawling in the bay and the vi-bration shook dust and soot from the rafters.

The Barbary Spar advertised a circulation of twenty-five thousand. That figure was based on the calculation that at least five people were exposed to each issue of the biweekly journal. At that it was an exaggeration, because of the five thousand copies printed, five hundred were returned for credit by the merchants who stocked them.

Updegraff was built close to the ground and looked as if he'd shriveled inside his clothes: His open waistcoat, yellowed shirt, and trousers swaddled him, and in fact had the day he'd bought them. He was indifferent to male fashion and thought Greenfield a fop for blacking his shoes and changing his collar twice a week. He himself had worn the same green eyeshade since Dakota, cracked and spliced with sticking-plaster. The cigars that had burned holes in his shirt had left furrows on every surface in the office except the lithographic stone. The only thing he was vain about was his eyesight. The wire-rimmed spectacles he used for reading vanished into a clamshell case whenever someone approached. He was forty-two years old when Abraham Cripplehorn made his acquaintance, carrying a sheaf of neatly written notes on Palace Hotel stationery.

ILLUSTRIOUS GUN MAN STOPS HERE.

by Jack Dodger

Mr. Francis X. Farmer, known to readers throughout North America as the shootist ensnared in a "blood feud" with Mr. Randolph Locke, both originally of Texas, since the spring of 1868, is stopping in San Francisco and hopes that Mr. Locke will be doing the same when opportunity permits.

Asked the reason for the long enmity, Farmer said, "That's between Randy and me. I don't see how it's of concern to anyone else."

When this correspondent went on to inquire as to the character of his esteemed opponent, he replied, "He was one of the hardest-working hands who rode for the old Circle X, and what he lacks in skill with a carbine or rifle he more than makes up for with a hand iron. I carry around evidence of that, for anyone who doubts my word."

Farmer was alluding, in addition to two ancient scars on his chest and back, to the artificial ear of expert workmanship that substitutes for that appendage, which was shot off by Locke in Abilene, Kansas, in 1869.

Locke has not gone unscathed as a result of these associations. He lost much of the use of a leg when Farmer shot his horse from under him in Wyoming, ruining him for ranch work. He's said to have made his living since hunting wolves and buffalo and as a ranch cook. . . .

"No, I've not lost my taste for the affair," Farmer said when asked if time had cooled his ardor. "I don't reckon Randy has neither, and if he hasn't turned into a yellow skunk by now, I look forward to taking up where we left off in Salt Lake City."

Major Updegraff snatched off his spectacles and looked up from the sheaf in his hand. His visitor was a bland-enough-looking fellow despite his elaborate Wild West Show rig-out and false eye. He looked like a barbed-wire salesman who'd gotten too close to his samples.

"You're Dodger?"

"Professionally, yes. The name is Cripplehorn in private life."

"I've heard of this pair. For my money there's been too much romanticizing of this kind of range rat already. It drives away business and puts the vigilantes on the prod."

"If you're not interested—"

"I didn't say that. I'm just warming up for an editorial. My readers like it when I get my back up. You don't say where Farmer's staying."

"He asked me not to. He doesn't want reporters camping out in the lobby, like what happened with Locke when he was in town."

"That's all right with me. I can't get hotel advertising. What brought you here? Why didn't you go to Gilbert at the *Examiner,* or Butler at the *Call,* or any one of a half-dozen others can buy the *Spar* out of petty cash?"

"They all wanted to turn it over to one of their own reporters, rewrite everything, and copyright it under the papers' names. I didn't write it for someone else's glory."

"Well, it could do with editing. You got three pages in the middle of midnight rides and bloody gun battles, with no one to attribute it all to. Were you there?"

"No, but it seemed kind of puny without it. I couldn't get Frank to say a derogatory thing about Randy till the end, and that was tame. The idea was to get him out here and lay the thing to rest."

"I can see where Butler wouldn't have any of it. His people are Quakers. Is it your intention to be there when it happens?"

"In a manner of speaking."

The Major lit his cold cigar, releasing a fresh shower of sparks onto his shirt and waistcoat. He brushed at them and squinted at the other through a screen of blue smoke. "You one of those jaspers likes to attend public train wrecks?"

"I'm an entrepreneur. I make my money off those same jaspers."

"I'm not one. I don't pay for outside copy, if that's what you're thinking. If I was to start doing that and my reporters found out, I'd have to pay them regular."

"I'm not. Are you interested or aren't you?"

"I ought to send a man to interview him himself."

"He won't get past the door. I've got Frank's word the story's mine."

"The word of a man-killer?"

"He's been called that and other things as well, but never a welsher."

Updegraff picked up a page. "Who's Mississippi Belle?"

"A boat I used to own. The story needed a woman."

The newspaperman drew a line with a soft black pencil and Belle was gone.

"How do I know you didn't make the whole thing up?"

"Isn't this the paper that printed the headline CUSTER'S VICTORY IN MONTANA?"

"That was the War Department's fault. They withheld the details so as not to spoil the Centennial celebration in Washington. I had to run a retraction. You don't develop a taste for crow, I can tell you."

"You can send a man with me to talk to Farmer. He'll convince him who he is quickly enough."

"Probably scare him out of town and leave me short-staffed." Updegraff's cigar had gone out again when the hot ash met saliva, but he didn't appear to notice. "Well, I can't use it as written, starting with the headline. I write those myself, and it has to fit the column. Most of the rest reads like a cheap novel. All this Buffalo Bill hogwash has to come out."

"That's acceptable, as long as you keep in the quotations and put my name on it."

"Don't you worry about that. One place you've got him talking like Henry Ward Beecher and another like Davy Crockett. If I asked any of my people to claim credit, he'd up and quit."

"Will you send it out on the wire?"

"Oh, hell, yes. The eastern journals will be on this like buzzards on a dead elephant. I'm going to copyright it— don't get your bowels in an uproar, we'll share ownership— so they'll have to mention the *Spar*. I may have to increase my print run to what it says on the masthead."

12

Bad company is like a pox, and the unafflicted would be wise to avoid it.

The railroad man's name was Herbert, Henry Herbert. Right off Randy was disposed to dislike a man who hadn't a last name.

He was enormously fat—sideshow freak fat, the kind of fat that made a stranger turn to watch him, slack-jawed, as they passed on the street, like a runaway train on fire and passengers jumping off the vestibules to sure broken necks to get free. Globs of him pushed out under the hickory arms of his swivel chair, which groaned agonizingly like a cow breech-birthing, and if he had on a cravat—as seemed likely—you couldn't see it for the concertina folds of fat under his chin. Randy wondered why the man bothered. He was sweating in his office on the second story of a bank building in Phoenix, Arizona Territory, with the windows open creating a cross draft of pure furnace air, a slippery mess of overfed catfish who might just lubricate himself free of the chair if he weren't wedged in tight as a tick.

"I know your dealings with Frank Farmer," Herbert said. "To be honest, I'd rather be talking to him. This is more in his line of work, and I'm concerned about that leg."

"Just what *is* the job? The notice in the paper just said you wanted an unmarried man."

"A bit of drama, suggested by my partner; to get attention, he said. He was right. Since it ran I've turned away dozens of applicants. We're building a spur from Elgin to Calabasas in Pima County, a stone's throw from the Mexican border. We need someone to discourage the Apaches from endangering the workers."

"One?"

"I'd prefer a squad, but the treasury won't cover paying men just to stand around waiting to be needed. Some of the workers are experienced with weapons, so you won't exactly be alone. Of all who have come forward you're the most promising—if you're who you say you are—but, to be honest—"

His favorite phrase, it developed, like a profane man slinging around Jesus. "I don't shoot with my leg," Randy put in. "I'm best at close range, but I shot wolves and buffler from three hundred yards. I reckon I can scatter a batch of yammering savages on those scrub ponies they straddle down here."

The railroad man's chair groaned this way and that; thinking with his ass. Finally he swiveled to face his desk, dipped a pen in a squat bottle, scribbled something on rag paper with the name of the railroad printed across the top in bold letters with doodads on them, sprinkled sand from a pot on what he'd written, and blew away the loose grains. "Give this to Ralph Potter, the foreman. Go to Elgin and follow the tracks west. You'll need travel expenses."

A black iron safe with gilt lettering squatted in a corner. Grunting and blowing, the railroad man crab-walked his chair over to it on squealing casters, leaned forward, and worked the dial. He took a tin box from inside, opened it, counted out banknotes from a stack, put back the box, shut the safe, and gave the dial a spin. "One hundred dollars. That should cover the fare to Elgin—I'd give you a pass, but that stretch belongs to a competitor—provisions, and whatever other incidentals you'll need."

Randy took the sheaf of notes, stuck it in his worn cowhide poke, and put it in his hip pocket. The railroad man asked him if he wasn't going to count the notes.

"I reckon it's all there. You train men don't steal by the dollar. Anyway, I can always find my way back here."

It was March, although by the standards of most places it was July, especially the farther he went south across that parched territory, where through passengers got out at every poke-hole station to unstick their shirts from their backs and drink water from a pump. At every stop lay the same yellow dog in the shade of the station overhang, sprawled on its side as if dead, the same plug-hatted Indian wrapped in a blanket sat with his back to the station wall, the same litter of scrawny boys wearing ropes for suspenders flocked around the alighting passengers looking to run an errand for a penny. Sixty miles of that, from Phoenix to Elgin, with nary a stick of wood in sight except what was required for support and couldn't be fashioned from the native mud like everything else. All the stations were made of it, frequently whitewashed although not always, with the red mud bleeding pink through the white.

Elgin was more of the same. The names of the businesses were generic: MERCANTILE, SALOON, LIVERY STABLE, BANK, as if the sheer dirt-pounding pressure of arid heat shriveled the imagination like the string of chili peppers hanging from every porch post, and painted directly on the dried mud. There was one mercantile, one livery, one bank, four saloons, with it seemed every horse in the vicinity tied up in front of the latter, heads hanging in the heat.

A fat blue fly landed on Randy's cheek while he was collecting his bedroll from the brass overhead rack, waited resignedly for him to swat it. When he didn't bother, it rubbed its front legs together, tested one wing, then the other, and lifted off, floating on the heavy air.

"You get used to it," said the old man in a split-bottom chair tipped back against the station wall, another fixture at every stop. "It's dry heat, not like Kansas or Missouri."

The newcomer finished mopping the back of his neck with a bandanna. "It's dry in a Dutch oven, but the biscuits burn just the same."

He entered the livery, where the cool dimness fell across him like mist. The attendant, a wiry sixty in filthy overalls, sat on an overturned bucket scooping sardines from a can into his mouth with his fingers.

"Buggy's hired," he said, eyeing Randy's game leg. "Expect it back at sundown."

"I need a saddle horse."

"You can have Patty. She's old but she's gentle."

"I said a horse, not a rocking chair. And a decent saddle, not one of them dishrags." A row of brittle-looking saddles drooped from a wooden rail, cinch straps stiff as straw. He'd sold his good one in Lincoln for the fare to Arizona Territory; he'd had his fill of cold and thought he might try his luck prospecting for silver in Tombstone or Bisbee. But the money ran out in Phoenix, just in time for him to see the notice in the *Herald*.

The livery man frowned, tossed the empty sardine can into a pile of manure, wiped his hands on his overalls, and got up to trot out a short-coupled sorrel mare with thick haunches. Randy looked at its teeth, felt its fetlocks, and inspected it for fistulas. "How much?"

"For the day or the week?"

"For the horse. I don't figure to be coming back here."

They traded, agreeing finally on thirty for the horse and ten for a McClellan saddle that looked as if it might last to Calabasas. Randy lashed his bedroll wrapped around the Ballard rifle behind the cantle and swung into leather, awkwardly on account of his leg but fast enough to satisfy the livery man he wouldn't fall off in town and bring shame to the enterprise.

Ralph Potter, the foreman, was a lean man in a leather waistcoat and whipcords, with stovepipe boots and a flat-brimmed, round-crowned hat like a town Indian's. He wore a self-cocker in a stiff cavalry holster on his hip. His pale blue eyes looked like steel shavings caught in cracks and he was burned deep cherry from sweatband to collar and from wrists to fingertips and likely was creamy white everywhere else, like an honest man. Randy figured he was honest enough, but disliked him on sight. He was inhospitable, but that was neither here nor there. There was something lacking in the man—not as obvious as a missing limb or a blind eye, but easy to spot just the same.

Decency, that's what was missing. Randy had seen it before, often enough to know better than to argue himself out of the suspicion.

"Goddamn it, I told 'em the Apaches are down in Chihuahua, holed up in caves avoiding General Crook. I'd sooner they sent a good working jack."

"Well, I'm here."

They had tents set up, the nearest shade being where they had come from and where they were headed, which was about the same distance. The graders were hauling their drags, the gandies dropping the rails into place with businesslike clanks and swinging their sledges, the Irish singing something from the old country, the Chinese working silently, no jabbering like their fellow expatriates who worked in town. A Negro boy in a flop hat and overalls carried around a bucket of water from which the Irish took a dipper and drank or sloshed it over their heads or both. The Chinese never sloshed, and some of them skipped their turns at a drink, seeming almost annoyed at the interruption to their labors. There was a covered chuck wagon and a dray loaded with barrels of water. Randy wondered what sort of man was in charge of the chuck.

Damn, now he was even *thinking* like a cookie.

Potter watched him watching the crew.

"The chinks are hard workers, and dependable as clap in Kansas City. They don't get drunk, don't fight among themselves, never go on strike, and stay away from whores."

"What about the Irish?"

"Ignorant as mules and twice as stubborn. Oh, they give you a week's work in a day, when they ain't hungover or beating each other's brains out or got a bee up their ass over some little thing. If I could breed 'em with the chinks, cross the micks' muscle with the yeller boys' sense of responsibility, I'd have this spur finished. The Irish are talking strike, just when I need 'em to work through Sundays before the monsoons shut us down for a month." The foreman shot a stream of tobacco, just missing the toe of Randy's boot; testing the distance, thought the other, between his indecency and Randy's patience. "Seeing's how you're here, you can draw your pay at the end of the week, then go wherever you like, so long as it ain't here."

"I was promised six weeks."

"Not by me, you wasn't. I can't stand to see a man drawing pay sitting in the shade. It gives the Irish ideas."

"What shade? That rake handle over there wouldn't keep the sweat off a sand flea. I didn't come all the way from Nebraska for no twenty dollars. I spent all the up-front money on trains and that fat town mare holding up a Yankee saddle."

"You got them, and you got to see some country. I was you I'd leave it at that." Potter laid a hand to rest on the handle of the self-cocking pistol.

Randy considered it; but he was saving that fight for someone else. "I'll draw that twenty now."

"At the end of the week, I said."

He pushed his hat back on his head, exposing pale skin from where it had rested to his thinning widow's peak. "Then I reckon I'll stretch out under the chuck wagon. Have somebody wake me it's supper, will you? Me, I'd pick one of the Chinese, but I don't like to tell a ramrod his business."

The foreman's left cheek caved in, getting the works between his teeth. Randy saw a couple of the Irish looking their way, getting ready to lean on the handles of their shovels. Finally he dropped his hand from his weapon and jerked his head toward the biggest of the tents.

The respective cool of the interior dried the sweat on the back of Randy's neck. There was a campaign table and chair, a leather-reinforced canvas bag like postmen carried tied in a Gordian knot by its handles to the center pole with a lock securing its flap, a cot, and a ledger the size of a plat book spread open on the table. It was where the foreman doled out the pay. He sat in the folding chair, hoisted a bottle from under the table, and slid it across the table. "No glasses. No fandango dancers neither. Just Old Pepper; and if the micks smell it out they'll beat each other to death trying to get it."

Randy made sure a nearby powder keg was empty and lowered himself onto it. "If you're looking to drink me under this table to avoid paying me, you better dig a hole." He uncorked the bottle, tipped it up, and let it gurgle.

"No. Hell, no. Out there I got to behave like it's coming out of my own poke, but to me it's just rebel scrip. I was to do the company out of a dime, they'd hunt me to China and take it out through my kidneys. I reckon you and I can reach an agreement."

"The Irish?" Randy wiped the back of his hand across his mouth and scooted the bottle back across the table.

"When the day's work's through and they ain't stripping the hide off each other's faces with their bare knuckles, they're talking strike. I can't take 'em all on, comes to that. But if an example can be made before they sort out their minds on the subject, I might could buy time, at least till the monsoons. By then we'll be so close to Calabesas I can finish with the chinks if I have to." He took a pull and pushed the bottle Randy's way.

Randy left it there. "I hired on to shoot injuns on the warpath. I won't murder a white man just to make a point."

"That's surprising talk, considering what I heard about you; but I'd never ask you to shoot an Irishman. They come in litters and we'd both be fighting 'em off the rest of our lives, which wouldn't be long."

"What, then?" But he was beginning to suspect.

Potter got up, went to the tent flap, and drew it aside. The view descended a slope to where a group of Chinese in flop hats and overalls were carrying twenty feet of iron rail.

"Take your pick," he said. "They're all of 'em alike."

Randy said nothing. The foreman looked back at him. "It'd convince the Irish we mean business. A chink today, maybe a mick tomorrow. It ain't as if the yeller boys ain't got a hundred cousins pouring in from Frisco every day."

Randy considered; then stood, scooped up the empty keg, and swung it at Potter's head. The staves collapsed like the sticks they were and one of the iron hoops lit on its side and rolled out the flap and down toward the latest patch of railroad, where it excited some interest, but only for a moment. Then the clank of the rails dropping into place and the clang of the sledges striking home the spikes resumed, echoing in Randy Locke's mind miles after it had faded from actual hearing.

In his poke he carried the six weeks' wages he'd hired on for, freed from the bank bag with the aid of his old worn Bowie and his own two hands, worn as well but still of service. Apprised of the atrocity by a wire from Ralph Potter, recuperating from a broken jaw in a mission hospital in Elgin, the railroad man in Phoenix posted a reward for his capture; as was typical of that industry, the amount settled upon was ten times more than had been lost.

Randy stopped for rest in a town that was so Mexican he suspected government surveyors of erring in drawing the line south rather than north of it. Every day seemed to be a cause for fiesta: the birth or death of an important saint, the anniversary of some skirmish between patriots and some tyrannical despot or other, thirteen whelps born to an old unparticular bitch thought barren, and she with teats enough to serve the bunch. All the signs were in Spanish and some bored woodcarver had hacked a monkey-faced Christ out of a saguaro cactus at the village entrance. The cantina where he found a room was run by a short broad Mexican with his hair cut in bangs and little triangular moustaches at the corners of his mouth. He put aside the Spanish-language newspaper he was reading to open the registration book. When he spun it his way to read the signature, his eyes stood out from his head.

"*Señor* Randy Locke?" said he. "*Randolph* Locke?"

"Not Randolph. Not to my face. Not in twenty-five years. *Por qué?*" A man couldn't remain in Arizona long without picking up some of the lingo.

The little man spread the newspaper on the cracked piñon surface of the registration desk, pointing a ragged nail at an item in *El Noticias Telégrafo*. The first English word Randy spotted quickened his pulse: *Farmer*.

"How's your English?"

The little man glanced out the open front door, which looked out on the Rio Grande, brown and sluggish under the burden of violent history; Mexico three hundred yards away.

"*Señor*, I am not certain which language I am speaking now."

Randy stabbed a finger at the paper, cutting a cicatrix in the brittle newsprint with the nail. "Read it. In English." He stood a cartwheel dollar on its edge and spun it with a flick of the same finger. It made a white blur, mesmeric to the little man behind the desk, who snatched it up in mid-spin and turned the newspaper back his way.

"San Francisco, December eleventh," he read . . .

13

**There is no better way of determining a
friend's true character than to spend three days
under the same roof.**

San Francisco had lost nothing of its ability to separate
a man from his capital; if anything, it had refined the
process since Randy Locke's visit.

As damp, foggy winter melded into foggy, damp spring,
the rates at the Palace had hollowed a deep gouge in Abraham Cripplehorn's Chautauqua earnings. Frank Farmer's
more modest poke was reduced to the same state by the
demands of the lesser hotels near the crumbling harbor. After some palaver, the two pooled their resources and went
partners on a rented house occupied until recently by a
shanghai agent known locally as Black Louie, and more recently still as a guest of the gallows. The walls were sufficient to hold up the roof, but held out neither noise nor drafts,
and the roof itself had the unique property of releasing rusty
water onto the tenants' heads even when the sun shone.

"How the devil is such a thing possible?" complained
Cripplehorn, when a fresh gout teeming with iron particles
and live wigglers suddenly seasoned his soup.

"A proper roof don't slant to the middle," Frank explained. "This one leaves pockets. Think of 'em as un-
planned cisterns. If this was New Mexico, you'd be happy
to have 'em."

"Well, it isn't, and I'm not. What's your reasoning on the
rats? This morning I found a litter of them in my valise."

"Half this town's built of busted ships. I reckon the critters just come along with the timbers."

"What's keeping your friend? Updegraff says that piece

went out on the wires two months ago. Maybe he's turned into that yellow skunk after all."

"I didn't say them words. That was pure Jack Dodger fiction, and if you remember right I was agin it. Randy's a lot of things, but he never tucked his tail 'twixt his legs and he ain't dumb enough to believe I ever said he did; not that it would keep him from coming here shanks mare if he had to. Either he's so far out in the high country he hasn't got the word or he's dead." Frank finished a game of Patience and peeled the dirty pasteboards off a dirtier oilcloth, one by one. "Either this table needs a new cover or I need a new deck. One more hand and I'll want a spatula."

Cripplehorn upended his last bottle of peach brandy into a tin cup that had come with the house. He ran a finger around the inside of the neck and sucked on it. "I entered this venture intending to clear enough to meet all the crowned heads of Europe. Instead I'm incubating vermin and eating nail soup."

"Don't forget the baby meskeeters. A man needs meat."

"Do you really think he's dead?"

Frank shuffled the deck; or to be more precise, broke it free of itself from time to time like a batch of sliced bacon and rearranged the rashers.

"Nope. I know Randy better than anybody. He might let himself be swallowed up by a grizzly, if he got bored with the contest, but he'd come out that bear's ass with his Colt in his fist, asking after me."

"Can I quote you on that? It would read so well in *Harper's Weekly*."

Frank pasted a jaded queen of hearts to the disreputable oilcloth. One of her eyes, thumb-smeared and stained with soot, appeared to be winking at him, with the tired automatism of an overqualified whore. "You come out here looking for color, you said. You wasn't specific as to the picture it got painted with."

Cripplehorn drained his cup, wobbled the last taste of civilization around inside his mouth, plucked his last cigar from his waistcoat, which needed mending at the seams, and lit it off the greasy flame from a coal-oil lamp that smoked like a rendering plant. Frank Farmer, he'd discovered, was less than the ideal roommate. He kept to his grooming, barbering his imperials, brushing his suit of unmatched pieces, and bathing when necessary, but as to the rest, living with him was like sharing quarters with one of those wild men one read about, raised by wolves. The outhouse was only ten paces from the back door, but when nature called, the nearest window would do: All the whitewash was eaten off the wall beneath every fenestration on the premises. He seemed to regard passing gas the supreme compliment to a meal well prepared (Cripplehorn considered himself a passably good cook, a condition forced upon him by self-sufficiency), scrubbed out his longhandles in the same sink where Cripplehorn washed his vegetables, and hung them from the same hook that supported the big frying pan in which most of their meals were prepared, dripping onto the iron stove and leaving circles of rust and essence of Frank Farmer on the surface.

It was about as far a cry from the crowned heads of Europe as could be imagined.

Frank, in his turn, found Cripplehorn fell short of pards he'd lived with in past times. His coffee was so weak a fly could swim around on the surface, practicing its dog-crawl and floating on its back like some Oriental put'n'take, and it wouldn't wake a man up from a daydream. When the man retired, hanging up his clothes and fiddling with them so the pleats were just so, taking out his Dutch eye and polishing it with a little cloth and sinking it in a glass of water, he thought he might as well be living with a high-toned woman, only without the expected benefits.

The worst of it was that eye. On nights when the fog

didn't stand between the house and the moon, a shaft passed through the window and lay on that glass. Ivory didn't sink, and so the eye floated on top, drifting this way and that, the way a real eye did in a human face, and lighting on Frank where he lay on his bunk. He couldn't shake the feeling that Cripplehorn was in charge of it and what it saw, and he couldn't sleep with a man staring at him wide awake from the bunk next to his.

This night he turned away from it onto his back. He stared up into the darkness beyond the red glow leaking from the poorly joined barrel stove and prayed to the Lord for Randy's safe conduct.

14

No man who has someone he can call upon for help is truly poor.

WANTED
Randolph Locke
is Sought for
Assault and Robbery
in Elgin, A.T.
A REWARD OF $1,000
is offered for information
leading to his arrest and conviction.

Randy spotted the shinplaster tacked to a corkboard in a combination general store and post office in San Diego. His description—height below average, thickset, full-faced—was right enough, but his own mother couldn't identify him by the pen-and-ink sketch that accompanied it. If he were the manhunting type he could keep pulling men off the street with vapid expressions and faces traced around the bottom of a whiskey bottle all day long and come away empty-handed. The storekeep, who was also postmaster, gave him not a second glance when he filled his order.

Not that being wanted signified anything. The more miles he put between himself and Arizona Territory, the less economically feasible it was for anyone to attempt to claim the thousand. He'd burned off most of the wages he'd had coming to him for refusing to shoot a Chinaman just getting that close to San Francisco and Frank. If he wanted to arrive with any stake at all he was looking at better than three hundred miles in a cattle car.

But worse was to come.

The guards aboard California trains had no regard for tramps. They made a thorough examination of the rolling stock before it moved, which meant jogging along and grabbing on outside the yards before the cars got to moving too fast. With his bedroll slung by a rope across his back, he missed on the first try and was falling behind when someone already aboard hung halfway out the open door of the car by the handle and stuck out a hand in a sooty fireman's glove. "Grab on, brother!"

Randy lunged for the hand, but he was at his limit, stumbled, and would have had to wait for the next train if another man aboard didn't take part. He got a grip on the edge of the door, linked hands with the first man, and hung on while the first man leaned out another six inches, grasped Randy's outstretched hand, and with the added strength of his friend jerked Randy off the ground, through the door, and into a sliding skid across the straw-strewn floor that knocked the wind out of his lungs. He was still scratching for breath when the two men, aided by a third, robbed him of his bedroll, his Colt, and his poke, snatched him by his belt and the back of his collar, and slung him back out the door. He felt the first rib let go when he struck ground and lost count before he stopped rolling.

He was discovered by a kindly tramp who'd grown too old to ride the rods, scraping out a living picking up lost or discarded items along the cinderbed, fixing what could be fixed, and selling it in town. The old man loaded him aboard his wheelbarrow and delivered him to a free hospital run by a Mexican doctor who hadn't a license to practice in the United States. Felipe Guzman—"Doc Flip" to his white patients—stitched up his gashes, bound his rib cage with thirty yards of bandage, gave him a bottle of laudanum for the pain, and discharged him, apologizing that he couldn't spare the bed.

Standing on the boardwalk in front of the hospital, which still had part of a cow painted on its bricks from its butcher-shop origins, Randy went through all his pockets and came up with a dollar and change. He spent it in a Western Union office.

Abraham Cripplehorn went to the Palace Hotel on a daily basis, hoping for some word from Randy Locke. He was in the act of turning away from the marble-topped desk, having gotten the usual answer, when the clerk said, "Don't you also go by Dodger?"

STRANDED IN SAN DIEGO STOP NEED CASH TO GET
TO FRISCO STOP WIRE GENERAL DELIVERY

R LOCKE

"It could be a scheme," Cripplehorn told Frank. "Somebody read my article and is using his name to raise easy money."

"It ain't." He was still looking at the yellow flimsy.

"What makes you so sure?"

"On account of I can't afford not to be."

"He does have fifty coming. Trouble is, I don't have it."

"How much you got?"

Cripplehorn opened his wallet, cordovan with gold corners, and got out two banknotes, a twenty and a five. A search of his pockets turned up a dollar in change. Frank found two limp singles and a cartwheel dollar.

"That should get him as far as Los Angeles."

"If he don't starve first. Hold on." Frank sat down on the wheezy old mattress, pulled off a boot, and went to work on the inside with his pocket knife. He came up with a twenty-dollar gold piece.

"Holding out on me?"

"I near forgot I had it. I had it stitched into the lining for when I tapped out again. It's from the fifty you gave me up front."

The entrepreneur took it and laid it on the tacky oilcloth with the rest. "I can get twenty for my watch; twenty-five if Goldfinch is in a good mood. He's my local bank when I need a stake."

"If I know Randy he'll need fresh duds. They're always last to go. He ain't the dress hoss I am."

"We don't make rent this month."

"If you ain't full of sheepdip, we'll be in the Palace before it's due."

The gunsmith in San Diego, a Swiss whose blond beard encircled his face like a wreath, handed the customer a Colt with most of the bluing gone. It was a .44 like the conversion he'd lost, only chambered for cartridges at the factory, and with a four-inch barrel.

"Got anything full-size?"

"That Smith and Wesson there on the wall."

"I mean a Colt."

"Just that custom piece in the case."

Randy looked at it through the glass. It had a stag handle and gold chasing on the nickel plate. The tag said fifty dollars.

"I'll get used to it." He turned from the counter, extending the short-barreled pistol from the shoulder, cocked it, and snapped the hammer on an empty chamber. "Trigger pull's tight."

"I can fix that. Dollar and a half extra."

He'd bought decent clothes and booked a day coach. He could just cover it and the purchase. "How soon?"

"Come back around three. I have two ahead of you." The gunsmith indicated a stockless Winchester in his vise and a Derringer in pieces on his bench.

Seeing the carbine gave Randy an idea. "Buy much off the street?"

"From time to time."

"Anybody come in trying to peddle a Ballard rifle?"

"Just yesterday. I turned him down. I didn't like his look."

"Leave his name?"

"No, but his kind generally hangs around the Sisters of Charity down on Ash."

"He didn't by any chance have a Colt to sell."

"No."

"How much to hang on to that short-barrel?"

"Five."

He put a banknote on the counter. "Hold off on that trigger till I get back."

He didn't entertain much hope. That train had been heading out of town. The bunch that jumped him wouldn't likely have circled back to turn his gear into cash. But men weren't as predictable as wolves and buffalo.

The neighborhood was worse than he'd seen in any dirty mining camp: lawyers with smut under their nails handing out cards on the corners, tramps sleeping in doorways, the kind of whore that was last to leave when a vein played out, ugly as half-broke sin. The buildings looked ready to fall down when a rat farted; they made a man want to walk down the middle of the street and take his chances with the drunken wagon drivers. He identified the Sisters of Charity by the line of unwashed men waiting for handouts.

One caught his eye, leaning without much hope against the iron railing of the front steps. Randy hadn't gotten a good enough look at those tramps to pick one out of a crowd, but this fellow was the only one carrying a bundle big enough to contain his Ballard. It was wrapped in an overcoat holier even than his clothes. He smelled of all kinds of human corruption, with an overlay of boiler soot, and someone had taken exception to his face sometime and tried to take it off with an axe or a big knife; the scar was old and puckered and ran from temple to chin. He had on dirty fireman's gloves, which rang a bell somewhere in the murk, but you couldn't kill a man just for what he wore on his hands.

Not with so many others present anyway.

Randy crossed the street to a boarded-up building and took a position in the doorway.

The line moved slowly, but in twenty minutes the man with the bundle was inside. Randy gave him twenty more to get to the front of the line, give Jesus His due, and eat his soup, then another twenty when that twenty ran out. His bad leg began to throb from all the standing; before long the pain would be fierce and constant.

But he forgot about it when the man came out and descended the stairs with a little more spring in his step than he'd had going in. Randy waited for him to hit the pavement, then crossed the street and fell in behind. They were two blocks from the charity house in a section empty of people when he quickened his pace and drew abreast.

"I'll have a look at that bundle."

The vagabond had better instincts than anticipated. Without pausing to look at the stranger he made a move for the inside of his torn overalls. Randy backed up a step, but he still had his Bowie. The blade parted the man's shirtsleeve and carried away flesh from his elbow to his wrist. The bundle fell from under his arm, but Randy caught it and shoved the tramp the rest of the way off balance with his other hand.

There was something hard inside the holey overcoat. He grasped it, fingers closing around the familiar pistol-grip stock, and shook his rifle free. In the same motion he smashed the barrel across the man's face just as the man was scrambling to his feet, doubling the force of the collision. He went down hard on the ground, stunned.

Randy bent and searched his reeking clothes—not forgetting the pockets of the coat the tramp had used to swaddle the Ballard—but there was no sign of his Colt, just the clasp knife he'd intended to plunge into Randy. He threw it into a patch of weeds across the street.

He made a cane of the rifle, leaning on it to brace his bad leg, kicked the man in the side, snapping ribs, and went back to the gunsmith's shop for his new sidearm.

15

A man needs a close companion, if only to spare him from his baser instincts.

"Mr. Cripplehorn, may I expect payment this time in reasonably short order?"

The tailor, a tall Levantine with a scholar's stoop, wore the standard uniform of open-necked lawn shirt, striped trousers suspended by braces, and yellow tape measure around his neck. Pearl-headed pins glittered like captain's bars on his collar. He was on one knee beside the carpeted rise before the triptych mirrors, making chalk marks where the entrepreneur's uncut deckle-edged trouser leg crumpled at the instep.

The customer narrowed his working eye at his image in the basted-together morning coat; he prided himself on his ability to view himself with total objectivity. "Of course, my man. My allowance is due next week."

The tailor made a small adjustment in a measurement and recorded it in his little notebook, abandoning the discussion as pointless. With the forty-niners dying out and their grown sons making the Grand Tour to visit Italian statues and order suits in London, much of his business came from wayward progeny supported by payments from their respectable eastern parents to stay away. Since North America ran out at the Pacific, San Francisco was where they lighted. It was a generation that favored silk next to its skin and considered it bad form to settle a tailor's bill in less than a year. Meanwhile the Levantine's daughter wore hand-me-downs and his son was reduced to shaming his father in public wearing suits from Monkey Ward's.

His fitting completed, Cripplehorn resumed his last good

suit and stepped out into a rare patch of Barbary Coast sunshine, absently groping for his silver-plated watch before he remembered. A glance at a tower clock told him he had an hour before the 3:45 got in: time enough to meet with his other partner.

"I was beginning to think you fell in the bay."

One glance at Frank Farmer said he was drunk and in a foul mood. The saloon, on Mission Street near the harbor, was a bare-bones affair aimed at mariners, with whitewashed walls naked but for a poorly wrought painting in a chipped gilt frame of a schooner caught in a storm at sea and shelves of whiskey cut with salt water from the Pacific, a beneficial combination, as it turned out: The liquor burned the throat, the brine cured it. Frank sat red-eyed at a corner table with a smeared glass in front of him and a nearly empty bottle at his elbow.

"Our arrangement was informal." Cripplehorn hung his Stetson on the hat tree and pulled out a chair. "If my session ran long, I would go straight to the station."

"I reckoned you'd growed dependent on that stem-winder and lost all track of time. In another fifteen I was fixing to meet the train myself."

Cripplehorn frowned.

"We agreed you're not to set eyes on each other until the contest. It's been years, and one or the other of you might lose sight of our objective in the heat of the moment."

"You saying I can't keep a hobble on myself?"

Not in your present condition. Aloud he said, "I'm less acquainted with Locke, based on our one conversation. We've a long way to go before the event. We need financial backing, and the legal matters will require money and time."

"Right now you can't raise the price of a drink even in this pisshole. What makes you think you'll find someone who can?"

"I've my eye on a young fellow I met at my tailor's. He's the man who gave me the idea to identify myself as the prodigal son of a wealthy and exasperated family, to forestall inconvenient questions about the condition of my finances: textiles, if I understood him correctly. He was in an inebriated state at the time, but he ordered three separate suits of evening wear and a half-dozen shirts made in Paris. He's a sporting man as well. I managed to separate him from ten dollars at euchre while we were waiting for a fitting. With a bit of finesse I hope to interest him in an investment that will grant him a measure of independence and a healthy return on our labors."

"Well, you just spent five times that ten in words. I lost a dollar to a man running a shell game in Denver during my Regulating time who I reckon swallowed the same dictionary."

"Then you see the value of my intentions."

"I knocked him flat and found the pea that belonged under one of them shells in his watch pocket. Being the nearest thing to law in that room I took back my dollar and fined him five more for being a tinhorn."

"You haven't met Sheridan Weber; of the Rhode Island Webers. He couldn't knock flat a blade of grass. Research the history of any one of these second-generation robber barons and you'll find his father strained him through a sheet."

"The cattlemen's association I worked for in Colorado was run by a fellow with consumption and a geezer couldn't hear a powder charge going off in the next room. You calculate this Sheridan wouldn't hire five men like me to take his investment out of your hide?"

"I think you should leave the business part to me and stick to your target practice."

"I'll take it up with Randy. He's a buffalo turd, but I'd rather sit downwind of him than listen to you gab about all the textile millionaires you met standing around in your long-handles."

Cripplehorn stretched himself, studying the men lined up at the bar out of the corner of his eye. He felt inside a pocket, counting coins. He pushed out his chair and stood. "We're talking in circles. Why don't I get you something to soak up that skullbender and see if that bartender has a bottle of peach brandy he's keeping for medicinal purposes?"

"I ate yesterday. Just fetch me another one of these here, seeing's you're so good at euchre." Frank poured the rest of the whiskey into his glass.

A city policeman in his tight blue tunic and postman's cap stood with his foot on the green brass rail, drinking beer. As was the way of such establishments he had his end of the bar all to himself. Cripplehorn came up next to him and asked what varieties of liquor the bartender had on hand.

That individual stopped polishing a glass with a rag that left the glass in worse shape than when he'd started. He looked as if he'd stepped out of a sporting print, by way of too much butter and too many eggs. His nose was turned west ten degrees of his face and his apron hung straight down from his hard belly. "You got two choices, mister: bottle or glass."

"Glass. Not that one," he said, when the man set down the one he'd been working on and picked up a bottle. "One of those behind you." The pyramid of one-ounce glasses standing on the shelf looked as if he'd started them earlier in the rag's ruination.

"Ten cents."

He pushed a dime across a resistance of spilled whiskey turned into mud from the grit on the bar and leaned in close to the policeman, who was staring into his beer and chuckling quietly at the exchange. Lowering his voice to a murmur, Cripplehorn said, "Officer, do you see that fellow sitting at the corner table?"

"I saw him. I don't miss much. This is my first drink to-day." He might have brought his brogue straight off the boat.

"What do the local statutes say about carrying firearms in the city?"

"They're to be checked at the station upon arrival and picked up upon departure, on pain of fine or incarceration." He appeared to have memorized the official language. "It's a peaceful place, mister, mostly. Anything you heard about road agents and vigilantes is way out of date. We confine all that truck west of Montgomery Street, where we know where to find the bad element when required." A pair of gray eyes set in a young hard face with black sidewhiskers took in the man making the inquiry. "What's your interest? You look like a hideout man to me."

Cripplehorn smuggled a look over his shoulder. Frank sat with his hands wrapped around his glass and his face almost touching it, his hat entirely obscuring his features. The entrepreneur knew the danger posed by men who appeared to be in torpor. But he wasn't looking in the direction of the bar.

Carefully, Cripplehorn unbuttoned his coat and spread the tails for the officer's inspection. "I don't have use for percussion weapons. The knife is for my personal protection."

"The ordinance don't say nothing about knives, so long as they ain't put to use. I'm waiting for an answer." He was standing straight facing Cripplehorn, his beer forgotten.

"I suspect that man I pointed out of wearing a pistol under his coat."

"Ain't he your friend?"

"It's for his own protection I'm asking. If he could be placed in a cell until he's sober, you'll find him a model citizen upon release."

"Gus, see to them at the other end."

The bartender had moved to within earshot of the low conversation. He nodded and carried the bottle to where a group of men dressed like teamsters was staring at the schooner in the painting waiting for it to sink.

"You see the pistol?" asked the man in uniform.

"No, but I can't imagine him without one."

"What's his name?"

"Frank Farmer."

The stiff-visored cap moved back, propelled by the muscles in the officer's forehead. "The gun man?"

"Retired."

"I never heard of such a thing happening this side of a churchyard."

"He's not wanted anywhere, if that's your concern."

"Farmer, huh?" He tugged at his sidewhiskers. Cripplehorn could read the man as easily as an amateur card player: No one wanted to be a street patrolman forever. Finally the officer threw a coin on the bar.

"Keep him here if you can. I might need help."

"Try not to hurt him. He's a white fellow when he isn't in his cups."

16

**Partnerships are based on personal regard
and mutual trust. Where one is missing,
the other is inconsequential.**

He spotted Cripplehorn's exaggerated hat before the train rolled to a stop. Alighting, he avoided shaking hands by carrying his bedroll by its strap with one hand and his Ballard with the other. "Where's Frank?"

"He's arranged accommodations. Have you?"

"I ain't got the price. I'll camp outside town. I sure do hope you wasn't lying in that newspaper story."

"There's no need to worry about that."

"I like to worry, Dodger. It's got me this far."

"It looks like you took the rocky road."

"I ran into some excitement, but I'll heal. I won't ask you again about Frank."

"You'll have to accept my word he's in town. I can't take the chance of old associations come to grief before their time."

"That's a fancy way of saying I can't keep a fence on my own self."

"I never doubted it, but I'm not so sure about Mr. Farmer."

"You like to light both ends of the match, Cripplehorn."

"I'd consider it a favor if you'd call me either Cripplehorn or Dodger; not both. I'm told the vigilantes are inactive at present, but aliases have a way of exciting old passions. Are you hungry?"

"I could eat the stink out of a skunk."

Randy checked his gear in the station. They went into the Harvey House, where a hostess in a crisp white apron offered to help Randy into an alpaca coat from a rack.

"No thanks. I ain't cold."

Cripplehorn said, "It's a house rule. They won't seat you otherwise."

"What else do I need, a plug hat and a monkey stick?"

"Just a coat."

He thrust an arm into a sleeve. "Place sure has got toney since I was here last. Next time I'll have to bring along a brass band."

"I think you'll find the food's worth it."

"I won't appreciate it. I been eating my own cooking so long I can't tell a potato from buffler hump."

They were seated in a clean bright room with checked

tablecloths. Another young white-aproned woman took their orders and moments later set roast sirloin and boiled sweet potatoes in front of Randy and a pile of blue-point oysters before Cripplehorn. Everything was on Santa Fe Railroad china. Randy watched his host pick up a half-shell and slide an oyster into his mouth. Cripplehorn noticed him staring and raised his brows.

The other shook his head. "Just curious to see if you bothered to swallow."

"They're a fine source of iron."

"You can get that sucking on a horseshoe nail." He cut off a piece of steak. "This is a fair spread. You must be in tall cotton."

"The meals here are seventy-five cents apiece."

"Six bits, that's what I'm worth to you?"

"A moment ago you thought it was two dollars. It's still the same steak, is it not?"

"It should be, but it ain't. Cow lives its life, maybe she knows she'll wind up on a plate somewheres, ask her does she want to go for a banknote or pocket jingle? I reckon it's all in the way you look at it, providing you're a cow and got no vote in the election."

"Is it necessary always to be colorful? It must be a constant drain on the imagination coming up with all these frontier aphorisms."

Randy chewed his steak, letting the juice slide down his tongue. "Finding the time ain't much of a challenge. To read your books, a man'd think there wasn't time to use the outhouse for all the gunnies and greedy bankers and injuns on the warpath slinging lead like it grows on trees. I counted eighty-seven rounds from a six-shooter in that Brimstone Bob thing."

"I've never pretended to a knowledge of firearms. Blame my editors."

"It don't signify: I'm talking about the life. I never read

a word about all the time spent pushing the same two dollars around a card game in some line shack watching the snow pile up or sitting around some shit town playing mumblety-peg from noon till sundown waiting for the two-fifteen to get in from Cheyenne. I spent a year in Bismarck betting on when a busted gate would fall off its hinges. I reckon some of the boys are still there waiting."

"There's such a thing as literary license."

"It needs renewing."

Cripplehorn slid another oyster down his throat and chased it with coffee. "I'm sure the world is holding its breath until you publish a novel of your own, with all the slow time put in. Against my advice, Pat Garrett insisted on putting that same lethargy into his life of Billy the Kid. *Petticoat Betsy, the Bandit Princess,* with all its relentless action and dearth of introspection, outsold it a hundred to one."

Randy swirled a piece of steak in its juice, watching the fat coagulate.

"You know something?" he said. "I don't believe you ever met Garrett. I'm starting to believe the closest you ever got to a Jack Dodger book is them copies you sling around like grain seed. Fact is, Mr. Cripplehorn, I don't think you ever done a thing in your life a man could brag on. You're so full of compost I'm surprised you don't grow beans out your ears."

"I won't argue the point or we'd be here all day. Past performance doesn't guarantee future results, as they say in New York City. You know as well as I that what's between you and Farmer is mother's milk back East. People are plunking down their hard-earned dollars from Philadelphia to St. Louis just to see Buffalo Bill and his red-eye-swilling cronies pretend to shoot each other with cap guns onstage. They'll tire of that soon enough and start demanding the real thing. I have ancient Rome as an example to back that up. Those old emperors filled arenas larger than Madison Square Garden to see Christians try their luck against African lions; knowing all the time how the contests would finish. I'm—we're—going them one better. No one can say who will come out standing from a blood duel between Randy Locke and Frank Farmer."

Randy scooped a forkful of sweet potatoes dripping with butter into his mouth and followed it down with a pull from the pint of Old Pepper he'd bought in San Diego.

"Well, I thank you for the top billing." He grinned at Cripplehorn's sudden interest. "Didn't think I knew about such things, did you? It so happens I'm a reading man. When I plunk down a dime for a newspaper I get all the good out of it, from President Garfield getting shot to who's playing the Bird Cage in Tombstone. But I know who'll come out standing. Frank's an artist with a Winchester, but if I was a fair man I'd give him a second's head start when it comes to hip guns. Not that I would," he added, chewing steak. "You don't ever give the other fellow a break when it comes to killing, like in them books you claim you wrote."

"I know an alienist in Chicago who'd pay to cut up your brain and see what's inside," Cripplehorn said; "but I have my standards. I want you to sign this." He drew a folded sheet of rag paper from his inside breast pocket and pushed it across the tablecloth.

"What is it?" Randy left it where it was.

"Look it over. It's not a rattlesnake."

He wiped his hands on his shirt, picked up the paper, and snapped it open, holding it out at arm's length until the type-written letters arranged themselves into language. His lips moved as he read.

"What is it?" He put it down.

"Merely a letter of agreement, attesting to the terms we've discussed: an equal division of the proceeds from your competition with Mr. Locke, between myself and the survivor, or his designated heirs should he encounter a fatal wound as a result. You can read, can't you?"

"I told you I read newspapers. I stuck through fourth grade like everyone else. Did Frank sign this?"

"He's considering it, as would any man of foresight. You may take as much time as you like, and consult an attorney if you want. There's nothing in it we haven't spoken about already."

Randy refolded the paper and pushed it back.

"I'll sign it when Frank does."

Cripplehorn twisted his face into something he hoped was ironic.

"He said the same about you. Are you sure you haven't been in contact with him since Salt Lake City?"

"If I was he'd be dead; or *I* would, if he catches luck. But we both worked for the old Circle X, and there was never nothing between the outfit and its hands but a handshake."

"That was then. Times have changed. You can't put a handshake in a safe."

"A paper can burn up. A handshake never does. Some things don't ever change."

"But there must be a record!"

"What's that, when one or both of us is in the ground? You city folk put too much store in records and such. They won't grow flowers on any of our graves. I won't sign it, and neither will Frank. I reckon I know him that well, if nobody else does."

Cripplehorn picked up an oyster; put it back. He wiped his hands on his napkin. "I'll never understand your type."

"That's the difference between us, Mr. Cripplehorn—or Mr. Dodger, whichever it is—Frank and me, we understand your type right down to the ground."

"A handshake it is, then; against my better judgment." He stuck his hand across the table.

Randy took it, in a grip that brought water even to Cripplehorn's false eye. When the entrepreneur tried to pull himself free, Randy increased the grasp. An iron tooth showed in a bunkhouse grin.

"You know why us frontier types put so much store in this here ritual?"

Cripplehorn shook his head; at a loss between freeing his phalanges from their punishment and Randy Locke's use of the term *ritual*.

"On account of if you don't hold up to it, the next time we show our hands is around the handle of a six-shooter. That's what this western hospitality you're always hearing about has to do with. If you don't prove yourself to be a gentleman, you gave up your right to be treated gentle."

He let go then, and mixed a forkful of rare sirloin with sweet potatoes. His face registered full approval of the flavor.

"I don't know why a man'd drop two bucks in New York City on six bits' worth of grub like this in Frisco," he said. "I reckon that's the difference between a railroad baron and a man works for plain wages."

Abraham Cripplehorn kneaded feeling back into his fingers and wondered for the first time if his wits and a belt knife were sufficient for survival in the American West.

17

Diplomacy is crucial to enterprise. Many a promising arrangement has failed for lack of a judicious word.

One watch, tin," said the clerk behind the bars.

Frank said, "Platinum, you ignorant son of a bitch."

"One wallet, empty."

"I had a dollar in it when I got here."

"Take it up with the day man."

"Forget it. I'd as lief start over clean anyway."

"One Remington Frontier Model revolver, forty-five caliber. You need to replace those grips."

"I'm used to 'em."

"One cartridge belt and holster, cowhide."

He strapped on the belt and slid the weapon into the worn wraparound holster.

"One quarter, two nickels, one penny: thirty-six cents total. Sign here."

Frank Farmer scribbled his name on the receipt the clerk had thrust through the opening in the bars and left the jail. No one was waiting for him outside the ironbound oak door leading to a back street. His clothes were rumpled, his imperial whiskers blurred with stubble, and one eye was nearly swollen shut, although he allowed as he'd given as good as he got when the men in uniform dragged him out of the saloon; one had gone over the bar into the bottles in back, he'd elbowed another's nose flat, and the drunk-and-disorderly they'd dumped into the neighboring cell the next day said he'd heard a third man wound up with a splint on his arm.

A judge with hair sprouting from his ears had sentenced Frank to three days underground for concealing a firearm and tacked on another ten for resisting arrest. He'd been given the choice of paying a fine of fifty dollars instead, but being as how he'd had only a dollar thirty-six cents to his name it wasn't a choice at all.

A wooden barber pole scratched all over by men striking matches hung outside a brick building on the corner. He turned in through the door. "Shave."

A man in striped shirtsleeves with his hair parted in the middle looked up from the newspaper he was reading in a chrome-and-leather chair and took him in from head to foot.

"Fifteen cents."

Frank slapped a quarter on the counter, stirring loose hairs there. The barber got up, made change from a General Jackson cigar box, and snapped the creases out of a cotton sheet.

The shop was all white enamel and black-and-white tile, with oak cabinets containing personalized shaving mugs and foo-foo juice in ornate bottles with glass stoppers. It smelled of citrus. Advertisements on the walls illustrated various sports with splendid curls and elegantly curved moustaches, and signs assured customers YES, WE CUT WET HAIR and offered special rates for children under age ten. Men wearing tights struck pugilistic poses inside pasteboard frames—showing off, thought Frank, for the lady in her underwear in the middle.

Reclined looking up at the pressed tin ceiling, he eased the Remington out of its holster and rested it on his lap under the sheet.

The barber whipped up a lather in a mug with a badger brush. "Interest you in your own mug? Fifty cents. Your name on it in copperplate, script, or fancy old English."

"What's wrong with the one you're using?"

"Nothing, only it's common. Folks come in, see your name there in the rack, they know you're quality. I could stand here all day and tell you the business deals got made right here on the premises."

"I'm certain of that, this place being so close to the jail. Slap on the soap and don't mess with my beard and moustache. I do my own trimming."

The razor's gentle scraping lulled him into a half-doze. When the street door opened, tinkling the copper bell mounted on it, he came awake and tightened his grip on his revolver.

Abraham Cripplehorn glanced around the room and smiled when he saw Frank. He was panting a little.

"You're next, mister," said the barber. "Today's news-papers there in the basket."

Cripplehorn nodded, but his eyes remained on the cus-tomer. "I took a chance you were here when I missed you at the jail. They let you go early."

"I got ten minutes off for good behavior. You got ten sec-onds to talk me out of drilling you where you stand." He lifted the Remington, making a bump in the sheet.

Cripplehorn riffled a pad of banknotes. "Barber, give this man your best shampoo and haircut."

The bump flattened.

It came about this way:

After seeing Randy off on a cable car to the Oakland side of the bay, Cripplehorn called upon Sheridan Weber in his permanent suite at the Eldorado. French doors opened on a balcony overlooking most of the city, and his family crest, griffin rampant on a field of flax—aged artificially to disguise Weber *père*'s recent purchase—hung above the four-poster. Cripplehorn held the door for a waiter push-ing out a butler's caddy heaped with silver-covered dishes.

Young Weber stood in the middle of the Oriental rug in his underwear, curling a pair of black dumbbells. The ex-ercise appeared to have made no difference in his hollow chest and slight paunch. His red hair was arranged in ring-lets to disguise encroaching baldness and his attempt at re-creating his father's rich muttonchop whiskers had so far been no more successful than his fitness programme. He wore a monocle, of all things. His visitor thought the real Jack Dodger, whoever he was, would blush to write such a character into one of his books.

"'Morning, Abe!" Weber strove to be as democratic as his sire was autocratic. "You're up and about early."

"It's five P.M., Sherry. The nighthawking life has thrown your internal clock off the rails."

"Ah, well. Sundowns are as pretty as sunrises, I'm told; and one is awake to appreciate them. What have you there, the opening of another blood-and-thunder novel? I can't keep up. I'm still slogging through Brimstone Bob."

"This won't take long. It's only two pages, and the wording is the same on both." He thumbed the sheets in his hand to demonstrate their brevity.

"Your last will and testament? Am I to witness the division of your worldly acquisitions?"

"That would be even briefer."

Weber tossed his dumbbells onto the bed, mopped his face on the towel draped around his neck, and took the sheets. From the lines of concentration on his forehead his visitor realized he was one of those men who had difficulty reading when someone was watching them. Cripplehorn strolled out onto the balcony, gazing out over the city spreading out from Telegraph Hill and across the bay; from his perspective, a handspan alone separated Frank Farmer from Randy Locke. He'd felt far more at ease when half a continent stood between them.

"Excellent!" said Weber, when he came back inside. "I'd thought these frontier types never put their names to anything."

"It took some convincing." Cripplehorn privately prided himself upon his ability to make two signatures appear as if they'd been written by different hands; he'd even thought to use two different colors of ink. He was grateful that actual specimens of the men's script were unavailable for comparison. "What about your end?"

"What sort of expenses are we talking about?

"A thousand, to start."

"Indeed, that much?"

"The situation is unique. On top of printing, advertising, travel, and accommodations, we're bound to encounter resistance from the authorities."

Weber returned the contracts and took a shirt off a hanger in the wardrobe. "My father is always entertaining public servants in Providence. My observation is they're sporting men."

"Many of them are, but they answer to the public. Wives in particular are opposed to exhibitions involving violence. You can't stage a legal cockfight in Texas, whose state bird ought to be the one-eyed rooster. In Washington there's a move afoot to outlaw prizefighting anywhere in the country. You can imagine the hue and cry when we propose a duel to the death."

"Women can't vote."

"Their husbands can. You'd be surprised to know how much influence a domestic arrangement can exercise in the privacy of a polling booth."

"You propose to bribe the authorities?"

"A man who can be bribed is a man who can double-cross you. He must be bought."

"And you think we can do this with a thousand dollars."

"I'll do the horse-trading. That's my end."

Weber stepped into a pair of checked trousers, tucked in his shirttail, and pulled braces over his shoulders, observing the effect in the full-length mirror on the wardrobe. "Just how much do I stand to clear from this arrangement? After all's said and done, it doesn't seem as if it will be enough to earn independence from my father."

"Mr. Weber, I think you want his approval more than anything else; to prove to him that you, too, can be a self-made man. The fact that the opportunities aren't as plentiful as they were in his time enhances the success. In addition to attendance fees, I intend to charge newspapers and magazines for interviews with my clients and will offer an exclusive with the survivor—if there is one—at auction before the event. I have contacts—subscriptions, anyway—with several of the major eastern newspapers, as well as *Harper's Weekly, Frank Leslie's Illustrated Newspaper,* and *Ned Buntline's Own,* and expect to hear from others once the news gets out. I estimate our enterprise will clear at least a hundred thousand once all the dust has settled." He twisted his face into a mask of concern. "I must warn you that there will be an inconvenience."

The young man—he was thirty, but a chronic adolescent—paused in the midst of tying his cravat. He watched Cripplehorn's worried reflection in the mirror.

"I know you're a modest man, Mr. Weber, who would go to any length to avoid sensation. That may not be possible in this case. I'm very much afraid that the journals will attempt to portray you as the greatest promoter of entertainment since P. T. Barnum. Your likeness will appear in the vulgar press, your every movement recorded: the entertainment venues you visit, the men and women who accompany you. Reporters will gather around you wherever you go. Your opinion will be sought on every subject. I'll understand completely if in the light of this intelligence you decide to abandon our business arrangement and avoid the nuisance."

There was always risk involved; a man pushed his chips into the center of the table and fought the urge to hesitate before taking away his hand. It was like standing on a bridge railing and looking down into a creek that didn't appear nearly as deep as it had before he'd accepted the boyhood dare to jump. A rocky bed and a fragile tailbone spelt disaster. Sometimes he wondered if that wasn't why he lived the way he did, for that heart-stopping moment when fate could go either way, and that the money was just another way of preserving it in a scrapbook. It was a test of courage, and it made a man understand what drove a Randy Locke and a Frank Farmer.

The time for the shakes and self-recrimination would come later, after the moment passed. And then he would plan his next.

The moment this time was briefer than usual. He saw the light of glory in Sheridan Weber's dull eyes.

"Barnum, you say?" He resumed dressing. "Coarse bounder. They say he lived openly with Jenny Lind."

"They say a great many things. It's all very vulgar, and so—public." Cripplehorn almost shuddered, then thought better of it. A man could go too far even with the idiot son of a pompous ass.

"Indeed. But I suppose one must take the lemon along with the sugar."

"You're most unselfish. Now, I may be able to keep your name out of it. Mind you, these journalists are tenacious, and can be thoroughly unscrupulous. I can't promise to be successful, and I wouldn't want to influence you with false—"

"That would be an expenditure of effort far beyond its worth. There's too much else to be done if this venture is to succeed." He shrugged into a Prince Albert coat cut for a younger man, put on a gray bowler, and selected a gold-knobbed stick from an assortment in a hollowed-out elephant's foot beside the door. "The money's downstairs in the safe." He reached for the knob.

Cripplehorn beat him to it. "Allow me."

18

The human element is the open question in any transaction; one cannot allow for it, only prepare for difficulties.

I'm back; did you forget me?

No reason you shouldn't. My life would make a diverting book, but not as fast reading as Mr. Locke's or Mr. Farmer's. I wouldn't be its hero, only its narrator.

I'm the fellow who brought this whole affair to your attention, back when the West wasn't anyone's never-mind but the two men at the center. I reckon I should have took out the copyright when I had the chance.

Apart from a couple of wranglers working the Wild West crew, I'd had no contact with any of my fellow Circle X hands in sixteen years, and nearer seventeen. They didn't remember me, for which I was grateful, given the extent of my contribution to the outfit.

That season I'd helped birth a foal—getting in the way mostly, ranch work and me being casual acquaintances at best. It's a wonder that critter isn't still in there.

I think of that colt from time to time: scrawny thing, more leg than anything else, and not sure what to do with them except try to stand, and for the first half-hour or so he found that challenge enough, doing splits like an acrobatic dancer I paid a nickel to see in a shack in Dry Fork they called the Opera House. He's dead now, most likely, or worse, tied up to some damn tinker's wagon, hanging his head and waiting to be rendered down for glue to stick a heel on some lady's pumps. I hadn't any contact with Randy or Frank in all that time, but I sure knew what they was about.

The Buffalo Bill outfit was touring Europe. For those of

us in the press corps—what manager Nate Salsbury called it, after the crew in Washington that was writing down everything President Arthur had to say, which for pure interest wouldn't fill anyone's idea of a book worth peddling— the time dragged. A man got his fill of empty palaces, fallen-down temples, and busted statues in museums, and after a while even the spectacle of plains Indians chasing pigeons around St. Mark's Square for supper lost its charm. What time I didn't spend embroidering on Cody's career for press releases and souvenir pamphlets I whiled away reading newspapers, for whom Farmer and Locke never seemed to lose appeal. They came in bundles by ship from the States; but even the journals in London and Paris and Rome picked up items of general interest by way of the Trans-Atlantic cable. I still have cuttings in which *Monsieur* Locke and *Signor* Farmer are prominent. I can't read them myself. How those old emperors and popes managed to take over so much of history talking gibberish is beyond me.

See, nothing much of real interest had happened in the creaky Old World since *Herr* Bismarck whupped Louis Napoleon more than ten years ago, and what with "Bison William" and Annie Oakley and their passel of red Indians splashed across posters on every vertical surface from Buckingham Palace to the Parthenon, it seemed Europeans couldn't get enough of scalpings and gunfights and other colonial truck; it reminded them of Guy Fawkes and other excitements they'd got too civilized to let happen again, and missed, for all the pettifogging in Parliament and the Hague. Scuttlebutt said Salsbury approached Cody with the idea of inviting Frank and Randy to join the excursion, but Cody was agin it; seems he'd had his fill of taming such folk after Wild Bill Hickok shot out an acetylene spotlight from a Chicago stage because it hurt his eyes, showering sparks over the paying customers.

I was sorry to hear it. I'd grown weary of injecting nonexistent Indian battles and physically impossible feats of marksmanship into the official record, and could have done with some unadorned anecdotes from the Genuine Article. So I took my excitement from pallid, third-person accounts of that contest that had been going on since before the smoke had cleared from the War of the Rebellion.

That pair was about as hard to track as a grizzly through dry cornstalks. They left their sign on every scrap of newsprint those tramp steamers could carry without sinking. I reckon them that sank, when they're discovered and raised, will be found to have ferried their share, all clumped together like Spanish coin. Frank and Randy would shake their heads at the places their names had gone where they never did; some places they probably never heard of.

I knew about Abilene and Salt Lake City, though I craved for details I wouldn't know for many years, when I was able to collect them from what the legitimate historians call "primary sources." When all the pomp connected with placing the whole business before a paying audience came about, I learned the name Abraham Cripplehorn (and made up my mind about that fellow's character based just on the scanty evidence presented between the lines; I was on a personal basis with Ned Buntline, that unprincipled sot, and had built my opinions on that model). I followed his efforts to settle their differences—for the price of a ticket—before the court of public opinion, and thought about it long and hard when my company visited the Coliseum, hoping to stage the exhibition on the site where all those gladiators had made their last bloody stand. Nothing had changed except the tin hats.

And I read about that business in San Francisco, where the impetuous behavior of the principals nearly brought it to an abrupt end.

* * *

A fellow had to travel a fair piece from the city of Oakland—and on foot to boot—to find a place to set up camp. The whole state was settled worse than Ohio. Randy had begun to think he'd have to walk clear to Nevada for unclaimed country when he found a grown-over vineyard with a weathered house and barn leaning towards each other like a couple of drunks looking for support and a sign in front where a bank had slapped its brand. He busted up the sign for firewood and after he'd cooked and eaten some beans and bacon and drunk coffee he found a cozy spot inside the barn among some old straw. The barn looked as if it would fall down about the same time as the house, but he had a cowboy's superstition about empty houses and ghosts: No one ever heard of a haunted barn. He lay on his back on his blanket, watching blue twilight steal in through the loft, and shot the first bat that showed itself, for the practice. The odor of sulfur and cordite lingered and lulled him towards sleep. A night like that made a man feel in harmony with existence. When the thing was done and Frank was in the ground, he reckoned he'd spend his cut on a grand house on top of some mountain and camp out in the backyard every night.

In the morning he walked a mile into the town the bank belonged to, all brick with a school and a library and even a Catholic church, and sent a wire to Cripplehorn letting him know where he could be found. He asked the clerk for the location of the livery.

"There isn't one."

"What kind of town don't have a livery?"

"Our kind. Most folks have their own horses. We're carriage trade here. I can't remember the last time I saw a man sitting smack-dab on top of a horse." His eyes flicked over Randy's range gear.

"Well, what do you do when you need a carriage pulled?"

"You might ask Lyle Miller if he's got a horse to spare."

"Where's his spread?"

"He's not a rancher. He owns the local milk route."

He got directions to a windowless building with wide double doors at the top of a wooden ramp. A sign reading SIERRA FARMS FINE DAIRY PRODUCTS ran across the front.

The doors were spread open. Randy climbed up the ramp into a place that smelled like a well-kept stable. Horses occupied ten stalls and five wooden milk wagons stood in a neat row along the back wall with the company's name painted on their sides. Tall milk cans gleamed spotlessly in a ten-tiered wooden rack erected across from the horses. In a little office built from two partitions in a corner, a squint-eyed old runt wearing a white shirt and necktie tucked inside clean overalls and a by-God Panama hat looked up from a ledger on a tall desk that was designed for standing behind, grinned, and said, "Howdy, cowboy. What can I do you for?"

"You Miller?"

"I favor Lyle. Miller's my father. Yep, he's still alive. Ninety-eight last month."

"Maybe he's dead and you just didn't notice. Where's the farm, Lyle?"

"Oh, the name? That's just for the customers. No one wants to buy milk from a factory. I get my stock from all over the county, depending on who's selling it cheap. You looking for a job delivering? You don't look like much of a milk drinker to me." His merry old eyes took in the rifle and belt gun all over again fresh. He chuckled.

"I'm through having anything to do with cows. I need a horse if you're selling."

Lyle took a short yellow pencil from a row of them in his bib pocket just to scratch his temple with the eraser.

"I'm considering pasturing Mabel. She's getting so old she practically has to deliver by the glass."

"She stand a rider?"

"Sure. A man ain't a load of full milk cans."

"I'll have a look."

The white mare was huge, with thick shaggy cannons and teeth worn down to brown stubs, but there was muscle under the loose and shifting skin. She'd do until a proper mount came along; or for that matter an ox with spirit.

"I'd sell you a stepladder if I had one," Lyle said, watching Randy make his inspection. "She's Percheron stock. That's the closest thing you'll find to royal blood around here."

"How much?"

"Ten dollars."

"I'll go six. She may be the nag queen of England, but in horse years she's older'n your old man."

"I could get eight from the dog food people in San Francisco; but my heart ain't in it. I started with Mabel and fourteen customers. She's family."

"She's barely a horse. Six."

"Make it seven and I'll throw in a pair of blinders."

"Six and you can keep the damn blinders. I ain't fixing to sell butter and cottage cheese. It's a saddle horse I'm after."

"Oh, you'll need the blinders. She wouldn't know what to do without 'em. You can kick her all day long and she'll just stand there like a knot on a fence."

"You don't know much about horse-trading, Lyle. I'm about to go down to five."

Lyle stroked the mare's broad face. "Don't you listen to him, old girl. You're going out more dignified than I will."

Randy gave him a banknote and a cartwheel dollar.

"Where's your saddle, mister?"

"I sold it in San Diego. You can't carry one and hop a freight too."

"Bareback, hey?" Lyle shook his head, stuffing the money behind the pencils. "Ride 'em, cowboy."

Mabel clopped down the wooden ramp with Randy hanging onto the reins as much to stay upright as to steer the horse. He hadn't ridden bareback in years, not since before he hurt his leg, and riding the tall mare was like sitting on the driver's seat of a stagecoach; the ground looked far away. It made him feel like a stunted boy his first time aboard.

On the road outside town he tried to spur the old girl into a trot—a gallop was too much to count on—but apart from blowing indignantly through her nostrils she showed no result, plodding at the same pace that had taken thousands of gallons of milk from door to door. For once in his life he hoped he wouldn't run into Frank. Seeing his old foe sitting a giant draft horse with blinders on might just kill him with laughing, which would be an unsatisfactory end to their contest.

He could make as good time on the soles of his own feet, but he had too much cowboy in him to choose walking when anything at all was available on four legs.

"Whoa!"

The mare, a tribute to obedience, stopped so abruptly he almost fell off. He drew the rifle from the bedroll he'd strapped across Mabel's neck and shouldered it, but held off on the trigger when he recognized Abraham Cripplehorn's Pike's Peak of a hat on the head of the man standing between the tumbledown house and barn where he'd staked his camp. A horse about half the size of Randy's stood between the traces of a two-wheeled buggy on the side of the road.

"What's that you're riding?" asked the entrepreneur as Randy approached him. "It looks like something from Homer."

"It's from Lyle, and I'll thank you not to disparage a man's mount. You must of hit paydirt, all dressed up and renting that town rig." The man was wearing a stiff new suit, royal blue almost to the point of purple, with yellow piping, and oxblood boots with flaps over the toes. The hat was the same, but freshly blocked and brushed. He looked like the circus had gone off and left him behind.

"I have, after a fashion: a mother lode named Weber. I thought you might be running low on money for supplies and provisions." He slid a sheaf of banknotes out of his inside breast pocket.

Randy was swinging his good leg over, figuring how to drop to the ground without landing on his bad one, when something made the decision for him. It passed so close to his face that his first thought was someone had struck a match off his nose. The sound of the shot came cracking after, by which time he'd thrown himself all the way onto gravel.

19

When your rosebush grows nothing but thorns, don't condemn your bad luck. Pierce them and sell them as needles.

Get down, you ignorant son of a bitch."

Cripplehorn had remained standing, staring toward a line of chestnut trees to the east. When Randy, already flat on the ground, snatched the nearest ankle and jerked it out from under him, he went down hard enough on his back to knock the wind out of him. Comically, his absurd Stetson came floating down afterward like a child's handkerchief parachute.

The entrepreneur wheezed, reinflating his lungs, and rolled over onto his stomach beside Randy. "Who is it?"

"Who you think?"

"No. He wouldn't be that rash. I gave him more money just this morning."

"You tell him where I'm fixed?"

"Of course not."

"Then he followed you. The trouble with you easterners is you never turn around and look where you come from. You might as well of been borned with no swivel in your neck."

"You said there was a reward from Arizona for your capture. Maybe it's a bounty man."

"If it is he's a fool. They want me alive, which we sure won't both be if he tries to wrassle me all the way back there."

"But you said Frank would never use a rifle on you because of the unfair advantage."

"Maybe he's changed."

"I don't believe it. Yours has always been an affair of honor."

"I wouldn't put it as toney as that, but I agree it ain't like Frank. Then again, that slug missed me. Could have been just his way of announcing himself. There's one sure way to find out." He planted his palms on the ground.

"What are you doing?"

"Getting up to fetch my Ballard."

Before Cripplehorn could put words to his astonishment, Randy stood, brushed himself off, and slid the rifle from the bedroll strapped to the mare. He patted her big neck. Muscles rolled beneath his palm. "I talked you down some earlier. I'd be obliged if you'd forget it. I never had a horse stand so close to a bullet without jumping. On the other hand, maybe you're deaf."

Mabel blew again, contemptuously.

"Or lazy. I don't reckon no milk horse gets shot at regular." He checked the load in the breech, then rested the barrel across the mare's slightly swayed back. The smoke had drifted away from the trees, so he addressed the whole bunch at the top of his lungs.

"Frank, I ain't got all day!"

Silence stretched; Cripplehorn hugged the earth and wished for a hole. When the answering shout came from the trees he flinched as if it were gunfire.

"How do I know you won't plug me when I show myself? I reckon I owe you that."

"Horseshit, Frank. If you meant to put me under with that Winchester, I'd be under. So howdy right back at you."

"You're lucky I sold the rolling-block I had in Colorado. I could of shot you from there and let it fester till I caught up."

A breeze damp with bay combed the distant leaves. Then a figure appeared, moving slowly in their direction, small against the towering chestnuts. A brass-action carbine dangled from one hand, muzzle pointing groundward. Randy socked the Ballard back inside the bedroll.

Curiosity got the better of Cripplehorn's sense of self-preservation. He rose to his feet, sidling until the horse and buggy stood between him and the approaching figure. After what seemed an hour, Frank Farmer stopped just inside pistol range. The tail of his frock coat was swept behind the Remington in his holster. Randy stepped out from behind the big mare.

"How do, Randy. That a horse or you shave a buffalo?"

"Shaving it weren't the hard part. The hard part was slapping on the bay rum after. I heard you taken up with a woman."

"It didn't stick. I heard you turned down the opportunity to shoot a Chinaman."

"I didn't think that was knowed outside the camp."

"I still got friends with the railroad. There ain't much to do in a roundhouse but play cards and jabber. I heard that spur went bust."

"Did it? It don't surprise me. That jasper I knocked flat with a powder keg wouldn't stop talking about the Irish going on strike. No wonder the line put up so much reward over one skinny foreman."

"It wasn't striking done it. The Apaches came back, meaner'n bloody turds. Though I can see why they'd take on so about your claiming six months' pay for one day's work; if that's what you call caving in the straw boss's head."

"It was six weeks, not months. I'm surprised it isn't ten foremen by now, and there was powder in that keg."

Frank nodded, rolling a cigarette, with the Winchester cradled in the crook of his arm. "You ready?"

"God's sake!" said Cripplehorn. "You're undoing the work of years! Can't the pair of you control yourselves for two more months?"

Randy slid his Colt out of its holster, cocked it, and thumbed the cylinder around, checking his loads. "Ready."

Frank stooped to lay his carbine on the ground and checked his Remington. When he was standing with his feet spread and the pistol hanging at his side, Randy adopted the same pose. He was raising the Colt when Abraham Cripplehorn jerked the buggy whip from its socket next to the driver's seat and, holding the ironwood handle by the whip end, hit him on the back of the head with all his might. Randy dropped, out as cold as his pistol.

BLOOD FEUD COMES TO SAN FRANCISCO.

by Jack Dodger

Randy Locke and Frank Farmer, who are well-known to these columns, brought their enmity to San Francisco yesterday when Farmer made an attempt from ambush on Locke's life.

Locke narrowly escaped death when a ball fired from

cover passed within inches of his head as he was dis-
mounting at his campsite west of Oakland.

The incident might have ended in tragedy had not an
uninterested party, Abraham Titus Cripplehorn by name,
took action, disabling Locke with a blow before he could
return fire. His opponent, observing that the match was
over for the time being, made the following statement to
Cripplehorn:

"You tell that little skunk when he comes around I'll
fight him anywhere, anytime, out on the desert with only
the scorpions to bear witness or on stage at the Bird Cage
Theatre in Tombstone."

" 'Bear witness,' he said that?" Major W. B. Updegraff,
resting his stiff leg on a leaf of his heaped rolltop, looked
up from the pages in his hand.

"Something on that order. I wasn't taking notes at the
time."

"It seems to me you hinted months ago about a public
contest between Farmer and Locke. Are these desperadoes
always so accommodating, to advertise your intentions in
the press?"

"It isn't as if they ever made a secret of their antago-
nism."

"You made yourself a part of the story?"

"Fortunately I always write under a *nom de plume*. I was
told once journalists should remain in the background."

"There's a simpler way." The man in the cinder-burned
waistcoat found a stub of orange pencil behind one ear and
scratched out the byline. "This is straight news, not human
interest. I don't assign credit. I see you've annexed Oakland
to San Francisco. I thought that authority belonged to the
city superintendents." He struck San Francisco from the
lead paragraph and crossed out the headline entirely. "I

don't like it, Cripplehorn, or Dodger, or Puddin' 'n' Tame, or whatever you're calling yourself Tuesdays and Thursdays. After that first piece ran, I received a visit from a member of the Committee of Safety."

"Vigilante, I suppose."

"You suppose right, and you wouldn't be so smug about it if you were here in '77. The only reason you still see Chinese in town is there were more of them than Denis Kearney and his Pick-Handle Brigade had hickory handles. Back then it was the Tongs had the Committee running about reading the law at the end of a stick; now it's pledged to keep blood sports out of town, like cockfights and bearbaiting and public duels. If they get the notion I'm encouraging barbarism, they may just decide to bust up my press and me along with it."

"I'll take it to the *Bonanza* then, on the assumption the publisher hasn't been threatened yet." Cripplehorn held out his hand for the pages.

"People only buy Ted Sullivan's rag to start fires. I didn't say I wouldn't run it. Kearney's star has set, and this new litter skeedaddles when a cat yowls in a black alley. Even if they were a blister on the arse of the original Committee, I wouldn't let 'em tell me what I can print and what I can't. That's my name on the flag on Page Two: *W. B. Updegraff, Publisher and Editor-in-Chief.* I don't see any of their names there."

"I'm glad you see it that way. I was bluffing about Sullivan. He turned me down the first time."

"I know. He told me over whiskeys at the Bella Union after I ran it. Did you really coldcock Locke, or was it something on that order, like that Farmer quote?"

"There wasn't anything heroic to it. I hit him with a buggy whip handle when his back was turned."

The Major showed yellow teeth around his cigar stump.

"Too bad Kearney didn't know you five years ago. He drafted the city ordinance against carrying firearms, but he liked his bludgeons."

"It's a pleasure doing business with you, Major. When I've made all the arrangements I'll place a full-page advertisement in the *Spar*."

"Like hell you will. I don't approve of your design any more than the Committee. If you come in here waving money in my face promoting murder, I'll throw you out through my one and only window."

20

The success of any venture is measured by the size and number of obstacles overcome.

Cripplehorn had said nothing to Frank while Randy was senseless. Where reason was missing, recriminations accomplished nothing. Frank withdrew, leaving the entrepreneur to await Randy's awakening.

"What in hell did you hit me with?" He sat up, feeling gingerly the knot on the back of his head.

"Does it matter?" Cripplehorn was seated on the driver's seat of the buggy, drinking peach brandy from a silver-and-pigskin flask.

"Where is he?"

"Gone."

"Gone where?"

"Why, so you can finish what he started? I always heard you cowboys were as good as your word."

"Talk to him. He's the one broke it."

"As would you have, given the opportunity. You two are worse than a philandering husband. He can't keep his pecker in his pants and you can't keep those hoglegs in their holsters. I'm splitting you up until the time of the contest."

"Where you sending me?"

"I'm putting you up at the Asiatic for now. The reporters will be looking for you at the Palace and the Eldorado. I know how that annoys you."

"Hell, I thought you was going to say South America or somesuch place."

"Frank's the one broke the bargain. I'm sending him out of the state until I can get things worked out in Sacramento. There will be resistance, but I'm counting on Weber's money to soften it up."

But secrecy was a luxury infamy could not afford. An old acquaintance from his cowhand days recognized Frank on a railroad platform in Boise, and by the time his train crossed into Montana Territory, reporters were gathering at every station clamoring for his comments. He avoided them by staying aboard until the engine gushed to a stop in the mining town of Butte, where he stepped down carrying his valise and his Winchester in its scabbard.

"Frank, you running away from Randy?" asked an unpressed gentleman of the press from Chicago.

"Say that again and I'll drop you where you stand."

The representative from the *Billings Gazette* asked him if it was true he intended to shoot Randy in broad daylight in public.

"I'd shoot him in the dark if I could see in it."

"Aren't you concerned you'll be arrested for murder?"

Frank, bathed, brushed, and barbered, smiled in appreciation at this vision from the *Omaha Herald,* a trim young woman in a becoming traveling suit and a flower patch on her straw hat. Spots of color appeared on her cheeks.

"I'll cross that crick when it counts."

The reporter from the local *Miner,* in pinstripe suit and stovepipe boots, asked him what he thought of Butte.

"I'll let you know once I find it under all this muck." Every surface in sight bore traces of smoke from the smelting plants: A finger left a track through the grime.

"Where are you stopping?" asked the same journalist.

"Someplace clean, I hope."

"Good luck with that."

Frank registered at the Copper Palace, a four-story hotel decorated almost entirely with material from the local mine: The ceiling in the lobby was made up of pressed sheets of copper, all the hardware and even the chandelier were copper, and copper covered the desk, behind which stood a clerk who might have been fashioned from the same reddish metal, although this was probably an illusion created by reflection from all that copper. That evening Frank dined in the hotel restaurant with the comely female reporter from Nebraska Territory, who after he said his good-byes in a voice that carried, followed him up to his room as the waiters were clearing the tables.

"Abraham Cripplehorn?"

The entrepreneur took in the small, fussily dressed man standing outside the open door of his room at the Palace. On his waistcoat hung a brass star attached by tiny chains to an engraved plate containing his title of office. "You have the advantage, sir."

"I'm Connie Post, sheriff of San Mateo County. I'm here to serve you."

"How very generous."

The irony of this response found no purchase on the little man's spade-bearded face. He handed the guest a roll of parchment covered with Spencerian script and embossed with a seal.

"This is an injunction, signed by Judge Webster Bennett, prohibiting you or anyone else from conducting a murderous exhibition in this county. You've been served."

"Indeed I have. Bennett, you said?"

"Webster Bennett, district judge."

"Thank you."

That individual, horse-faced with white sidewhiskers combed out to shoulder width, entertained Cripplehorn from behind the desk in his chambers in a county courthouse dripping with limestone gewgaws and bronze statuary, some grafter's dream of wealth come to life. The glass eyes of antelope heads stared down from the walls. Going by his obvious threescore and ten, the jurist had bagged the creatures back when San Francisco was still in swaddling clothes.

"Don't think I'm ungrateful for your offer, Mr. Cripplehorn. I'm retiring at the end of this term and do not intend to seek reelection. Mr. Cable, the prosecuting attorney, is running for my party, but he isn't in a position to reverse the injunction I ordered. Any donation from you would come entirely from your interest in good government."

Appeals were telegraphed to all the other counties in California. Some were rejected by return wire, others after local debate attended by concerned citizens, many of them women. ("Supporters of the event should not hold their husbands accountable for opposing it," wrote the correspondent from the *Examiner*. "Faced with overwhelming numbers, a wise general withdraws from the field.") Still others were considering the request when Sacramento intervened:

BY ORDER OF THE GOVERNOR OF CALIFORNIA, NO CONTEST INVOLVING HUMANS THAT IS DESIGNED TO CONCLUDE IN THE DEATH OR SERIOUS INJURY OF ONE OR MORE OF THE PARTICIPANTS SHALL

TAKE PLACE ANYWHERE IN THE STATE. ANY AT-
TEMPT TO STAGE SUCH AN EXHIBITION WILL BE
MET WITH THE FULL WEIGHT OF THE LAW. THE
STATE MILITIA IS HEREBY ORDERED TO STAND
READY TO DEFEND IT, IF NECESSARY WITH DEADLY
FORCE.

"Please correct me if I'm mistaken in my understanding of this proclamation," Cripplehorn told the press in the
conference room at the Palace. "Is it the governor's intention to prevent killing by killing?"

Badinage, however, was ineffective, and after conferring
with Sheridan Weber ("Don't ask me about politics, Abe; I
haven't voted since Grant"), the entrepreneur looked into
substitute venues.

However, no sooner did the news enter the telegraph columns than representatives of the neighboring states and
territories declared that they would not host so callous a
display of savagery. Oregon, Nevada, Arizona, and Utah
warned that all three principals would face arrest the moment they crossed their borders.

"Arizona wasted its breath," Randy said. "It's my neck
to visit the place anyway."

The rest of the country followed suit. In the governor's
office in Albany, New York, Grover Cleveland signed a bill
banning the event by name, the first law in that state's history aimed directly at three U.S. citizens in particular.

Cripplehorn was indignant. "This kind of thing wouldn't
have been possible before the Rebellion."

Randy was bemused. "I wisht my old man was alive.
He'd be proud to think his son had been declared war on
all on his own."

"We just lost Rhode Island in the *Bulletin*."

"We lost Delaware and Ohio in the *Call*. I'm almost
afraid to look at the *Examiner*."

"I can't see why you find this so amusing."

"You're the one wants to be the Cornelius Vanderbilt of gunning folks. All I want is Frank in the ground, and that always was against the law."

Mexico and Canada came next. Under pressure from Washington, President Díaz mobilized the *federales* to turn Cripplehorn & Company back at the Rio Grande. Ottawa, not to be outdone by the rest of North America, announced that the Northwest Mounted Police would eject them from the Dominion of Canada as undesirable aliens. In Butte, Frank bought a round of drinks for some journalists and remarked that he felt downright hurt: "I never wanted to go till they told me I couldn't. Now I got a hankering to ride up there and shoot some moose, and maybe a Mountie or two. I seen a picture once of British soldiers in a history book. Those red shirts make an easy target."

Unlike Randy, "the dandified gentleman from Texas" not only didn't mind the attention, but sought it out. He couldn't stand five minutes at a bar waiting for someone to recognize him without identifying himself, and didn't have to pay for a drink the rest of the visit. He bought a new suit and a pair of boots with fancy flaps like he'd admired on Cripplehorn, had a gunsmith replace the old cracked grips on his Remington with ivory ones, and had just left the shop when his gaze fell upon a frame building with photographs on display in the front window.

Butte, M.T., September 16—Mr. Frank Farmer, the notorious Southwestern gun man, had his picture struck last week in O. C. Nordstrom's studio on Silver Bow Street last week. He posed before a Swiss alpine backdrop with pistol and rifle on display, and most who have seen it agree that he is a fine figure of a man for an assassin. Straightaway several of the local citizenry offered to buy prints of his likeness for souvenirs, and by the end of the week they were selling for a quarter apiece. It is rumored that should the mines play out, the city fathers can increase revenue by inviting all of the celebrated frontier pistoleers to come in and have their likenesses made for sale to tourists.

"That's something you and I should consider." Cripplehorn looked up from the telegraph column in the *Bulletin* at Randy, stretched out in his sock feet on his bed in the Asiatic. "All the famous bad men have sat at one time or another. People would take it against your reputation if you don't."

"How do I know you won't sell it to the papers?"

"They can't use them; they bleed, Updegraff says. The paper's too coarse and absorbent."

"You asked him."

"We can't all hole up in a hotel breaking wind all day. Someone has to keep up the momentum."

"I ain't doing it. Some son of a bitch in Arizona's sure to put it on a shinplaster and double the reward on account of I'm famous."

"You get more mileage out of that old business than any bounty man. For all you say about disliking the attention, I think you enjoy being wanted."

"Well, I don't like reporters. They ask impertinent questions and they all smell like moldy cardboard."

Randy was using the name George Purdy, borrowed from the mule-headed Circle X foreman who'd fired him for shooting Frank the first time and leaving the outfit shy one man; thereby doubling the deficit. He was unwilling to leave the hotel except to walk the stiffness out of his leg, and then only after dark. But in the midst of all the world telling him how unwelcome he and Frank and Cripplehorn were, he got restless and went out for a ride, looking all around for journalists when he exited out a side door and keeping his head down with the brim of his old weather-stained hat obscuring his features.

The man who operated the Golden Gate Livery left off his whittling and said, "That horse of yours died last night. You owe me for a week plus the cost of dragging out the carcass."

Randy went into the stall to see for himself. Old Mabel lay on her side with her eyes gone glassy and flies crawling on her.

He patted her side. "Damn if I ain't sorry. I used you for a shooting stand and you didn't even blink. The army lost a good mount when they hooked you to a damn milk wagon." He went back out and asked how much to put her under.

"There's a dog food place downtown'd give you cash for it."

Randy gave him a banknote. "I'll be asking 'em if they bought an old white mare from the Golden Gate Livery. If the answer ain't no I'll come back and kill you."

San Francisco, Sept. 22—The Spanish governor of Cuba has informed the U.S. State Department that he will arrest anyone intending to stage a blood duel in his jurisdiction. This is undoubtedly a reference to the Messrs. Locke, Farmer, and Cripplehorn, whose search for an arena in which to work out the fatal differences between the first two men has appeared regularly in these columns. With President Arthur having banned the contest from these United States, this brings to a total of four countries, thirteen individual states, and eight territories to declare they would not host so callous a display of savagery. The editors of the *Examiner* note that the principles of the good Christian faith still prevail in these uncertain times.

Asked by reporters over liquor and sandwiches in Cripplehorn's suite in the Palace if this latest blow meant the end of his plans, the promoter smiled. "The Cubans sacrifice a bullfighter every few months and I've never heard a word of protest from Santiago. Still, it's a big old world."

"Are you saying you're taking the show abroad like Buffalo Bill?" asked the man from the *Call*, around a mouthful of liverwurst.

"I can't take the risk of putting Locke and Farmer on the same boat. I'd rather avoid the complication of arranging separate crossings with so many other preparations to be made."

"Where, then?" The *Chicago Tribune*.

Cripplehorn swallowed peach brandy and responded with two words.

"The Strip."

21

Education begins with books and instruction and ends with travel. It is a rolling classroom.

I suppose some desperadoes, all tucked into their hideout beds, say their prayers before sleeping. Contrary to the assumptions of the editors of the *San Francisco Examiner,* there are Christians on the run from justice. When a damned soul prays, I don't reckon God ever gave him a more satisfactory answer than the Cherokee Strip.

Although I'm no more an authority on how the Congress works than the senators and representatives themselves, I imagine the discussion went something like this:

THE HON. CONSTANT FLAPDOODLE: What do we do
   with that piece of the Indian Nations? It just kind of
   sticks out like a gingham patch on a Sunday shirt.
SEN. EVERLASTING PETTIFOG: What's it got? Gold,
   silver, timber?
FLAPDOODLE: Just red clay and scrub, far as I can tell.
SEN. FENCE STRADDLER: How come we ain't give it
   to the injuns?
FLAPDOODLE: Which tribe? We divvied up the rest of
   the territory among 'em.
PETTIFOG: Hell, let's just toss it up in the air and let
   the bastards fight over it amongst themselves.
FLAPDOODLE: Makes sense to me. Second the motion.
FENCE STRADDLER: All in favor?

It was a rectangular slice of the Indian Nations, about
the size of Greece. As to woods and prairie and rocky outcrop, it was a fair example of the rest of the frontier. Flapdoodle, Pettifog, and Straddler didn't know it from darkest
Africa. Declaring it the communal property of the area
tribes meant it was officially unassigned, the only piece of
the United States left up for grabs, and therefore no one's
property at all. It stood outside the law, federal, territorial,
and local, which made it a bolt-hole for every wanted fugitive in America.

The fugitives took notice. Before Fence Straddler's gavel
stopped ringing, the Strip filled fit to bust with murderers,
rapists, wife-beaters, train robbers, and common road
agents who'd worn out their welcome everywhere else in
the civilized world except on scaffolds. Since there was no
reason to lay low with no one looking for them, they helped
themselves to whatever was handy and seldom left witnesses. The grittiest of U.S. marshals hesitated to go there
except in armed convoys. Policemen appointed from among

the Five Civilized Tribes—Cherokee, Creek, Seminole, Choctaw, and Chickasaw—done their damnedest to keep order, but their authority was limited and they were scattered like buckshot.

An army fort might have helped contain the atrocities. However, through an agreement between the Indians and Washington that no one really understood, the military was banned from the territory. In any case, there was no precedent for the cavalry protecting Indians from United States citizens; generally the situation was opposite. It was No Man's Land, utterly lawless.

Where better, Cripplehorn reasoned, to stage an outlaw entertainment?

"It's a fair piece off," said Randy, "and aboard a hot train. Where's Frank stand on the matter?"

"I wired him in Montana. He asked the same question about you."

"Hell, I'd go clean to China to have it out with him for the last time."

"I felt certain you would. I answered him along those lines, and he said just what you did; only in his case it was Russia."

"I'm surprised you didn't just crack us both on the head like you done me in Oakland and dump us aboard a fast freight."

"There are a thousand things to be done. I haven't time to waste running back and forth carrying messages. There's no telling when Washington might change its mind and annex the Strip, placing it under civil authority."

"Can we stop on the way for a bottle of Old Pepper? That fruity horse piss of yours gives me the two-step worse than cooking grease."

* * *

It was a hot ride as predicted, and hotter still as they chugged down the eastern side of the Divide and stopped in Pueblo, a town noted for its salubrious climate—but not in September—to take on water. Randy sat in a wallow of sweat, screwing up his face against the glare through his window, and allowed as how he'd had his life's portion of dusty towns, burnt grain served up as coffee, and sour women.

Cripplehorn got up from the seat beside him. "I won't be a moment."

"What for, you want to borrow a cup of dust?"

"I need to send a telegram."

"Give Frank my regards and tell him to keep breathing till I get there."

"He's already on his way. I'll fill you in later."

Randy felt he was in the Nations before he saw the place: a brief whiff of brimstone, a tightening in the chest, a sickness in the stomach carried by old miseries not necessarily his. The territory had been born in tears and irrigated by them ever since.

Then again, he might simply have been train sick.

"You've been staring out that window for miles," Cripplehorn said. "What's wrong?"

He turned his head away. "My mother said I had injun blood back on her side; Iroquois, I think she said. I reckon some great-great grandpappy just walked acrosst my grave."

"It never occurred to me you had a mother."

"She died when I was fourteen and I ran away."

"Because of your father?"

"No. We never met."

"You're lucky."

In the town of Cimarron, named after the river separating the white and red territories, the entrepreneur excused himself again. The place was built of new yellow wood just waiting for a spark to come along and burn it to the ground. Randy watched through the window as Cripplehorn shook hands with a fat man in a suit too heavy for the climate and a hat with a rolled brim, bright metal doodads dangling from his watch chain. He accepted a cigar from a battery of them in the man's breast pocket, wagged his chin little, and nodded lots. From his gold-cornered wallet Cripplehorn slid a fistful of banknotes, folded them into a little square, and shook the man's hand again, coming away with nothing in his. He got back on board just as the whistle blasted its first warning.

"We're stopping here." He took his carpetbag down from the overhead rack and reached for Randy's bedroll.

"Don't touch my gear." Randy sprang up and fetched it himself. "What's in Cimarron, besides a dose of clap?"

"Our home, for the time being. It's all arranged. We've got a two-month lease on a farmer's field not two minutes from here."

"What we fixing to put in, oats or potatoes?"

"Neither. Planting's done. I just sealed the deal with the banker who foreclosed on the place. He's the one I sent the telegram to from Pueblo, to arrange this meeting. The Choctaw who worked it put in corn, but the hot summer burned up his investment: The stalks grew tall enough, but the kernels wouldn't form, and he ran out of extensions."

"I don't know why he thought he could raise anything in this country."

"Just a cry of despair. We're going to plow under what's left and stake a great big tent to discourage freeloaders."

"Whose working the plow, you?"

"The farmer himself. Banker Anderson says he's willing to do it, and whatever other odd jobs come up, just for letting him and his family stay in the house through the winter."

"And I reckon his wife will knit us the tent."

"That's the beauty of the plan. We'll sell advertising on the canvas, inside and out. With the house we're expecting, any smart merchant would chase us all the way down the street to stuff our pockets in return for space. It will cover our overhead and more."

"We're selling empty space?"

"That's how it works."

"I'll be damned."

"That's foreordained."

"Don't leases and such need signing papers? I didn't see nothing change hands but cash money."

"It's that kind of deal. A case might be made for conspiracy should the situation change. A trail of paper could prove an embarrassment."

"Well, we wouldn't want to embarrass a banker. How do you know he won't crawfish?"

"That part called for diplomacy. I reminded him there would likely be one gun man left standing when the thing was done. That whole business of honor among western gentlemen has always been based on the lead standard."

"You draw me and Frank like a gun."

Cripplehorn fixed him with his good eye; though Randy had the strange impression there was life in the one carved from ivory, cold as it was. "You were what you are before I met you both. Don't pretend I'm worse than either one of you."

The whistle shrilled twice as the train prepared to pull out.

"I ain't renting no place with you, if that's what you're thinking."

Out on the platform, Cripplehorn stopped and turned. Randy leered.

"Didn't think I knew about that, did you? Frisco's nothing more than small towns all bunched together. Folks talk. Frank must of got soft not to of shot you weeks ago. I almost done it on sight last year."

The promoter raised his voice above the plunging pistons, holding down his hat against the suction of the departing train. "It's not the Palace, or even the Asiatic. The Cherokee Rest is the best Cimarron has to offer."

"As opposed to what else? I didn't count but four blocks, counting the town pump."

"A boarding house or two, but there's no privacy there. I can't promise a private bath or even hot water, but there won't be any false eyelashes in the basin."

"I'm sorry to hear that. It was my only female companionship that whole time. What about Frank?"

"Oh, I'm putting him up in an adjoining room so I can sleep in the crossfire." Cripplehorn mounted the steps of a wooden front porch and opened a door, jingling a set of sleigh bells strung from the inside knob.

Dust motes hung motionless in the sunlight slanting in through the front window. A squaw rug, most of its color gone, lay on a plank floor and the moth-eaten head of a boar tusker glared down from the wall above the stairs.

A loud smack sent Randy groping for his Colt. Then he saw a clerk scraping a dead fly off a rolled-up newspaper against the edge of the desk. He let his hand fall from the pistol.

"Wherever he is, it better not be no Eldorado, that's all I got to say."

22

The theater's unrespectable reputation is undeserved. The amount of labor and dedication involved in preparing a production is a test of character.

The dilemma of what to do with Frank was as vexing as any of the arrangements necessary to ensure the success of Crip's Folly, as the press had christened the enterprise. (It was coined by John Clum, editor of the *Tombstone Epitaph*, as a way of drawing fire away from that city's sinister recent history, and spread from paper to paper like smallpox.) Wherever he wound up, his inability to resist attention was bound to announce his whereabouts, and the situation had increased to the point where anywhere in the Nations was too close.

The solution was so simple it's no wonder a confidence man whose train of thought ran in twisted circles took so long arriving at it: Cripplehorn told Frank to stay put. He could hold court in the Copper Palace as much as he wanted, and distance alone would prevent Randy's native impatience from boiling over.

The reporter who covered the Strip for the *Fort Smith Elevator* was a bandy-legged rooster with a horse-collar beard who looked like Walt Whitman and swore like Jo Shelby. He wore an out-at-the-elbows morning coat, Confederate trousers with a stripe, and a Union forage cap. He was a veteran war correspondent whose thirst for action had led him down to Mexico to cover the revolution, and when that ended too soon he'd come back north and traveled from one boomtown journal to the next, mostly on foot, before finding satisfaction in the worst part of the

Nations. None of his colleagues would willingly roam those caves and thickets poking into other folks' affairs, so he enjoyed a freedom of movement unprecedented in his profession.

Caleb Munch interviewed Abraham Cripplehorn in his room overlooking Cimarron's main street. The visitor sat in the room's only chair with his legs crossed. It was hard to tell where his limbs left off and the spindle legs started. His subject sat on the bed with his back propped against a pillow and his legs stretched out in front of him to keep his trouser creases straight. He was smoking the cigar he'd gotten from banker Anderson.

"You spend most of your time separating your clients like a couple of fighting cocks," Munch said.

"More like a pair of unruly children, which is worse. Where is your notebook?"

"I kept losing them, so now I just remember." Munch was an unsmiling man who had no patience with humor, a clutter in speech as it was in written copy. "You stand to sacrifice your whole investment if Locke and Farmer tangle too soon."

"Is that a question?"

"I never ask them. Around here you get out of the habit."

"Doesn't that make it hard for you to conduct an interview?"

"It hasn't yet."

"These next three weeks will be the most difficult. But the closer we get to the event, the easier it will be to keep them under control. They've been out to kill each other so long, another day shouldn't matter. Tempers tend to cool when money becomes imminent."

"I've yet to read a word about why they're so determined to destroy each other."

"I've asked, but all I ever got was a glib answer. I think

they've forgotten themselves. They've been at it so long I don't suppose it matters."

"No one's ever explained what a dog has in mind when it chases a cat. You know, Cripplehorn, people compare you to those blood-crazy Roman emperors. There are other ways to make a living."

"Not for me. Not the way I want to live."

"I want to sit down with Locke."

"I don't advise it. Reporters rank just below Farmer on his list."

Munch untangled himself from the chair. "I think I'll knock on his door. You don't object."

"I never step between another man and a mistake."

Fort Smith, Oct. 1—Caleb Munch, our correspondent in the Indian Nations, inquired of Randolph Locke, the prominent duellist, as to the nature of his antipathy toward Frank Farmer, also of that profession. He was unable to obtain an answer, but both Munch and Locke are recovering at present from injuries sustained during the interview.

"I got thirty-one bad teeth, and that fellow with the whiskers knocked out the good one." Randy, standing with his braces down before the mirror above the washbasin in his room, inspected the gap. His upper lip was puffed up twice normal size and he had sixteen stitches above his right eye, swollen also.

"How'd he get that close?" Cripplehorn asked.

"I opened the door to shoo him out and he hit me square in the mouth."

"Where was your gun?"

"I dropped it out of pure astonishment. Nobody's crazy enough to hit a man holding a pistol."

"I saw him coming out after the commotion. He had a sleeve torn off and there was blood in his beard."

"Next time it'll be a slug in his chest. Maybe not, though. It's bad luck to kill a crazy man."

The tent was the biggest thing the local wagon-sheet maker had ever attempted. He stitched together most of his stock, solving the problem of waterproofing by overlapping and understitching, and staked it out in the field where the exhibition was scheduled for the printer to stencil the advertising. When a team of laborers erected it, it stood taller than any building in town and encompassed almost the entire plowed patch of ground. Trumpeted the *Elevator*:

DEATH TENT BIGGER THAN
CODY'S WILD WEST.
Locke *v.* Farmer
Arena Compares to Madison Square Garden.
Largest Construction in the Nations.
"Blood Coliseum," Declares the Hon. Isaac Parker.
Our Famous Jurist Decries
Official Inefficacy to Prevent Barbarous Display.

A squad of carpenters abandoned construction of an Episcopal church to build bleachers for the spectators, who could read of the miraculous properties of Edison's Elixir, consider the Blue Plate Special at the Kickapoo House, admire a giant shoe illustrating the wares of Gabriel & Sons, Cobblers, and ponder the marble monuments available from C.C. Cox, Stonecutter. There were notices printed on both sides of the canvas.

Cripplehorn spent more time with the printer than anyone else. He had tickets made with legal waivers on the backs, indemnifying the exhibitors against damages in the event of injury or death as the result of a stray bullet, and designed posters to be placed in every shopkeeper's window for miles around (EXHIBITION OF THE CENTURY! A DUEL TO THE DEATH! FRANK FARMER AND RANDY LOCKE, TOGETHER FOR THE LAST TIME! NOV. 10, 1882. TICKETS $1.00 [ONE DOLLAR] Jack Dodger, Programme Director).

"What kind of stock?" asked the printer, holding the sheet scribbled by his customer.

"Something that will take this." Cripplehorn handed him a stiff-backed photograph of Frank, looking the proper bad man with his ivory-handled Remington poking above his belt and the butt-plate of his Winchester planted on the floor, the Matterhorn for some reason in the background.

"Take good care of it. I had to send for it all the way from California. I want Farmer's name underneath in twelve-point type. I've been spending a lot of time with news-papermen, and know the lingo."

"What about the other one?"

"He's camera shy. Do what you can with this."

The printer took the wanted poster with the bad sketch of Randy. "This reward still good?"

"It won't be after the tenth."

23

Philosophy is just another word for regret.

Frank's train got in late. The station was dark, and the few people left to greet the passengers looked like phantoms in the light leaking from the windows of the coaches.

"What happened?" said Cripplehorn.

"Tree fell across the tracks forty miles back. We sat in the dark two hours waiting for the crew to chop it loose.

Some folks will do anything to keep this here extravaganza from happening."

"Impossible. No one knew you were on the train."

"I sort of let it slip in Billings. I reckon there was a fellow or two from the press mixed in amongst the regulars. News sure spreads these days. Hard to believe it took a month for some to hear Lincoln got shot."

"Just out of curiosity, what would it take to make you keep your mouth shut?"

"Hell, I thought you'd be pleased. You spent most of our stake advertising this shindig. I got you the same thing and it didn't cost a cent. Where's Randy?"

There was no reason not to tell him. The Cherokee Rest had been in all the papers after Randy's interview with Caleb Munch. "In the hotel. He gave me his word he'd stay away from you until the day after tomorrow. I want yours. Thirty-six hours, that's all I ask."

"I stayed in jail longer than that. I reckon I can wait a day and a half out of sixteen years."

"Your word?"

"You got it."

"Seems to me I had it once before. You know how that turned out."

Teeth flashed in Frank's whiskers. "You ever broke a bone?"

Cripplehorn touched his cheekstrap, an involuntary gesture. "Yes."

"Then you know oncet one's broke and knitted back together it's stronger than it was."

"You westerners and your homilies. You can't shoot the moon, it's unlikely you'll ever see an elephant, and a promise isn't a bone." He shook his head. "I never will understand this regional concept of honor, especially when it might get you killed."

"That's easy. You go back on it, you're kilt for sure."

They stopped before a shallow two-story house, white-washed with green trim. BED AND BOARD read a wooden sign suspended from the porch roof. It was dark but for a coal-oil lamp burning in a ground-floor window with a furious moth batting at the glass.

Cripplehorn said, "I took the precaution of arranging a separate accommodation. I hope you're not offended. I've played the percentages all my life, and human nature being what it is—"

"The trouble with you slick talkers is the words come too fast and too many." Frank shoved his valise into the other's arms. "You carry it the rest of the way. I'm as tuckered out as if I was swinging an axe right alongside that crew."

"You'd better get your rest. And go easy on the whiskey. That legal waiver won't stand up in court if an innocent bystander stops a bullet fired by a drunk who can't shoot straight."

Frank shook his head. "There ain't no such thing as innocent bystanders."

"I'm curious about the Swiss backdrop." Caleb Munch crossed his legs in a bent-arm rocking chair, circles of sticking-plaster on his forehead, one cheek, and a pink patch shaved out of his beard. He looked like Walt Whitman after a run-in with John L. Sullivan. He showed Frank the photograph from Butte.

"It was hot. My boots was so full of sweat they squished when I walked. The fellow with the camera kept pulling down canvas sheets from rollers, asking which I liked. When I got to that one it was like a north breeze. Greek temples sure didn't do it, nor palm trees on a pile of sand."

"I don't suppose you'd care to tell me what it is about Randy Locke gets your back up."

"I ain't just sure, only I took a dislike to him the minute we laid eyes on each other. Hell, you catch my loop. I read where you went to get his story and wound up dancing with him Texas style."

"I'm conducting this interview. Not liking a man seems a poor reason for murder."

"It wouldn't be murder. We neither of us never made a play without warning and without both of us was heeled."

"Cripplehorn says in Oakland you shot at Locke from cover, without announcing yourself first."

"That *was* the announcement. It was to get his attention."

"Readers of the *Elevator* will need some assurance of that."

"Hell, he's alive, ain't he?"

"Old Gideon." Cripplehorn stood the quart bottle on the pinewood chest of drawers. "It's the closest thing to sipping whiskey you can get down the street. Did you know saloons are illegal in the Nations? Not that it matters in the Strip, where everything's so far outside the law it's a law unto itself. Just tonight I've seen two men threatened with death and had to sprint to avoid being tackled and raped by a lewd woman who'd dress out at three hundred pounds."

"I know Maude. You should of let her catch up." Randy, busy with one hand disassembling his Colt on the nightstand, pulled the cork with his teeth and spat it in the general direction of nowhere. "Want a snort?"

"Lord, no. The last time I drank liquor that hard I woke up in Juarez with a burro in my bed."

"I hope it was a jenny. How bad's the news? Every time I get a gift from you it costs me."

"I want you to pose for a photograph."

"We had this conversation. You just wasted the price of a bottle."

"Hear me out. That half-ass sketch of you in Arizona must have been made by a demented child. The proof the printer showed me demonstrated the contrast. It was ludicrous. Surely you want to come off as well as Frank."

"I will and more, oncet he's in hell."

"You haven't heard the rest."

"There's more?" He took a swig, put down the bottle, and thrust a pipe cleaner through a chamber. The acidy stench of the solvent warped the air in his room.

"I want you to pose with Frank."

Randy paused in mid-thrust. Then he chuckled.

"You got yourself a deal, Mr. Cripplehorn. I never miss an opportunity to catch up with Frank."

"There's one condition."

"There usually is, and mostwise more than one." He extracted the pipe cleaner and blew through the chamber. A low whistle resulted.

"No loads in your weaponry. I've petitioned the town council for a deputy marshal to be on hand to inspect it."

Randy finished his cleaning and started in with the oil. A pleasant scent of vanilla took the edge off the acrid odor of the solvent.

"Hell. I was afraid you'd have me strip to the skin in case I had a belly gun stuck up my ass."

Cripplehorn reacted as he usually did once his fish was on the hook; pushing his luck. "You'll need a new wardrobe. That hat of yours wouldn't even make a good bucket, filled with holes as it is, and your trousers look like a band of gypsies moved out of them."

"My hat keeps the sun off my skull and the pants cover my ass. That's as much as any man can ask of his personal gear."

"You're right, I suppose. Frank ordered himself a new suit of clothes from Montgomery Ward, and a bootmaker named Bluewater is fixing him up with a custom pair made from the indigenous cottonmouth. He'll come off a clown next to you in your honest rags."

Randy started putting the Colt back together. He paused to pull from the bottle.

"I won't wear a chimney tile like Ben Thompson, nor a beetle hat like that dude Luke Short. Maybe a good Texas crown with a plain band, and a coat that don't make me look like a tinhorn or an undertaker. I reckon I could use a new pair of boots. Bluewater, you say his name was?"

"Still is, I imagine."

"Well, I sure don't want no snake; its mate might come looking for him. There's a yard or two of buffler hide left, I wouldn't mind wearing it. Them shaggies kept me in tall corn."

Cripplehorn felt that old orgasmic thrill of conquest, head to toe. "I'll ask."

The camera was a big wooden box propped on a steel tripod in a small studio smelling of caustic chemicals, with men's and women's clothes hanging from a pipe rack on casters, hats enough to open a haberdashery, a forest of walking sticks in a bamboo umbrella stand, and various items of weaponry from a Confederate officer's sabre to a large-bore rifle that fired elephant rounds; although many of those who booked a session provided their own costumes and props. One wall was covered with pictures of grim-faced wedded couples, firemen gathered around pump wagons, a locomotive laboring up a grade, and a twister, a spectacular composition.

The photographer, a young Osage named Andrew Fox, ducked under his black cloth to inspect the focus. Refracting mirrors gave him an image of two men suspended upside down, one in an upholstered chair with a floral print, the other standing beside the chair with one hand resting on the back.

Randy and Frank had watched the Osage pulling down landscapes painted on canvas attached to rollers, rejecting a pagan temple in Rome, palm trees, Versailles, and the Pacific Ocean before agreeing on a meadow shaded by tall oaks.

"Looks right peaceful," Randy said.

Frank said, "I clumb trees just like them back in Pennsylvania."

"Too bad you didn't fall out of one and bust your neck."

"Gentlemen," said Cripplehorn, in a warning tone, nodding toward the two off-duty city deputies he'd hired to observe the session. They stood at opposite ends of the room, wearing heavy-handled Colts in stiff holsters. One had a ten-gauge shotgun broken open over the crook of one arm.

"You said there'd be just one. We got no rounds." Randy bit off the words.

"That Bowie of yours is too picturesque to leave out, but it's more than just a stage property. I know about Frank's clasp knife."

"That's just for whittling," Frank said. "We don't settle our scores with cutlery. We ain't Mexicans."

"These men are here merely to protect you both from those base instincts we all possess in some form."

Frank said, "I never been insulted in such pretty words."

As the shorter man, Randy posed standing, wearing a stiff new Texas pinch hat, a striped waistcoat over a lawn shirt with plain garters gathering the sleeves, and whipcord trousers tucked inside knee-length glossy brown boots, his worn old spurs on the heels. His Colt hung in his soft leather holster and he held his Ballard with the stock resting on the floor. Frank, in his new suit, fancy flap-toed boots, and tall-crowned sugar-loaf sombrero, sat with his Winchester across his lap. Both flinched when Andrew Fox raised a hod heaped with magnesium powder and touched it off with a candle, plunging the room into bright dazzle followed by acrid smoke; but the shutter was faster than even their reflexes, capturing them in the moment, calm and resolute.

For a time, the original plate was on display among other assorted hardcases in a museum in Guthrie, but it was destroyed in a fire soon after Teddy Roosevelt turned the Indian Nations into the State of Oklahoma. But you can still find a print in a junk store if you're looking, or pick up one of the posters Cripplehorn had made, all curling and fly-specked with the faces faded to blank ovals.

You can get a good price, too. The men are forgotten now, like the buffalo and the Great Plains Wolf and the range where they all wandered.

24

Avoid cards and spirits, or stand in the crossfire of ruin.

The day of the event, Abraham Cripplehorn sat at a campaign table in front of the gargantuan tent with several rolls of tickets and a strongbox, the off-duty deputies posted to see no one ran off with either. He set up at 9:00 A.M. and by noon had sold out, with two hours to go before the tent opened for business. There wasn't a room to be had in Cimarron, whose streets were filled with strange horses and buckboards and carriages from throughout the territory and places beyond. He'd hired a brass band made up of volunteer firemen and a talented local stock clerk to juggle bright rubber balls to open the show.

At quarter to two, Cripplehorn sent the two deputies to escort the featured players from their rooms. He inspected his new gold watch several times, listening to the band playing "The Garryowen," before the deputies returned without them.

The Rusty Bucket Saloon operated openly and illegally on the south side of the tracks, where from time to time a satisfied customer was run over by the Katy Flyer while weaving across the rails. It was the original railroad station before the new brick one was built on the north side, a fine solid construction of lath-and-plaster, and long enough to accommodate a paneled mahogany bar and scrolled backbar that had been brought in, dismantled, in freight wagons before the coming of the railroad. It offered two gaming tables with green baize tops and steel-engraved pictures in frames chronicling the triumphs of George Washington. The owner was an Irishman married to a Creek woman, who bought his stock from whiskey runners who managed to elude Judge Parker's marshals by entering the territory directly from the west and north without crossing their jurisdiction.

Today it was deserted except for the Irishman and a short-coupled customer in new clothes with a Colt on his hip. Everyone else, apparently, was either in Cripplehorn's big tent or on his way there to take in the show.

"You're fixing to be late, Mr. Locke," said the man behind the bar, a fine-boned example of lace-curtain stock who kept order in the place with two feet of billiard cue and a shotgun nearly as short.

Randy directed his scowl first to the bartender, then to the poster with his and Frank's picture on it propped up in the front window. "Well, they can't start the ball without me." He thumped his glass twice on the bar. The man came his way with a bottle and filled it to the top. "You know this John Barleycorn doesn't mix with shooting."

"You might be right. I disremember even asking you for the advice."

"Holy Jesus, Mary, and Joseph." The bartender stood with the bottle in one hand and the cork in the other, staring at Frank coming in the door.

"Well, if they weren't in their rooms, you should've gone looking for them," Cripplehorn said. "The town isn't that big."

One of the off-duty deputies, tall and rangy with handlebars and a little paintbrush beard, moved a plug from one cheek to the other. "My mama didn't raise me to go looking for no puma in no thicket. You wanted 'em to stay put, you should of posted guards at their doors."

"The marshal didn't have any more men to spare and I don't trust civilians I don't know. Find them. Please."

"That's better. It's a little-bitty word, don't cost nothing, and does so much." He loosened his pistol in its holster, looked at his partner, and jerked his head over his shoulder. The other deputy, a Chickasaw half-breed with deep pockmarks on his face, slammed shut the breech of his ten-gauge and they moved off away from the brumping band inside and the clerk juggling bright-colored balls.

Randy's hand dropped to his weapon, but Frank spread his hands away from his leathered Remington, palms forward. Randy rested his hand on the bar and Frank hooked a heel on the brass rail next to him. He nodded at the bartender, who realized he was still holding the bottle and cork and filled a fresh glass.

"How many's that?" Frank asked, tilting his head toward

Randy's and meeting his gaze in the mirror mounted on the backbar.

"My second. I stop at two now, just enough to take the sting out of my leg."

"I do regret that. That horse you had throwed up its head or I'd of just kilt you instead of making you lame."

"Well, I taken your ear. I know how much store you set in good looks."

"It slowed me down some at the start, but since I got famous I ain't wanted for companionship."

"What about that woman you stole from her sheriff daddy in Colorado?"

"I left her and she died. That's another regret. Whenever I think of you I clean lose my good manners. As I recall, you always had a way in that department. I seen the most looksome women with the ugliest toads."

"They come, but they never stick. They expect you to put 'em first, leastwise when you're together. If it's another woman they can always scratch her face and pull out her hair, but they can't fight what they can't see. I never could commit to one like I do you."

"You might send flowers now and again, seeing as how you're so sweet on me."

"Go to hell, Frank."

"You first."

The tall deputy came in the door, his hand resting on his gun handle. His partner, the half-breed, stood on the threshold with his shotgun leveled. Frank and Randy turned to face them.

Randy said, "Gents, you better be as good as you think you are."

The tall deputy took in the two men with their hands hovering near their pistols. "How good you got to be with a street sweeper at your back?"

Frank said, "That's the trouble with a long narrow room

like this. If he cuts loose, we all three go down squirting blood with all our inwards outside. So that makes two of us you got to take down all on your own."

The man with the paintbrush whiskers switched cheeks on his plug, switched back. He leaned over a little and shot a brown stream into the nearest spittoon. He caught his partner's eye in the mirror. The man with the shotgun backed out the door and turned away, followed by his partner, moving backwards also.

When they were alone with the bartender, mopping his face with his swamp rag, Frank said, "Can you get that pistol out of that soft holster in under two minutes?"

"If I hold the holster down with one hand and jerk hard."

"Me, too. We ought to ask Cripplehorn where he got them slick holsters and tie-downs he writes about in his books. I reckon them boys are readers."

"Hell, I don't believe he ever wrote even one. Got time for a hand?"

Randy jerked down the rest of his drink. "Always."

They sat at one of the gaming tables while the bartender brought a deck of cards.

"I heard they grow their lawmen tough in the Strip," Cripplehorn said. "Is there no end to these myths?"

The half-breed Chickasaw cradled his shotgun. "We chose badly."

"I understand how you feel. You hear that?" The entrepreneur tilted his head in the direction of the tent. The band was still playing, but above the thumping brass and boom of the bass drum came the regular chugging beat of a freight train at full throttle. "They're pounding the bleachers with their feet. Before long they'll come streaming out screaming for their money back. The vendors have been plying them with beer all afternoon. I may be the first man ever strung up on a complaint of disappointment. What were they doing when you left?"

"I looked back in through the window," said the tall deputy. "They were playing cards."

"Locke and Farmer?"

"Yup."

"Playing cards."

"Yup."

"What kind of place is this, where men are shooting at each other one day and socializing the next?"

The half-breed rolled his shoulders. "If you spend enough time out here, you get used to everything."

"I've been crisscrossing the West for more than ten years. I'm not used to it yet."

"You just need more time."

Frank, who sat facing the window in the Rusty Bucket, shielded his eyes against the lowering sun. "Half-past two or thereabout. I forgot to wind my watch this morning; ain't used to wearing one after all them visits to pawnshops. Two cards." He laid down two.

Randy dealt him two off the deck. "That's what's good about the sun. It don't need winding."

"It's dependable, that's certain. Everybody knows when the sun'll come up and bed down; it's in the Almanac. But the moon comes and goes on its own and nobody knows when."

"That's on account of God made the sun, and He's an orderly man. The moon's the devil's work. Dealer takes one."

Both men raised the stake. The bartender came around with the bottle and a fresh glass for Randy, but Randy shook his head and Frank cupped his hand over his, preventing him from pouring. He returned to the bar and sat on a stool, dividing his attention between the *Fort Smith Elevator* and the Regulator clock clunking out the minutes on the wall opposite.

Frank asked Randy if he was thinking what Frank was.

"If I was, I wouldn't own to it."

"I'm thinking Cripplehorn's got no leave to poke around in what's between you and me, and nobody else neither."

Randy concentrated on his cards. "We gave him our word."

"Till day after tomorrow, we said. That's today."

"I never wanted this folderol to begin with," Randy said. "I only went along with it because I needed money at the time."

"Same here. It just feels like we're standing in downtown Denver in our long-handles with the flaps down. I don't figure he bought the right for that. Call."

Randy spread his cards on the green baize. "Two pair, jacks and deuces." The fifth card was the five of clubs.

Frank's teeth showed in his imperials. He laid his hand down faceup. He had two jacks and deuces and the five of hearts.

Randy said, "I've played poker all my life and watched a thousand games. I never saw such a thing before. I never even heard it could happen."

"That tears it, don't it?"

Randy looked up and smiled. "Who invited God into this game?"

25

Nature is a random force, disaster
its close cousin.

They selected the railroad tracks for the contest, Frank on the north side, Randy on the south. That placed the sun to Frank's left and Randy's right and at a disadvantage to neither man. No trains were scheduled before early evening. They took off their coats and laid them on the ground, Frank folding his carefully according to the creases, Randy letting his fall in a heap; that gave their arms freedom of movement. Randy, unaccustomed to his new hat, took it off and dropped it on top of the coat to avoid distraction.

The band music and the noise of hundreds of customers pounding the bleachers reached them from a distance, as of a storm on the other side of a mountain range, lightning pulsing and thunder a dull thud, dumping torrents, while they stood in the sun, utterly detached from someone else's tempest.

They squared off, raising their pistols to shoulder height and extending them the length of their arms, hammers cocked.

"Drop your weapons or I'll shoot you both where you stand!"

The man who had stepped around the corner of the brick train station on Randy's side of the tracks was hatless, with his thick blue-black hair cut in a bowl and a bright star on his blue tunic. He held a Henry rifle braced against one shoulder, his other hand resting on the forepiece. He had features the color of brick, and with the sun carving caverns in his cheeks and the flat planes of his temples, seemingly as hard.

Frank and Randy faced off the way they played poker, allowing nothing to draw their eyes from the game.

"I'm an officer with the Cherokee Lighthorse Police and it's my intention to prevent murder on grounds entrusted to me. Drop 'em!" he roared.

Walter Red Hawk's reactions were slower than his sense of probity, and were no match for Randy's relentless practice or Frank's experience in the field. The Cherokee managed to fire only one shot before two pistol bullets struck him full in the chest. He went down, reflexively cranking a new round into the chamber, which was still in it unfired when he fell into the gravel off the edge of the station platform. His slug had passed between the two men as they wheeled in his direction. The coroner's inquest the next day established death as instantaneous. Two rounds were dug out of the corpse, both of which had hit vital spots.

That event, taking place as it did in the more cramped venue of the Evangelical Church, was packed as closely as Cripplehorn's tent, with all the pews taken and spectators standing three deep in back. The dead man was known to most who attended, and popular. He'd supplemented his stipend from the tribal council working in the local sawmill and supported a Cherokee wife and two small children.

As the town had no jail, Randy and Frank were placed in custody in a room on the second floor of the hotel. The shots had drawn a crowd from the tent, who grasped the situation immediately and seized and disarmed them both; there were just too many of them to shoot and make an escape, so they held off. The city marshal, his deputies, and Walter Red Hawk's colleagues in the Lighthorse Police guarded the men in shifts while shouts reached them from the Rusty Bucket, which was the place of choice whenever informal hanging required discussion.

"They swung Spanish Bob in the church bell tower a couple of years back," the marshal informed his prisoners.

"I'm not just sure any of those Cherokees with badges would place themselves between you two and a lynch mob with practical experience."

The peace officer's name was Foster. He wore a gray suit and town shoes and his hair was prematurely white. Strangers mistook him for a banker until they got close enough to study his brown seamed face and empty eyes. He carried a Schofield revolver on his belt and a squat English Bulldog in a Wes Hardin rig under his left shoulder. In five years, the first two as a deputy, he'd shot eleven men and been acquitted of murder in one case where the evidence was doubtful.

Frank, who like Randy was stiff-limbed and swollen-faced from mishandling by the crowd, asked Foster what had become of Cripplehorn.

"He ran off with his cash box when the shooting started. I and my men were too busy keeping the pair of you from your appointment in church to look for him, and the Indian police didn't care. My thinking is he hid somewhere out in the trees till the eastbound came along and hooked it after it pulled out. Personally I don't give snake shit. If folks are dumb enough to shell out three days' wages to see two men try to kill each other when they can see it for free anywhere in the territory, it isn't my responsibility."

"What's to be done with us?" Randy asked.

"Assuming you survive the night we're putting you on the train to Fort Smith in the morning. I and my deputies will ride with you as far as Buffalo, over in the Cherokee Nation, where we'll hand you off to the federals. They'll see you the rest of the way." Foster stood with one foot on a stool upholstered in petit-point embroidered fabric and one arm resting on his thigh, watching them with his empty eyes. "If I were you I wouldn't mess with Parker's marshals. Half of them had shinplasters out on them before they signed on and the other half is just plain ornery. They don't want to shoot you, because then they'll have to pay for the burial out of their own pockets, but that won't slow them down if they find you're not worth the trouble of delivery. I wouldn't count on them being as easygoing as Walter Red Hawk. I've ridden with them and I know."

It was a long night in their lives, with voices murmuring down in the street and the flicker of torches through the window throwing crawling shadows on the ceiling. The half-breed with the shotgun was posted in their room, the orange point of his cigarette moving now and again and glowing more fiercely when he drew on it from his chair in the corner with a view of the window. His tall partner sat outside the door with a chair borrowed from another room and the back tilted and propped under the knob, where anyone would have to go through him to get in.

Randy said to the breed, "Just be sure that street sweeper ain't pointed too general when the ball starts."

"Shut up."

Frank lay for a while in silence, stretched out on the bed with his hands behind his head, watching the muted fireworks. One of his ankles was shackled to the bed's iron frame. "Where do folks get so many torches, I wonder, and so fast? You reckon this is such a normal thing they keep 'em in a nice dry place, pitched and ready?"

The guard told him to shut up too.

"Damnedest place I ever did see," said Randy, seated on the edge of the mattress with his feet on the floor, one of them chained like Frank's to his side of the bed. "They got law, but it don't raise a finger to stop the show, only when we took it outside. You reckon Cripplehorn had a license and didn't tell us about it?"

After another little stretch of quiet, the breed spoke. "Walter had it in his mind to stop you in the tent the minute you faced off. He was on his way there when he spotted you two trying to spoil everybody's day."

"How you know that?" Randy asked.

"Hell, he talked about it for weeks. I don't reckon anybody thought he'd act on it. Them Cherokees like to hear their tongues rattle like a gourd. This is the first time one actually done what he said he would."

"He should of kept his voice down," Frank said. "You don't shout at two men with guns when all you got is one."

Randy said, "I like a nice polite arrest. I don't mind if it involves me waking up with a knot on my head from some hoglegs swung by somebody knows how to swing it. I sure don't like to be squawked at like I'm married to a she-bear."

"Go to sleep, Randy. That'd have to be one desperate she-bear."

The half-Chickasaw deputy told them both to shut up.

26

Justice is man's invention. The universe makes no such promise.

A sudden downpour, not uncommon in November in that region, doused the dudgeon of the mob, which broke up into individuals sprinting for cover. Although it had re-formed the next day at the train station, the presence of Marshal Foster, all four of his deputies, and as many Lighthorse Police, every man carrying a shotgun, kept things benign.

Frank and Randy were seated in facing seats, each shackled to a deputy. A fresh, green horse apple splatted against a window and the train began its journey through that feral country, where rocks pushed up like yellow-brown knuckles through the soil and half-naked trees clawed holes in the overcast.

In Fort Smith, Arkansas, where Judge Isaac Parker exercised federal jurisdiction over the Nations, the prosecutor and the attorney appointed to defend the prisoners debated whether the defendants should be tried separately (Parker overruled this), whether Walter Red Hawk had overstepped himself in attempting to arrest non-Indians (Parker allowed this argument to proceed), and whether two men can both be charged with the same homicide.

The celebrated "Hanging Judge" (twenty-five men convicted by that January of 1883, twenty-four hanged, one escaped) was intrigued by this argument. He'd presided over the court for seven years, and although the burden of his docket and awesome responsibility had streaked his hair and beard with white at age forty-four, a novel suggestion always brought him upright in his chair.

A partial transcript of the discussion between prosecutor Clayton, defense attorney MacElroy, and Judge Parker follows:

CLAYTON: Your honor, the coroner's inquest found both wounds fatal.

MacELROY: I submit, your honor, that whereas one bullet pierced the deceased's heart and the other punctured a lung, the first would have caused death immediately.

PARKER: Counselor, are you suggesting that one of your clients is more guilty than the other?

MacELROY: That would be unethical. I'm attempting to establish grounds for separate trials.

PARKER: I've already ruled on that. In any case, this court has no way of determining who fired which bullet. They come identical from the factory and are unrecognizable upon impact.

MACELROY: Your honor—
PARKER: Pursue another line, Counselor.

Whenever the trial recessed, Frank and Randy were returned, each man's wrists and ankles chained together, to their cells in the brick jail, which was built around a three-tiered steel cage, the latest in penal design with a gear-driven mechanism that allowed the guards to open or shut an entire line of cells just by throwing a lever. This made a hellish clang that had been known to break a man. The two men occupied different levels, with no way of communicating short of shouting, and the guards discouraged such breaches of the peace.

The remaining bone of contention—keenly observed by the reporters assigned from across the continent to cover the trial—was whether Walter Red Hawk, in interceding in an affair between white men, had exceeded his jurisdiction, which was confined to Indians by federal law. In his instructions to the jury, Parker left no question regarding his opinion on the matter: Notwithstanding the deceased's error in judgment, the willful slaying of a tribal officer and a ward of the U.S. government was a federal offense. After deliberating two hours, the panel of twelve returned a verdict of guilty. The defendants were sentenced to hang.

"Frankly, I wish it were from someone else's gallows," said Parker, raising his gavel. "We grow murderers enough here at home without importing more."

But the world wouldn't quit turning.

Things had changed since the days when Parker suffered no interference from Washington. In the early years of his tenure, no appeal existed between him and the president—or God Almighty, some said, because showing mercy to murderers cost votes, particularly in the wild territories; but the Judge had enemies in the Congress. They argued that no man's influence was greater than both houses combined, and pushed through a bill placing the infamous Eleventh District firmly in the appeals system that applied to other courts.

The eastern newspapers applauded the decision, while privately regretting the loss of sensational accounts of wholesale executions on the great Fort Smith scaffold. Such headlines as SIX MEN "JERKED TO JESUS" IN A HEARTBEAT did more for circulation than war with Canada.

And so those stalwart public servants Flapdoodle, Pettifog, and Straddler succeeded in gelding the old bull at last.

Seeing the advantage in publicity—for Abraham Cripplehorns are rather more common among attorneys than most other places—the lawyer who'd been appointed to represent Frank and Randy reopened their file. His name was F.S.T. MacElroy: "Feisty" to his fellow law students at William and Mary, and he had earned the nickname through more than just his initials. Feisty hired a jeweler.

The jeweler, Otto Weismann, wore a skullcap and a loupe hinged to his wire spectacles. He used his scales to weigh the two bullets that had been removed from Walter Red Hawk's corpse, which the coroner in Cimarron had placed in separate envelopes labeled HEART and LUNG. The slugs were both intact, although misshapen by passage through the flesh. The difference in weight was almost infinitesimal, but inarguable: The bullet that had penetrated the left lung—a long, agonizing death when left on its own—was a .45. The other, which had stopped the heart upon contact, causing instant death, was a .44. Weismann signed an affidavit swearing to his conclusions and it was sent to the court of appeals.

The newspapers reported the event, to keep alive a story

they'd missed covering, but overlooking its significance: It was the birth of modern ballistic science.

Frank Farmer had reason to be thankful he'd replaced his lost .44 New Model Remington revolver with a .45, cracked grips or no. That tiny difference in calibers spared him the gallows.

Armed with this information, F.S.T. MacElroy wrote to Chester Alan Arthur, who at the time was stinging from public accusations about his wardheeling past and needed a reputation as a progressive. He commuted Frank's sentence to life.

But the lawyer wasn't done. He filed a petition asking for a second trial for his clients based on his earlier argument that the slain peace officer had lacked the authority to arrest them. The petition was granted, but for unexplained reasons only Randy's conviction was set aside. The attorney's protests were ignored. Bail was denied. Randy languished in his cell until April 1885, when a new jury heard his case. Once again, Parker presided. His hair and whiskers now were nearly all white.

"Mr. Blood, did you say in the presence of the defendant that you tried to talk Walter Red Hawk out of attempting to restrain Frank Farmer and Randolph Locke from shooting each other?" asked lawyer MacElroy.

"No." Deputy Marshal Billy Blood, the half-Chickasaw from Cimarron, sat in the witness chair with his feet flat on the floor and his plate star shining on his blue tunic. "What I said was I didn't believe him when he said he would."

"Objection."

"On what grounds, Mr. Clayton?" Parker asked the prosecutor.

"Leading the witness."

"Sustained."

"I'll rephrase the question. Why didn't you believe him, Mr. Blood?"

"Cherokees are all talk and no action. Everybody knows that."

"Objection! Conclusion on the part of the witness."

"Sustained. Mr. Blood, old antagonisms between the tribes are of no interest to this court."

The defense attorney repeated the question. Billy Blood fidgeted, then said:

"Walter always went by the book, and the book says Indian officers can't touch white men. They're for U.S. marshals and deputized city policemen."

After the summations, Parker addressed the jury, reiterating what he'd said in the first trial about the killing of tribal officers and wards of the government.

Whether because his iron rule had been challenged by the Congress or for other reasons known only to the jurors, the Judge was less convincing this time. Three days of deliberation ended in deadlock. A mistrial was declared and Randy was returned to custody to await a third trial. In December of the same year he rose before the judge of the Third District Court in Fort Scott, Kansas, and learned he'd been acquitted on grounds of self-defense.

He was free, while Frank was removed to the Federal House of Corrections in Detroit, Michigan, to serve out the rest of his days at hard labor.

"That ain't fair," said Randy.

He was back in Fort Smith to claim his belongings, including the Ballard and the Colt, which had been removed from three years in evidence.

MacElroy, a son of the Commonwealth of Virginia who smoked cigarettes in a long onyx holder to avoid staining his fair Van Dyke beard, nodded. He'd invited his client to his office, a cramped room smelling of dust and rotted bindings overlooking Garrison Avenue, to give him the news. A heating stove intended for a much larger room made the air oppressive.

"It's worse than unfair; it's indifferent. The implication is Frank's case was closed when he was taken off Death Row."

"What you fixing to do about it?"

"Oh, I'll write letters."

"That's it?"

"It was sufficient to save you both from execution. I might wear them down. You never know. I have a reputation for perseverance."

"That son of a bitch Parker had us both measured for the rope. I still like him better than this bunch in Washington. You know he cried when he said we'd be hung by the neck till dead, him that'd said the same thing twenty-five times already?"

"He's a sentimental old ogre. Prays in the Methodist church for the souls of the men he sent to hell."

"I bet Chet Arthur never shed a tear when he buried Frank alive."

"Well, there's a new president. I doubt Cleveland would have granted my petition."

"He's the sixth since Frank and I been fighting."

"I expected you to be pleased. I've been through the transcripts of your double trial so many times I can recite them chapter and verse. I never read of a kind word passing between you."

"Just because you want a fellow dead don't mean you want him locked up in Michigan."

"I'm afraid your gentleman-duellist's ideas of honor don't apply to the criminal justice system."

"It's criminal all right."

27

Time is worse than a thief. It murders youth and hope.

Fifteen years plodded past, pulled by oxen. At times they seemed to stop utterly, caught in mire or forced to wait for water to recede. The pace was the same for both men, outside as well as in.

The world spun around them. It was like being stuck trackside with a busted wheel, watching trains hurtle past, all the faces in the windows a blur.

Geronimo, a great butcher and liar to his people, surrendered himself and his band of thirty Chiricahua to General Miles in a place called Skeleton Canyon, turning himself from a bloodthirsty savage to a celebrity overnight.

Another fierce winter, worse than the one that had closed the Lazy Y and most of its competitors in 1882, swept away the last of the open range, leaving behind fenced ranches, truck farms, and hundreds of tons of bloated cattle carcasses to be buried in mass graves.

The *San Francisco Examiner* ran out of gunfights and published a poem by Ernest Lawrence Thayer called "Casey at the Bat."

The Indian Nations, now known as Oklahoma Territory, hosted a barn-burner of a horse race: Hundreds of would-be homesteaders whipping teams and mounts into a lather to claim 160 acres apiece in free land. The Cherokee Strip vanished overnight, its original settlers pushed aside and the scum of the earth fled to Canada and Mexico.

The Congress and President Benjamin Harrison sliced Dakota in two, bunched it in with Montana, Washington,

Idaho, and Wyoming to bring the total of U.S. states to forty-four.

A gang of Oklahoma stick-up artists experimented with bank robbery in Kansas, and got themselves shot to ribbons for stepping outside their specialty, which was robbing trains. Four men paid for it with their lives, including two brothers named Dalton.

The first copies of *The National Geographic* found their way into barbershops, where the African issues wore out faster than the edge on a razor.

A nobody named Selman shot John Wesley Hardin to death in El Paso, prudently from behind.

A battleship went down off Cuba and that fool McKinley declared war on the whole goldarn Spanish Empire.

Meanwhile, Frank slept nights in an eight-by-five cell in Detroit and busted rocks days to pave the streets for automobiles, and Randy tried suicide.

It's difficult to say which man suffered more: Frank, because of the unremitting hardship and monotony of incarceration, or Randy, because the purpose of his existence—to end Frank's—had been stolen from him with the flick of a little wooden mallet.

In Sedalia, Missouri, he aimed his Colt at his temple, but owing to his drunken condition missed and shot off the end of his nose, resulting in copious bleeding but not death. The woman who ran the boarding house found him, and charged him for the ruined bedding after the bandages came off.

Suicide was against state law, although no one who'd succeeded had ever been prosecuted. Instead of jailing him, the city police put him in a lock ward at the hospital and strapped him to a bed. When after three days he promised a foreigner in a white coat with a billy-goat beard he wouldn't repeat the offense, he was released and his weapon

returned to him. He'd sold the Ballard for grocery money
a year earlier, the West being wolfed out and Randy so far
outside rifle range. He kept the pistol to shoot rats and such,
his usual accommodations not measuring up to the standards of the Eldorado.

One night, lying wide awake amongst the vermin in a
five-cent-a-room palace in Jefferson City, his Colt out to
protect his boots from the men snoring in the surrounding
beds, he got a brainstorm from a pint bottle: Everybody was
always trying to break out of prison, but nobody ever tried
to break in. They wouldn't be expecting that.

Hopping trains wasn't as easy as it was once. The new
coal-burners were greased lightning, and with the country
going through one of its panics all the guards were on the
prod for tramps. After several false tries he managed to grab
a handle on a westbound, and to jump off when the train
slowed for a curve outside Pawnee, O.T. There he walked
into a hardware store run by a husband and wife from Wisconsin, place cluttered with rolls of barbed and baling
wire, hickory axe handles, and Sears, Roebuck catalogues,
shot a hole in a nail keg, and demanded cash. But the husband was unfamiliar with the new cash register, brass
and bronze and big as a plow, and terrified besides. Randy
was watching him fumble for the magic combination of
keys and crank that would open the drawer when the wife
crept up behind the desperado and swung an axe handle at
his head, putting a crack in it and ruining his Texas hat.

In the Fort Smith courtroom, he fingered the lump where
his head had been shaved, stitched, and plastered and
waited for Parker to come in, adjudicate, and ship him off
to Detroit. Once he was in the House of Corrections, he
reckoned, any sort of makeshift weapon would save the nation the expense of boarding Frank Farmer for the re-
mainder of his natural span.

But he hadn't read a newspaper in months and didn't

know that Judge Parker had died in office after twenty-one years on the bench. The squirt who showed up looked like a little kid in the big horsehair chair behind the massive cherrywood desk. He gave Randy three to five years in the federal penitentiary at Little Rock, four hundred miles from his target.

Meanwhile, a letter arrived at a cramped overheated office overlooking Garrison Avenue in Fort Smith:

OFFICE OF THE ATTORNEY GENERAL
WASHINGTON, D.C.

Dear F.S.T. MacElroy, Esq.:

In response to your letters regarding Francis X. Farmer, please be advised that this office is considering your request for a hearing to determine whether parole is indicated. . . .

The honest Indians of Oklahoma Territory mourned Isaac Parker, who had brought swift justice so many times on their behalf. Not so the Congress. Its members picked over his carcass, divvied up what was left of his jurisdiction, and reviewed all his decisions starting with when Hector was a pup. Some were let stand, others reversed and the prisoners granted either new trials or a presidential pardon. Still others were paroled. On June 5, 1900, Frank Farmer walked into a mostly empty room where five men sat behind a long table from a Masonic lodge and walked out a free man.

The news got five lines from editors who vaguely recalled the drama of Locke *vs.* Farmer. The *Barbary Spar,* owned and operated still by Major W.B. Updegraff, bald now and stone deaf, made use of improved photograph reproduction and accompanied the piece with the picture taken of Randy and Frank in Cimarron, cropped to the size of a postage stamp. The one-column headline read:

FRONTIER ERA GUNMAN RELEASED.

Newspapers were banned in the Little Rock penitentiary, to avoid exciting the inmates with stories of crime and pictures of Russian ballerinas in tights; but if you had the contacts and had put back a little money you could get anything. Randy hadn't had much to put back, but what he scrimped on tobacco makings he saved for news from the outside world. With things moving so fast all around, you never knew when the status quo might make a square turn.

His stomach sank when he found the teeny piece about Frank in the telegraph column of the *Little Rock Gazette*. Luck and timing had been against him so long he reckoned the Lord had it in for him for all those times he'd taken His name in vain. But then his heart quickened. If he behaved himself, he, too, would be out in eighteen months; no time at all when you stood it up against twenty-five years.

28

An ocean voyage is the best remedy for the stagnant soul.

Frank Farmer thought San Francisco the biggest, fastest, loudest place in the world: the boldest whores, the busiest streets, saloons the size of cotton warehouses.

Then he saw Nome.

It was a sprawl bigger than Creede or Deadwood in their

time. The beach was a sea of tents, enough canvas to make a thousand as big as Cripplehorn's show tent outside Cimarron. With nothing to separate them but duck stretched over frame, the tin-tack pianos, banjos, and string bands made a racket like a trainload of kettles tumbling down a ravine. The place had more whorehouses than Dodge City, Denver, and Tombstone combined, some of them honest-to-God cribs where a hostess entertained you in the little wooden rick where she slept, stacked one on top of the next in rows like crates in a warehouse, and you could track the progress of what was going on in each house from ten doors down. There was no escape from the bustle except the hop joints, where a man could crawl into a bunk and smoke up unobtainable women and colors that didn't exist.

Someone had stubbed his toe on a nugget in Alaska, and the rest of the world came running.

Back in Frisco, where the ships set sail, you couldn't cross a street without taking the chance of being run over by a carriage or a buckboard or a by-God automobile, squawking its horn and choking on its own exhaust with a bang that throwed your heart into your throat, thinking you'd been dry-gulched. You could walk across the harbor, stepping from schooner to steamship to tugboat to barge and never get your feet wet. It might've been that way clear to Alaska, but it wasn't. Frank bought a berth on a steamer called the *Pelican,* and found himself on the ocean for the first time in his life.

If Randy was alive—and he was sure he'd know if he wasn't—Nome was where he'd be found.

Neither man could resist going someplace where people gathered in herds. It was the best place to look. Big mining interests had claimed the gold fields of California and Colorado from under the feet of individual fortune-seekers, the silver mines had played out or flooded, and for all the annoyance they brought with them the ticking of horseless carriages was still too faint to excite much interest in the vast pools of oil slumbering beneath Texas and Pennsylvania. Best of all, Nome had few laws and fewer men still to enforce them. It was like the old Cherokee Strip without that pest Cripplehorn to spoil things.

It was a rough crossing. The sea stood up on its hind legs and pitched over onto its forefeet, arching and twisting, sunfishing like an unbroke mustang by Beelzebub out of a waterspout. Frank got right well acquainted with the lee rail of the *Pelican* and decided if Randy didn't get lucky and kill him he'd find his way back home on foot somehow.

His first day outside, Randy broke another law.

He spent the wages he'd made working the mangle in the prison laundry on a day coach and crossed the state line four hours later, violating the terms of his parole.

"Where you off to, old-timer?" asked the man in the seat facing his, a fellow in a striped coat and straw boater who looked like one-fourth of a barbershop quartet.

"North."

"You caught the wrong train. This one's heading west."

"It was the first one out of the station."

"What's your hurry?"

He allowed himself a bitter grin. "Gonna get rich up in Alaska."

It was a long way, a man had to eat, and the jobs didn't come in a straight line. He loaded bales of cotton and barrels of molasses aboard flatboats in New Orleans, spread tar on the streets of Houston, cleaned and polished cuspidors and swamped up vomit in a saloon called La Perla in the Spanish peninsula of Baja, California. The Mexican government appeared to have lost interest in banishing him from the republic. He slept in barns and stables and out in the open. He was a ghost, a figure of derision in rags with a short nose. He spent a night in jail in Yuba City for jerking his pistol on a gang of boys who pelted him with gravel and horse apples.

Randy hated boats and such truck; losing his horse and gear when that ferry capsized by Fort Benton in '77 was as close to a sailing man as he ever cared to get. But unless they built a bridge, he knew he'd have to put up with some ocean. There was too much of it between Frisco and Nome, so he set his sights on Seattle.

He got as far as Puyallup, collapsed in the street, and lay there two hours before someone noticed and took him to a hospital for the indigent with as bad a case of pneumonia as had ever been admitted there. A month later, still weak but turned out because his bed was needed, he rode with a pile of fish to Seattle, where he put in for cook's helper aboard a sealer bound for the Bering Sea.

The captain was clerkly looking, with graying burnsides. He sat with his tunic buttoned to his neck at a table in a room stacked with sacks and barrels and smelling of the sea.

"Before you sign, understand we're not putting in at Nome. I've had trouble with gold fever and desertions. If you try going over the side, I'll invoke maritime law and have you shot."

Randy signed.

The cook had about the same talent as his helper, although he made better biscuits. Randy labored visibly climbing to the captain's cabin carrying dishes on trays, stopped frequently in passageways to lean against a bulkhead to catch his breath, sweated buckets. By the time the ship passed the Aleutians, its master and crew were no longer paying him any attention, except to wonder if they'd have a corpse to send over the side.

"He's a curious cuss, that's certain," said the first mate. "Always asking landlubbers' questions and watching how we do things."

The captain frowned. "Ordinarily I'd tell Cookie to give him something useful to do with all that spare time; but he's one played-out fish. Serves me right for taking pity on an old man with only a bedroll to his name. I wasted a lecture."

They were creeping along the territory's northwest coast, the man in the crow's nest watching for ice floes, when the bosun pointed the stem of his pipe at a glitter in the otherwise solid black off starboard. "Nome."

Randy waited until the man went below, then swept the canvas sheet off a lifeboat stored with supplies and provisions pilfered from the galley and sea chest, climbed in, and lowered himself by pulleys to the water.

It was a hellish voyage: What the crew considered a calm sea was to him a tempest, he was clumsy with the oars, and the scudding fog obscured the lights ashore for minutes at a time, during which he was certain he'd come around and was rowing away from land. That terrified him more than being shot to death; more than prison. A Texas cowboy had no business drowning in a frozen sea.

When at last the incoming tide took over, drawing the boat into the shallows, he couldn't wait for it to ground. He bundled his foodstuffs and personals in an oilcloth slicker, got out, and waded.

Once on the beach, pale in the light from the settlement, the wire broke that had been holding him together. He dropped his bundle and followed it down to the ground.

Lying on his back chasing his breath, he saw a ragged sliver of moon through a tear in the clouds.

Everybody knows when the sun'll come up and bed down; it's in the Almanac. But the moon comes and goes on its own and nobody knows when.

*That's on account of God made the sun, and He's an
orderly man. The moon's the devil's work.*

"Well, Frank," he whispered, "I shoveled puke, scoured
grease, spit up blood, and crossed a goddamn ocean. If you
ain't here, I'll track you down and kill you twice."

29

**Upon encountering an old friend after a
separation of years, resist the urge to remark upon
how much he's aged. The chances are he's
thinking the same thing about you.**

The gaunt, moustachioed barkeep of the Broadway Saloon sighed when he recognized Frank shoving his
way through the crowd to the bar.

"No, mister," he said, "I ain't seen no mangy piece of
wolf bait today. Leastwise not one answering to Randy
Locke."

"Who the hell was that?" asked a prospector drinking a
beer, jerking his head toward the departing man.

"I forgot his name the minute he give it. Been in every
day for a month asking the same question."

Frank worked all the way down Front Street, asking the
same question in the Dexter, the Cosmopolitan, the Acme,
and all the rest; identical, every one, hung with moose
heads and snowshoes and smelling pungently of unwashed
wool steaming in the heat of a cookstove. He got the same
answer, as he had every day since he'd arrived in Nome.

There was no reason to leave a description of the man
he was looking for. Neither man had ever shied from
leaving his true name, and in all candor any description
he might give would fit half that population of frostbitten

prospectors caked with blue clay to their boot-tops, even if it was any good after fifteen years. When Randy did show up, he'd make the same rounds Frank had, asking after him.

The next day he started in fresh, not even having to ask the question now and leaving without a word after the answer. In the Parisian he was already turning away when he realized he'd hit paydirt.

"I ain't just certain," said the barman. "He was drunk and mumbled the name. I locked him up in the storeroom to keep him from getting his throat cut for what was in his pockets."

"Mighty big of you."

"I'm a Christian, mister."

Frank watched him unlock the door to the room behind the bar and followed him through. Randy lay spread-eagled among the barrels and crates, snoring loud enough to rattle the empty bottles awaiting refilling on the shelves.

"He's high-smelling. I'd be obliged if you'd take him on out of here."

Frank sent him away with a cartwheel dollar and hauled Randy to his feet by one arm. An empty bottle of Old Pepper slid to the floor and rolled to a stop against a rat trap, springing it with a loud snap.

In the New York Kitchen Frank half-dragged, half-carried him to an oilcloth-covered table and dumped him into a chair. Two men seated at a nearby table picked up their plates and moved to the other side of the room.

A waiter with a full beard and a white apron that hung to his knees appeared.

"We don't serve tramps. You want to buy him a bowl of soup, you send him around back."

The muzzle of a Remington revolver planted itself against the waiter's forehead.

"Mister, you got two choices."

"What'll it be?"

Frank lowered the hammer and holstered the pistol. "Coffee. Bring the pot."

When it came, Frank filled a thick china mug, pulled Randy's head up from the table by his hair, and poured coffee into his open mouth. He choked, sputtered, shook loose of the other's grip, and slapped at his hip. Frank slapped him harder across the face and went on slapping until Randy's eyes came into focus.

"You son of a bitch!"

"That's what my daddy said." He sat down, filled the mug again, pushed it across the table, and watched him raise it to his lips with both hands. They shook. His shirt was full of holes and he smelled as if he'd rolled in a puddle of rancid grease. "You keep on with that skullbender you'll cheat me out of what I got coming."

"It's the only thing here that's cheap."

"They stir it up on the spot and refill the bottles. You can buy two for the price of an egg. When'd you get in?"

"Last night late; waded in. I had to thaw out. This place is colder than the winter of '81."

"They say it gets worse come November." Frank pushed some banknotes across the table. "Finish that pot and buy yourself some decent clothes. I can't shoot you in this condition."

"Struck it rich?"

"It'd surprise you how much money you can make busting rocks fifteen years. I didn't spend none of it inside and I'm camped out on the beach. You can look for me there when you stop shaking."

Frank was almost at the door when a hammer cocked behind him. He spun, clapping his holster with one hand and snatching out the Remington with the other, just in time to see Randy's Colt blow a hole in the waiter's apron.

The man was still holding his sawed-off shotgun when he hit the floor.

When Randy laid the pistol on the table, Frank leathered his. "Obliged."

Randy lifted his cup, steadily now with one hand.

"I didn't spare you nothing you ain't got coming."

Frank was dousing his nerves in the Broadway when a miner came in wearing muddy overalls. "Your name Farmer?"

"Who's asking?"

"You better come get your friend. He's over at the Sitka, drinking out the joint and calling all the customers every kind of a son of a bitch. They're fixing to bust him to pieces."

The Sitka stood at the end of Front Street with an eight-foot totem pole beside the entrance. Frank ran inside, just behind the Remington. From old habit he ducked the big tin hurricane lamp that hung too far down from the low ceiling, but failed to duck the hard object that struck him from behind.

When he came to himself, wrists and ankles bound and slung facedown across a pack saddle, he knew himself for a fool. The leader of a party of fur-clad locals who dumped him into a snowdrift north of town explained to him that he had been posted out of town under the laws of the State of Oregon for disturbing the public peace.

"This ain't Oregon." Cut loose, Frank sat up, packed a snowball, and pressed it against the tender spot on the back of his head. His rubber ear was missing.

"Alaska's governed by Oregon law," said the man, built bearish with icicles in his beard. "By order of the Organic Act of 1884. We're special deputies sworn to uphold it."

"What peace did I disturb?"

"We don't like our waiters getting shot."

"I didn't shoot him. Anyway, he was fixing to bushwhack me when Randy gunned him."

"He's dead on account of you, and since he is, we can't post him out of town. Anyway, Nome needs waiters more'n it needs gun men. We're running out of rope."

"How's Randy? Last I heard he was about to get whupped by half of Nome."

"That was a story to smoke you out of the Broadway. The bunch that hangs out there disagree with the Organic Act of 1884."

"What drift you throw him in?"

"None. We pulled him out of the New York Kitchen and put him on the last boat headed to the States till spring."

"Where do I go till then?"

The man said something in a language Frank had never heard before to a man with features the color and apparent texture of iron. The man said something back, pointing into the teeth of the stinging wind.

"There's a party of Eskimo hunters camped a couple miles due north," the icicle man said. "I was you, I'd get there before sundown. We got wolves make the ones down south look like squirrels. That's why we let you keep your iron. Good luck with grizzlies. You don't want to know how big we grow *them*."

He took it out carefully, saw that the chambers were empty. "I don't reckon you know what become of my ear."

"That what that was? I stepped on it without knowing and it broke. I thought it was a small king crab got away from the New York Kitchen."

"It got brittle. No hard feelings, Sheriff."

"I ain't a sheriff. Sheriff's back in Portland. I'm a special deputy, and if you try coming back to Nome, I'll make it my special responsibility to shoot you on sight. There will be hard feelings then."

It was an Aleut camp, actually.

By day the men, their faces pierced and plugged with ivory ornaments, walked miles out onto the icepack to shoot seals with their bows while their women tended the cook fires and mended and made warm coats from the skins of their prey. By night they slept in skin huts with snow plastered on the outside to keep out the cold. Their chief, who had been baptized into the Russian Orthodox Church, wore a crucifix carved from ivory on a sinew thong around his neck and smoked tobacco through a ptarmigan-bone pipe with an ivory bowl. He had no English, but was eloquent in sign.

Frank spent the winter, skinning and doing chores for his keep. He traded his extra cartridges for a coat and the fur boots they called mukluks. The women pried loose the bullets and mixed the powder with water for ink to tattoo their chins. Sometimes, when gales raged, howling like the icicle man's giant wolves and slinging razors of ice, the seal-oil lamps made it so hot in the huts Frank slept naked and sweating.

He saw one of the icicle man's gargantuan grizzlies at a distance, playfully batting around a walrus that bellowed and died and the bear ate it. He calculated it stood twelve feet high on its hind legs. However, he was under the influence of a native remedy made from otter piss filtered through fermented trade grain, and distrusted the sight. Alaska was so far out on the frontier it was almost civilization.

Frank didn't begrudge the time lost. He'd been snowed in before, and prison taught a man patience or it broke him.

Come what would of the frontier, there would always be strikes and industry, and towns grown up around them overnight. He'd find Randy in one.

He just didn't know it would take as long as it did.

30

Opportunity is a cat, not a dog. It won't come to you; you must go out and bring it back.

The calendar shed leaves like buffalo hair, singly at first, then in clumps. Buckboards receded from the road, nudged aside by Model T trucks. Mercantiles became markets, filling orders placed by telephone. Electrified streets glowed bright as day in the dead of night. A Johnny Reb named D. W. Griffith moved into the vacancy left by P. T. Barnum, a good Yankee. It seemed the only place you saw an Indian was on a billboard selling chewing tobacco. In Dodge City, they tore down the Lady Gay Dance Hall and put up a roller-skating rink in its place.

When the first gusher came in at a place called Beaumont, Texas, Frank Farmer took a job protecting wildcat oil wells from slant drillers, driving away anyone attempting to build a derrick within twenty-five yards of his employers' with volleys from his Winchester. He asked around for Randy—a big chore in a town that had grown from nine thousand to fifty thousand souls in two years—but he never showed. He couldn't know that his old adversary was stuck in Glenn Pool, Oklahoma Territory, recovering from eight broken ribs on Indian land suddenly no longer worthless; before that he'd worked as a cook for the West Virginia Oil Company, and spent his time off asking for Frank. He'd decided to pack it in and try his luck in Beaumont when a block-and-tackle failed and dropped ten feet of pipe on him. That was in 1905.

In 1909, after performing much the same duties with his Winchester, Frank got a job helping to transport portable jail cells to overnight boomtowns that lacked such facilities on a permanent basis. The cells were made from iron strips riveted together and looked like big chicken coops when they were loaded aboard the wagon. Communities paid top dollar for the cages, so the wages were good and it was easy work; the recipients were so eager to accept shipment they did the unloading themselves. At every stop, Frank bent over the faces of drunks chained to trees while they sobered up, but none belonged to Randy.

When Randy, making some of the same stops, got into a fight with a drunken Osage oil millionaire in Cushing Field, O.T., he spent a night in one of Frank's portable cells, but couldn't sleep for restlessness. He was unsure why.

Frank tried speculating on his own in 1912. He reckoned that if dry places like Texas and Oklahoma gave up oil, so would Nevada, where he'd be the first to try his luck. He borrowed money from a banker who was impressed with the well-dressed middle-aged man who wore his hair over his ears and tied into a little queue in back, bought equipment, and freighted it to Carson City in a wagon.

He was checking into the Empress Catherine Hotel when a signature farther up the page caught his eye. He hooked on a pair of spectacles and read Randy's name in a big round hand. His own hand shook when he tapped the name with his spectacles. "What room's Locke in?"

The clerk slid his own spectacles down his nose to read upside down, then poked them back onto the bridge. "He checked out night before last."

"Say where he was headed?"

"He said to tell anyone who asked to look for him in Californy. That's how he said it, with a *y*. Your friend isn't very well educated."

"He's ignorant as a drift fence, and he ain't my friend. I'm checking out." He picked up the pen again and drew a line through his name.

"California's a big place, mister. How do you expect to find him?"

"In a big crowd."

Frank unhitched a horse from his team and wired the banker to tell him where he could find his equipment. The banker hired the Pinkerton National Detective Agency to find him and arrest him for fraud, but when other speculators went bust looking for oil in Nevada, he considered himself fortunate things turned out as they had. He called off the investigation.

Understand, much of this is guesswork on my part. I got some of the story from Frank in Los Angeles where we were both working for the studios, some from cowboys and wranglers employed by them also who had worked ranches with them after they left the Circle X, and filled in the rest from imagination leavened by personal experience. I don't pretend that this is a true account; but I challenge anyone else to do better.

Frank was friendly and liked to talk about himself. He was too old to wrangle or herd, but he was kept busy working as an extra in what they called outdoor dramas. Directors liked his looks, with his Buffalo Bill whiskers and long silvering hair worn long to cover the hole where one ear was missing, and used him to dress up saloon sets and necktie parties; he looked good in his range clothes holding a flickering torch and was usually up front for Bill Hart or Tom Mix to shoot him first and dispel the mob.

I asked him why all the fuss with Randy. It was no surprise he had an answer ready.

"You ever try to drive a nail and it just won't go in straight? It's never the fault of the nail; there's a knot in the wood or you just ain't a good nailer. But you blame the nail anyway, just like it's a bad man or an ornery dog. You just plain hate it, and for no good reason.

"Well, sir, that there's Randy in a nutshell."

I never could get Randy to sit down and talk. He ignored me the first time, growled at me the second, and as I approached him for one more try he gathered up his cook's apron in one hand and rested the other on his Colt. He was an extra part-time—if you went to the pictures and saw an old man smoking a pipe and rocking on a front porch, it was him more than likely—and did some cooking for the cast and crew when a company went on location.

He was a disagreeable old cuss, and his enemy genial; but I liked Randy better. Frank was full of himself, and I suspect he pumped up his personal exploits considerable. I didn't dislike him so much as I thought he was a clumsy liar, laughing self-consciously at his own tall tales like a poker player who couldn't bluff. Randy didn't care what folks thought of him, which is an appealing trait. We might have been friends if Frank had never left Pennsylvania. Like any good hunter, Randy thought only of his prey.

I was going to write a scenario about their generation-long feud; I had a story editor at Triangle mildly interested in it as a possible vehicle for Mix and Carey. But I never did. There was no redemption in it to iris out on at the end.

Hollywood, California, was the last western boomtown. It had all the vices you expect of such places, but they got played up more in the newspapers because the people who practiced them had their faces plastered on full-color posters in neighborhood theaters across the country and grinned and snarled and wiggled their eyebrows on screens where their faces were blowed up twenty times life size. You saw them on the covers of magazines, read about what they slept in and how they ate and what kind of automobiles they drove, so when a matinee idol got arrested in a men-only brothel or a little sweetheart fell down a flight of stairs with a snootful of cocaine, the story drove President Taft clean off the front page.

There was killing, too; and long before those sordid cases involving fat actors and big-time directors.

Westerns were the moving pictures' most popular product. After the industry moved to California to take advantage of the light, it found all the mountains and deserts it needed to represent any territory in the old frontier without having to paint a single backdrop. And it struck paydirt in talent. When the last of the great ranches stopped hiring, all the boys gathered up their gear and headed to where the jobs were. They looked after the picturesque livestock for wages, sometimes wandered into a shot or were invited into one because of their look, and the outfit saved on wardrobe and equipment because they came with their own. A few of them even became stars. Will Rogers and Hoot Gibson went straight from scratchy bedrolls to silk sheets.

There was no lack for work. At a saloon called the Watering Hole in the heart of Los Angeles, a man with range experience could stand on the corner for a couple of hours and see everyone he knew, doing rope tricks and such to attract the attention of a passing casting director. A tenderheel from back East named Harry Carey hung around stealing authenticity.

I never could find the tracks in publishing after I left the Cody outfit. I think those marathon Indian fights and saving homesteaders' daughters from runaway horses ruined me for writing literature under my own name. I killed more men in a chapter than Crazy Horse at the Little Big Horn. When my money ran out in Dayton, Ohio, I left behind a trunkful of manuscripts and another trunkful of rejections and joined the westward migration. In no time at all I landed a spot polishing a scenario for Thomas Ince on his five-thousand-acre backlot north of Santa Monica—the place was rolling fat with actors and directors but thin on writers—and after *Custer's Last Fight* came in under budget and ahead of schedule I was offered a steady job. I accepted; the work was easy, and because no words were spoken on film, except on title cards when explanation was needed, a forty-four-minute two-reeler ran about ten pages. It paid better than working cattle and you could do it in your long-handles.

Biograph was paying better, though, so I quit and went there. But Griffith didn't like my writing—said it read like a Ned Buntline dime novel—and in less than a week I was through with the best outfit in the business. That's how I came to be a fellow employee of Frank's and Randy's for the first time since 1868.

Neither man was interested in meeting featured players; *stars,* folks were calling them now, and the feeling was mutual on the stars' part.

The years since they got out of the oil business had not been kind to Frank and Randy. They'd been up and down, down more than up, which is where aging sets in. Frank kept his hat on inside and out because that long hair the directors found so photogenic lost its glamour when you saw his scalp poking up through it. Randy was getting bent, his leg dragged worse than always, and that patch of frost-bitten skin that hadn't patched itself up since buffalo days leaked into his scraggy beard. The sight of it put some off their feed, and so he drifted from one studio commissary to the next, still practicing making biscuits.

It was 1913. They'd been shooting at each other for forty-five years, longer than many friendships and most marriages. The death of either man—no matter if they were separated by a thousand miles of prairie or a city block—would be known for certain to the survivor the instant the spirit was divided from the body. So deep was their bond of hatred, the only consistent thing in their lives, and to which they were entirely faithful.

They had, in fact, been separated by considerably more than a thousand miles, and by something less than a city block. For a time, Frank Farmer had joined one of the lesser Wild West exhibitions ("Arapaho Bob's Frontier Extravaganza and Confederation of Bordermen, Indian Princesses, and Savage Riders of the Plains! No Whitewash, No Hogwash, No Washing of Hands!"), shooting at blown-glass balls with his aging Winchester and not missing many, and toured with the troupe to England while Randy was driving an ice wagon in Bismarck. When Randy Locke lay near death from malaria in Panama City, contracted while digging the great canal, Frank, who'd been stranded abroad when the exhibition went bust, was working his way home by way of Nova Scotia, shoveling coal into the firebox of a tramp steamer.

Once, when Frank was chasing a rumor that Randy was laying a natural-gas pipeline in Wichita Falls, Randy was on his way to Amarillo, where Frank was said to be doing the same. Their trains passed only yards apart. (Each felt a chill on the instant.)

Fort Mescalero was shooting outside Palm Springs. The carpenters had gone and built a stake fort in what was supposed to be the Arizona desert, where everything was made of mud because the nearest tree was in Colorado; but then the Apaches all wore Cheyenne warbonnets and five minutes into the first reel the shadow of an aeroplane can be seen sliding across a wagon train. The director was known for never doing retakes and bringing productions in on time.

Frank was cast as an old mountain man to balance out the cigar-store Indian standing on the other end of the bar in a tent saloon. A canopy made from the same canvas had been staked out to keep the Mojave sun off the necks of the players and backstage personnel when they broke for lunch. They lined up along a trestle table crowded with covered pots heated by cans of Sterno: Indians in feathers who last week had been centurions in armor for DeMille, stunt gaffers with limps almost as bad as Randy's, women in homey bonnets, the same women next day in whores' silk, codgers with whiskers, tinhorns in tile hats, carpenters, painters, electricians, cowboys dressed as cowboys, and an undertaker in a morning coat who for some reason looked like Woodrow Wilson. They ate whatever the company brought from town, packed in ice in the original chuck wagon that appeared in the film and prepared by professional cooks.

The third day on location, Frank held out his bowl and stared at the man in the apron ladling clam chowder into it from the other side of the table.

"Long time no see, Frank," said Randy. "You want crackers?"

31

In some languages there is no word for good-bye. One cannot help but think it was a conscious decision, and reflect upon its wisdom.

Well, I sure don't want no biscuits. There's a cowboy working for Famous Players still digesting it from Colorado."

Randy turned to his assistant, a tall bony kid with pimples like smallpox pustules. "Finish this out, will you? I'd go easy on the chili. I didn't put in no green ones, but it's commencing to look like a Christmas wreath. No sense poisoning no stars."

He helped himself to a bowl of chowder and a cube of cornbread that looked like rotten concrete and accompanied Frank to another trestle table, away from a group of wranglers sweetening their coffee from a bottle. Frank asked if they should borrow it.

"Go ahead if you want. I give up that hoo-head john after Nome."

"I don't much need it. Once you drank otter piss in an Aleut camp it ruins you for everything else." They were sitting across from each other. Frank blew steam off a spoonful from his bowl. "What you been up to, Randy?"

"This and that. You?"

"Same thing, I reckon. You still lugging that smoke-wagon?"

"Been wearing it so long I took it into the shower last week. Still got that Remington?"

"It's my good luck piece, saved me from the rope in Fort Smith. What become of that Ballard rifle?"

"Sold it for grub. What become of that Winchester?"

"The same. Country's got so crowded you don't need no long gun to drop a man."

"Yakima Jim died last week of pure mean and blood poisoning over a poker game; little bitty belly gun fired so close it set his shirt afire. World's shrunk and no mistake."

"You still unattached?"

"I taken up with a woman in Glenwood Springs. We never said the vows, but she used my name and had a kid she said was mine, but I got my doubts."

"I hope you're right. I wouldn't want to think there's another Locke running around pretending to be a human being. She leave you?"

"Sure did. The doc said it was dropsy, but she told me

near the end it was a broken heart and I was the reason. I was always running off, leaving her alone to chase down some rumor of you."

"I believe that."

"Maybe so, but if her heart was broke it sure didn't affect her appetite. By the time she took sick I bet she bent the scale at two hunnert. Galloping her was like trying to hang onto a sack of beans in a runaway wagon. What about you? Ever marry?"

"Yes, sir. Still am."

"Hell you say."

"Even so. We sleep in what you might call separate bedrooms. Hers is in Boston, Massachusetts."

"Same issue?"

"There was several, but I calculate that one topped the list." Frank swallowed a hunk of clam; it went down without chewing. "Ever hear from Cripplehorn?"

"I heard he tried to get into pictures, then went back East and died."

"I heard the same, though it was a tame fit of apoplexy. He's laying in a Sisters of Charity home in Atlantic City, New Jersey, drinking his supper through a straw."

"I don't envy them sisters. I don't know how you put up with him in that shack in Frisco."

"He was a big sissy. I took the borrow of his toothbrush once and never heard the end of it. He was always saying how when he got rich he was going to trade that ivory eye for a glass one made in Vienna, hire some fellow named Mo-nay to paint it."

"I'm surprised you didn't shoot him."

"I considered it, but he talked so pretty I figured I'd miss him. It was like listening to Scripture."

"He was a tinhorn through-and-through. I don't believe he ever read a book, much less wrote one. He got himself into some silk-hat company somehow and remembered everything he heard."

"He weren't stupid. Them vendors in that tent in the Strip kicked back half of every pail of beer they sold. He kept the tally in a bitty notebook."

"I'd bet a good saddle he never showed it to that Sheridan Weber."

The assistant director, a consumptive-looking New Englander with a ladylike strut, blew his whistle. They had five minutes before the next take.

Randy said, "I'm going to shoot him next."

"He's just doing his job."

"I'm going to shove that whistle down his gullet first."

Frank changed the subject. "You know, we just missed each other in Carson City last year. I checked in to the Empress Catherine just after you checked out."

"I caught the last train to Gunnison. Sewing-machine drummer I run into in the vertical railway said he talked to a fellow named Farmer there last week. Said he packed a forty-five Remington."

"You should stay off elevators. One day that door may slide open and there I'll be."

"I thought the whole point of this confab was to put that to rest."

Frank paused with his spoon halfway to his mouth. "You talking truce?"

"No, sir, I don't speak that lingo."

They slurped soup in silence for a minute.

Frank said, "I don't like leaving no job half-finished. That director fellow says we wrap next week. He's hosting a party at the Watering Hole."

"I reckon I'll see you there." Randy stood and picked up his bowl. "Whatever happened to that Dutch ear, by the way?"

* * *

The place was got up like every saloon in the West, or what
some easterner thought it would look like. A fat naked
woman lollopped in a chaise longue in a scrolled frame
above the backbar, drilled through with authentic-looking
bullet holes, and an eight-gauge shotgun was growing dust
on a rack made of elk antlers above a Faro table where a
group of extras sat drinking and not gambling. The string
band that had played throughout the production to create a
proper mood played a piece composed for the piano players who would accompany the showings. The director
made a speech, said nobody's money was good in the joint
beyond the first two drinks, and sat down at a table with
the female lead and the brave lieutenant who'd led the suicide charge against about ten thousand Apaches, a young
Shakespearean actor from Hartford, Connecticut. The female lead didn't appear to object when the director put an
arm around her and squeezed a breast.

Randy had come there straight from the set, where the
assistant director was shooting second-unit to fill out the
rest of the reel, and cast him as a stove-up stagecoach
driver. He wore the costume he'd been given from the
wardrobe grab-bag—sweat-stained Stetson with the brim
turned up in front, shirt made of ticking, patched dungarees tucked into stovepipe boots with the heels ground
down by dozens of pairs of feet. He spotted a pair of
slumped shoulders he knew as well as his own at the end
of the packed bar. He left the fake Indian he'd been talking with in the middle of a drunken gripe and went over
to tap one of those shoulders. He wore his Colt in a prop
holster, his old one having worn out in the Oklahoma oil
fields. The new one was stiff enough to hold a flagpole;
the pistol slid out every time he'd mounted to the driver's
seat.

No tap was needed. Frank sensed his presence and turned quickly from the bar, resting his hand on his Remington. He had on a regular suit of clothes and a pearl-gray bowler he'd swiped from Wardrobe, also a stiff slick holster just like Randy's, with a tie-down that made a two-handed draw unnecessary and a hammer thong to keep the pistol where it belonged.

"How do, Frank?" Randy spoke as if they hadn't seen each other only last week.

"Not so bad, Randy. Yourself?"

"Middling."

"I forgot to ask you how you found L.A."

"I got off the train and there it was."

The conversation lapsed. Both men looked embarrassed after this exchange. They'd talked themselves out in the tent commissary. After so much time they had only the one thing in common.

"Where you want to do this?" Randy asked.

"It's still light out."

They went outside, Randy first on account of his leg. He'd sooner expect a priest of the faith to backshoot him than Frank.

It was suppertime. Traffic was light. They waited for a streetcar to pass, then stepped out onto the asphalt and faced off.

There was no need for talk or signals, no whenever-you're-readies or dropping of bandannas: That was for Jack Dodger books and moving pictures. When each man was satisfied the other was set, they went for their pistols.

Both men were at a disadvantage. They were unfamiliar with the fast draw, which hadn't existed before eastern fabulists invented it, and slower than any movie pistoleer; but Randy had an edge. Frank forgot about the hammer thong, and fumbled with it when the Remington didn't clear. Randy's slug pierced his heart just as he got the rig loose. Frank fell cruciform on his back in the middle of Cahuenga Boulevard and didn't twitch.

Randy didn't bother to check for signs of life; he'd known the outcome the moment the pistol pulsed in his hand. He dropped it back into its holster and turned away.

A crowd gathered around the dead man, some of them cowboys from the Watering Hole drawn by the familiar sound of gunfire. The director and his two leads hung back in the doorway. A police officer in harness came blasting his whistle to clear a path. No one paid any attention to the elderly bean-slinger hobbling in the opposite direction.

On the sidewalk, Randy whistled an old cattle lullaby, waiting for the next streetcar to come racing along. When it did, he stepped out in front of it.

The Adventures of
Johnny
Vermillion

For Robert C. Jones,
a gentle giant with the wit of a banished elf

Our interest's on the dangerous edge of things.
The honest thief, the tender murderer,
The superstitious atheist, demirep
That loves and saves her soul in new French books.

—ROBERT BROWNING,
"Bishop Blougram's Apology"

I

The Prairie Rose Repertory Company

1

Most of what follows took place in the West.

    Not just any West.

It was the West of legend and suckling-memory, where drifters caked head to heel with dust swilled red-eye whiskey at long mahogany bars, punching holes in the tin ceilings with their big Colts to impress their half-naked, quartz-eyed hostesses; where buffalo rolled thunder across gaunt desert, grass ocean, and the great mountain ranges where the earth showed its tusks, stopping only to splash in the wallows and scratch their burlap hides against the cowcatchers of the Central and Western Pacific and the mighty Atchison; where red-lacquer Concords barreled down the western face of the Divide, pulled by teams of six with eyes rolling white, whips cracking like Winchesters above their heads; where glistening black locomotives charged across trestles of latticework oak, burning scrub-wood in greasy black streamers and blasting their arrogant whistles; where highwaymen in slouch hats and long dusters pulled bandannas up over their faces and stepped suddenly from behind boulders, firing at the sky and bellowing at shotgun messengers to throw up their hands and throw down the box; where all the towns were named Lockjaw and Busted Straight, Diablo and Purgatory and Spunk.

A West where gamblers wore linen and pomade and dealt aces from both sides of the deck and derringers from inside their sleeves; where cowboys ate beans and drank coffee around campfires to harmonica music, and everything was heavily seasoned with tin. At sunup, drowsy and stiff, the cowboys drove undulating herds of grumbling, lowing, high-strung longhorns past ridges where feathered warriors balanced their horses square on the edge, bows and lances raised against the sky while the brass section blared and kettle drums pounded. Gun battles cleared busy streets in a twinkling and bullets rang off piles of rock in the alkali flats with a *p-tweeeeee!,* kicking dust into the eyes of lawman and outlaw alike. The U.S. Cavalry was invincible, and bandits and gunfighters were celebrities, trailing battalions of paparazzi in brown derbies: Custer had yet to stand on his hill, Jesse to turn his back on Bob, and Wild Bill to draw his fabled hand. All the wagon trains came with concertinas, and all the undertakers and hangmen looked like John Carradine.

It was a West where prospectors, cotton-bearded and toothless, led mules over foothills riddled with shafts, Russian grand dukes shot buffalo from Pullman cars, bandidos wore their ammo belts crossed and flashed gold teeth in duplicitous grins and called everybody Gringo; where women baked bread in gingham and looked cute in buckskins and spilled like ripe peaches out of corsets and sequins and wore feathers in their hair. Train robbers shinnied up telegraph poles, tapped into the lines, and rapped out misleading messages to citizens' vigilance committees on the barrels of their six-shooters. Posses sprang up like cottonwoods, lynch mobs stormed jails, fiddlers played "Little Brown Jug" at church raisings, and legions of tin-tack piano players knew all the notes to "Buffalo Gals" by heart.

A West, this, where cattle barons gathered in clubs and railroad magnates sat in parlor cars to smoke cigars and plot mayhem; where assassins in their employ took target practice on grangers and Chinamen and shot at the heels of tenderfeet to make them dance. Where tall saguaro cactus grew everywhere, even places where it had never existed; where saloon mirrors were in inexhaustible supply and every bluebelly sergeant was named O'Hara and wore his hat brim turned up in front. Men rolled cigarettes and spat into cuspidors. Most of the lumber went into saloons and gallows and markers on Boot Hill.

Sam Grant was in Washington, soldiering his way through his troubled second term, chain-smoking General Thompsons, drinking Hermitage by the case, and wishing he'd never heard the name Bill Belknap. Lily Langtry was on tour. So were Lotta Crabtree and Jenny Lind, and Edwin Booth was performing as Prospero in Denver. Judges Bean and Parker adjudicated in Texas and the Indian Nations. Ned Buntline guzzled Old Gideon, philandered with married women, and wrote reams of frontier claptrap that sold millions in New York and San Francisco. Wyatt Earp was in Dodge City getting a tooth pulled by Doc Holliday. Chiefs Crazy Horse and Gall rested on the Powder River, watching old Sitting Bull smoking up dreams with a blend of open skepticism and hidden contempt. These things are matters of history and bear no direct application to our tale, but they help set the stage for the rip-roaring action to come.

It was a West of ruthless ranchers, patient housewives, crooked sheriffs, courageous pioneers, eager hellcats, leather-lung bullwhackers, scheming carpetbaggers, spinster schoolteachers, blacksmiths, gunsmiths, wheelwrights, farriers, dressmakers, swampers, grave diggers, and prostitutes with hearts of gold; also of ice and iron. One out of three men answered to Frank or Jack or Billy, regardless of whether his real name was Henry or Leander, the women all seemed to be either Sadie or Jane, and any cowpuncher worth his found knew which one to kiss and which to marry. Everyone seemed to walk around wearing a sandwich board advertising his or her true nature: card cheat, music-hall lecher, bushwhacker, army deserter, wife beater, husband poisoner, snake-oil merchant, newspaper rat, whiskey trader, reader of French novels. All wore the uniform of his station: the top hat tilted at a disreputable angle, the garish waistcoat, the rhinestone buckle on the pointed shoe, the leaded walking stick, the boots with flaps over the toes. But it was also the West of elaborate obfuscation. Dry-goods stores sold muffs with pistol pockets in the linings, spring-operated wrist holsters, and knife scabbards to be worn on lanyards around the neck. Unescorted women walked the streets in safety, but the theaters and ballrooms dripped with murder. It was possible to purchase arsenic in quantity and pistols small enough to conceal in the palm of one's hand. The West's reputation for politeness and hospitality was based on the threat of imminent death for transgressors.

It was the West also of rampant optimism. The consumptive in search of a cure, the criminal in quest of redemption, the failure in pursuit of a fresh start, the bigamist in flight from his wives; each found a fresh page upon which to start his journal anew. A world bereft of records, fingerprints, and the ubiquitous camera, and a blank amorphous map labeled the Great American Desert, offered panacea to a variety of ills. Not since Alexander fled the shadow of his father into the vast reaches of the Known World had our solitary planet so plainly beckoned to the wanderer to cast aside his burdens and press on.

It was the West of Daniel Boone, Kit Carson, and Billy the Kid; but it was also the West of William S. Hart, Roy Rogers, and John Wayne. It was big enough to encompass the bombastery of Buffalo Bill and Cecil B. DeMille and the skullduggery of the bloody brothers Harte.

This was Johnny Vermillion's West; a West that should have been, but never quite was.

2

Tannery, Nebraska, was a good place to sin, and now it's gone.

A few overgrown foundations, a well fallen in and filled with topsoil and chaff are left, and they're invisible from the traffic whirling past on the state highway. But for a few years, before the buffalo vanished and the farmers took their trade west to Omaha, Tannery roared like a young bull.

It boasted fifteen saloons, buck-toothed whores, a Masonic Temple, two banks, and a theater called the Golden Calf. This last seated six hundred, with triple-decked boxes nearly all the way around, but it stood vacant during the warm months when the hides were ripe. Stacks of them two stories high surrounded the tannery itself, attracting flies and repelling visitors not directly involved with the industry. The larger theatrical troupes passed the place by from May to November, leaving the citizens to manufacture entertainments of their own. A sporting lady known only as Roberta once rode a tame buffalo named Ambrose into the taproom of the Metropolitan Saloon and halfway up to her quarters on the second floor when the stairs collapsed under the weight; but show me a ghost town without a buffalo-riding whore named Roberta in its past and I'll show you a town that plain bored itself out of existence. Our story is more original than that.

Nothing in the short stormy history of Tannery ever compared to the night the Prairie Rose Repertory Company performed *The Count of Monte Cristo* at the Golden Calf. People who claimed they were present that night were still talking about it years later, after the town had been dismantled and reassembled on the south bank of the Platte under the name Plowright.

Sadly, Plowright proved no more durable in its second incarnation than it had in its first. The spring runoff following the disastrous winter of 1886–87 swept the entire town downriver, drowning one-fifth of its population and scattering the survivors from Ohio to Oregon. But journals and letters carry the story, and aged participants close to the principals were candid in their memoirs.

During the frosty autumn of 1873, in response to a telegraphic exchange between Tannery and Kansas City, Isadore Weaver, proprietor of the Golden Calf, posted the first new bill to garnish the front of the theater since Mabel North, the Yankee Belle, had trilled "Listen to the Mockingbird" to the accompaniment of a live canary on its stage the Saturday after Easter. This was sensation. By the time he brushed out the last blister, a crowd had assembled, exhaling clouds of steam as they read the legend aloud:

FIRST WINTER TOUR

J. T. VERMILLION'S

PRAIRIE ROSE REPERTORY COMPANY

PRESENTS

"THE COUNT OF MONTE CRISTO"

(ADAPTED BY MR. C. RAGLAND FROM THE CLASSIC NOVEL

BY ALEXANDRE DUMAS *PÈRE*)

FEATURING

MR. J. T. VERMILLION

MISS APRIL CLAY

MAJOR EVELYN DAVIES

MME. ELIZABETH MORT-DAVIES

MR. CORNELIUS RAGLAND

ONE PERFORMANCE ONLY

A separate notice was plastered across the bottom, informing interested readers that the play would take place

Saturday, November 7, at 8:00 P.M., and that all would be admitted for the sum of fifty cents.

"Never heard of any of 'em," huffed Lysander Hubbard, publisher of the *Tannery Blanket* ("We Cover the Plains"); the poster had come by rail and not from his shop. "What've they done, I wonder?"

Stella Pardon, who ran the general merchandise with her husband, blew her red-lantern nose into a sturdy handkerchief. "Honestly, as long as none of them shot Lincoln, what does it signify? I'll be there, with or without Loyal."

That, demonstrably, was the general sentiment. Weaver pasted up a SOLD OUT notice three days later.

On the Friday before the performance, the westbound U.P. panted to a halt beside the Prince Albert Memorial Depot and stood with steam rolling off its boiler while porters unloaded trunk after trunk onto the platform. Each piece of luggage was stenciled with the theatrical company's name in large, easy-to-read letters. Taking shelter inside this Stonehenge from flying snow, the five new arrivals introduced themselves to the consumptive young staff reporter for the *Blanket* and a large sampling of residents and transients that had been gathered there for more than an hour.

The chief spokesman, identified as Mr. John Tyler Vermillion of Chicago, was a tall fellow a year or two shy of thirty, slim as a trotter. When he removed his hat, a fine soft black one with a broad brim, his longish fair hair whipped about him like a young Byron's. He wore silken moustaches and an imperial in the hollow of his chin, and even the yoke-shouldered buffalo hiders present acknowledged him uncommonly presentable. Existing photographic portraits indicate chiseled bone and eyes of that crystalline shade of blue that always reproduces pale in black-and-white. He must have made a fine figure that day in his gray ulster and beaver collar, Wellingtons shining on his narrow feet. Even Stella Pardon's eyes glistened like steamed plums.

"May I present Miss April Clay," said he, sweeping every gaze with his hat toward the woman who had just joined them from aboard the day coach. "She will be playing the unattainable Mercedes; and may I warn you, gentlemen, she remains in character offstage as well as on."

A chuckle coursed through the group, warmest in the throats of the "gentlemen" thus admonished. Bowler, badger-piece, and filthy slouch hat came away as one, in some cases exposing crania covered since All Hallows' Eve. For Miss Clay was a dainty daub, in the language of the day; a strawberry blonde with skin like milk, dressed to the fashion in a tweed traveling suit and cape, with an adorable little hat pinned to her upswept hair. She was then in her twenty-second year, five feet four in tiny patent leathers with a hint of heel. Her eyes were hazel, slanted gently (her grandmother, it was said, was Russian), and as large as asteroids.

"Where did you appear last?" inquired the young man from the *Blanket*.

The wind gusted. Miss Clay swayed and placed a slender hand in a suede glove against the reporter's waistcoat for support. She asked his pardon, withdrawing the hand. "The Tivoli, in Kansas City. I assayed the role of Viola in Mr. William Shakespeare's *Twelfth Night*. I was Maria as well, and briefly a sailor."

Her voice was astonishingly low for one of her stature. The reviewer for the *St. Louis Enquirer* had compared it to "a bassoon in heaven's ensemble."

"Three parts in one play? How did you remember all the lines?"

"The sailor was nonspeaking," said Mr. Vermillion. "We are a small company, but versatile. Each of us seldom portrays the same character twice in succession, and we often perform double and triple duty. In the hierarchy of the stage, repertory is solidly working class. In that, we are very like your own fine panners and prospectors, sifting the streams and prowling the hills all round for gold."

Someone in the audience pointed out that Tannery was a buffalo town, not a mining camp. The leader of the troupe was unabashed.

"Your noble stalkers and skinners, if you will, conquering the brute and refining its outer shell for personal comfort. We come before you, ladies and gentlemen, to distract and amuse, to provide a brief holiday from the trials of daily existence."

Applause crackled. He bowed and swung his hat. "Madame Elizabeth Mort-Davies, who has charmingly agreed to strain credulity and appear as the hero's silver-haired mother."

Mme. Mort-Davies' hair was, in fact, a rather alarming shade of violet, piled high and caught cruelly with combs; it was not observed to move even when the wind toppled a large valise from the mountain of luggage. She was nearly as tall as Mr. Vermillion, straight-backed and buxom, and fifty-five if she was a day. Matrons were her specialty, but she had been known to don a beard for Polonius, and strain credulity to cracking to allow Miss Clay to abandon the ingenue for a smaller part that offered more challenge. Saturday night, she would also pull a set of false whiskers as the venal warden of the Château d'If.

Her husband, introduced as Major Evelyn Davies (emphasis on that first long E), formerly of the Queen's horse guard, stood a head shorter and round as a barrel hoop in a buffalo coat and morning dress, dove-gray gaiters on his square-toed boots. He wore white handlebars and carried a gold-headed stick. His responsibilities included the beleagured Edmond Dantès' aged father and also the Abbé Faria, Dantès' fellow prisoner.

"Finally, Mr. Cornelius Ragland, the plain sturdy band that holds together our quartet of gems. Tomorrow night you shall know him as the villainous Danglars, and perhaps recognize him among an army of coachmen, stewards, and prison guards. However, impersonation is not the sum total of his genius. He is the playwright who distilled Dumas *Père*'s great work into three manageable acts, with time for intermission."

Young Mr. Ragland was plain as tin, but far from sturdy; he made the hollow-chested journalist look burly by comparison. Stoop-shouldered, bespectacled, with ears that stuck out conveniently to prevent his hat from settling onto his shoulders, he appeared miserable in the cold, and his suit of clothes was far from clean. At every glance he belonged to that genus of sickly male described as Too Fragile for this World.

"What do *you* play, Mr. Vermillion?" someone called out. "The Chateau Deef?"

The leader of the troupe laughed with the others. "It will be my privilege to ask you to accept me in the person of Edmond Dantès and his alter ego, that mysterious, haunted fellow, the Count of Monte Cristo." He bowed deeply, and those in witness could do naught but clap their hands. Frontier audiences were notoriously generous.

Isadore Weaver arrived, crimson-faced and puffing, apologizing for certain entrepreneurial details that had delayed him at the Golden Calf. He made the company's acquaintance and explained that accommodations awaited them at the Railroad Arms; a brace of stagehands was on its way to transport their costumes and stage properties to the theater. Mr. Vermillion seemed prepared to resume orating, but Miss Clay tugged at his sleeve and asked the fellow from the *Blanket* for the time of day. Among the crowd on the platform there was a furious scramble for pockets.

The reporter alone came up empty-handed and bewildered by the situation.

Miss Clay smiled and produced a battered turnip watch and chain from her little reticule. "It's a handsome time-piece," she said. "I couldn't resist a closer look."

Blushing, the young man accepted its return, along with her sweet apology. Miss Clay, explained Mr. Vermillion, was a gifted parlor magician whose father had studied un-der Monsieur Robert-Houdin in Paris. His listeners ap-plauded the charming demonstration of legerdemain, and not one noticed the blue-icicle gaze he fixed upon the pretty conjurer.

When the fire curtain rose Saturday night, bearing with it its wallpaper pattern of advertising ("TROPICAL FRUIT LAXATIVE, THE GENTLE PERSUADER, AVAIL-ABLE AT BOYLAN'S DRUGS"; "ELY & SONS PRES-ENT SUMMER AND WINTER SUITS FOR MEN AND BOYS"; "SHARPS METALLIC CARTRIDGES BY CASE OR GROSS, ORDER AT PARDON'S GENERAL MERCHANDISE"), a capacity crowd cheered everything, even the set.

The set, at least, benefited heavily from anticipation. Back then, itinerant actors traveled much more lightly than the Broadway road companies of the present day, depend-ing upon theaters to supply all but their costumes and makeup and some hand properties specific to the produc-tion. The Golden Calf appealed in turn to its patrons, who built and painted sets and donated odd sticks of furniture, some of which came from the trash heap behind the Old Cathay Saloon after its biweekly brawl. As a result, the home of Edmond Dantes in Act I was more reminiscent of a Victorian jumble sale than of the play's French Empire setting, and when Edmond bearded Danglars in his own den in Act III, a number of sharp observers noted that the villain appeared to shop in the same places as his mortal enemy. But it was the performances that mattered.

Whatever his thespian challenges—he tended to speechify, and Mr. Ragland's script indulged that tendency—Mr. John Tyler Vermillion of Chicago cut a dashing figure in tights and delivered his soliloquys in a ringing tenor, punctuated by clashing blades and much athletic hopping about during the fencing scenes. Miss April Clay captivated the women with her courage and the men with her decolletage; a bit of modest lace in the last act, and a dash of talcum to her temples, supported the passage of years. Poor Mr. Ragland was a weak and unconvincing swordsman, but spoke his lines with a serpentine hiss (and a bit of a lisp) appropriate to the dastard of the drama. All agreed that the Madame and the Major were rather fine, and the choice of material fortunate. During the quiet stretches, a great many fewer shots were fired into the ceiling than usual.

At intermission, those consulting their programmes for the first time were startled to learn that Miss Clay and Mme. Mort-Davies had disguised themselves as prison guards to dispose of Faria's earthly remains. It had been assumed those mute parts were played by men of the cast.

The *Tannery Blanket* and its readers joined in declaring *The Count of Monte Cristo* a successful opening to the winter theatrical season. The review would have claimed the entire first column had not someone robbed the Pioneers Bank & Trust midway through the second act.

3

I t is an established fact of American town life that one neighborhood is singled out as the best among three adjoining, that one of two identical houses is regarded as superior, and that traffic is heavier on one side of Main Street than on the other. The Pioneers was the more successful of Tannery's two banks simply because its competitor, the Planter State, stood on the side where Grand Street entered Main at a right angle, interrupting the pedestrian flow. Even rugged settlers, once settled, tend to follow the path of least resistance. That path led to Horace Longnecker's institution three doors down from the Golden Calf Theater.

Alvin S. Geary was on duty the night of the robbery. As the cashier in shortest residence, he'd been ordered to come in that night to correct a shortfall of sixty-two cents in Friday's deposits, an assignment accepted with ill grace. Geary suspected Old Longnecker had pocketed the difference in order to force Geary to surrender his ticket to *The Count of Monte Cristo* to Longnecker's married daughter. He was sufficiently bitter to attract suspicion, but his refusal to change his account eventually persuaded City Marshal Fletcher to broaden his search.

According to Geary, he had the deposits spread out on the large worktable in Longnecker's office, counting the notes and coins and comparing the sums to figures in the ledger, when he heard the street door open and close. Certain he'd locked it securely, Geary stepped into the lobby to investigate and found himself facing a cloaked figure pointing a large revolver directly at his chest.

The intruder gestured toward the office. Hands raised unbidden, Geary backed inside, followed by the visitor, who produced an oilcloth sack from a coat pocket. No explanation was required. The cashier took the sack and scooped the money into it. The figure with the gun took back the sack, gestured for Geary to sit down behind Longnecker's desk, and backed out, reversing the key in the office door and locking him inside. The episode was over in less than five minutes, with no words spoken.

By the time Geary broke free, some thirty-four hundred dollars in notes, gold, and silver had vanished without a whisper.

The bandit wore a soft dark hat with the brim pulled down and a coarse scarf wound around his lower features, with a bulky coat that hung to his heels. He stood under the average height and the coat was far too big for his slender frame; the sleeves were turned back twice and the revolver appeared too heavy for the delicate wrist that stuck out of the right. Geary had the impression he was a youth, aged no more than sixteen.

"You're stout enough," said the marshal. "You ought to have tried to outwrestle him."

"Not for Old Longnecker's money. The gun was stouter."

Marshal Fletcher was forty and unpleasantly fat, a fixture in outlaw tales of this type. Picture him in a horizontal heap behind his desk, batting at flies with a paper fan given out by the local undertaker, soup stains on his vest and egg crusted on his badge of office. A fly lands on his neck; he swats, but he's too slow, and the insect takes flight, insolent and drowsy in the heat from the potbelly stove. A pot of coffee has simmered there since morning—when it's poured you could tie a knot in the stream. There is the usual gun rack and the usual bulletin board shingled with plug-uglies and offers of reward, with no restrictions as to their condition upon delivery.

Lazy fat men are commonly dismissed as cowardly and stupid. This was not true in Fletcher's case, although in most circumstances he preferred to sit still and acquire the reputation than stir himself to correct it. Against that, he had a drawer full of fans given him by the undertaker, and a board stuck in Boot Hill for every one. A fly is not a desperado.

Once he was satisfied of Geary's innocence, the Law in Tannery took the obvious next step and presented himself at the Golden Calf.

The cashier had insisted that the robbery took place at five minutes past nine, nearly an hour before the theater let out; but Fletcher knew a bit about the comings and goings of actors in performance, even if he didn't care for entertainments of that nature. He'd read somewhere, possibly in the *Police Gazette,* of Edwin Booth absenting himself from *Richard III* in New York City long enough to get smashed at the Knickerbocker bar and staggering back onstage just in time for his cue. He reckoned that an experienced imbiber would be twenty minutes at such a task; the Pioneers bandit had needed just five to remove thirty-four hundred and change.

Fletcher sheltered no prejudice against theater people, only strangers. He was a community booster, confident in the belief that most serious felonies were committed by people from out of town.

Summoned to the lobby, Isadore Weaver was unhappy to learn that the marshal intended to interview the cast of the splendid play that was then whirling and crashing toward its final curtain. He was unhappier still that Fletcher wished to detain all six hundred members of the audience until they'd been questioned and released. He became obstreperous on the second point. A compromise was reached: The public would be allowed to go home after leaving their names with the head usher and information on where they could be reached. The owner beckoned to that fellow, told him what was needed, and conducted the marshal backstage.

The Golden Calf retained two dressing rooms, each generously proportioned according to the standards of the time. Mabel North, she of the duet with the canary bird, had had one all to herself and her partner in its cage, but the Farrell Family of tumblers, high-wire performers, and dog trainers had crammed themselves in eight to a room, plus six poodles. Gallantly, the male portion of the Prairie Rose Repertory Company shared the smaller of the two chambers and gave the other to Mme. Mort-Davies and Miss Clay. Marshal Fletcher smoked a cigar in Weaver's office and questioned them one by one, starting with the men.

He found Mr. Vermillion cooperative and pleasant. Wan Mr. Ragland was nervous; many of his responses were mumbled and unintelligible and had to be repeated for clarity, but Fletcher was experienced with uncertain youth and did not reckon it a mark against him. He positively disliked the apoplectic Major Davies, who challenged him constantly, thumping the floor with his stick and answering every question with one of his own. Fletcher had to smack Weaver's desk hard with his hand to startle the man into submission. All three assured the marshal they had not left the theater from first curtain to last, nor witnessed any of the others leaving.

Vermillion smiled. "Do you understand repertory, Mr. Fletcher?"

"Marshal. I think I do. You shuffle yourselves like cards and play each other's parts."

"And whatever parts are called for beyond the first and second leads: grooms, nurses, Lord High Mayors, lunatics—spear-carriers, we call them. Most plays have five or six such characters, nonspeaking usually, but essential to the business onstage. Some have dozens. We play them all. There isn't time to step outside for a smoke, much less rob a bank."

Fletcher struggled upright. "Who said anything about robbing a bank?"

"A theater is a leaky old barn, Marshal. Rumors fly in and out like sparrows."

Ragland, too, knew Fletcher's purpose; the audience had been lined up as far back as the stage, waiting to give the head usher the information he wanted and get out. He'd overheard them talking on his way there from the dressing room.

Asked if he also was aware of the situation, Major Davies thumped his stick and demanded to know if his wife was to be subjected to this infernal inquisition.

Miss Clay resembled a little girl with her makeup scrubbed off and a silk scarf over her head, a smart coat covering her robe. She was sweet and answered questions readily. Mme. Mort-Davies, who had had time to fix her face and hair and put on street clothes, provided direct responses, offering no details beyond those requested. Their sessions went swiftly.

At the end, the marshal felt he had a clear picture of what each player had been doing at the time of the robbery. A score of interviews conducted at random over Sunday convinced him that none of the players had been outside the view of six hundred witnesses long enough to have committed it; but lazy men, once they've overcome inertia, are thorough. Before he led a posse out of town in pursuit of a lone fugitive, he directed three full-time deputies to search the theater, the company's rooms at the Railway Arms, and their many trunks and bags for the missing money, which contained too much gold to conceal on the person. The Prairie Rose arsenal of fencing foils and stage pistols was impressive but hardly conclusive, as everyone owned firearms. Their props were numerous and varied and included a bicycle. The bandit's attire, so vaguely described by Mr. Geary, might have been anywhere among the dozens of costumes and accessories so tightly packed in pasteboard drawers and placed upon thin wooden hangers, or nowhere at all.

Neither the search nor the posse was successful. On Monday morning, butt-sore and lighter by several inconsequential pounds, Marshal Fletcher apologized to the players for their inconvenience and escorted them to the depot. As the train pulled away, he saw his employment future leave with it. For once, the swarm of flies that overhung Tannery had given way to a cloud of doubt concerning the local system of law enforcement. Every merchant in town had lost some portion of his profits while the Count of Monte Cristo was busy settling old scores, and all Fletcher had managed to do was discourage him and his party from ever coming back to free the town from its travails.

Eight miles due west of Tannery and a brief, kidney-rattling buckboard ride north of the U.P. tracks lay the hamlet of New Hope, now entering the late stages of dissolution. An establishing shot lingers significantly on a plank sign with a black X painted through "NEW" and "NO" lettered above in the same dismal shade. The town's founder had undertaken to swindle E. H. Harriman in a business transaction, and without pause to reflect, the dyspeptic force behind the Transcontinental Railroad had altered the construction by a quarter-inch on the surveyors' map. New Hope withered.

As their transportation slowed to negotiate the prairie-dog town that had taken up residence on the broad single street, April Clay frowned prettily in the shade of her parasol.

"Johnny, it's deserted. There's no one to protect us from Indians."

Vermillion, seated facing her on the bench opposite,

reached out and patted her knee. "Of course there is, dear. You've met Gunderson."

Their driver, a representative specimen of frontier color introduced as New Hope's mayor pro tem, wore a Union forage cap and the greatcoat of a colonel in the Confederacy. He'd appointed himself to fill the vacancy left by the founder's suicide.

"It's a damn Whitechapel in the desert," declared Major Davies, gripping his stick. "There are *rats* in the *street*." He was always in bad cess when his wife was absent.

"Those aren't rats, old fellow. They'll keep the rattlesnakes out of our beds."

"You don't mean we're to stay here overnight!" April glared defiance—a showstopper in the third act.

"That depends on Liz. She doesn't pedal as fast as she used to."

"She rode the high wire in Atlantic City in sixty-three," said the Major. "My part against yours she'll be here by dark."

"Even so, there's no train before morning. I've slept outside on Blue Island. We'll survive."

"It will be an adventure," said Cornelius Ragland.

All eyes turned to the fragile young man, who had not spoken since before they left the train. He sat next to Gunderson on the driver's seat. His eyes, large as pears in his thin face, gleamed through his spectacles.

"Corny's our pioneer," Vermillion confided. "There's nothing for him back East but the sanitarium."

They drew rein before a gaunt barn in a community of dun-colored clapboard. Gunderson hopped down among the obligatory tumbleweeds and reached up to help Vermillion unload their single trunk; all but it and April's leather train case had remained aboard the train, bound for their next port of call.

"Oh, Johnny, a *barn*?"

He bared his polished teeth. "I think you'll be pleasantly surprised."

Inside, a lantern burned on a table inside a circle of barrel stoves, an island of warmth in the dank vastness smelling of grain. There were chairs, a pile of bedrolls, a picnic basket, and a foil-wrapped glass neck sticking up out of a galvanized bucket filled with chunks of ice. The Major drew out the bottle of champagne and squinted at the label. "New Jersey." He let it slide back.

"The French have yet to discover the charms of Nebraska." The leader of the troupe uncovered the basket, took out a tinned ham, a loaf of bread, and a jar sealed with beeswax.

"Them's peach preserves." Gunderson twisted the corncob pipe in his gray beard. "I couldn't get the cheese."

"Quite all right." Vermillion handed him a small drawstring bag. Silver clanked. "We're waiting for the rest."

The mayor pro tem left, and the company sat down to their meal, filling tin cups with water from a canteen. They saved the champagne for later. April avoided the ham, but took her bread in small pieces spread with preserves. Ragland ate with appetite, Vermillion with exaggerated fastidiousness. The Major said American peaches were no substitute for Sussex marmalade.

Nearing dusk, they heard a noise outside. April drew a derringer from her reticule, a fine Remington with silver plating and ormolu grips. Vermillion opened the door and peered out, then spread it wide. "Merely our prodigal daughter. You may stand down, dear—although I must say that piece looks more comely in your hand than the Colt."

"That horrid thing. I'm sure if I pulled the trigger it would flip me over onto my bustle." She returned the weapon to its pocket in the lining.

Mme. Mort-Davies entered, pushing her bicycle. She'd strapped down her generous bosom with canvas and pulled on a heavy ribbed sweater and tan riding breeches of the kind worn by Western Union messengers, gathered tight to her calves with high lace-up boots. She made rather a homely man with her abundance of hair gathered up inside a tweed cap. Her cheeks were flushed from the cold.

"About time, my pet. Thirty minutes more and you'd have pedaled all this way for nothing."

She fixed her husband with a stony gaze. "I've made it clear to Johnny these wagers of yours don't include me."

"In any case I didn't agree to it." Vermillion plucked the oilcloth bundle from the bicycle's wicker basket while Ragland went to work with a wrench. In three minutes the front wheel and basket were off and the entire vehicle was packed in the trunk. Vermillion waited until he finished, then dumped the bundle out onto the table. Packets of banknotes lay among the silver dollars and glittering gold double eagles. April sighed.

The Major was the first to speak. "Next time, we must get inside the vault. I made more than this at the Old Vic."

4

Who is Johnny Vermillion?

The history of the American theater makes no mention of him or the Prairie Rose, and his name occupies barely a footnote in the constantly metastasizing library of Western outlawry, with inaccurate information appended. For answer, we must depart from the written record and borrow a technique from the medium of film.

The color bleeds to sepia and we observe a sprawl of maverick construction on the swampy shore of Lake Michigan, far more impressive for its size than its architecture; for it appears to be without limit. Grain elevators tower above its few wooden stories of houses, shops, barns, and municipal and county buildings, the first generation of brick warehouses on the lake, and long horizontal columns of depots built of native sandstone. There are stacks and chimneys, of course, and smoke lies in coppery layers like the sunset. Locomotives chug high and low and all about like toy trains. Superimposed on this, a virile legend: CHICAGO 1844.

Not, perhaps, the Chicago we expect. The eye searches in vain for the stockyards, slaughterhouses, and gingerbread mansions of iconic memory; they are yet to be built. This is an agrarian center, serving wheat and cotton and flax to the East on rails still shining and fresh. Its days of butchers and barons and grotesque wealth lie twenty-five years in the future. But it is a young force, brawny with plans.

We are drawn, as by the Ghost of Christmas Past, over roofs, past lines of washing, and through a window on the third floor of the Winston Hotel, which will perish, along with its mahogany and crystal and miles of green velvet hung in swags, in the Great Fire of 1871. We cross the glistening tessellated floor of the ballroom, littered with confetti in heaps like cornstalks, and stop at last before an Empire chair supporting the prosperous corpulence of Scipio Africanus McNear, assistant city comptroller and chairman of the local Democratic Party. His collar is sprung, his waistcoat unbuttoned to provide egress for his grand belly. A tower clock chimes four; all his colleagues have retired to their beds, leaving him to smoke a final cigar and sift through a pile of telegrams congratulating him upon the election of James Knox Polk to the presidency of the United States. He has been a tireless supporter of the gentleman from Tennessee ever since John Tyler gave up his own bid for reelection, and McNear has delivered Chicago to the Democrats at the expense of fifty tons of coal distributed in the South Side and a number of fractured skulls in the disputed precincts. He expects much from Washington in exchange.

However, the telegram we find him reading is not from a crony, but from the head of surgery at St. Patrick's Hospital downtown:

> YOUR SON BORN TWO TWENTY THREE A M EIGHT POUNDS SEVEN OZ STOP MOTHER CHILD WELL RESTING STOP AWAITING NAME

Boss McNear, as he is pleased to be known to the press and public, has a pawkish sense of humor. Chuckling, he produces the pencil he used to tally the vote and scribbles a name on the back of the telegram: "John Tyler McNear, Esq."

He reckoned he never knew a better day, and that fate demanded a steep price. In 1860, the year the Republican Party gave Abraham Lincoln to America, McNear's wife, Geneva, a daughter of one of the city's founding French families, was killed when the streetcar she was riding jumped the tracks; she was pregnant with a daughter, who perished also. McNear was serving as a state senator, and came home from Springfield to find himself a stranger to his fifteen-year-old son, a dreamy sort of lad who had spoken French exclusively until he was five. He was promptly shipped off to a boarding school in Rockford. There he failed consistently at mathematics, humiliating his father, the former comptroller, but scored well in history and drama, where his performance as Dr. Faustus on the school's amateur stage drew an enthusiastic review from the *Rockford Evening Gazette*. McNear, who did not attend, consoled himself that the young man might become a decent orator, but his hopes were shattered when John was expelled for theft.

Summoned before his father to explain himself, he confessed that after his exit in Act IV, he'd removed a number of valuable items from pockets in the cloakroom, and that a silver snuffbox belonging to a patron had been found in his rooms. McNear beat him severely with his belt, and later beat him again when the school superintendent wrote to report that Master McNear had not committed the crime in person, but had seduced the young lady who played the Good Angel into performing the task while he was soliloquizing onstage; the young lady had come forward upon her own, hoping that the truth would lead to Master McNear's reinstatement.

"You filthy pup!" sputtered the old man, when his arm faltered. "Is that what they taught you up in Rockford?"

John Tyler, it's said, touched his torn lip with a handkerchief. "Actually, I believe it was in your suite at the Winston, the night the party nominated Douglas. I learned a great deal that evening."

That evening, Scipio Africanus McNear suffered the first of several strokes that would force him to retire from public life at the age of fifty-eight. His investments during the cattle boom that followed the War Between the States allowed him to live the life of a wealthy invalid on Lakeshore Drive, with nursing care around the clock, and to pay his son an allowance to keep him away from home. Then came the fire. When the company through which he'd insured his pens and meatpacking plants defaulted on all its claims, the prospect of an impoverished old age brought on the stroke that killed McNear on the eve of his seventieth birthday. His former colleagues contributed to a collection to bury him in Mt. Carmel Cemetery, sparing him a pauper's grave on Blue Island.

John Tyler did not attend. He spent the day of the funeral

in a banquet room at the newly rebuilt Palmer House Hotel, treating his friends to a champagne supper with the last of the money given him by his father. For years, he'd used his mother's maiden name, Vermillion. None of his guests knew of his loss, and his women friends, who imagined they shared the secrets of his heart, were not aware he was related to one of those vulgar political creatures their fathers condemned at garden parties.

His descent from that point was vertical.

His male friends were not disposed to help him out. For some time, objects of value had had a habit of going missing when he was present—a watch here, an unattended banknote there. Such trinkets were considered dispensable in their set, and their principles differed sharply from those of the previous generation. Like John's, their family connections had released them from military service during the war: Honor, to them, was rather a remote concept, like the elaborate burial practices of the early Egyptians, and they looked upon it with the same combination of amusement and contempt reserved for last year's collar. When they confronted him, they were contented to accept his markers, just as they were when any of their peers lost at cards or arranged a loan to hold them over until their next allowance. Some of the items were returned, in fact, and some debts repaid. But after he was locked out of his rooms for nonpayment of rent, the reality of his financial condition barred him from both their company and their hospitality. Turned away from their doors with nothing but the clothes he stood up in, Johnny Vermillion perceived that his country was headed in a harsh new direction, to a place whose customs were dictated by money, and not by whether one's French ancestor had sailed with Drake or fought the British at Ticonderoga.

It was a lesson for which he'd been prepared all his life. From an early age, he had witnessed the comings and goings in his father's house of ward leaders and building contractors, bearing satchels of cash to and from Boss McNear for favors asked and services rendered. He'd spent the summer before his mother's death running errands for the Democratic Party, and had seen the unsheathed greed on the faces of elder statesmen whose pen-and-ink likenesses graced the sober columns of the *Chicago Sun* when tariffs were discussed and hospitals under construction. Money was the ammunition of the Industrial Revolution; whether it was acquired with a pistol or scooped in buckets from the public treasury seemed less to the point than getting it and spending it. He had not so much a disrespect for the rights of property as a lack of awareness that any such rights existed.

The loss of Geneva Vermillion McNear, a creature above and apart from the soiled coinage that kept the political system tinkling like a player piano, had severed whatever connection this sensitive, good-looking, queerly observant boy had maintained with the catechism of *Père* Argulet, the spiritual guide of his youth at St. Patrick's. The boy was a clever thief by birth and an uncommonly skilled one by education. He'd stolen far more from his acquaintances than they ever suspected—they'd blamed carelessness and attrition—and pawned it to support a standard of living somewhat greater than his father's subsidy had made possible. Now he was denied access.

His female friendships, although less altered (his father, a strikingly handsome figure before the overindulgence of his middle years, had given him a straight nose and a narrow waist, his mother her fair hair and all the charms of the Parisian court), offered even smaller hope for shelter. Many were married ladies, and those in single circumstances had strict landladies and rigid curfews. He had neither the training to enter a profession nor the endurance to withstand sixteen hours of physical labor daily. The spark of dramatic ambition that had glowed briefly at school had long since guttered out. That left either vagrancy or thievery from strangers. Prison fare, he'd heard, was bad for teeth and ruinous to the complexion, and certain other rumors that had come his way concerning life inside he found not worth the candle. The wastrel's way beckoned.

By the winter of 1872, he was sleeping on streetcar benches and begging for coins. A successful day's panhandling bought him a "flop" for the night on Blue Island. This was a dirtfill in a canal leading from the lake and a hotbed of malaria, saloons, brothels, and that variety of lawyer that existed mainly to give abortionists and white slavers a reason to feel superior. The island itself was in a constant state of erosion, retarded only by the addition of fresh manure swept from the streets. To take a turn there was virtually impossible without kicking up a bone belonging to some indigent buried by the city. Even the Great Fire had gone around it as a waste of destructive force.

On a pewter-colored morning in late November—it might have been early December—Johnny awoke to a prod from an impatient toe and stirred himself to clear the doorway where he'd sought shelter from the wind an hour before. The visitor, however, made no motion to step past him. He was a stout, ruddy-faced party in a tall Mormon hat with an eagle feather in the band and a preposterous fringed coat trimmed with an otter collar, crumbs in his moustaches. Johnny thought he looked like a third-rate hotel waiter reciting *The Song of Hiawatha* in concert. The waiter fixed the man at his feet with an alcoholic glare.

"You look as if you'll clean up well enough." He held up a silver dollar. "How would you like to be an Indian?"

The man's name was Buntline, plainly a *nom de caprice* under which he practiced professionally. To hear him speak, in a four-wheeler growling over brick pavement into the heart of furious construction downtown, he'd been just about everything *but* a hotel waiter: naval officer, newspaper publisher, duellist, inciter to riot, temperence lecturer, popular novelist, and, currently, producer and playwright. Johnny shared the carriage with four other recent recruits in varying degrees of sartorial and hygienic neglect and learned their employment was temporary. A bill posted outside Nixon's Amphitheater had promised a spectacle involving authentic frontiersmen and genuine red Indians. However, there had been an oversight, and although the former were available, the latter were not. Until such time as the real article could be procured, he explained, "you gentlemen present will wear feathers and paint and carry on like wild dogs for the sum of two dollars per week."

Scouts of the Plains opened under Nixon's roof, a canvas rig as temporary as the nonspeaking cast, on December 18, led by an uncommonly beautiful former scout and buffalo hunter named Cody. He was two years younger than Johnny, with the identical straight figure and even features, and wore his chestnut hair to his shoulders, a closely cultivated Van Dyke, and buckskins tailored to his measure. An execrable actor who stammered and forgot his lines, he was nonetheless a powerful presence; beside him, his fellow rude thespians, a man called Texas Jack and Buntline himself, faded into the painted prairie backdrop. The effect upon the audience, male and female, was electric. Johnny himself, behind the clay-colored pigment that smeared his face, developed a bit of a crush on Cody that evening; a manly one, to be sure, with no suggestion of unnatural attraction, but a crush just the same. But he was not so besotted as to fail to study the phenomenon and isolate its ingredients. In forty years in public life, Boss McNear had prided himself on his ability to make stew from toads, and this, too, was his legacy. Cody himself seemed unaware of his charms, which was a contributing factor in its success. Years later, touring the great cities of the New World and the capitals of the Old, the star would learn to apply them to queens, kaisers, and Sioux chiefs, real ones; by which time Johnny Vermillion could provide lessons of his own.

The play was folderol, an amateur freak show seasoned with "blanket-stretching" tales from the border told around a synthetic campfire and a slapstick Indian raid with rubber tomahawks and popping stage pistols, and a sensation. Notwithstanding withering reviews in all the Chicago papers, the engagement sold out and was held over for weeks. Johnny was bored to stupefaction by the unscripted antics of his fellow "supers" and himself, and not a little embarrassed by them. But his salary allowed him to sleep indoors and eat regularly, and he put his time in the wings to good use, analyzing the stuff of mass popularity. Although he and Cody never exchanged a word, Johnny observed that he never left the theater after a performance without a different attraction on his arm, decked in ruffles and touched with scent, parasol in hand. The young man from Blue Island out of Lakeshore Drive bought a suit of clothes in a secondhand shop, a decent fit, and let his hair grow, even though he could afford an occasional visit to a barber. He was content to have it trimmed only when it curled over his collar, a Byronic effect. He knew from instinct he could not pull off the part of a backwoods Adonis; his accent was solidly Midwestern, and his French too good.

The show closed out its extended run and prepared to embark on a tour of the eastern states. The "Indians" were not invited, possibly because New York's Bowery and the Tenderloin of Boston promised their own sources of two-dollar-a-week performers. Johnny wasn't disappointed. He'd determined to exploit his skills as a mendicant and borrow money to open a show of his own.

5

He had, of course, no prospects among his former friends, from whom he'd stolen hundreds. Wasting no time in lament—a foreign emotion—he took the five-dollar gold piece he'd received in severance from an ebullient and unusually munificent Buntline, sewed it into the lining of his new suit coat, and boarded a boxcar bound for St. Louis.

In the restless years following the end of hostilities between North and South, not all of the pioneers who ventured West did so aboard day coaches and wagon trains, the latter already fading from the landscape in the glare from the flashpans at Promontory Point. Something in excess of fifty thousand maimed and impoverished veterans sought berths in freight cars and on the naked rods between the wheels hoping for work on the frontier. A rare whole man in that company of cripples, many of whom were younger than he, Johnny felt shame—for the fathers who were either unwilling or unable to secure their sons' exclusion from the draft. He concealed his unbroken condition in the fluttering shadows.

Fortunately, conversation was limited to a barter system of smoking materials and flasks of paint-strip whiskey, and one lively auction over a paperbound novel, filthy and tattered, begun by an entrepreneurial fellow who wore a bandanna over one side of his face, ruined by grapeshot on some forgotten field; boredom was the overpowering complaint on that endless trek. The story—*The Prairie Rose, or A Maiden's Journey Among Savages*—eventually sold for two cents and a half-consumed plug of Levi Garrett's. Johnny admired the title.

In St. Louis, he spent his stake on a shave, a bath, laundering, a press, and a room above a printing shop on Pike

Street. A wallet lifted in bustling pedestrian traffic yielded a slim bounty, from which he paid his landlord, the printer, to provide him with twenty-five cards printed on good stock:

J. T. VERMILLION, ESQ.
The Prairie Rose Repertory Company

The printer fingered the notepaper upon which the order was written. "What about an address?"

"I hope for better quarters presently."

The first to receive his card was a banker named Argyle, whose name Johnny had read in an advertisement in the *Dispatch*. Explaining that he had no appointment, the visitor sent the card into his office through Argyle's private secretary, a thin young man, pale as porcelain, who wore his spectacles on a black ribbon pinned to his waistcoat, and sat down to read *Frank Leslie's Illustrated Newspaper* and wait. At the end of two hours, during which a procession of roseate gentlemen in boiled collars passed in and out through the private door, he was granted an audience of five minutes. He found Argyle, an emblem of the type in white side-whiskers and a liverish hue, behind a leather-topped desk looking quizzically at his card. Introductions were brief, and Johnny lost no time in placing his proposition before the banker.

"Young man," said Argyle, "the theater is an unstable enterprise. This institution—"

"Pardon the interruption. Are you not related to Walter C. Argyle, the Chicago financier?"

"Walter was my brother. He is deceased." The liver went gray around the edges.

"The same Walter Argyle who threw himself beneath the wheels of the Michigan Central at Union Station in eighteen fifty-nine?"

"A tragic accident." He stole another glance at the card. "Vermillion. The *Chicago* Vermillions?"

"On my mother's side, actually. My father was S. A. McNear."

There was now no trace of healthy organ meat in the banker's face. "I—I understood he had no offspring."

"That was his conceit. I was a disappointment. However, I apprenticed to him for three months in fifty-nine. Your brother was a valued contributor to the party, right up until his partners learned their own contributions got no closer to the Douglas campaign chest than his office. The money never surfaced. There was talk of an unknown accomplice, but those rumors died out, as they will when there is no foundation. I hope I'm not upsetting you with these unhappy recollections."

Peter Argyle was a man with a keen grasp of the realities. It was this instinct that had led him to St. Louis, and to shift his allegiance to the Republican Party a full year before the election of Ulysses S. Grant. Without further conversation—indeed, before the five minutes allotted to the interview had elapsed—he signed and handed the young man a bank draught in the amount of five hundred dollars.

St. Louis, it developed, was fertile ground for past guilty associations. Johnny was not always successful. He retired from one second-floor office when the man behind the desk rose and offered to propel him through the window, and there was an anxious moment near the levee when the newcomer had reason to be grateful for the rough education he'd received on Blue Island; he blacked the eye of one attacker and scaled a fence to elude his partner. Others were more cooperative; some negotiated. At the end of his first week on the Mississippi, Johnny Vermillion had reason to close old accounts with his late sire and to open the door to a suite of comfortably furnished rooms on Fifth Street. The time had come to begin assembling his troupe.

Here, as it had in the form of Buntline's toe, fate prodded him. Struggling against the pedestrian flow on Market Street following a successful interview with a regional vice president of the Santa Fe Railroad, he bumped into a petite lady in a becoming white dress, tipped his hat to her in apology, and fought his way upstream for a hundred yards before he realized a roll of banknotes was missing from his inside breast pocket. The railroad man had paid him in cash. Instantly he reversed directions and gave chase.

The lady was fast on her feet and graceful, but had shown faulty judgment in her choice of dress; like a marine rescuer fixing on the ripples where a swimmer has gone down, her pursuer kept his eyes on the white vision fluttering in and out among the duns and grays and blacks of business dress, toppling hats and jostling old gentlemen off their canes as he plunged ahead to close the gap. By the time he caught up with her, rounding the corner of Third, he'd lost his own hat, and his hair hung over his eyes. The scream he stifled by clamping his hand over her mouth and pushing her into a doorway was genuine fright. He stuck something into her ribs, or rather the stays that bound them.

"A knife is a wicked weapon," he whispered. "You have something that belongs to me."

She made a noise full of *m*'s against his palm. Pinned against the door by his weight, his hand covering the lower half of her face, she was warm, and tense as a coiled spring. She glared fire at him from under a white hat with a sweeping brim, the veil pinned up on one side. It was a most becoming hat. He could feel her heart beating clear through him.

The tension went out of her body all at once. She nodded. He withdrew his hand and turned it palm upward.

Suddenly he stiffened. The object she drew from the reticule wound by its drawstring around her wrist pressed hard against his abdomen. It made a crisp *snick* when she thumbed back the hammer.

"A pistol is a wicked weapon," she said. "I'll have yours."

He laughed and showed her the harmless card case in his other hand. Stepping back, he opened it and held up a card.

She read it without taking it. The silver-plated derringer remained in place. "Where is your theater?"

"All over this great land. Tell me you have not dined."

April Clay, neé Klauswidcsz, was the daughter of Polish immigrants, although she insisted her grandmother had belonged to a noble family in St. Petersburg. Her father was a prodigal, and had not been heard from in ten years; her mother had been dead for two. April was currently supporting herself at the Steamboat Theater, assisting a magician billed as Gandolphus the Great, with whom Johnny assumed she had a romantic arrangement, but apparently not a satisfying one financially.

Johnny could hardly believe his good fortune. Here was a beautiful young woman with stage experience, her own demonstrated talent for sleight of hand, and none of the cumbersome baggage of honesty. If she could act—but what did that signify? She would look comely in ruffles and tights.

They ordered the sauteed duck at the Planter's House, with a dessert of roasted peaches served in champagne sauce—his first taste of that delectable libation since the day of his father's funeral, and a harbinger of change. By the time the coffee was served, she had agreed to invest half of the money she had separated from Johnny into their joint venture, and also to pay the bill, as it had been the only cash he'd had on his person.

He suggested they seal their partnership in his rooms,

over the remaining portion of their bottle of wine. She declined sweetly. Commerce, she explained, was a difficult undertaking without the additional complication of a personal relationship. Thus, from the beginning, was set the tone for the association. He saw her to a hansom, and did not realize his card case was missing until he returned to his rooms.

The next stage of recruitment presented more challenge. They needed character players, capable of comedy and drama, and versatile enough to support a multiplicity of roles. The dignity of age would supply authenticity and gravity, but good health was crucial, to withstand the rigors of travel under often primitive conditions. Add to this the necessary cavalier approach to probity and virtue, and the difficulty increased. During the long days and nights that followed this declaration of their requirements, both Johnny and April wondered, fleetingly, whether honesty weren't the simplest policy after all, if not strictly the best. It was a passing consideration as noted, gone with the sunrise.

Separate and in tandem, they haunted the theaters and melodeons of St. Louis, taking in matinees and evening performances and comparing notes afterward. They avoided the popular shows in the bigger theaters, concentrating instead upon the barely respectable houses on the tattered fringes of the entertainment district, with no lines at the box offices and FINAL NIGHT plastered in an indolent diagonal across the performers' names. This was Desperation Alley, where the weak and defeated straggled behind the herd, to be picked off by predators. It was also, unfortunately, a burial ground for the hack, the charlatan, and that pathetic breed of entertainer that should have never been allowed closer to the proscenium arch than the third row of the orchestra. The pair endured more banana-handed jugglers, broken-arched dancers, tone-deaf singers,

overcautious acrobats, and harelipped elocutionists in one
six-block area than in all the theaters of the East; April confided that she'd have put them all out of their misery (and
hers) if her little Remington only had the range.

Success came to them both simultaneously—or almost.

Johnny sat through a dreary afternoon bill at the Empress, a cramped collar box of a music hall that had survived the riverfront fire of 1849, and still smelled of char, as
well as generations of cooked cabbage; tearing his programme into a string of paper dolls to keep himself from
screaming profanities at the abominations onstage. With
two acts remaining, he'd reached the end of his patience
and got up to leave, only to be arrested at the door by a series of perfectly round vowels projected from behind the
footlights. He turned around and watched a corpulent old
fellow, in full dress with top hat and the scarlet sash of a
dignitary, proclaiming his passion for a woman taller than
himself and straight as a plumb, dressed in the simple gray
of a mature maidservant with a white apron. The placard
on the easel downstage right was redundant to the action:
THE DIPLOMAT DEPOSES. The woman waited, hands folded
before her apron, until he finished—and declined his pro-
posal of marriage, wringing a collective gasp from the scattered audience, and general applause as the curtain rang
down on the old gentleman with head hung low.

The performance impressed Johnny less than the response from the orchestra; he found it mannered and
laughable, as was its subject. *The Diplomat Deposes* had
been around for years, an old dependable harness horse of
the stage. His own school turn in *Dr. Faustus* had followed
the one-act piece, and he had sat through three hideous ver-
sions in the last ten days alone. That a pair of actors whose
best years were demonstrably behind them—he reckoned
their combined age would stretch back to the Revolution—
should manage to wring such a reaction from so jaded a

gallery was remarkable. That their position near the bottom of a fifth-rate bill in a tenth-rate theater placed them in straits he considered approachable was encouraging. As a stagehand shunted the placard to the back, exposing the next and last, Johnny made haste to record the two names in his leather notebook.

Ablaze with his discovery, he was exasperated not to be able to find April. The old dragon who stood sentry in the lobby of the women's hotel where she lodged reported that she'd been out all day. Their preferred table at the Planter's House, where they met regularly to commisserate, was occupied by a middle-aged German couple with faces as sour as *braten*. He decided that April was scouting an evening performance, but could find no mention of where in his notes. He returned to his rooms and paced the floor until the hour when the theaters let out.

Back at the Planter's, he drank a quick brandy and ordered another. It had not yet arrived when April swept in, ravishing in green satin, her cheeks afire with excitement. She was seated opposite him before he had time to rise. They both started speaking at once; stopped, laughed distractedly, and started again: "I've found what we've been seeking."

Johnny played the gentleman and sat back to hear her out. She'd been talking less than a minute when he lunged forward and grasped her wrists, cutting off both her circulation and her narrative. "Don't tell me their names," he said. "I shall guess. Major Evelyn Davies and Mme. Elizabeth Mort-Davies."

Nothing in their association, including accosting her on the street and threatening her with a knife, ever so astounded her in his presence. Her mouth formed an adorable crimson O and her unforgettable eyes widened to their full extent. He struck a mental photograph of the expression, and was loath to dispel it with an explanation; but theirs was a professional enterprise, with no place for egoism outside of costume. Through an oversight, Johnny and April had duplicated each other's effort, attending both the matinee and evening performances of *The Diplomat Deposes*. It was proof of the unity of their vision that both had recognized the object of their goal when it presented itself.

Ambuscaded at the stage door following the next day's matinee, the Major and the Madame were sufficiently motivated by the beauty and charm of their admirers to join them for supper. Once again, dessert—pears this time, panfried and drizzled with maple syrup shipped at fabulous expense from New England—worked its magic. The Major, who claimed service with Queen Victoria's horse guards before the Call drew him to the London stage, was hesitant in regard to the larceny, as his knowledge of law enforcement was based upon the compact efficiency of Scotland Yard, but by that time it was clear he was not the one who made the decisions in that union. Mme. Mort-Davies quizzed them closely concerning practical details. She'd been an acrobat and high-wire artist until age alone had directed her into spectacles less demanding physically, and she was far more interested in mechanics than risk. Accord was reached, and of morality no mention was made. Exchanging observations later in private, Johnny and April agreed that the Davieses' account of their years on the circuit had been edited to remove a veritable cross-country crime wave of petty proportions.

She lifted her glass. "To the Prairie Rose."

He shook his head. "That would be premature, and bad luck. We still need a second lead: a Tybalt. The prospect of Major Davies bounding about with a foil would provide comic relief where none is required, to say nothing of its effect upon the boards. We must appear to be legitimate."

"Oh, dear. More auditions."

"Take heart. Now that we're four, we each need attend half as many."

Fate spared them even that ordeal. The next morning Johnny, deeply regretting last night's overindulgence, stumbled out of bed in his nightshirt to answer the door and found himself facing a physical manifestation of his own fragile condition. The young man on the landing was a half inch shorter, disregarding his stoop, and underweight; sunlight seemed to shine through him as if he were made of bone china. His ears stuck out from his cropped head and a black ribbon dangled from his wire spectacles.

"Mr. Vermillion, my name is Cornelius Ragland. We've met."

"I think you're mistaken." Johnny was on his guard. This fellow in his shabby suit, holding a shabby hat before him in both hands, bore all the marks of an extortionist, with his guilty evidence stuffed inside the even shabbier leather portfolio pinned under his left arm. Perhaps he'd been betrayed before he'd even begun.

"I am Peter Argyle's private secretary. I showed you into his office some weeks ago."

Johnny was certain now of his suspicions. He did not remember the fellow, but Cornelius Ragland appeared easy to forget even when he was standing in front of one. Argyle had been the Prairie Rose's first reluctant investor; perhaps he'd left his transom open during their transaction, and here came his secretary to turn the tables. He did not represent Argyle. The banker had gotten off easy at five hundred dollars. He stood to lose far more by exposing their arrangement.

Abashed by Johnny's silence, the visitor stammered ahead. "I—I couldn't help but remember your card said you were with a theatrical company. I've been asking around for you ever since that day. Your address wasn't on the card."

He drew the portfolio from under his arm, dropping his hat in the process. There was some funny stage business during which he dropped one, then the other in trying to retrieve it. Johnny wondered if he ought to crack the fellow on the head with a water pitcher while he was bent and search his case. Perhaps it contained Argyle's canceled bank draught.

He was muzzy-headed, however, and did not act. Upright again, Ragland untied the portfolio and sorted through the mass of foolscap inside. "Here is *Sleepy Hollow,* and *The Count of Monte Cristo,* and two of Dickens', abridged of course. A full staging would consume several hours."

"*What* are *Sleepy Hollow* and *The Count of Monte Cristo*? What manner of game are you playing, Mr. Ragman?"

"Ragland." Red spots burned on the stranger's cheeks. Johnny guessed he was consumptive. "They're adaptations, Mr. Vermillion. Stage plays, based on great novels. I'm a playwright."

"I thought you were a secretary."

"That's temporary. I—I've heard that repertory players are always in need of material. I thought—perhaps—" He muttered something apologetic and turned to leave. The tips of his ears had turned as red as his cheeks. He'd mistaken stunned relief for rejection.

"One moment, Mr. Ragland."

The young man turned back swiftly, nearly losing his hold on his bundle of loose pages. He let his hat fall in order to grasp the case with both hands. Johnny's misery fled before an urge to laugh. Ragland amused him to the bone.

"We're a small troupe. We ask everyone to pull a deal more than his own weight. If—and I mean *if* according to Mr. Webster's definition of the word—if we decide to use your scribblings and employ you to scribble more, we will expect you to perform other duties as well."

"What would they entail?"

"Have you studied fencing?"

6

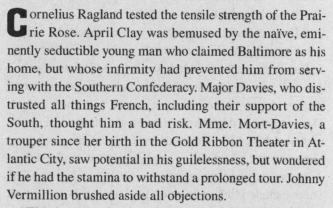

Cornelius Ragland tested the tensile strength of the Prairie Rose. April Clay was bemused by the naïve, eminently seductible young man who claimed Baltimore as his home, but whose infirmity had prevented him from serving with the Southern Confederacy. Major Davies, who distrusted all things French, including their support of the South, thought him a bad risk. Mme. Mort-Davies, a trouper since her birth in the Gold Ribbon Theater in Atlantic City, saw potential in his guilelessness, but wondered if he had the stamina to withstand a prolonged tour. Johnny Vermillion brushed aside all objections.

"This conversation is pointless," he said. "I've told him he's hired."

"We don't even know if he can act," said April.

"I don't know if *you* can, dear. You've all expressed your opinions as artists of the stage, which is an attitude I encourage. However, you've overlooked young Mr. Ragland's principal value to our company of players."

"His writing talent?" The Major blew out his moustaches. "A monkey can scribble."

"*The Diplomat Deposes* is evidence of that. I'm not referring to his literary skill."

"Certainly not his presence," said Mme. Mort-Davies. "He is barely there."

"That can be manufactured. But you're right; it isn't that either."

"What, then?" demanded April.

"He and I are roughly the same height."

This announcement was met with the silence of self-recrimination. With proper coaching, particularly as to posture—identical costumes, and an expert application of makeup, Johnny and Cornelius could stand in for each other onstage while the man the audience thought it was watching stole away to perform elsewhere. In the flurry of rehearsals and arrangements, the troupe leader alone had remained on mission.

"Mind he doesn't turn sideways," grumped the Major. "He'll vanish into the backdrop."

They engaged the tumbledown Empress Theater for their debut. It was located near the levee—a factor of prime importance—and the rental fee agreed with their budget. The purchase of duplicate costumes, and of material for the versatile Mme. Mort-Davies to add certain features to those costumes that could not be duplicated, had strained their resources, to say nothing of the cost of hand properties. These included foils, a brace of duelling pistols, and a Colt revolver large enough to impress patrons in the back row and cashiers at close range. The costumes were Elizabethan. The Major, a superstitious old thespian, held that no successful season had ever begun without a Shakesperean comedy; he would not budge from the position, and so Cornelius Ragland's original scripts were laid aside in favor of selections from *Twelfth Night,* scaled down to the size of the company. April squealed in delight. She'd seen Ada Rehan on tour in the role of Viola and since then had worshipped at her shrine.

"You'll have more than her measure your first time out," Johnny said. "I'll warrant Rehan never played Maria in the same production. You'll make a fetching sailor as well."

He assigned the Major to the role of Sir Toby Belch, with a walk-on as a priest. The Madame—Lizzie, as Johnny made bold to address her—fitted Shakespeare's description of Olivia quite nicely, and would wear whiskers as Viola's sea-captain friend. Cornelius, who had no stage experience, was confined to the part of young Sebastian, which would be challenge enough; although he would double for Johnny as Orsino for one brief scene.

"And who will you play other than Orsino?" April asked.

"So far as the printed programme is concerned, I shall appear in a variety of undemanding roles apart from the lead, but the programme is a fraud. I shall perform only two."

She asked what was the other. He smiled.

"You won't find him in the dramatis personae."

Rehearsals were intense, and twofold: This troupe must not only block out movements and commit the Bard's lines to memory, but also practice switching costumes backstage. Many a long night was spent in a swirl of flying fabric until, within seconds, countess became captain, lady fell to maid, knight ordained himself priest, Viola's brother became her lover. This last transformation was performed with the most ease, as they had managed to procure duplicate costumes for Orsino and Sebastian, and the pair had only to exchange sashes to complete the substitution. With the plume of Johnny's hat covering half of Cornelius' face, and with his back turned toward the audience for most of the scene, the illusion was satisfactory. Madame Lizzie, a gifted scold, berated the former secretary to stand straight and dissemble his stoop. She was also a talented seamstress, and with scissors and string had reengineered all the one-of-a-kind costumes so that they came off with a twitch and refastened in a twinkling.

Bald head streaming, the Major groped in vain for a handkerchief. He'd forgotten he was dressed as a priest and that the cassock had no pockets. "At this point, we could empty five safes during the first performance."

"We'll start with one, during the last," Johnny said. "We're virgins, don't forget."

Twelfth Night—An Abridgment opened at the Empress the second week of October 1873, to uninspired reviews from a press that had seen Henry Irving in a full-scale production of the same play. Audiences trickled in, as did water; the sky wept through all six performances, the roof leaked, and at times it seemed more seats were occupied by buckets than people. None of the city papers mentioned the show's closing, at the end of the Monday matinee. They needed the space to report the daring daylight robbery of the steamboat *Czarina Catherine* by a lone bandit that afternoon. The vessel had docked at St. Louis to take on fuel and passengers, one of whom, described as a tall man in a long coat with the collar turned up and the brim of his hat turned down, produced a large revolver in the purser's cabin and demanded the contents of the safe. The purser, alone at the time, complied, and the mysterious stranger left carrying six thousand dollars in a satchel, an amount deposited for the most part by professional gamblers hoping to squeeze one more profitable season out of a mode of transportation made obsolete by the railroads.

The owner of the Empress, more tidy in his dress and grooming than in his finances, clucked over the Prairie Rose receipts, a disappointing four hundred dollars and change. "You didn't even make back your investment."

Johnny was sanguine. "St. Louisans are overentertained and jaded. I expect a warmer welcome out West, where diversions such as ours are rare. And the weather will be kinder in the dryer reaches."

"People starve to death on the plains."

"You underestimate our little party. We intend to develop a system for living off the land."

* * *

You've seen it before: a succession of stoked boilers streaking toward the screen, intercut with close-ups of charging wheels and plunging drive rods. On the soundtrack, short cello strokes imitate the chomping of pistons and steam whistles blast from the brass. Depot signs loom at us from the far perspective: KANSAS CITY; OMAHA; SIOUX FALLS; CHEYENNE; SALT LAKE CITY. Quaint old-fashioned broadsheets spin and stop long enough to display headlines: BOLD ROBBERY OF THE FARMERS TRUST (*Kansas City Times*); LONE BANDIT HOLDS UP STOCK SHOW (*Omaha Herald*); WELLS, FARGO OFFICE RAIDED (*Sioux Falls Journal*); CATTLEMAN'S BANK STRUCK BY DESPERADO (*Cheyenne Leader*); MORMONS FORM VIGILANCE GROUP FOLLOWING OVERLAND OUTRAGE (*Deseret News*). Solitary figures in big hats and bandannas appear and dissolve, gesticulating with a revolver (can there be just one?). They are tall and short, comically fat and thin as water, substantial and slight. We pan past actors in elaborate costumes making faces, fencing, and soliloquizing, across a row of frightened clerks and cashiers raising their hands, around an auditorium filled with people clapping hands, dissolve to a pair of hands scooping piles of money into gunnysacks and satchels. Stacks of banknotes and gold coins grow before our eyes. Bottles of champagne foam over in the dressing room of some frontier theater—steer horns hung among the generic collage of playbills and atomizers—where our little band has gathered to commemorate the success of their inaugural tour. And out.

We leave them, reluctantly, for another establishing shot of Chicago. This time, the stockyards and slaughterhouses are in place, and a great many more buildings constructed of brick, so we'll have no more nonsense about great fires. We dolly in toward an imposing edifice of gray stone and a brass plate mounted at eye level, engraved with the omniscient eye of the Ancient and Honorable Fraternity of Free and Accepted Masons and this legend:

PINKERTON NATIONAL DETECTIVE AGENCY
"We Never Sleep"

Well, you knew it had to make its appearance sometime.

The window we creep through on this occasion belongs to a small, sparsely furnished office and a man seated behind a desk, industriously clipping an L-shaped hole out of a newspaper with a pair of shears. He places the cutting on a stack to his right, stuffs the rest of the newspaper into a wire wastebasket packed already to bulging, and slides another newspaper off the stack to his left. The only decoration in the room is a portrait, overpoweringly large in a massive gilt frame, of a resolute face with a Quaker beard on a sloping body buttoned tightly into a three-piece suit, glaring over the man's shoulder from the wall behind the desk. We shall meet him in the flesh presently.

The man doing the clipping is named Philip Rittenhouse, and he is not popular at Pinkerton headquarters. Numerous times he has made use of his authority to cancel leaves of absence upon short notice, and his humor is of that sarcastic bent that rarely endears. Moreover, he is an ugly man. Absolutely clean-shaven, including his head, he has deep hollows in his temples that throw his brow into prominent relief, pale and gleaming like polished bone. His nose has a predatory hook ending in a barb, and although his teeth are quite good, he bares them only on one side when he smiles, like a dog snarling over its dish. Thick lids sheathe his eyes; it is because of these that a departing operative referred to him as "Reptile house." Those who stayed behind have shortened it to "the Reptile."

He has, in fact, only one admirer in all the Pinkerton

National Detective Agency, and that is Allan Pinkerton himself, the subject of the portrait on Rittenhouse's wall. For the Reptile is an uncommonly fine detective. Seldom leaving his office, working almost exclusively by wire and through the post, moving his field agents about like pieces on a board, he has broken a coal miners' strike in Pennsylvania and brought to justice sixteen fugitives whose names marred the lead columns of newspapers throughout the United States and its territories for months. This in itself might have attracted the old man's attention, but not necessarily his affection. *That,* Rittenhouse has secured by refusing to communicate with the press when a major case is closed, referring all requests for interviews to Mr. Pinkerton or one of his sons. The challenge in the agency is to rise to a level approaching genius without casting a shadow across the face of its legendary founder, and the bald man in the little office has met it to the degree that if one of Mr. Pinkerton's male offspring developed a dislike for him and demanded his father to choose between them, Rittenhouse himself would not place a wager upon the decision.

He has contributed significantly to the stack of cuttings, diminished substantially the pile of unmutilated newspapers, and altered the shape of his wastebasket beyond all hope of restoration, when the patriarch of the Pinkerton clan, somewhat grayer than his painted image but if anything more resolute in appearance, opens Rittenhouse's door and steps inside. He never knocks, and none of the doors in the building contains a lock to bar him from entering its remotest corner.

Pinkerton observes Rittenhouse's project. "I'd wondered about that item in your budget: subscr-riptions." If anything, the old man's Glasgow burr has increased in prominence during his three decades in America.

The Reptile's manner is familiar, but respectful. "You mustn't be a Scotchman in this. They whisper in my ear from a thousand miles away, and seldom raise their rates. Unlike paid informers."

"Rest your eyes from the small print a moment and tell me what you think of this." Pinkerton draws a square of yellow flimsy from his watch pocket and places it between the stacks on the desk.

Rittenhouse does not pick up the folded telegram. A man with inexhaustible patience for details, he has none for redundancies. He asks what's in it.

"It's from Mr. Hume, of Wells, Fargo, and Company. He wants us to look into a robbery that took place at a freight office in Dakota Territory last month. The bandit made off with thirteen thousand in gold." He waits, but no response is forthcoming. "That's bandit, not bandits. There seems to have been a r-rash of this lone wolf sort of thing out that direction."

"Hume is their chief of detectives. Good man. Why does he need our help?"

"His hands are full with gangs: the James-Youngers and the Reno brothers and this fellow Brixton and his band. Hume's people are spread thin. That leaves a gr-reat many holes for a one-man crime wave to slip through."

"Shall I close them?"

"Not your usual way, Philip. Stagecoaches are on their way out. This agency's personnel is committed to the railroads and banks, so there will be none of this broadcasting agents about like seeds just to close one case. One man is responsible, and one man may ferret him out where an army may not. I want you to go to Sioux Falls and handle it personally."

"Very well."

Pinkerton's thatched brows twitch upward. "I thought you might offer argument. You've been a fixture here since before they laid in the gas."

"That's just it. I haven't had a holiday in three years. That's unhealthy."

"This is no holiday. Field work is exhausting, to say nothing of dangerous. It is also deadly boring; interviews with uncertain witnesses, dead ends, waiting hours for suspects who never appear. You must have the constitution for it."

"I've been exhausted and bored right here. A little danger sounds to me a nice tramp. I'll make arrangements immediately."

"Draw what you need from Dorchester downstairs. I want reports by the week and a thorough accounting first of ever-ry month. Stay in boardinghouses wherever possible. I fail to see why a highwayman should take his chances with the Wrath of Pinkerton, when running a hotel allows him to do the same thing with impunity."

"Shall I draw a bedroll as well, and sleep out under the stars each night?"

But Rittenhouse's superior is impervious to his sting. "Don't forget to requisition a pistol, though I caution you not to use it. Going into the field does not make you a field man. When you have your evidence and a location, turn them over to the local authorities for apprehension. Mind they give credit to the agency."

Following the old man's departure, the Reptile thinks for a moment about underwear and Pullmans, then makes inventory of the cuttings he's taken. They are from newspapers in St. Louis, Kansas City, the *Tannery Blanket*, Omaha, Sioux Falls, Cheyenne, and Salt Lake City; the week-old copy of the *Deseret News* arrived only that morning. He skims through the dense paragraphs once more, noting names, dates, and other salient material on a writing block in his own encryption, then drums the scraps together and slips them into a pasteboard folder upon which is displayed the Pinkerton Eye and a notation in his own tidy hand: *Solitary Thief.*

From those same publications, he's cut also dramatic reviews calling attention to a series of entertainments presented by a troupe of traveling actors skilled in the special requirements of a small company saddled with large casts of characters. These, too, he reads again, makes notes, and places the cuttings in a second folder labeled *Prairie Rose.*

Closing the cover, he lifts his lip on one side to show his teeth. "One man." He slides the two folders inside a leather briefcase that has seen all its wear so far traveling back and forth between that room and his cold-water flat on South Clark.

II

The
Ace-in-the-Hole
Gang

7

Before we forget Marshal Fletcher of Tannery, wise beyond his weight, let us move in tight on the bulletin board in his office and linger for a moment upon one of the prognathous, razor-challenged faces posted there. It's a peculiarly savage likeness of a type once epidemic on the covers of *Action Western* and *Flaming Lariat*: jaw sheared off square at the base, boot-scraper beard, eyes like dynamiter's drill holes in granite. The name beneath the pen-and-ink sketch is Black Jack Brixton, and it should come as no surprise that he's wanted dead or alive. His activities include assault, armed robbery, murder, and burning entire towns to the ground.

Dissolve to a real face, strikingly identical, in glorious Technicolor on a screen thirty meters wide: Brixton in the flesh, under a gray Stetson stained black with sweat, a blue bandanna creating a hammock for his aggressive Adam's apple. His expression is intense. He is watching something we are not privileged to see until we cut directly to the explosion.

In the enormous ball of smoke and fire and dirt, we pick out flying sections of steel rail and shattered oak ties, uprooted trees, and what may be a human body, flung high and flailing its limbs like a piece of shredded licorice before it disappears under a heap of earth and sawdust and pieces of sets left over from previous productions.

As things clear, we see a locomotive hurtling toward the destruction. The engineer's face, leaning out of the cab, pulls tense with shock. A sooty fist hauls back on the brake lever. The steel wheels shriek, spraying sparks. The cow-catcher grinds to a halt inches short of the bent and twisted ends of the rails. Steam whooshes out in a sigh of relief.

"Yahoo!" cries Brixton, smacking his horse on the rump with the ends of his reins and firing his six-gun into the air for added incentive. The animal bolts, leading the charge down the hill.

"Yahoo!" cry his subordinates, galloping out of the dense stand of trees on the other side of the tracks. More bullets fly.

As several men board the train to pacify the paying customers, the rest take charge of the engineer, his fireman, and the fat conductor. They are herded out onto trackside and Brixton threatens at the top of his voice to blow their heads off if the guards in the mail car fail to open the door by the count of five. On "four," hammers click. The door slides open then and the guards emerge with hands high. Foolishly, one lunges for the revolver in his holster. Brixton shoots from the hip. The guard snatches at his abdomen, drops his weapon, and tumbles to the cinderbed.

A bundle of dynamite makes its appearance. A match flares; the fuse is ignited. The spark travels ten feet and the door flies off a black iron safe embossed with a gold eagle. Sacks of coins, bars of bullion, and bales of banknotes— big, square, elaborately engraved certificates, much more impressive-looking than our modern bills—vanish into canvas bags and saddle pouches. More cheers and shooting as the horsemen clatter away.

These are a few minutes in a day in the life of the Ace-in-the-Hole Gang, infamous in newspapers in both the East and West and in a flood of cheap novels printed in Chicago and New York City. Somewhere in a cattle camp or saloon

or velvet parlor with a piano, an uncertain baritone is singing its ballad to a melody plagiarized from "Blood on the
Saddle."

Like so many others of his day, Jack Brixton's story began in Missouri, where he rode with the Bushwhackers,
holding up Union trains, blowing windows out of banks
filled with Yankee gold, taking target practice on Jayhawk-
ers, and generally giving civil war a bad name. Witnesses
say he left that crew because he considered Bloody Bill
Anderson too lenient.

Accounts of how he spent the years between the end of
the conflict and the spring of 1874, when his trail crossed
with Johnny Vermillion's, are mostly hearsay. He's said to
have rustled cattle in Texas, hunted Apache scalps in Arizona, shot a couple of dozen Mexicans south of the Rio
Grande, and introduced the sport of lynching to Wyoming
Territory. It was about the time the Wyoming story got
around that people started calling him Black Jack.

It was a name no one called him to his face. Transients
and newcomers to the gang found that out right away, at
the butt of his Smith & Wesson .44 American, a weapon
endorsed also by Jesse James and Wyatt Earp for use as
both a firearm and a bludgeon. Brixton had a superstitious
horror of nicknames. Frank "Hole Card" Handy, the gang's
original leader and also the inspiration for its name, had
been so called because of the Butterfield derringer he carried for emergency use in a special holster sewn inside the
crotch of his trousers. Drawing it one night during a dis-
pute over a hand of poker, he shot off the end of his penis
and bled to death before he could be brought to a doctor.
His successor, Apache Jim Weathersill, who was no part
Indian but had been rechristened to avoid confusion with
the better-known Jim Weathersill of the Turkey Creek Outfit, took a double load of buckshot in the belly from a
pimp who'd mistaken him for the original Jim, and Redleg

Johnson, the most athletic of the Ace-in-the-Hole boys, miscounted his coaches while loping along the top of the Katy Flyer looking for the mail car and ran off the end of the caboose to a broken neck. Brixton had come to the conclusion that living up to one's professional name involved ceasing to live at all. He considered it bad luck to pass one of his wanted posters without slowing down to obliterate the "Black" with a fusillade of lead.

In addition to his daring, ruthlessness, and bad temper, Black Jack Brixton was notorious for his escapes from the law. He'd been captured in Missouri by McCulloch's cavalry, by the sheriffs of several counties in Kansas and Colorado, by a succession of town marshals (which he didn't count), and by a deputy United States marshal in the Indian Nations, and had wriggled free every time, a phenomenon he credited to his talent for dislocating both wrists. No matter how tight the manacles, he had only to slip his bones out of joint to slide them over his hands and off. He'd employed this trick so many times his wrists had a habit of slipping out on their own, often at inopportune moments, as when his gun arm gave out under the weight of his big American in a bank in Grand Junction and he shot Mysterious Bob Craidlaw, his best man, in the foot. After that, he'd acquired a pair of Mexican leather cuffs with brass studs and buckled them on tight before going to work; Mysterious Bob acquired a permanent limp.

Bob kept his own counsel to the extent that no one in the bank apart from Brixton and himself knew he'd been shot until the gang reunited in a line shack twenty miles from the scene of the robbery, when he pulled off his boot and poured out a pint of blood. The suddenness of the report, in fact, had startled Tom Riddle into shooting a cashier, which raised the reward for his capture to fifteen hundred dollars.

There was nothing secretive in Mysterious Bob's past.

Much of it was public record, and his list of criminal accomplishments filled a paragraph in his circular going back to age twelve. He just never talked about himself. Although he'd spent three years with Brixton in the service of Missouri guerrillas—an opinionated group, who punctuated their arguments with gunfire—none of the men who slept and ate and rode with him had ever been able to determine just where he stood regarding slavery and states' rights. Arch Clements, his immediate superior, thought he was a mute. When Brixton, who knew otherwise, asked Bob point blank why he never set Clements straight, the quiet man let a full minute pass, then said, "I reckon he didn't ask." He made his best remarks with his Winchester, and like his tongue he never used it until he was certain of the effect. He never missed.

Tom Riddle did enough talking for them both, and for that matter all the rest of the crew. Short and compact where Bob was tall and lanky, he'd once spent most of a week stuck in a badger tunnel in California, where he'd been sent by his prospecting partners, larger men all, to look for color. He'd survived on roots and earthworms, talked to himself the whole time to keep from going loco, and acquired a taste for his own conversation, if not for earthworms and roots, which he frequently and at length compared to the meals they were forced to eat on the trail. He also avoided going into vaults and other tight places. Tom was a good man with dynamite, and a little deaf from the explosions; his speech was loud as well as incessant. "Shut up, Tom," was a phrase repeated wherever the group bedded down, usually in chorus.

In enterprises of this nature, there is in all likelihood a man called Breed, who demonstrates the less fortunate traits of his white and Indian ancestors. They wear their hair unfettered to their shoulders, resist hats, and clothe themselves in fringed leather vests and striped cavalry trousers stripped from the carcass of some unlucky trooper like the skin of a slain animal. Ace-in-the-Hole's Breed spent his leisure hours curing the ears he'd sliced off bartenders who refused to serve him whiskey and stringing them on the buckskin thong he wore around his neck during robberies, which had a dampening effect upon individual heroism. He had *Mother* tattooed in a heart on his right bicep and *Father* encircled by serpents on his left, and prized his big Bowie knife above all other weapons. Brixton, who had balked at Bloody Bill's "spare the women and children" policy, found Breed's company distinctly unpleasant.

The Kettleman brothers, Ed and Charlie, had fled Texas one step ahead of the Rangers, who sought them for running guns to the Comanches, and of the Comanches themselves, who were eager to talk to them about the quality of their merchandise. They'd commandeered a wagonload of Springfield rifles with rusted actions and broken firing pins on its way from Fort Richardson to the Fort Worth scrap yards and traded them for a total of four thousand dollars in buffalo robes. They were businessmen who always got the best price for bonds, bullion, and other items that could not immediately be converted into cash, much of which they won back off their companions at poker. In action, they worked in perfect union, as if they shared one brain, and also at the table, where each had a sixth sense for what cards his brother held in his hand. They were the least popular members of the gang and the most indispensable. Identical twins, slack-jawed and skinny as rails, they looked in life very much as they did in a picture the Pinkertons took of them in 1875, propped on a barn door with seventeen mortal wounds between them.

These five formed the unchanging center of Black Jack Brixton's band of desperadoes; ten thousand dollars on the hoof to the bounty hunter foolhardy enough to dream of capturing them. The authorities and outraged commercial interests responsible for this reward were parsimonious, as always. Acting separately and in concert, the wanted men had looted a quarter of a million from legitimate concerns and circulated it back into the economy by way of saloons, women of casual character, and the army of camp followers who supplied them with arms, ammunition, horses, and shelter. Counting temporary help and onetime alliances with other gangs, a million dollars had passed through the hands of between twenty and thirty individuals associated with Ace-in-the-Hole. It was never at a loss for recruits, because in the bleak aftermath of the Panic of 1873, banditry was the fastest-growing cottage industry in America. Bicycle sales placed a distant second.

The bold daylight robbery of the Chicago, Rock Island & Pacific Railroad near Council Bluffs, Iowa, which we have witnessed, removed sixteen thousand dollars from the hands of its rightful owners, the robber barons of New York City and San Francisco. When word reached civilization, the sheriff of Pottawattamie County—rock-ribbed and sunburned, dumb as salt pork—assembled a posse of the usual hotheads who convened in the Boar's Neck Saloon to burp up pickled eggs and damn the Republican administration. They mounted up, milled around the town square making speeches and terrifying the horses, and rode out, whooping and waving torches and shooting up private property.

By the time they reached the stranded train, Black Jack Brixton and his companions had been gone for hours. The sheriff's men followed their tracks half the night, stopping briefly to set fire to barns and smokehouses along the way, and wound up back at the train; whereupon they straggled back to town and wired the Pinkerton office in St. Louis.

Ace-in-the-Hole, meanwhile, had scattered like so many cards.

Anticipating a hot reception to so successful a raid, they sought bolt-holes as far south as Louisiana and as far west as California. The Pinkertons, who lost no time in identifying the train robbers, were just as quick to declare the trail cold, and counseled waiting until Brixton's men struck again. The board of directors of the Chicago, Rock Island & Pacific howled at the delay, and bumped the reward up a hundred dollars per man.

Money won in the course of a few minutes' work, however intense and fraught with peril, spends quickly in sinful Barbary and the deadfalls of New Orleans. Fifteen men had taken part in the raid, and sixteen thousand divided so many ways melts like grease in a skillet. As winter broke up beneath the heavy rains of early spring, six men in shining slickers waded their horses through the muddy streets of Denver and tied them to the rail in front of Nell Dugan's Wood Palace. Inside, Brixton, Mysterious Bob, Tom Riddle, Breed, and the Kettlemans took their pleasure out of what funds they had left and blocked out a plan to rob the Overland office in Salt Lake City.

That same day, the Prairie Rose Repertory Company commenced rehearsals of *The Legend of Sleepy Hollow* at the Salt Lake Theater, directly across the street from the Overland.

8

Salt Lakers who happened to be looking out across the flats that morning saw a half dozen men on horseback, small as clothes-pegs and shimmering through ribbons of heat; a few swore they heard ghostly flute music, but that was probably just the Denver & Rio Grande blowing its whistle.

By noon the riders appeared no closer. Then suddenly they had passed Temple Square and were clattering down Main Street, using their reins as quirts and sending Mormons and Gentiles alike scrambling for the safety of the boardwalks. Elder Sterne, who'd been expecting revenge for Mountain Meadows for twenty years, dove into Browning's gun shop and had to be subdued by three employees to prevent him from running back out with a Whitney double-barrel.

They saved his life. Rounding a corner onto State Street, the riders surprised a dog into lunging at their horses' legs and pumped eleven bullets into it in a group no larger than a man's spread hand.

Daniel Oberlin, who managed the Holladay Overland Mail & Express Company office across the street from the theater, thought at first the men in dusters with bandannas over their faces were fellow members of the Zion Club come to play a trick on him; nobody in the history of the company had been robbed twice in twenty-four hours, and it was just the kind of low humor he expected from that society. He changed his mind when the man with the words, a big fellow with eyes as empty as the safe, backed him to the wall behind the counter and stuck the muzzle of his big revolver against the bridge of Oberlin's nose.

"Open the safe or I'll open your skull."

Oberlin opened the safe.

"Where the hell's the money?"

"I gave it to a fat fellow last night. He had a gun as big as yours."

"Kill the son of a bitch." This in a hissing tone from one of the other gunmen, who wore his black hair long like an Indian.

"I swear it's true! All he left was the petty cash in the box."

"Hand it over."

He gave the man the tin box he kept on the shelf beneath the counter. It contained forty-five dollars and seventeen cents.

On the way out of town, the Ace-in-the-Hole Gang registered its disappointment by shooting out windows in several establishments, including the temple, where city commissioners and church elders were meeting to discuss forming a citizens' vigilance committee to deal with outrages such as the freight office robbery the evening before. (The motion passed unanimously after the dignitaries crawled out from under the table.) Mysterious Bob Craidlaw entered the lobby of the Deseret Hotel without bothering to dismount and removed six hundred dollars from the safe at the point of his Winchester, and one of the Kettlemans separated an employee of the Salt Lake Theater from his right index finger as he was taking down a bill advertising last night's performance by the Prairie Rose Repertory Company. Breed had to be restrained from going back and slicing off Daniel Oberlin's ears.

They'd left provisions and fresh horses at a disused Butterfield stage stop ten miles east of town, where they stopped to divide their small gain.

"I got more'n this out of that badger hole in Sacramento," said Tom Riddle, fingering his shallow stack of banknotes.

Breed said, "I still want the ears off that son of a bitch. I bet he stole it himself when he heard us coming."

"He'd of said it was a dozen men," Brixton said. "You don't make up one fat man with a pistol in your face."

"It wasn't the James boys." Ed and Charlie Kettleman spoke in unison. Ed, older by two minutes, continued when his brother fell silent. "This is a piece off their range."

"The Renos neither," Riddle said. "They always work in a bunch."

"Turkey Creek," suggested Breed.

Brixton shook his head. "They always leave a dead man behind. That's how you know it's Turkey Creek."

Riddle said, "We sure as hell left a dead man behind at Council Bluffs."

"He committed suicide." Brixton threw a fistful of pennies against the wall, knocking a piece out of the adobe. "When I find out who the fat bastard is, I'll skin him and use his belly to carry away the cash."

"I bet he's local," Riddle said. "It costs them Mormons plenty to take care of all them wives. What you figure makes a man want more than one?"

"Maybe he done it to get out of the house." Once again, the Kettlemans spoke together, and fell to wrestling playfully. Breed put an end to it by sinking his Bowie up to its hilt in the rotten wood of the tabletop.

"One of us ought to go back into town and poke around."

Five pairs of alkali-reddened eyes swiveled toward Mysterious Bob. They were the first words he'd spoken since Denver.

"It's still all in one place," he said. "One man's easier to stick up than a whole freight company."

Nearing the middle of a spartan but comfortable bachelor's life, spent almost entirely within a brief streetcar ride of the house where he was born (which, like him, had stood through the fire among others that had not), Philip Rittenhouse discovered to his surprise that he quite liked traveling.

It posed its challenges. In the weeks since Allan Pinkerton had assigned him to investigate the robbery of the Wells, Fargo office in Sioux Falls, the bald man with the carrion-bird profile had put out fires in his clothes ignited by sparks from a dozen locomotives, cracked a tooth jouncing over the Bozeman Trail in a succession of stagecoaches (none of them the fabled Concord "Rocking Horse of the Plains"), been bitten by species of bedbugs unknown east of the Mississippi, and lost a valise containing his best suit to a thief in the train station in St. Louis. He was peeling from sunburn, shivering with the ague, and a suspicious fungus had begun to grow between the second and third toes of his right foot. A woman uglier than he, in a dirty satin dress, had called him "Phizzle-Face" when he'd declined her advances on the street in Kansas City, and an attack of food poisoning had forced him to crouch over a chamber pot all through the night he'd spent in Omaha. It was a splendid adventure. He intended to ask the old man to assign him more fieldwork once he'd lain this case to rest.

He'd been more bored in Chicago than he'd let on, even to himself. For years, those brief few moments of satisfaction he'd experienced upon the successful closing of an investigation had more than compensated for the hours, days, and weeks spent at his desk, clipping items out of newspapers, reading reports and telegrams, drafting responses, and maintaining stoic patience in the presence of minds slower by far than his own—turtle-brains, to be blunt; William Pinkerton, Allan's second son, was particularly chronic in this regard—but of late, as he'd come to realize that half his span was behind him, the prospect of merely repeating himself throughout the second half depressed him deeply. For the first time, he understood the motives of the men he'd brought to justice who had thrown over decades of good behavior for the lure of a dollar unstained by the sweat of honest labor. It amused him to consider that he, who turned down such harmless temptations as a free meal for his part in exposing a thieving restaurant employee, might have turned highwayman but for this opportunity.

There'd been no danger of that; he didn't even stray so

far as to enter a personal expenditure of a nickel into the account-book he kept for the agency. But he entertained himself with the conviction that he'd have made a criminal of the first rank. In order to apprehend one, it was important to understand his mental processes, and in effect to think more like a thief than a thief-taker. In this he had a decade of experience. Certainly, that approach had proven most useful during his interviews thus far in his journey.

Being of an honest temperament, Rittenhouse would most likely have become a senior file clerk in some business concern but for the chance encounter that had brought him to the attention of the nation's foremost detective. He never read a newspaper without a pen and a pair of shears close to hand, to underscore and remove items of interest for closer study, and the pigeonholes in his desk in Chicago were packed with lists he'd compiled of mundane details connected with larcenous events, compiled from reporter's accounts and replies to telegrams he'd sent requesting further information: calibers of firearms, the bandits' dress and idiosyncracies of speech and behavior, the nature of the containers in which spoils were carried away; there was no end to his patience with regard to such minutia, and he had a mesmerist's skill for gleaning data from witnesses who insisted at first that they'd been too preoccupied by personal danger to notice whether the robbers were right- or left-handed or what they wore on their feet. Nothing was without interest, and no observation too unimportant to record.

He applied this same thoroughness to his daily reading of out-of-town newspapers. While other agents satisfied themselves with a cursory examination of the criminal columns, Rittenhouse made it a point to scan the inside pages containing local advertisements, notices, and items of human interest. When the announcement of a visit by a group of itinerant actors calling itself the Prairie Rose Repertory

Company appeared in issues of both the *Kansas City Times* and the *Omaha Herald* reporting the robbery by a lone bandit of first the Farmers Trust Bank and then a livestock auction, he was alerted; when he learned that the Prairie Rose players had been present also at the time the Wells, Fargo office was struck (again by a man acting alone), he was committed. A close study of papers from Cheyenne, Wyoming, and Tannery, Nebraska, settled the question as far as Rittenhouse was concerned.

He was encouraged rather than put off by the variant descriptions of the robber involved in each outrage. Here he was tall and well-built, there thin and stoop-shouldered; elsewhere, he left the impression of an adolescent boy. He knew a little something about repertory players and their skill at playing one another's roles upon short notice, and from the more detailed reviews of the company's performances he was satisfied that the cast fulfilled all the body types mentioned in the criminal accounts, to wit:

> In the role of young Master Pip in Mr. Ragland's ingenious abbreviation of *Great Expectations,* Miss April Clay engagingly and convincingly reverses the Elizabethan conceit for placing young male actors in the guise of women. Had your correspondent not spoken with the lady in costume shortly before the curtain went up on last night's performance, he would have invoked Holy Scripture to maintain that the company had sneaked a boy into the cast, and unwittingly committed blasphemy.

So read the notice in the same number of the *Cheyenne Leader* that had reported the robbery of the Cattleman's Bank the previous evening. Rittenhouse wasn't put off by the robber's description, tall and rough-voiced. It would have been begging the question to present Miss Clay as a boy in both places. The company was bold, but not incautious.

Rittenhouse shared his certainty with no one, not even the old man. Pinkerton responded to his wire reports with querulous telegrams, demanding to know what in thunder he was doing wasting fares and accommodations visiting such flea specks on the map as Tannery, when his orders were clearly to begin his investigation in Sioux Falls. The fledgling field agent replied that all would be explained in the fullness of time, knowing the tightfisted old Scot would bite through his own lip before he'd incur the expense of withdrawing him and replacing him with a more easily intimidated subordinate. However, he knew also the boundaries of Pinkerton's patience, and conducted his business posthaste, seldom staying in one place overnight before moving on to the next location.

Marshal Fletcher of Tannery, Nebraska, was a man after his heart. An unprepossessing figure, fat and lethargic, and manifestly out of favor with the town council, which allowed him to remain in office only until an adequate replacement could be appointed, he impressed Rittenhouse with how quickly he'd acted to investigate the Prairie Rose the night the Planter State Bank was robbed. Although authorities in some of the other towns had taken the same course, none had done so with such alacrity, and still others had ignored the company entirely, choosing instead the standard action of assembling a posse of amateurs to go haring all over the countryside looking for incriminating tracks among the scores leading into and out of the city limits. Moreover, Fletcher remained confident about the propriety of his decision, even as he was at a loss to explain why a thorough search of the Prairie Rose's traps and possessions failed to turn up so much as a silver dollar that couldn't be accounted for. Asked for an inventory of what had been found, he produced a sheet from his desk, transposed in his own hand from notes taken by the deputies who'd conducted the search.

"I won't trouble you to return it," said the marshal. "I won't need it clerking at Pardon's store."

Rittenhouse thanked him, and rose to leave. At the door, he turned back and retraced his steps to give Fletcher his card.

"I can't promise anything," he said. "Mr. Pinkerton prefers his men fit."

"I expect Stella Pardon'll work some of the tallow off me." Fletcher stretched out an arm and tucked the card into the corner of the bulletin board next to the picture of Black Jack Brixton.

The detective reread the list frequently, riding in day coaches, hanging onto straps aboard the Butterfield, and resting his sore muscles on lumpy boardinghouse mattresses. None of the inventories he procured elsewhere was as exhaustive; Kansas City's was oral and vague, and in Cheyenne and Sioux Falls the actors had not even been questioned, let alone submitted to a search. Instinctively, he felt Fletcher's list contained the answer to the mystery that troubled him, keeping him awake even though he'd become inured to the bedbugs' torment and spoiling whatever appetite he'd developed for watery dumplings and chunks of undercooked chicken floating in curdled gravy. His quest for the solution wore the paper to pieces and continued to elude him long after he'd committed every item to memory: four large trunks; one army dispatch case; two train cases; six satchels, various sizes; one pr. duelling pistols; one Colt's revolver, .45 caliber; four fence foils; one bicycle; many, many items of clothing, each detailed within the limits of a frontier lawman's knowledge of such things; and etcetera.

Any one of the satchels could have been used to carry

away the money from those robberies where satchels were reported. The company seemed to prefer oilcloth sacks, but there was no mention of one on Fletcher's list. Even if there had been, it didn't explain just how they'd gotten the notes and gold and silver out of town. Whatever plan they used, it would be in place as well in the communities where they hadn't been searched; they could never be sure they wouldn't, and this was one gang that took no unnecessary chances. They might have buried it, but that would mean returning to the scenes of all their robberies, braving the very risk they'd taken careful steps to avoid the first time. This wasn't a bunch of guerrillas, shooting up the town and hollering and riding hell-for-leather into open country, saddle pouches stuffed with cash. The means to retrieve the spoils had to be as clever as the means they'd used to acquire them in the first place. For the first time in his career, Philip Rittenhouse was—well, *baffled*, as the sensational press often said of the police back East. It was an uncomfortable feeling, and of late he'd become enough of a connoisseur to assign it a rare vintage.

Pondering the problem again after his interview with the Wells, Fargo manager in Sioux Falls, he stopped to buy a copy of the *Deseret News* in a mercantile that carried several territorial newspapers. The stacked headlines had caught his eye:

DOUBLE OUTRAGE AT THE OVERLAND
FREIGHT OFFICE STRUCK TWICE IN A MATTER OF HOURS
SECOND BAND FORCED TO LEAVE EMPTY-HANDED
REIGN OF TERROR FOLLOWS
PERSONAL RECOLLECTIONS OF MANAGER OBERLIN

Sipping weak coffee—it might have been strong tea—in the window of a restaurant looking out on Main Street, Rittenhouse chuckled over the account of the hapless second gang's reaction upon finding they'd been outflanked by a rival. He strongly suspected they were Jack Brixton's Ace-in-the-Hole marauders. Salt Lake City was a plausible ride from Denver, where they were known to patronize Nell Dugan's Wood Palace; much good that did, with Nell's lips sealed as tight as her corset. He recognized Breed's description.

That was the old man's headache, with his obsession for protecting railroads, a frequent Brixton target. But he'd wire the office. There was no telling if anyone was reading the farther-flung papers in Rittenhouse's absence, and in any case Pinkerton wasn't likely to pay much attention to what happened at Overland. He'd written off stage companies as a vanishing source of income.

Turning the page, the detective was excited, but not much surprised, to read half a column about the presentation by the Prairie Rose Repertory Company of *The Legend of Sleepy Hollow* at the Salt Lake Theater.

He lifted his gaze across the street to rest his eyes from the dense print; at this rate he would soon need spectacles to read. He watched a dusty fellow in range attire lead his equally dusty mount up to a community trough, watched it plunge its muzzle into the water and suck.

Rittenhouse thought of his memorandum book then, and the notes he'd taken from newspaper accounts and eyewitness testimony concerning the robberies. He saw Marshal Fletcher's list, as clearly as if he hadn't discarded it when it had grown too tattered to read. He spilled his coffee, burning his hand. He let it blister. He knew how the thing had been done, and how it was still being done, as recently as Salt Lake City.

9

Charlie Kettleman got the job.

He was the obvious choice. Mysterious Bob's conversation skills were lacking, Tom Riddle was too loud and too deaf, Brixton's face was too well known, and Breed—apart from the fact he stuck out among all those Mormons like an ear of Indian corn in a tin of peaches—was far too likely to let his Bowie knife ask his questions. Charlie, who'd stayed outside to watch the horses, was the least likely to be recognized by the Overland manager. In addition, the Kettlemans were experienced negotiators who came away from the table with more than they brought. Charlie got a fresh mount from the corral behind the fallen-in stage stop and rode back into Salt Lake City to find out who had stolen the money that was properly theirs to steal.

He went to the Overland office first. That was the test. If the manager had happened to look out the window and could place him, he'd have to cut his losses and run. He tethered his horse in front and went inside, resting a hand on the Forehand & Wadsworth in his coat pocket.

"If you've come to rob me, you'll have to take a seat. I haven't had the chance to go to the bank."

Charlie hesitated. Then he saw the beaten look on the face of the man behind the counter, no recognition there, and knew he'd made a feeble joke. Charlie took his hand out of his pocket and drew the door shut behind him.

"I heard you had a run of bad luck. I just came to ask when the stage leaves for Ogden."

The glum-faced manager exhaled. Clearly, he was relieved to respond to a normal query from an ordinary customer.

"We canceled that route two years ago. You can take the Denver and Rio Grande straight through."

"Oh. It's been three since I was here last. My name's Cuthbert. Denver Mining Supplies." He stuck out a hand.

"Oberlin." The manager took it listlessly. "You rode here clear from Denver?"

Charlie was ready for that one. His horse could be seen through the window and there wasn't much he could do about the alkali dust on his clothes. "I rented a mount at the livery. I like to go out riding after sitting on a train."

"I didn't know Ike Gunther had horseflesh like that."

"I reckon I got all the luck intended for you." He moved on quickly. "I wonder you don't quit."

"I gave notice today. I'm only staying on to break in the new man, whoever he is. He better be Wild Bill. This country's gone to the devil."

"That's what I hear. Two gangs in one day."

"Well, the second was gang enough. The first time it was just one man."

Charlie whistled. "He must've been eight feet tall."

"He was as long as he had that big gun, as far as I'm concerned. Without it he was shorter than you, and twice as wide."

"Fat man, you say? He can't have got far on horseback."

"He doesn't have to since the railroad. Hop on in Denver or someplace, stop off in Salt Lake City, say, 'Stick 'em up,' then hop back on and ride all the way to San Francisco. Why spend money on board and feed when fares are so cheap? You're in the wrong business, Mr. Cuthbert. Mining's on its way out. Robbery's the coming thing, and you don't need riding lessons."

" 'Stick 'em up,' that's what he said? I thought folks only talked like that in the dime novels."

"Well, he never did. 'Hand over the swag,' that's what he said."

Charlie laughed. He was that surprised.

Oberlin's face darkened. "That's what he said. Like a pirate in a play."

From there, Charlie went to a barbershop and then a bathhouse, where he gave the boy a quarter to brush some of the Utah Territory off his clothes while he soaked the brine out of his skin, but all he overheard from the other customers were stories about the robbery of the Deseret Hotel and the shooting spree that had followed the unsuccessful raid on the freight office. Over a plate of fried chicken in a restaurant he heard a man had lost a finger and a dog its life, but he'd known that already. He learned Mormons were no better cooks than anyone else. That was all there was to get from the locals.

When he came out onto the boardwalk, picking pinfeathers from between his teeth, dusk had slid in. He wondered if he should ride back in the dark or take a room. Night riding was the worst part of being a desperado, but he couldn't be sure if Oberlin wouldn't check his story about hiring his horse from the livery and alert the town; lynch mobs scared him worse than Texas Rangers and mad Indians. He'd just about decided to mount up and leave when someone came down the street pedaling a bicycle.

Bicycles interested him. Back in Fort Worth, he and Ed had seen an advertisement in a catalogue and had discussed stealing a shipment somewhere and selling them to Comanches, but had abandoned the idea because Indians were suspicious of the wheel. He still thought there was profit in it, if robbery got too various and there was a way to do it without the stigma of legitimate commerce.

Instinctively, he dropped his toothpick and backed into the shadows as the rider passed. In the light coming through the window from the restaurant, it was a tall fellow in a cloth cap, heavy sweater, tan britches, and boots that laced to his knees. Charlie figured he was a telegraph messenger.

Charlie was about to turn away toward where he'd left his horse when the rider lifted his feet off the pedals and coasted to a stop next to the boardwalk. He alighted in front of a dry goods store, shut up and dark. There was no one there to accept a telegram.

The fellow got off, and something about the way he stood looking up and down the street moved Charlie to take another step back into the dark doorway behind him. He watched as the rider leaned his bicycle against the hitching rail and bend down over the watering trough in front of the dry goods. He turned his head left and right again, then tugged up one sleeve of his sweater, stuck a hand inside the water, groped around, and pulled out something heavy. Water ran off it in a sheet, splashing back into the trough. Oilcloth glistened.

Charlie couldn't believe his luck.

As the rider slapped the bundle into the wicker basket attached to his handlebars, Charlie stepped that way, taking the revolver out of his pocket.

His luck didn't hold. The restaurant door opened and someone came out, bumping into him from behind. "Beg pardon, brother."

He stuck the revolver back into its pocket. Startled by the sudden activity, the rider threw a leg over the seat, pushed off from the hitching rail, and began pedaling like mad. Charlie pushed the clumsy fool from the restaurant out of his way and took off in the other direction, sprinting toward where his horse was tethered.

"Gentile!" The man from the restaurant stalked off down the boardwalk.

The bicyclist was nowhere in sight when Charlie came back that way aboard his mount, but he held it to a canter. The salt flats threw back moonlight like a fresh fall of snow, and that single tire track made a dark line down the center of the road leading west of town, running parallel to the railroad tracks. He had the thing put together now; the man he was after wouldn't turn aside from that route.

Outside the city limits, he broke into a gallop. The bicyclist came into view, a vertical mark with reflected light from the great lake bouncing down from a sheet of cloud, bright as Abilene on Saturday night. Charlie drew the Forehand & Wadsworth and fired a shot high. It rang clearly in the dry air.

The bicycle wobbled. The driver twisted in his seat, then turned back forward, bent over the handlebars, and made the pedals whir. Clearly, this was not the fat fellow who'd held up the freight office, but Charlie wasn't confused. He didn't believe in lone bandits; there was always a silent partner somewhere, and usually several. He let the man gain a few yards, then smacked his reins across his horse's withers, took aim, and squeezed the trigger again. He didn't expect to hit the man, and he didn't, but the bullet must have struck close enough to remind him that a bicycle can't outrun a good horse. The rider went another ten feet at top speed, then slowed to a stop and got off. He let the bicycle flop over and stood on the side of the road with his hands raised.

Charlie was hauling back on the reins when one of the hands swung down. Something gleamed, but he didn't waste time trying to bring his own weapon around. He let go of it and launched himself out of the saddle. A hot wind smacked his ribs. His momentum snatched the man off his feet, they struck ground with a *woof,* and rolled over and over. It wasn't until Charlie had the man's gun arm pinned to the earth and his body trapped beneath his own weight that he realized he'd been wrestling with a woman.

"It *looks* like snow," April said, "but it isn't. Still, I'm cold. Explain that." She'd drawn on Katrina's shawl from *The*

Legend of Sleepy Hollow and paced the hardpack floor of the miner's shack hugging herself, and incidentally stealing glances at her fetching image in the window's single unbroken pane. Beyond it stretched the white flats, ending in an abrupt line where salt met black sky.

Major Davies took a pinch of snuff. "Self-mesmerization. Your brain tells your heart it's salt, but your heart is unconvinced. It's a condition of womanhood." He blocked a powerful sneeze and swept away tears with a handkerchief bearing someone else's initials.

"The other explanation is we're in a desert." Cornelius Ragland sat at the warped table, filling sheets of foolscap by coal-oil light and pausing to dip his pen. "It's a scientific fact that the grains are too loose to hold the day's heat. The result is the same whether it's sand or salt."

"Rubbish. If that were the case, I'd cool my soup by shaking salt into it rather than blowing on it. I am a man, ruled by my brain and not my heart. Therefore I'm not cold."

"You're fat," said April. "You ought to be hibernating. Look at Corny, shivering like a leaf. Does that make him a woman?"

"He's consumptive. When he isn't burning up with fever he's freezing."

"Actually, I'm neither. This is rather a stirring scene and I've let it get the better of me." He sat back, removed his spectacles, and wiped them on his sleeve.

April bent over the page before him. "What is it this time? Not Dickens, I hope. Except for old hags and insufferable little girls, all his women are simpletons. Lizzie's Miss Havisham blew my Estella clear off the stage."

"This one is an original story, based upon the tragedy of Joan of Arc."

She gasped. "Oh, Corny! I take back everything I've ever said about your acting. Will I get to bob my hair and wear a breastplate?"

"That will be up to Johnny. However, if we simulate the flames properly while you're burning at the stake, you'll have cover and time enough to slip out and hold up the Denver Mint."

As if he'd heard his cue, Johnny came in from outside and rubbed his hands above the chimney of the lamp. "Cold out there. You'd think it was snow and not salt."

"Rubbish!" The Major took snuff.

"Oh, Johnny, I'm going to play St. Joan!"

"Good God, Corny. Why not write about the Virgin Mary and make the challenge impossible?" He caught April's wrist in midswing. "No, dear. Smite the English."

The Major blew his nose. "What news?"

"Not a sign. She ought to be back by now." Johnny took off his coat, black broadcloth with three capes and a red silk lining. He'd seen a photograph of Irving wearing one like it and had had it made to his measure in St. Louis. He looked dashing in it, and with his long flaxen hair and moustaches a bit like a buccaneer.

April said, "You don't suppose she's been arrested."

"We always knew that was a possibility. Hers is the riskiest part of our plan."

"Your plan, not mine. A posse could be on its way here at this moment." She touched her throat.

"What of it?" asked the Major. "There's nothing here to incriminate us."

Cornelius laid down his pen. "She has the money. That's incrimination enough."

"Only for her."

Everyone looked at the Major, who shrugged. "She would say the same thing, if our situations were reversed. That's the solid foundation upon which our relationship rests."

"Are you two even married?" Johnny asked.

"We exchanged the necessary vows. However, I have my

doubts about the minister. He played Horatio for five weeks in Philadelphia."

"We're sitting hens if she peaches," said April, "or even if she does not. Someone is bound to recognize her, and the rest will follow. I've said all along we should include horses in our arrangements."

"I haven't been aboard a horse since Harrow."

Johnny said, "The Major's right, dear. He's too fat to ride, and Corny's too delicate. The more players we leave behind, the greater our chances of conviction and imprisonment. Even if you and I make the train, the authorities will just wire ahead. We'll be arrested at the next stop. It's our word against Lizzie's if it's just her, and something else if it's two against three."

April sighed. "A fine honorable lot of thieves we are."

Johnny laughed. "There's no honor anywhere. I've seen the other side." He unshipped his watch. "We'll give her half an hour, then start searching. Perhaps she fell and broke her leg."

Cornelius picked up his pen and dipped it. "Let us hold on to that hope."

Thirty minutes of silence followed, interrupted only by April's pacing and the scratching of Cornelius' pen. Johnny looked at his watch for the twentieth time, then snapped shut the face with finality. "Right." He threw on his coat.

The door opened then and Mme. Mort-Davies came in, pushing her bicycle. The front wheel was bent and her sweater was torn. The Major struggled to his feet. Johnny lifted the lamp, casting light on Lizzie's face. One eye was swollen almost shut and blood crusted her chin.

Johnny took the bicycle while April and the Major helped her into the Major's chair. Cornelius reached inside the picnic basket and gave Johnny the bottle of brandy they'd been saving to celebrate. Lizzie winced when she opened her lips to receive the bottle; the lower one split open afresh and trickled more blood onto her chin. She took two more sips, and between them reported what had happened on the road outside Salt Lake City.

"He got all of it?" demanded Johnny.

"He didn't offer to divide it. Search me if you like."

"Don't take offense. If you stole from us, you wouldn't stop at one day's profits. What about the Colt?"

She tugged up her sweater, pulled a small revolver from under the belt of her trousers, and gave it to him. "He took it, but I found that after he left; he lost it when he jumped off his horse. I'm afraid it wasn't much of a trade."

The Major asked if he'd assaulted her. She looked at him piteously.

"He knocked me to the ground, cut my lip, and blacked my eye."

"You know very well what I meant."

"No, Evelyn. I'm still the same unsullied girl you married."

"You were living with a fire-eater when we met."

"Don't think I don't miss that."

The Major balled his fists. "That fellow should be behind bars."

"So should we," said Johnny. "Did he say anything?"

"He said, 'Teats! Jesus Christ!' Either my disguise is better than I'd hoped or I'm not as comely as I once was."

"Is that all he said?" April asked.

" 'Hand over the swag.' "

Johnny's watch ticked loudly in the profound silence.

Lizzie smiled sourly, gasped, and touched her lip. "*Annabelle and the Pirate*. It brought down the house at the Metropolitan in Detroit in fifty-eight. They held us over ten days."

"Twelve," murmured the Major.

Johnny glared at him. "Just what did you say in the Overland office?"

"I don't remember."

"If you say anything at all, you say, 'Reach for the sky.' We rehearsed it."

"It's hackneyed."

"It's intended to be. Swag! By God! You might as well have appeared in full costume and handed the fellow a programme. You might have autographed it."

"What's the point in directing him now?" April said. "This is terrible, Johnny, terrible. If the manager told this—this bandit what the Major said, he's told everyone. We're found out."

"Quite likely." He walked over to the table and lifted one of the sheets Cornelius had written on, read for a moment. "This is good. I'm sorry we won't be able to use it this season."

"It needs work in any case. My French is rusty."

A whistle blew, drawn thin by distance. Lizzie pawed at her attendants and got up to help put the bicycle in its trunk. Cornelius found his wrench.

"We have a few minutes," Johnny said. "Major, the lantern."

A railroad lantern with a red lens was produced. Johnny lit it from the table lamp. "So much more convenient than waiting at the station," he said. "Ladies and gentlemen, it's been a successful tour. We're long past due for a holiday."

The Major blew out his moustaches. "There are no holidays in the theater. Except Sundays, of course. Lizzie and I haven't had Christmas off since the Coliseum burned down in Baltimore."

"I'm declaring one. I'd intended to, anyway, after Boise. We're carrying too much gold and paper to distribute among ourselves and in the strongbox and claim it as box office receipts much longer. The time has come to place it in a bank in Denver. Since we've demonstrated that none of us can be trusted to do it alone, we shall all go. I see no reason why we shouldn't spend some of it while we're there and entertain ourselves for a change."

April buttoned her traveling cloak. "Does this mean the end of the Prairie Rose?"

"Just for a season, while we cede the headlines to a more conventional breed of blackguard and brigand." He put on his soft black hat and smoothed the brim. "And then—"

"The show must go on," said the Major.

Johnny smiled. "If only you remembered all your lines as accurately."

10

We glide down Pike's Peak, bluer than the ocean beneath its white coronet, into a hurdy-gurdy metropolis of macadam and brick, teeming with surreys, streetcars, beer wagons, top hats, and spinning parasols, "O Susannah!" fiddling on the soundtrack, white letters with square serifs on the scrim: DENVER. Crowding in for a tight shot of the scripted legend on a sign, swinging crazily from chains attached to a porch roof trimmed in gingerbread, we remove our hats, pat down our hair, and prepare to enter the Wood Palace. We step back a moment to allow a burly party in shirtsleeves and handlebars to hurl a drunken saddle tramp out through the swinging doors, then join the customers inside.

The main room, two stories high and hung with a chandelier that doubles as a trapeze, features green baize gaming tables, a mahogany bar as long as the *Mayflower* and more cunningly carved, a stage, and a high ballustraded hallway with stairs cantilevering up to it; nymphs and satyrs randy about in oil on canvas at the top, bordered by bronze cherubim. All the tables are in use and none of the

six bartenders is idle. The usual chubby quartette gallops
in sparkling leotards onstage; if we strain our ears, we may
detect the anachronistic notes of a can-can. This is an entertainment after all, and not a historical tale.

We're just in time to see that high railing collapse and a
pair of battlers fall ten feet to the table beneath, demolishing it and interrupting a lively game of faro. Once again
the burly fellow goes to work.

We suspect, of course, that all this is staging. The Wood
Palace's real business is conducted behind the numbered
doors lining that second-story hallway. From one of them,
if our fortune continues (and this is the same as catching a
glimpse of Victoria passing through the Buckingham gate
in her coach), Nell Dugan may make an appearance before
the last drunk is swept out.

Late in life, when the laws of time and nature had packed
off with those physical charms that had made her a doubtful subject for serious journalism, Nell told a reporter from
the *Post* that she'd come to America at fourteen with just a
dollar and forty cents in her pocket. Matronly vanity gave
her license to pare six years off her age, and social discre-
tion to leave out mention of the letter of introduction she'd
sewn inside the lining of her shabby coat, addressed by the
mayor of Limerick to Michael McFee, president and principal stockholder of the Denver Topical Mining Company.

It was an arrangement of convenience for all three parties. The mayor's wife had become suspicious to the point
of certainty, and Nell had placed in safekeeping a number
of letters of an indiscreet character written to her in his
hand. McFee, a confederate of the mayor's before emigrat-
ing ten years before, lived like Vanderbilt so far as the
scale of life in the Colorado Territory could support, and
desired both a mistress and a taste of the companionship
of old Erin; Nell chafed at the restraints placed upon her
by a puritanical father and a farmer husband who stank

perennially of sod. "It was like going to bed in me own grave," she told the reporter, who recorded the remark in his notes but forebore to publish it. The mayor stood her passage to New York, McFee her train fare to Denver, where the question of her accommodations pivoted upon the impression she made. It was a gamble; but like any good gambler, she was well aware of the odds, and that they were in her favor. A photograph made at the time the article appeared in the *Post* suggests, beneath the folds of fat of a prosperous middle age, something of the stake she brought to the table at twenty. Forty years of good Irish whisky, half-dollar cheroots, and carnal calisthenics may thicken the waist and coarsen the skin, but can neither alter the impudent tilt of the nose nor dim the devil in the eye.

McFee was a gambler as well, and knew a good hand when it was dealt. He set Nell up as titular owner of a former boardinghouse on Holladay Street that had been converted first into a hotel for prospectors weary of canvas and thrice-boiled coffee, then into a saloon, and finally into a "melodeon"; a designation made popular by San Francisco, promising all the entertainments of a debauched civilization adrift in the wilderness. Opium could be consumed there, as well as liquor in the original bottles, women who did not smell like bacon fat and their last customer, keno and cards, and music by the best third-rate orchestras west of the Gaiety in Kansas City. It was a profitable enterprise, reducing the strain on McFee's pocketbook, and ran smoothly enough on its own to place Nell's charms at his disposal whenever his business affairs got the better of his nervous system. Seen in this light, his situation makes it difficult to look upon his untimely death as a tragedy.

"The Wood Palace" was a misnomer with a legitimate pedigree. Built of brick to comply with the new city ordinance requiring all new construction to be of sturdy, noncombustible material, it occupied the site of its original namesake, which had been swept away by a flood in 1864, rebuilt, and consumed by fire in 1870. It was one of the city's more enduring institutions, respected for its tradition of survival, if not for the nature of its business.

The Panic of '73—brought on by greed fueled by the economic boom following the Union victory in 1865— brought thousands of investors from private Pullmans down to shank's mare, without a penny for a streetcar, while the speculators who had precipitated it found themselves forced to order champagne of a less fashionable vintage. It was in this climate that Michael McFee paused to confer with his attorney before the offices of the *Denver Times,* which had libeled him, and interrupted his consulta- tion to greet a pedestrian who recognized him from the most recent stockholders meeting at the Denver Topical Mining Company. Following an exchange of pleasantries, the stockholder produced a pistol and shot him twice in the stomach. McFee died six weeks later, raving for ice water and oysters; his assailant, who turned out to be a former clerk fired by McFee's company, took a short drop through a trapdoor and broke his neck.

Nell was saddened, but alert. Through a lawyer, she pur- chased the Wood Palace outright from McFee's estate, and continued as she had, only now with full access to the profits, which she reinvested in the business, securing its reputation as the finest establishment of its kind on Hol- laday, a wide-open street in a wide-open town.

Among the improvements she added was a suite of rooms in the basement, accessible only by a trapdoor hidden beneath a heavy Persian rug in the back parlor, where tenants were accommodated in absolute secrecy, at rates that rivaled those of the Astor House in Manhat- tan. Although none of the legendary Astor luxuries was in evidence, highwaymen could rest there in relative com- fort while heavily armed men combed caves and barns the countryside over looking for them. Nell did not keep a guest book, but had she done so, the signatures of the outlaw luminaries who had taken advantage of her hospitality would have crowned the collection of any autograph hunter of sinister bent.

As a result of her double income, Nell Dugan was the wealthiest unattached woman in Denver. Her dresses were cut to her petite frame from organdy of a quality that came dear after the collapse of the cotton industry in the defeated South—deep purple was her color of choice at night, lavender during the day—and she wore peacock feathers in her thick auburn hair, her best feature, for public appearances at her establishment. She kept her creamy skin pale beneath a vast collection of parasols, and her carriage-and-pair were the envy of Denver's newly rich. She made it a point to take them out often, and to drop as much as a thousand dollars on a dubious hand at poker, her only addiction, by way of inspiring confidence in her clandestine guests; a woman of such conspicuous means was far less likely to turn them in for the reward than the storied prostitute with a heart of gold. It was a reality of frontier economics that internal organs assayed out at considerably less than twelve dollars per troy ounce.

While the spring runoff was floating miners' tents on the eastern face of the Rockies, the entire Ace-in-the-Hole Gang stayed dry snoring and playing poker (for stakes much lower than Nell's notorious "thousand-burners") in the hidden rooms beneath the Wood Palace. The money Charlie Kettleman had reclaimed from Mme. Mort-Davies made the stop affordable, and the fuss the gang had created in Salt Lake City made it imperative. The Pinkertons had never stopped looking for them in response to the robbery of the Chicago, Rock Island & Pacific, and the wire Philip Rittenhouse had sent Allan Pinkerton after reading of the Overland fiasco in the *Deseret News* had announced their recent whereabouts to the national press. That very day, agents of the Denver branch had searched the upper and lower stories and the basement storage rooms on the other side of four feet of solid masonry.

"You should of put a round in her." Black Jack Brixton threw in his cards.

Charlie raked in the pot. "What's the point? We got the money."

"It would of put her fat friend in some other line of work. Next time we open an empty safe I'll shut you up in it."

"That's my job," Ed Kettleman said. "He ain't your brother."

"If he was I'd dig up my mother and punch her in the mouth."

Tom Riddle listened to the conversation with a hand cupping one ear. "You told me your mother's alive."

"I'd shoot her and bury her first."

Charlie said, "I never busted a cap on a woman or a child."

"You never busted a cap on a bottle of Old Gideon," Ed said. "You couldn't hit a three-hundred-pound Chinaman with a scattergun."

"Amateurs got to be discouraged," said Brixton. "You kill a man's woman, it takes the fight right out of him."

Ed shuffled the deck. "You ought at least to put the boots to her before you let her go, or brung her back for the rest of us. I do like to shinny up a tall woman."

"She had a face like Tom's bay mare."

"What's that? It was dark, weren't it?"

Breed said, "We going to jabber or play cards?" He was down a hundred and fifty.

"That bay mare's a good ride," said Tom, who'd only half heard what Ed said. "I ate the best horse I ever had in California. One time—"

"Jacks or better." Ed dealt. "You know, there's a mint

right here in town. I don't reckon them James-Youngers ever bought into a pot that big."

Brixton said, "That's because the federals got the whole army guarding it. This bunch can't even stick up Mormons."

"We got the money," Charlie reiterated.

"I don't appreciate being made to look the fool. You should of at least found out who the fat man was that got there first. We could of rendered him down and ate him with onions."

"I ate an injun once," Tom said. "He might've been a half-breed, meaning no offense to the breed present. California, it was. We'd been out prospecting—"

"Shut up, Tom," said the others in unison.

Ed said, "You could leave out California and make your stories shorter. Everything you done was in California before you joined up with us. What made you leave in the first place?"

A chorus of oaths followed this injudicious query. A hail of red chips bounced off Ed's slack-jawed face.

"There's a story behind that," Tom said. "It was up around Eureka; coldest place I ever been. Don't let no one ever tell you California don't get—"

"Why *not* the mint?"

Even Tom fell silent, waiting for Mysterious Bob's next remark. Bob, who disliked poker for the conversation required, sat on one end of a brocaded settee, most of whose springs were at odds with one another, lubricating an unidentifiable component of his Winchester with an oily rag. All the other parts were spread out on the cushions.

"I been fighting the army a dozen years, same as you," Brixton said. "They don't beat."

"New gold, that's all they care about." Bob traded the odd-shaped part for the barrel and peered inside. "I always wondered how those boys got paid, the workers and soldiers and such. You reckon they just scoop it out of the bin?"

Charlie said, "That'd make too much sense. The government don't work that way. They send it out from Washington, same as at Fort Lincoln."

"How do you know how the government works?" Ed asked. "You voted for Greeley."

Bob ignored Ed. "How you reckon they send it?"

"How's anybody send anything?" Charlie's face changed. "Holy Christ."

Breed looked up, frozen in the act of stealing a card from Tom's deadwood. "Goddamn."

"By train," said Brixton, who'd forgotten whose bet it was.

Bob began swabbing the inside of the barrel. He'd used up his conversation for the week.

We who are privileged to sources not available to historians and the makers of legend can enjoy the frisson of knowing that while the Ace-in-the-Hole Gang was planning what scholars argue might have been the most spectacular train robbery in American history, two-fifths of the Prairie Rose Repertory Company were enjoying the more celebrated diversions on the second story of the Wood Palace, two floors above their heads. Johnny Vermillion, looking more Byronic than usual with his shirt unbuttoned halfway down his smooth, hairless chest, greeted Cornelius Ragland from the depths of a tufted velvet chair in the sitting room of his temporary suite over a glass of Napoleon from Nell Dugan's cellar, which had recently been swept clear of Pinkertons. "Congratulations," he said. "I was afraid you'd succumbed."

Cornelius blushed and filled a glass from the decanter. "Only to conversation, which is quite as expensive as the other. Not that I'm consumptive; just weak. My father was a butterfly and my mother a wisp of smoke."

"You ought to write that down."

"It seems to me I did. Do you know I've submitted poetry and stories to every periodical in North America without a single acceptance? That requires talent." He slumped onto a divan with part of the Bayeaux Tapestry wrought in the maple frame. "You're the only man on God's fertile earth who hasn't tried to convince me I was born to be a secretary."

"You're a born thief. It's a natural mistake."

"I'm serious, Johnny. You're the first person in my life to look at me and not through me. If you told me to assassinate the Czar of Russia, all I'd ask is what method you preferred."

"A bomb, naturally. The only socially acceptable way of destroying an emperor is to blow him to smithereens. I often wonder where the Smithereens may be. In the Scottish Highlands, I suspect."

"You're drunk, Johnny. I've never seen you this way."

"You should have known me in Chicago."

The hall door opened and Major Davies tottered in. He wore his morning coat and his necktie was in disarray. Without preamble he plunked himself down beside Cornelius.

"You're as red as a radish," Johnny observed. "I thought you were back at the hotel with Lizzie."

"She's gone shopping with April. I left a note that I was going for a walk."

Cornelius said, "She'll see through that. You haven't walked more than ten feet from one chair to another since you joined the troupe."

"What you young single fellows don't understand is the stability of a seasoned marriage. She'll forgive me. Is that sherry?"

"Brandy. Pour him one, will you, Corny? I haven't any smelling salts."

The Major accepted a glass and drained it. "Mother's milk. I have a grand constitution, never fear. I shall be ready to rejoin the battle in thirty minutes."

"I only have this room for another fifteen. At this rate you'll be impoverished in a week."

"I doubt that. Lizzie keeps the books. Have you seen to-day's *Post*?" The Major patted his pockets, withdrew a fold of newsprint, and sailed it into Johnny's lap.

He unfolded it. It was torn from the front page and contained an account of that day's Pinkerton raid on the Wood Palace. A paragraph described the Ace-in-the-Hole Gang's reign of terror in Salt Lake City. Johnny finished reading and held it out for Cornelius to take. "I'd wondered what those fellows were about. I confess it gave me pause until I realized they had no interest in me or Corny."

Cornelius returned the scrap to the Major. "Lizzie had a near thing. Brixton's men are rough customers."

"Next time, one of you can ride the bicycle, or April. She's more accustomed to carrying a firearm than my dear Lizzie."

"We'll discuss it," Johnny said. "At least we can rest assured Black Jack and his gang aren't here."

Brixton dreamed he was back at Lone Jack, facing the entire Yankee cavalry with two empty pistols and no cartridges on his belt. He awoke with a yell and staggered out of his room to find Breed and the Kettlemans playing three-handed stud and Bob putting his carbine back together. "Where's Tom?"

Breed said, "He went upstairs for a drink. He said that badger hole in California ruined him for tight places."

"Why in hell didn't nobody stop him?"

"It's just so damn peaceful with him gone," Charlie said.

"Go fetch him. Anyone recognizes him, we'll ride our next train in irons."

"Deal me out." Charlie threw in his hand and rose.

"Don't *you* get recognized," Brixton called after him.

Charlie found Tom leaning against the wall just inside the bat-wing doors to the street, smoking a cigar. "Jack says come back. He got up on the wrong side."

"He went to bed on the wrong side. Let me finish my smoke first."

"Me, too, then. Nell's scared we'll set the place on fire we light up down there." Charlie got out his makings and rolled a cigarette. "What's the fight about?"

On the boardwalk in front of the building, a tall woman in a flat straw hat and a big bustle stood with her back to them, waggling a finger in Clyde Canebreak's big polished black face. Clyde, in his bright red Zouave tunic, greeted customers at the door and threw out undesirables, often two at a time.

"The old lady says her husband's inside, wants to talk to him. Clyde ain't having any."

"She ought to be happy he's still got lead in his pencil."

"I reckon she likes to have him do all his scribbling at home."

Clyde laid one of his coal-scuttle hands on the woman's shoulder and turned her gently aside from the door, toward the carriage she had waiting. Charlie recognized the gold device of the Coronet Hotel on the door.

He saw her face then. The match he'd lit stung his hand. He cried out and dropped it.

She started at the noise and looked his way. The blood slid from her face in a sheet.

11

Really, Lizzie," Johnny said, "this is a domestic matter between you and the Major. There was no reason to pull us all out here. Miss Dugan doesn't approve of messages from outside. I'm surprised you were able to talk Clyde into it."

"It cost me a double eagle. It was the first thing that came into my hand when I reached inside my bag."

They were seated in a private room at the Auraria Restaurant, the entire troupe gathered around a table cloaked in crisp linen and shimmering with silver. A heap of freshly opened mussels steamed in an enormous tureen in the center. April, fetching in a powder-blue suit she'd bought that afternoon, fretted. "*My* message was waiting for me at the hotel desk. None of us even had time to change for dinner."

"I wouldn't care if you were naked." Lizzie was in an agitated state. "I saw him."

The Major said, "My dear, you've drawn the wrong conclusion. I went to that place merely for male cameraderie. You have always been more than woman enough for me."

"Forget about yourself for once, you old goat. I don't care where you drop your seed or with whom. It was the lying I came to protest. You haven't gone out for a walk since the war with Mexico. The man I saw today was the man who knocked me down in Salt Lake City and stole our money."

Johnny put down his mussel shell still containing its prize and wiped off his fingers with his napkin. "Where?"

"At the Wood Palace. Why did you think I sent you that note?"

"I thought perhaps you were hungry. You're certain it was him? The description you gave that night was quite general."

THE ADVENTURES OF JOHNNY VERMILLION 303

"I haven't Corny's talent for word pictures. But I trust my eyes. Moreover, he recognized me. I saw it in his face."

Johnny said, "You mean to say he just stood there, a wanted man, knowing you could identify him to the nearest police officer?"

"I mean to say he darted away like a sparrow, taking his companion with him, a short fellow with a wizened face. I'm sure they went to report to their accomplices. That's why I sent that note and hurried here. My driver carried April's message back to the Coronet."

"Nell must have a priest's hole of some kind to conceal their like," said Cornelius. "But Denver is a big place, and they haven't the freedom to mount a search. They wouldn't know where to begin looking."

"I had the carriage from the hotel," Lizzie said. "I'm sure he saw it."

"Johnny!"

He patted April's hand. "There is every reason for optimism, and none for panic. These road agents are more frightened of us than we are of them. That's why they fled at the sight of Lizzie. They *have* the money. What else could they want from us?"

Lizzie said, "He knows I can identify him. You said so yourself. They'll murder me to prevent me from turning them in for the reward."

The Major sucked out a shell and daubed at his moustaches. "We've been overlooking an opportunity, and Lizzie has placed her finger square upon it. We should notify the authorities immediately and collect the reward for the whole gang."

Johnny said, "I question the wisdom of making ourselves too familiar with law enforcement. We're fugitives ourselves, don't forget. In any case those bounties are seldom paid in full, and we'll have made ourselves notorious for something less than we might remove from a safe in some fat mining town or cattle camp with a servicable theater."

"Guerrillas are territorial," Cornelius pointed out. "We pricked their pride in Utah. If they haven't forgotten the war in nine years, I doubt they'll have forgotten us in a few weeks. Lizzie isn't the only one who's in danger of their revenge."

The party fell into a grim silence while a waiter entered, removed the course, and glided out of the room.

"This changes nothing about our plan for a holiday, apart from the venue," said Johnny then. "We'll draw what we need from the bank for living expenses and separate. We'll meet again in Wichita and launch the fall season."

"Absolutely not." April set down her wineglass with a thump. "Cowboys pinch and grope and belch whiskey. They do everything but bathe."

"They also spend money as if it were grass," Johnny said. "Other rowdies, when they see something they approve of onstage, throw pennies; cowboys throw silver dollars. Sometimes more. In Amarillo, Lotta Crabtree fished a poker chip out of her bodice after a performance and redeemed it for a hundred dollars."

"I've seen Crabtree," said April. "She could fit the table stakes and the dealer in there as well."

"Do I detect a shade of green?" asked Lizzie.

"We can't all be cows."

Madame's cheeks colored. The Major choked, coughed, and spat a stuffed mushroom into his napkin.

"Dear me," said Cornelius, who preferred writing scenes to experiencing them.

"Yes. Separate holidays are best." Johnny sipped from his glass. "Shall we order dessert?"

* * *

Someone tapped three times at the door to the underground suite, paused, and tapped again.

"That's Charlie and Bob." Ed Kettleman got up to unlock the door.

His brother came in first, unhooking the wire-rimmed spectacles he believed provided an impenetrable disguise. An old photograph he and Ed had unwisely posed for in a studio in El Paso was floating around Texas, and although it had yet to appear on wanted posters circulated nationally, the spectacles came out whenever he separated from the gang, in case he ran into a lawman visiting from the Lone Star State. Mysterious Bob, known principally by his description, merely bent his legs to dissemble his height and put on a dirty bowler hat he'd shot a carpetbagger out from under in Dodge City. Together they looked like a pair of drummers no one wanted to buy anything from.

There was a general rattle of firearms being taken off cock and returned to their holsters; Ace-in-the-Hole hadn't much faith in such things as passwords and secret knocks.

"Put one in her this time?" Brixton was sawing at a longhorn steak with Breed's big Bowie and angry energy. The bill of fare at the Wood Palace posed no threat to Delmonico's, despite charging two dollars for a bowl of oxtail soup (twenty-five cents extra for evidence of an oxtail).

"She checked out," Charlie said; and yelled when the Bowie stuck in the lath-and-plaster six inches to the right of his head.

Ed said, "There ain't no call for that, Jack. He went soon as you told him."

"He's lucky Breed didn't throw it. I'm out of practice. He should of shot her when she was in range."

Breed put down his bottle of Old Pepper and got up to jerk his knife out of the wall. "You probably bent it cutting up that steak." He examined the blade.

"I couldn't shoot the old bat in the street," whined Charlie. "We'd be up to our ass in law."

"Nell's rules," Tom Riddle reminded Brixton, over a game of patience. "No trouble in the Palace."

"She didn't say nothing about out front."

Bob spoke up. "She weren't checked out yet when we got to the hotel. We talked to the carriage man, he said he dropped her at the Auraria Restaurant. We missed her there, and when we went back to the hotel, she'd checked out."

Brixton hauled out his big American revolver. Ed and Charlie scrambled for cover. Mysterious Bob scooped up his Winchester and levered a round into the chamber. "Hold on, Jack."

"If you two didn't have pig shit for brains, you'd of split up and covered both places."

"I needed Charlie along to point her out. If I went around shooting every tall old ugly woman I seen in hotels and train stations, I'd run out of shells."

"He's right, Jack." Charlie crouched behind the settee, covering Brixton with the Colt he'd taken from the old woman. His hand shook.

Tom Riddle said, "Let's all put up our irons now." He'd drawn his Remington.

When every muzzle was lowered, Brixton returned to his meal. "You at least get her name?"

"Elizabeth Mort-Davies," Bob said. "One of them two-part names, like that Englishman we strung up in Dry Gulch. You want to know who she checked in with?"

"If it was Ulysses S. Grant, I hope to hell you shot *him*." But Brixton put down the bone he'd been gnawing like a gaunt old wolf. Bob had never talked so long nor with anything close to enjoyment.

"Man named Davies. I reckon he's her husband. He's fat, the clerk said."

"Fat like the man stuck up the Overland office in Salt

Lake City?" Breed wiped his knife on his pants, smearing them with grease and plaster.

Bob ignored him; the only man in Breed's experience to do so.

"They weren't alone, neither," Charlie said.

He was the center of attention then. He was standing now, the Colt dangling at his side. You never knew when Black Jack would flare up again, like a heap of ashes in a campfire.

He said, "They're running with a bunch of actors. They all checked out at the same time. Waiter at the restaurant said they ate there together."

"Horseshit," said Brixton. "No bunch of actors ever stuck up no place. Whores and pansies."

"Shut up, Jack," Tom said.

A terrible quiet followed, like the space between a flash of lightning and the roar of thunder; but there was no thunder. Of all the members of Ace-in-the-Hole (except, perhaps, Mysterious Bob), Tom Riddle was the least likely to be shot by any of the others, even Brixton. It would have been like stopping a church bell. The awful empty silence that came after would have driven them all mad.

Tom alone appeared unmoved by his breach of outlaw etiquette. "Let's hear the rest, Charlie."

"They call themselves the Prairie Rose," Charlie said. "I wasn't sure I heard it right, so I made the clerk say it again. I remembered, on account of I heard folks talking about them that day in Salt Lake City. They pulled out right after the Overland was hit."

Brixton swallowed a piece of gristle and chased it down with Old Pepper. "They hit other places too, to be staying at the Coronet and eating at Auraria. They won't be hard to track. Those outfits cover the country with shinplasters telling folks they're coming and the papers write about them after they leave."

Tom said, "They're spooked now. They'll scatter to cover and stay there."

"They'll herd up again, just like we done. Gold don't go so far since the war."

Ed Kettleman said, "What good's tracking them? I never saw where they're wanted no place. They're probably selling us to the marshal right now. That rug won't keep the Pinkertons out of that trapdoor twice. We're the ones on the run."

"That's part of it," said Brixton. "They owe us for what we didn't get from that payroll train we didn't rob."

Breed scowled, looking exactly like the woodcut on his poster. "I want their hides as bad as you, but there ain't no market. They can't carry what they stole around with them any more'n we can. They've buried or banked it, or spent it same as us."

"Who said anything about taking it out of their hides? We'll just follow them around like we do trains and hit them next time they take on a big load. We don't have to worry about the Pinkertons or the law." He laughed. "Hell, it might not even be illegal. Just like milking a cow."

"Then we butcher it for the side meat," Breed said.

"Well, sure. I'm surprised you had to say it."

They arranged to take three separate trains spaced out over two hours and avoid gathering in a group at the station. Farewells were brief, with April and Lizzie embracing swiftly to indicate that all rancor was past and the men shaking hands. No personal plans were discussed, again by mutual consent, in order to prevent anyone from betraying the others' movements under duress.

"*The Merry Wives of Windsor,* I think, in the fall," Johnny said to Cornelius at parting. "We must acquiesce to the Major's superstitions, and you have to agree that

Twelfth Night started us off splendidly last season. Do you think you can winnow it down without inviting the Bard's vengeful ghost?"

"The merry *Wife,* perhaps?" The playwright's smile was sad; and then he was gone.

Somewhat to his surprise, Johnny realized he'd miss him most of all. The former secretary's awkward expressions of gratitude and loyalty at the Wood Palace, however inspired by the pleasure of conversing with whores, had moved him to an emotion he'd thought had died on Blue Island.

The Major and the Madame departed with all the pomp and fustian of exiled royalty, he popping his silk hat and directing the cabman with his stick like a concert conductor, she fretting aloud about the fate of the bags they'd sent on from the hotel. "San Francisco would be my guess," April told Johnny, waving as they rattled off. "*The Diplomat Deposes* and petty larceny the whole way."

"Just so long as the old ham doesn't try to hold anyone up at gunpoint," said Johnny.

To confuse pursuers, Johnny and April were traveling together to Colorado Springs as Mr. and Mrs. John McNear of Chicago. There, they would separate and proceed to their chosen destinations.

On their way to the station, Johnny had their driver stop twice to let him out on errands. The first stop lasted just long enough for him to hand a cash deposit to the clerk at the storage facility where they'd sent their theatrical costumes and properties on from Boise when their plans to play that city had changed. The second was longer, and he did not confide its purpose to April, who sat twirling her parasol irritably, then in alarm at the thought that he might have been waylaid. She started when he leapt back in beside her, and would have set her sharp tongue to work had he not held out a small square parcel wrapped in cloth-of-gold with a scarlet ribbon.

"The shade's a bit off," he said. "I asked for vermilion."

"If it's a key to your sleeping compartment, I shan't accept."

"It might have been in St. Louis. Those chivalrous buffoons I've been playing have had their effect upon my deportment in general."

"A few more, perhaps. There's still a bit of shanty Irish in your *g*'s."

"I hope to correct that over these next few months." He waggled the parcel.

She took it then and twitched loose the bow. Inside the pasteboard box was a container shaped like a miniature humpback trunk, covered in green velvet. "Oh, Johnny," Her tone was dubious.

"Opening it does not imply commitment."

She tipped back the hinged top. The garnet inside was the deep red of pigeon's blood, set in a band of twenty-four-karat gold (she knew her precious metals) with a delicate filigree.

"I had my mind set on a ruby," he said, "but they paled in comparison."

She snapped the lid shut with a smile. "I cannot, of course. Please take this advice for the future, as you might from a sister. Proposals are made with diamonds. This is for the wedding ceremony."

Johnny laughed. "Good God, woman! Don't confuse me with the parts I play. If we're to carry off the act of man and wife, we'll need a convincing prop."

She exhaled, relieved. "Take no offense," she said. "I'm fond of you. I loathed casting you in the role of disappointed suitor. Such a wasteful extravagance to fool a ticket clerk and a conductor."

Their driver cleared his throat loudly.

"One more moment, my good man." Johnny lowered his

voice. "I'd be inclined to agree, if it were them only. The concierges of London and Paris are far more sophisticated."

She stared at him with eyes like hazel planets.

"I don't know your plans," Johnny said. "If you could postpone them without serious inconvenience, I thought perhaps we might discover for ourselves whether the capitals of the Old World are as corrupt as the ones we know. Allow me." He unbuttoned her left glove and slipped it off.

She hesitated, then slid the ring onto the third finger. It was a snug fit, most flattering. "When you put it that way, I don't see how a lady can refuse."

As this pretty scene was playing itself out in Denver, rapid fingers were tapping on copper keys, sending messages streaking back and forth in high-pitched staccato surges along wires strung across fifteen hundred miles of desert, prairie, and crowded metropolis:

ALLAN PINKERTON
PINKERTON NATIONAL DETECTIVE AGENCY
CHICAGO ILL
WELLS FARGO TRAIL ENDS HERE STOP AM
SATISFIED IDENTITY PERSONS REPEAT PERSONS
RESPONSIBLE STOP REPORT ON WAY U S MAIL STOP
FOR REASONS EXPLAINED THERE THINK UNLIKELY
APPREHEND BEFORE FALL EARLIEST STOP SUGGEST
RETURN CHICAGO UNTIL THEN STOP PLEASE
ADVISE
RITTENHOUSE

PHILIP RITTENHOUSE
DESERET HOTEL
SALT LAKE CITY U T

RETURN NEXT TRAIN STOP TRUST REPORT
EXPLAINS NO BOARDINGHOUSES AVAILABLE THERE
PINKERTON

The detective took one last look at Salt Lake City through
the window before the train began rolling, after that first
curious backward lurch, as if it were as reluctant as he to
be heading back the way he'd come. He thought it unlikely
he would ever be that far west again. His adventure had
ended. Wherever his investigations led from there, genuine field agents would follow.

He swung down the patented Pullman footrest and settled in to read. He'd bought a copy of that day's *Deseret
News,* and seldom ventured anywhere without his pocket
edition of Tennyson bound in soft calfskin, but he left
them on the vacant seat next to his and slid the folded programme out of his inside breast pocket. A woodcut of an
obstreperous-looking rose decorated the front. He opened
it to read the one-line descriptions of the acts and scenes
of *The Legend of Sleepy Hollow,* adapted by Cornelius
Ragland from the story by Washington Irving, and the
names of the characters and cast. Once again, he drew out
his memorandum book and compared the names to the
list he'd made in his own hand. Next to each name was
penciled the initials of a city where the Prairie Rose had
played, based upon the description of the thief in the
armed robbery that had taken place there. Now he un-
capped his pencil and wrote SLC next to Major Evelyn
Davies. Then he put everything away and closed his eyes
to sleep.

III

The
Grand Tour

12

The 1875 London social season began splendidly for the pilgrims from America, with more invitations than they could possibly accept during their six-week stop, and ended on a sour note, with a challenge to a duel.

The S.S. *Columbian* docked at Gravesend in calm weather, at the end of three days of rough seas that left Johnny Vermillion grateful for the support of the fine alderwood stick he'd bought in New York City and April Clay powdered more artfully than usual to conceal a gray pallor. She had, nevertheless, been a popular dancing partner for many of the male passengers during balls, and Johnny had charmed the ladies over games of whist. They went directly from the boat train to the Langham Hotel in London and registered as Mr. and Mrs. John McNear of Chicago, U.S.A. The suite included gas fixtures, a bath with running water, a magnificent Regency four-poster bed, and a divan in the sitting room for Johnny to take his rest while April slept behind lock and key with her little Remington beneath her pillow.

This last was the only condition she'd imposed, and since her arm in his improved his social opportunities every time they appeared in public, he honored it without protest. Their arrangement had already furnished him with one shipboard liaison while the woman's husband was engaged at poker in the main salon; the absence of a romantic commitment spared Johnny chagrin at April's own conquest of a commander of the British Empire that same night. At breakfast the next morning they celebrated each other's success with champagne cups.

To those who'd heard it before, the name McNear was vaguely associated with power in the great Midwestern city whose beef graced many an English sideboard. Because politics and trade were forbidden topics of discussion in a class whose estates had benefited from investments made during the American Civil War, neither Johnny nor April had been required to utter a single untruth about their livelihood. This was a relief, since to confess to a background in the theater would hardly be more disastrous than to account for their activities in banks, express offices, and pursers' cabins over the past year. Whatever small gaucheries they committed in their new company were applied to their Yankee pedigree: "Quite charming, don't you know, and neither of them appears to chew tobacco."

In private, the couple made sport of their late acquaintances as they had their victims in the cities and hamlets out West.

"They're as witless as bullwhackers beneath the accents," Johnny had confided over that congratulatory breakfast. "One wonders if their cashiers and clerks are as ripe to pluck."

"Shopkeepers and clarks, dear." April pouted. "Don't forget, we're on holiday. And Scotland Yard is not a citizens' posse."

"You're right, of course. How old Scipio Africanus would chuckle to learn I've become a slave to my profession."

"It's time you emerged from his shadow. You're a better thief than ever he was."

"A successful run depends upon a talented cast; the leading lady above all."

They clinked glasses.

The connections they'd made at sea had provided them with introductions to West End society, and also created the necessity to drape themselves properly for garden parties, shootings on weekends, and evenings at the opera. They learned quickly that what was considered the zenith of fashion in St. Louis and Denver had had its season when Gladstone was at Downing, and that high collars, round lapels, and prominent bustles had become inexpressibly provincial under Disraeli. Standards (such as those that governed adultery) were relaxed during the transition of an ocean voyage and reinstated rigidly in Westminster. Johnny spent his first full day in London on Praed Street, being measured for morning dress and tails and wardrobes for both city and country, while April consulted a Regent Street seamstress among yards of taffeta and bolts of Chinese and Italian silk. Parcels and hatboxes piled up in their suite and their memorandum books filled with appointments for additional fittings.

The days sped past. April, striking in a new scarlet habit, took riding lessons in Hyde Park; Johnny shot at grouse at Fulham and clipped the elbow off a marble statue of Hermes; April saw a Russian grand duchess in a portrait in the British Museum whom she insisted was her fabled grandmother; Johnny lost his watch at darts in a public house on Northumberland; April dined at Simpson's with the third son of a baron and returned to the hotel the following morning to find the suite filled with carnations; Johnny sprained an ankle jumping from a balcony adjoining a married lady's boudoir in Kensington. They toasted and commiserated over kippers and tea, laced with cognac from a hammered silver flask Johnny had bought from a peddler in the Tottenham Court Road.

"What did you *say* to him?" She leaned forward eagerly.

" 'Well, which is it? Irving or Henry?' "

She laughed, turning heads at the restaurant as toward a fresh breeze through crystal pendants.

He looked rueful. "I'd overimbibed a bit. I daresay I won't be invited back to the Garrick, and I may strike Irving's name off my list of professional contacts."

"Poor dear. I'm afraid you've had the short end of things."

"Not a bit of it. I came to Europe for adventure and the old girl hasn't let me down."

His next encounter with Old World customs dampened his taste for exploits.

Johnny and April attended *Lohengrin* at Covent Garden; and more than a few pairs of opera glasses turned their way when they entered their box. Her fuschia gown was a flicker of rose flame and his black cutaway and snow-white waistcoat called attention to his broad shoulders and narrow waist. At intermission, he excused himself to seek lemonade for them both, but did not return until the lights were lowering for the second act. His face was nearly as pale as his collar and he was empty-handed.

"What's happened?" she whispered.

He looked at her in silence for a moment, then gave a short hollow cough of a laugh. "I saw a woman of my acquaintance in the foyer—and her husband, whom I did not know. It seems we're to meet with pistols tomorrow at dawn."

"Oh, Johnny!"

"Where the devil is Hampstead Heath, anyway?"

April said, "I don't understand why we don't simply cut short our visit and sail to France."

They were riding in a hired brougham through the predawn damp. He wore his caped overcoat, she an embroidered shawl over a white dress. A cold mist condensed into drops on her opened parasol, white also.

"The husband is something in shipping," said Johnny. "He'd have me pulled down the gangplank and shot under the blasted rules of chivalry."

"Next time you seduce a married woman, make sure you're not on an island."

"You're in awfully good spirits considering you're about to become a widow."

"Perhaps you'll win."

"The only way that could happen is if I shot at something else and hit him by accident. No statue is safe when I take aim at a bird just released from a trap." He tapped the driver's seat with his stick. "Stop here. I'll walk the rest of the way."

"Go on, driver. You know very well I can't walk far in these heels."

"Stop, I said. I'm doing the walking. You're riding back to the hotel. I don't know why I let you talk me into bringing you this far. Women don't attend duelling matches."

"I don't see why not. We're the cause of most of them."

The driver slowed the horses to a walk and twisted in his seat. "Which is it?"

"Stop."

"Go. I won't get out, Johnny, and you'll be late for your appointment. What do the blasted rules of chivalry say about that?"

"Oh, drive on. The least you could have done was put on something less conspicuous. When the sun comes up you'll stand out like a field of lilies."

"I should hope so. It's such a dour day. Where do you want to lunch?"

"Buckingham Palace. Or on top of the Albert dome, if you prefer. I'll have wings by then."

"Perhaps we'll dine in the suite. Ah! Here we are. Good luck, Johnny." She presented her cheek.

He took her face between his palms and kissed her on the lips. "Good-bye."

As he struck off through the wet grass toward where the party awaited him, she opened her reticule and repaired the damage to her makeup. Then she swung open the door.

"You'd best stay here, missus," said the driver. "You never know which way them balls will fly."

"Isn't that the truth?" She stepped down and lifted her hem clear of the mud. As she approached the slight rise where the men stood—Johnny, the aggrieved husband, his second, the man who'd volunteered to attend Johnny, and a tall, sallow-faced fellow carrying a doctor's bag—the sun broke over St. Pancras and the rain stopped. She folded her parasol.

The movement caught the attention of the men on the rise, who turned their heads her way and began gesturing animatedly.

". . . absolutely irregular . . ."

". . . rules . . ."

". . . no restrictions . . ."

"Yellow cad."

This last, from the husband, reached her ears all in one piece, unbroken by the open distance. Johnny made no response, but as no one approached her she assumed the controversy of her presence was settled.

Johnny selected a long-barreled pistol from a box in the hands of the husband's second and made a show of testing its balance and accuracy, raising it to shoulder level and holding it at arm's length, sighting along it; bits of business straight out of the third act of *The Count of Monte Cristo*. The husband, obviously unfamiliar with the production, seemed hesitant at this display of expert knowledge, but then Johnny spoiled the effect by dropping the pistol at his feet. A delay followed during which the second extracted the ball and wadding and damp powder, cleaned and oiled the weapon, and reloaded it. The sun by this time was clear of the distant roofs, and April adjusted her position.

At last the curtain rose on the action. Johnny and the husband, a burly brute with the erect bearing of an experienced campaigner, stood back to back with pistols elevated and started pacing.

"One . . . two . . . three . . ." Johnny's second called the count.

April loosened the drawstring of her reticule, dangling from her right wrist.

". . . seven . . . eight . . ."

A cloud crept in front of the sun. April took her lower lip between her teeth and held it until it passed.

". . . ten."

The duellists turned and leveled their pistols. April jerked open her parasol. The white lace caught the sun like a sudden puff of smoke. The husband, startled, jerked his trigger. Smoke shot out the end of the barrel. A yew tree twenty feet behind Johnny stirred its branches.

A brief silence followed, ending when Johnny's second cleared his throat. "You may take your shot, sir."

Johnny swayed, and April worried he'd been hit after all. Then he stiffened his stance, pivoted wide to the right, and fired at an uninhabited section of the heath.

April exhaled and tied up the reticule with her little Remington inside.

Johnny stood with arms akimbo among their packed trunks and valises. "Why don't we extend our stay a few days? Paris has waited for us this long. It will still be there at the beginning of next week."

"You're saying that only because you're the social lion

this week." April, seated at the secretary, circled an item in the *Times*. "As if surviving a ridiculous stunt carries any sort of merit."

"It was gallantry. I could have struck the fellow down but chose mercy instead."

"That was luck—and my parasol. You said yourself the only way you could hit him was if you aimed elsewhere."

"The parasol may have been unnecessary. Anyone so easily distracted is no kind of marksman."

"He's wounded three men in four years. And you're forgetting duelling is outlawed in England. We should have left yesterday."

Someone knocked at the door. Johnny said, "It's too early for the porter."

She directed him to step into the bedroom and went to the door to inquire who it was.

"New Scotland Yard, Madam."

The door to the bedroom drew shut with a thump. She undid the latch.

The little man in the hall removed his bowler and introduced himself as Inspector Gargan. He was accompanied by a constable in uniform. "We're here to ask your husband to come with us," he said. "He must answer for what took place at Hampstead yesterday morning."

"My husband has left for America. He took the boat train to Gravesend two hours ago."

His moustaches twitched, increasing his unfortunate resemblance to a rodent. "What ship, please?"

"The *Dolley Madison*, bound for Boston. Here, he's circled it." She turned briefly, picked up the *Times* from the secretary, and handed it to him. It was folded to the shipping column.

He glanced at the mark she'd made. "Why did you not accompany him?"

"We've separated. He was unfaithful to me, and nearly

killed another man for his transgression." Her lower lip quivered.

"Are all those traps yours?" He peered past her.

"Yes. I'm going on to Paris. Search the suite if you like." She stepped aside from the doorway.

The constable tugged at his helmet and took a step forward. Gargan stopped him with a gesture. "That won't be necessary. I'll wire Gravesend. Perhaps they've delayed departure. Thank you very kindly, madam. I'm sorry for your trouble."

Johnny came out after they'd left. His face was flushed. "That was taking a chance."

"Not really. They'd have searched the place on their own if I hadn't offered."

"What if they took you up on it?"

She smiled. "Then you'd have had your chance to play Sidney Carton. A 'far, far better thing,' and all that."

"You've bought us nothing but time, and little of that. They'll be watching the hotel and the boat train and the dock."

"True." She sighed. "Well, we smuggled banknotes and double eagles out of half a dozen towns out West. I'm sure we can smuggle you across the Channel."

The S.S. *Dover Castle* sailed with the tide for France. Inspector Gargan, his constable, and others were on hand to watch the passengers ascending the gangplank. The inspector lifted his bowler as April passed, her hat secured with a scarf tied beneath her chin to protect her hair from cinders drifting from the stacks. She nodded in response.

Her luggage arrived at her stateroom once the ship was in motion. She tipped the porter, twisted the latch on the door, and unstrapped the largest of the two trunks she'd held out from the hold. Johnny, in shirtsleeves and wrinkled trousers, unfolded himself from inside and stretched, cracking his joints. "I thought for certain they'd mixed up the instructions. I paid for first class, not baggage."

"Listen to you complain. *You* didn't leave half your London wardrobe for the chambermaid to find in the hamper. I'll need to start all over again in Paris, and I expect you to pay for it." April took a skirt from the other trunk and hung it in the closet.

"In that case, we shan't afford more than a few days in Rome."

"What of it? All anyone ever goes to see is the Coliseum and the Parthenon."

"Pantheon, dear. The Parthenon's in Athens. Really, you should read something besides the plays of Cornelius Ragland."

"Be grateful I read the *Times*."

13

While Johnny and April were taking in the wonders of the Old World and the authorities of Europe, Cornelius Ragland was taking the waters in Hot Springs, Arkansas, and writing *The Tragedy of Joan of Arc,* for which he hoped to be remembered. He spent an hour each morning parboiling himself in mineral water with steam pouring off it, then returned to his hotel room for a light breakfast in bed and spent the day filling sheets of foolscap, using his tray for a desk and stopping frequently to consult the thick research books stacked on the nightstand, all of them bloated with narrow rectangles of paper marking particular passages for review. In the afternoon he took tea only, saving his delicate appetite for supper in the hotel's excellent restaurant. He had a preference for poached salmon or boiled beef with steamed vegetables and bread pudding for dessert. Then to sleep. It was a most virtuous existence among surroundings sinfully decadent.

Cornelius was the son of a postmaster in Baltimore and had passed a civil service examination to clerk in the same post office before his health forced him to seek a position in the gentler climate of Missouri. He was asthmatic and suffered from chronic exhaustion, which a Baltimore physician had misdiagnosed as consumption, which had exempted him from the draft. A more cosmopolitan practitioner in St. Louis had corrected the record and recommended Hot Springs. However, accommodations were dear in that popular place for recuperation and recreation, and at the rate he'd managed to put money aside from his salary as private secretary to Peter Argyle, manager of the St. Louis branch of the Gateway Bank & Trust of St. Louis, Kansas City, and Denver, he'd calculated that it would take him five years to afford to stay there one week. Thanks to his association with the Prairie Rose Repertory Company, he had a suite for the season in the best hotel in town.

He was, he confessed to himself, a naïf, and still a bit shocked at how easily he'd been corrupted; but a perceptive observer of his companions and especially himself. He assigned whatever skills he had as a writer to that source. Johnny Vermillion held him in thrall. The disgracefully immoral young man from Chicago possessed many of the qualities Cornelius admired, and which he incorporated into the heroes of the plays he cribbed from the work of superior writers: charm, comeliness, audacity, athletic grace, elegant manners, and the sort of personality that drew men to him as well as women. These things gave him confidence Cornelius would never have, and the modicum of arrogance that was shared by most leaders of men. There was no telling how high he might have risen in politics had he followed his father's example.

A conscience he had not; and this, too, was a source of envy for a young man who was burdened with rather more than his share. He had witnessed far too much perfidy in banking to feel any sympathy toward the institutions from which the Prairie Rose stole, but that wisdom did nothing more than modify his own feelings of guilt. In the world that had come into being since the War of the Rebellion, he considered it more of an affliction than a virtue, and cursed himself as a weakling.

Much of Johnny had made its way into Cornelius' villains as well, although he doubted the man who had inspired them recognized himself there. It was a revelation how many traits knights and brigands had in common, at least when they were practicing their chivalry and treachery in front of painted canvas.

Cornelius could not be Johnny, as much as he tried to be, through the characters he employed in his plays. Failing that, he found it enough to be near him, and to consider him his friend. He had no others. The head of the company treated him with more warmth and regard than any man he'd known before, beginning with his stern, disappointed father. He praised Cornelius' writing, gave him courage and patient advice when his turn came to commit robbery—*armed robbery,* more terrible and exhilarating than his one experiment in the pleasures of the flesh, with a prostitute who'd accosted him on the levee in St. Louis— and in all things celebrated him as an equal.

Cornelius Ragland loved Johnny Vermillion.

His feelings toward the others were more ambivalent.

Mme. Elizabeth Mort-Davies intimidated him with her mannish height, large hands, and top-lofty ways, but on stage was a versatile character actress whose range permitted him to embroider heavily upon Dickens' grim dowagers, Shakespeare's dithering nurses, Dumas *père*'s fawning duchesses, and the long chain of sculls, dames, palm readers, hags, fishwives, nannies, landladies, daubs, frumps, flounces, and queen mothers who rattled and clanked through the distaff side of the British and American theater, to say nothing of the hordes of androgynous sailors, footmen, grave diggers, friars, churls, and sergeants at arms for which her statuesque build and husky contralto suited her. She could also, in a pinch, as when April Clay's less celebrated talents were wanted elsewhere (in seldom-traveled towns where a female of any description might pass as the Jersey Lily), play the heroine for one brief scene staged artfully; or more convincingly, the romantic lead. Still, he preferred to keep his distance, and to channel whatever suggestions he felt appropriate during rehearsals through Johnny, who proved a patient and persuasive director. The man's abilities appeared to be without limit.

Cornelius held Major Evelyn Davies in genial contempt, but found him the perfect blithering foil for Johnny's urbane swashbucklers, as clever at parlor banter as they were at swordplay and fisticuffs. When the time came to announce the ambassador from the Court of St. James, or the father of the bride, or the bishop who'd made one trip too many to the chamber where the sacramental wine was stored, the fat fellow with the preposterous white handlebars knew no peer. He was also an unscrupulous part-padder and stealer of scenes, and without Lizzie close at hand to still his unpredictable impulses, tended to boast about things best kept inside the company, at a level intended for the back row of the balcony. He made Cornelius exceedingly nervous, both as a playwright and as an accomplice to numerous felonies, each punishable by many years at hard labor. He enjoyed the Major's outlandish stories about the London stage (which he may or may not have experienced at firsthand), but was contented to leave his keeping to Johnny and the inestimable Madame.

April Clay was not so easily summed up by language; and language was all he had.

In the lexicon of melodrama, she seemed to be equal parts guileless maiden and scheming harpy—although a more passive and sweet-natured she-beast would have been difficult to find in the history of theater. She seldom raised her voice, never uttered so much as a mild oath, and apart from that tense hour outside Salt Lake City when Lizzie was thought to have been captured and their own freedom was in question, the playwright had never seen her more than mildly upset. She did not insist, she did not assert, yet there were times when she appeared to be leading the Prairie Rose, and not Johnny. Sex, of course, was the instrument, but there were no secrets in the close society of a company touring the primitive reaches of the frontier, with its shared dressing rooms and tight hotel quarters often separated by no more than two thicknesses of wallpaper, and Cornelius was certain the two were not intimate. But a woman whose merry glance could make a man's heart miss a step, and whose touch on his arm when he reached up to retrieve her train case from an overhead rack could turn his knees to water, could enslave him without unpinning her hat.

He was writing St. Joan with her in mind, and it would be one like no other. He could picture her neither listening to any voice outside her own nor succumbing to any flames not of her kindling. In Philadelphia, the authorities would shut down the opening-night performance before the end of the first act; in Wichita, where such Joans were Saturday-night staples in every saloon and bawdy house, the play might run six weeks.

It wouldn't, of course. With a sigh, Cornelius Ragland remembered that his was no ordinary repertory company, and that its concept of theater was more sophisticated than

most county sheriffs and committees of public vigilance
were prepared to embrace.

He sipped his tea, which had grown cold, and trimmed
his pen, which had caked. Just thinking about Johnny, the
Davieses, and April made one feel as if he'd been creating
vivid characters for hours, when in fact he hadn't touched
nib to paper.

The editor of the *Eureka Daily News* had a talent for cari-
cature, and had enlivened his column on last night's presentation of *The Diplomat Deposes* with an amusing and
accurate pen-and-ink sketch of the fictive elder statesman,
resembling a tulip bulb wearing a silk hat, and the erect
and somewhat equine object of his passion. At the moment,
copies of the sketch torn from the paper were clutched in
the hands of Wendell Zick, city marshal, and three of his
deputies as they watched passengers board the Northern
Pacific bound for San Francisco. They were eager to interview Major and Mme. Mort-Davies in connection with a
number of silver snuffboxes, gold toothpicks, and a fine
buffalo coat reported missing from the theater cloakroom,
and the matter of an unpaid hotel bill.

Traffic was heavy, with the loggers down from the
hills to shake off the effects of the long winter hiberna-
tion in the hellholes of Barbary with their accumulated
pay, and the Russians remaining from old Fort Ross hur-
rying to meet relatives for Easter services in the Orthodox
church, and all of them impatient to get away from the
mud and one another. Several times, Zick and his men had
had to lunge to pull likely candidates out of the stream
and compare their faces to the features in the illustration.
None of those thus delayed took the inconvenience with
good grace, and the press of those coming up behind led

to collisions, harsh words in a number of languages, and the intervention of officers to prevent fistfights and possibly a knifing or gunplay. Zick himself swore a German oath when a tall Russian in a fur hat and full beard ran over the marshal's instep with a wicker bath-chair bearing an old woman piled with rugs and wound to her white hair with scarves, a carpetbag in her lap. The couple continued on its way without pausing until a pair of porters stepped down from a car to help hoist woman and wheelchair aboard. Eureka, a rough place when Zick first came to it, but open and friendly, had since the completion of the spur to San Francisco turned as sullen as any of the Gomorrahs in the East.

As the train pulled out, the marshal sought his men, only to find them with empty hands and shaking heads, and stepped back to study the passenger windows fluttering past, but none of the profiles he glimpsed there drew a close enough resemblance to the sketch to warrant sending a wire to the next stop. He tore up the scrap of newsprint and walked off the platform, trailing the pieces like Hansel and Gretel in the wicked forest.

The Northern picked up speed coming down the coast and leveled out at forty with a long blast on its whistle, a catcall to those left behind in Eureka. The Russian couple sat in facing seats; the porters had removed the bath-chair to the baggage car on the assurance that the old woman could manage the trip to and from the water closet with a cane and the assistance of her companion. Major Evelyn Davies snatched off his white wig and scratched his bald head with a furious, motoring movement like a dog.

Elizabeth Mort-Davies blew exasperatedly through the mass of llama hair covering her face and leaned forward to take the wig and tug it back down to the Major's ears. "Wells, Fargo pays porters for information. If they suspect anything they'll have us held in Frisco and wire back to

Eureka if nothing comes of it, and something might. Don't forget Sioux Falls."

"You might at least have given me one without fleas."

"You might have foregone oysters in garlic sauce the last time you wore these whiskers."

At about the time Johnny Vermillion and April Clay were crossing to France and Major and Mme. Mort-Davies were riding the rails in disguise to San Francisco, the Ace-in-the-Hole Gang was in the middle of its worst run of luck since three of its more colorfully named members died under violent and ignominious circumstances, clearing Black Jack Brixton's path toward its leadership.

In a vainglorious moment during the robbery of the Pioneers Bank in Table Rock, Wyoming Territory, the president of that institution scooped a Schofield revolver from the belly drawer of his rolltop desk and shot Tom Riddle high in the chest. The rest of the gang responded characteristically, perforating the president with lead, but Tom did not benefit. Shock and loss of blood tipped him out of his saddle a mile outside town and they were forced to retreat to a cave to patch his wound and give him rest. By morning he was feverish and jabbering more than usual; it was clear he needed medical attention to survive. Brixton and Breed were in favor of finishing him off and skedaddling, but Ed and Charlie Kettleman voted to fetch a doctor, and Mysterious Bob broke the tie by throwing in with the brothers, possibly because he suspected his own habitual silence would become oppressive without Tom's garrulity to balance it. Internal tension had broken up more successful criminal associations than the Pinkertons and the U.S. marshals combined.

They sent Charlie. He'd proven himself capable of recovering the money from the Salt Lake City debacle, even if

he'd lacked the foresight to drive home the lesson by killing the woman he'd found in possession. He went without
protest. Brixton was still simmering over Charlie's failure
to secure the woman's silence in Denver, and when it came
to insubordination he'd been known to override the will
of the majority with a bullet.

Leading his horse down Table Rock's main street to
avoid spooking the recently robbed residents, squinting at
signs in search of "M.D.," Charlie caught a bit of luck when
a pudgy, gray-haired man in a rumpled suit stepped out the
front door of a private house carrying a small satchel just
as the bandit was passing. The man paused to touch his hat
to a woman standing just inside the doorway, who addressed him as "Dr. Edwin."

Charlie waited while the man set his satchel on the seat
of a worn buggy in front of the house, then when he turned
to untie the equally worn-looking horse that was hitched
to it, tethered his own mount to the back of the buggy,
stepped up behind him, and stuck the muzzle of his captured Colt against the man's ribs.

"You drive, Doc. I got a new one for your rounds."

Edwin put up a squawk, said he wasn't the doctor for
him, to which Charlie replied it wasn't for him, and put an
end to the palaver by thumbing back the Colt's hammer.
Edwin climbed onto the driver's seat without another word
and they rode out of town with the big revolver in Charlie's lap pointing at the driver.

In the cave, where the atmosphere was thick thanks to
Ed having mistakenly tossed a Douglas fir branch onto the
fire and filling the place with noxious smoke (and his companions with homicidal intent), Dr. Edwin goggled at the
sight of Tom stretched on his bedroll, babbling in his
stained bandages torn from a canvas bank sack. "What is
it you wish me to do?"

"Do? Dig out the slug, for chrissake!" Brixton looked

more disconcerting than usual with his bandanna tied over his nose and mouth to prevent asphyxiation. He'd taken the precaution of soaking it in Old Gideon and was inebriating himself further with each breath he drew. Needless to say, he was an unpleasant drunk.

When Edwin remained hesitant, Breed tore the satchel from his hand and dumped it out onto the cave floor to facilitate. Instead of instruments and bottles, books spilled into a pile, with Volume Five of Gibbon perched on top.

During interrogation, it developed that Edwin was a doctor of philosophy, retained by the woman of the house Charlie had seen him leaving to tutor her fourteen-year-old son in the history of Western civilization. More smoke ensued of the burnt-powder variety, and Erastus Edwin, professor emeritus of the University of Maryland, claimed his own footnote in history as the only Roman scholar to lose his life at the hands of frontier bandits.

Brixton's fury having spent itself on the unfortunate pedant, Charlie took his punishment in the form of a fresh horse and a third trip to Table Rock to correct his error. This time, he broke into the office of Benjamin Ruddock, M.D., at the top of a flight of stairs slanting up the outside wall of a harness shop, and finding it unoccupied spent his time while waiting for the proprietor's return satisfying himself as to the medical nature of the equipment and spelling out the script on a framed diploma on the wall above the examining table. When after forty-five minutes the door opened, he threw down on the rat-faced individual who came in carrying a cylindrical case and explained his errand. Dr. Ruddock shrugged and turned to precede him out the door.

"Hold on! Let's have a look in that there bag first. If it's full of books I'll plug you right here and save the trip."

Ruddock unlatched the case, spread it open, and held it out for Charlie's inspection. While the desperado peered at the probes, forceps, rolls of gauze, and corked containers arranged neatly inside, the doctor swept a two-pound medical dictionary off a shelf, knocked him senseless, tied him with bandages, and went for the county sheriff, whose office stood next door to the harness shop. Ruddock, as it happened, had just returned from an identical abduction to tend to a member of the Turkey Creek Outfit, who'd lost three fingers blasting open a safe in the mail car of the Santa Fe Railroad outside Bitter Creek two days before; he'd been hot, tired, trail-sore, and in no humor for another enforced house call so soon after the first.

Ironically, Tom Riddle survived. Breed, impatient over the delay, used his big Bowie to extract the bullet, not caring overmuch whether the surgery was fatal so long as it freed them to ride, and Tom's miner's constitution did the rest. When he was strong enough to sit a horse, Ed and Mysterious Bob took him to his sister's pig farm in Nebraska to complete his recovery and returned to help Brixton and Breed separate Charlie from the jail in Table Rock. This they managed to do while the sheriff was at supper, leaving an inexperienced deputy in charge. So pleased was the gang by this unaccustomed stroke of good fortune that it satisfied itself with binding and gagging the deputy and locking him in Tom's former cell instead of shooting him. (Ungratefully, the Table Rock Merchants Association added a hundred dollars a head to the reward for Ace-in-the-Hole's capture or destruction. The late president of the Pioneers Bank was a popular member of its poker circle.)

When Tom rejoined the gang, he had an anthology of new stories to tell, including a fanciful version of how he'd come by his wound despite the evidence of his listeners' own eyes, and an involved anecdote about his efforts to teach simple arithmetic to one of his sister's hogs. The others were grateful for the fresh material, and happy to be hearing something other than Bob's deadly quiet and their own stale thoughts. For a solid week, their "Shut up, Tom" lacked conviction.

But Charlie Kettleman was never the same after Table Rock. The blow from the medical dictionary had addled him, and during his occasional lucid moments he insisted that a bunch of those long words had leaked into his brain through the crack in his skull, tangling with his thoughts and making them come out incomprehensible and impossible to pronounce. This ruined him for horse trading; brother Ed was forced to increase his own skills twofold to keep the others from dwelling on the wisdom that Charlie had lost his usefulness and ought to be expelled.

Black Jack Brixton's theory about this latest setback was simpler than Charlie's. He was superstitious, it must be remembered, and had formed the conclusion that Ace-in-the-Hole's sour string had begun with its first encounter with the Prairie Rose Repertory Company, and would continue until they closed the curtain on its final performance.

14

In Paris, although they shared a suite in the century-old Hotel d'Hallwyl, Johnny and April were kept so busy by their respective schedules they rarely saw each other except to say good night on their way to their rooms. Each missed the other's company and perspective, and at length they decided to revive their St. Louis tradition and meet every day at a restaurant they both found pleasing, to renew their acquaintance and compare the details of their day.

Their choice was the Maison Cador, next to the church of Saint-Germain-l'Auxerrois and across from the east end of the Louvre, where Claude Monet had stood on a balcony to paint that Gothic pile eight years before. There in a cream-and-gold room decorated in relief and hung with crystal chandeliers, they sat in cane chairs at a pink marble table, sampling the patisserie's sweets and omelets and correcting each other's French.

"Another new frock?" said he one day, admiring her pearl-colored suit and gray silk shirtwaist. Her straw hat wore an abundance of intricately tied ribbons. "Shall we rob the *Banque de France,* or stow away in a lifeboat during the voyage home?"

"The *Banque* is impregnable to our method. I made a point of checking it out last week. In any case, you have our return tickets stitched inside the lining of that hideous caped overcoat. You oughtn't to leave it lying about."

"I don't consider hanging it in the wardrobe in my room leaving it lying about. You sewed it back up with admirable skill. I didn't detect it."

"I took it to a seamstress, and supervised her work."

He nibbled at a cream-filled pastry. "Did you think I was hoarding love letters? I'm beginning to think you're living your role. Repertory players are especially susceptible when they don't trade off."

"That's poppycock, and you know it. I wanted to make sure you weren't selling forged American railroad stock to gullible Europeans. You might end up in the Château d'If for real, and then where would I be, a woman alone in wicked Paree?"

"A bit less emphasis on the second syllable. I distinctly heard the double *e.*"

"It's pronunciation now, is it? Have you been taking French lessons behind my back?" She took a forkful of egg poached in white wine, made a little face, and sipped water to dilute the effect. Parisian food did not agree with her, much to her dismay; she felt it betrayed her American palate to the natives. In consequence, she ordered Parisian only, and bought peppermints by the half pound to put her stomach to rest afterward.

"Only indirectly. My fencing instructor has taken it upon himself to turn me into a *boulevardier.* He makes his vocabulary points quite literally." He touched a tiny scratch on his left cheek.

"I'd wondered about that. I thought you'd run afoul of a married marquis. Precautionary measures?"

"I think and hope I've fought my last duel. If challenged again, I'll choose parasols at dawn. I merely wish to improve my form the next time I cross swords with Corny onstage. He's gotten more graceful, have you noticed? It wouldn't do for Hamlet to lose to Laertes."

"Your poor beautiful face. Haven't those foils little round beads on the ends?"

"Buttons. Monsieur Anatole doesn't believe in them, nor in protective headgear. He considers fear of serious injury a useful learning device."

"*Un gros sauvage.* He'll put your eye out, and you'll play nothing but beggars and pirates the rest of your days."

"*Sauvage, oui. Gros, non.* He's scarcely your height, and I rather think you have the advantage of a pound or two. In all the most charming places, I hasten to add. He's damnably fast, and I think he has it in for men of greater stature."

"He'll kill you. Or give you one of those horrible white scars that look like tapeworms."

"I wonder which will distress you most," he mused. "You needn't be concerned about the former. I pay him only after each session, and then by cheque. He's an officer retired on half pay, with little more coming in thanks to his temperament." He sipped his coffee. "And what athletics have you attempted? Waltzing with counts?"

"I tired of the nobility the first week. The men all wear corsets and the women smell like mortuaries. My interests have taken a Bohemian turn. I've met the most interesting painter."

"Not one of those ragged Impressionists, I hope."

"He isn't that kind of painter. He specializes in houses and bridges, which in this city should keep him employed for life. He has muscles in places I didn't know they could be grown."

"You always fascinate me when you blush," he said. "It's a characteristic I've tried to develop, but in vain."

"For that, you have to have been raised in the Catholic faith."

"Oh, but I was. Every Sunday my father and I shared a pew with the governor, where Father delivered his graft by way of the collection plate. So will you surrender your citizenship and rear Anglo-French bastards on the Left Bank?"

"If I made that choice, they'd not be bastards."

There was no banter in this; her tone was cold and metallic. She attacked her eggs.

They finished the meal in silence. She was gone before he could rise, her skirts swishing over her curt good-bye.

Johnny finished his coffee in deep thought. He'd never known April to take serious insult to anything he'd said. He wondered if perhaps they shouldn't leave Rome to the philosophers and return home. Britain and the Continent had begun to corrupt them with its centuries of respectability.

Gilbert Anatole was a former colonel of the Second Empire, who claimed to have lost his right hand to Prussian grapeshot at Sedan, converted to Marxism under the Commune, and dedicated himself to the overthrow of the Third Republic in favor of a government run by the proletariat, of which as a humble soldier he considered himself a member in good standing. He was an ugly little man with a dark complexion who parted his scant hair in the center and wore a singlet and old-fashioned silk breeches that accentuated his womanly hips and a set of genitals all out of proportion to his small body. Johnny could not help looking at his crotch, to his own intense shame and near disaster to his person when they fenced. Fortunately, although he was convinced Anatole was a pederast, he himself was not the man's romantic preference. Valèry, the shaggy, paunchy gnome who showed up at the end of each session to drive him home, displayed proprietary interest, and his unwashed body left a tang in the air of the grubby little gymnasium in the Rue de la Glacière several minutes after their departure.

Preposterous as he appeared when at rest, Anatole was a demon on the mat; a whirling, lunging, unstoppable engine of destruction, lethal at every angle, as if he'd sprouted razor-sharp quills on all sides in addition to the single foil (épée, properly, since the tip was neither blunted nor rendered harmless by a button) in his remaining hand. In place of the other he wore a curious hook that ended not in a point but in an elongated loop shaped like a narrow spoon with a slot an inch and a half wide in the center. On the rare occasions Johnny defended himself sufficiently to lock blades in a tight clinch, the little colonel inserted Johnny's nose in the slot and gave it a savage twist that brought tears to the victim's eyes—and once a deviated septum, which Anatole later corrected by repeating the operation in the opposite direction, wrenching it back into place with a heart-stopping crack and nearly as much pain as the original injury.

"Damn your eyes!" Johnny sprang back with his hands to his face. Blood seeped between his fingers.

"*Devene un homme, Americain.* Be a man. I have left a piece of myself on every battlefield in Europe, and not a single tear. Did you not fight the rebel and conquer the red Indian?"

"Not personally. If Lee had armed his troops with contraptions like that, they'd be eating grits in Washington. Sometimes I think you forget we're only practicing. You confuse me with Bismarck."

"Ha. If you were Bismarck, they'd be eating crepes in Berlin. You poke when you should pounce. That is a sword, not a knitting needle. We go again. *En garde!*" He leveled his weapon, hook akimbo.

"On your own guard, you Gallic Attila. I'm through for the day." Johnny racked his épée and fished out a handkerchief.

Still, he progressed. He lost fat, although he had little surplus at the start, gained muscle, and straightened his posture; April commented on it at the end of his first week, before she learned what he'd been about. His reflexes improved rapidly, as they had to if he were to avoid decorating his face and torso with sticking plaster after each session, as he had after the inaugural. He was sore and sprained throughout that opening week, but ten days in he'd begun to acquire the kind of agility and economy of movement he'd only been able to affect onstage, naturally and without thought. Oddly enough, he first became aware of this not while fencing with Anatole, but on the ballroom floor, where a turn with the pretty daughter of a wealthy importer led quickly to her boudoir upstairs, where he could hear the violins still simpering below, and smell the smoke from her father's cigar in the sitting room of his chamber down the hall, where (she said) he was busy writing an eloquent letter to President Grant on the subject of tariffs. Johnny had never closed a seduction so promptly nor with so little conversation. Throughout that hour, he wondered at England's obsession with pugilism, when fencing was so much more rewarding. Monsieur Anatole was puzzled, and awkwardly pleased, when at the end of the course his student presented him with a splendid gold Swiss watch engraved with the master's initials; Valèry scowled.

Much later, in another hemisphere, Johnny Vermillion would ponder whether he ought to have given him much more. A watch, however beautiful and well-crafted, seemed poor payment for a life even so discreditable as his.

Allan Pinkerton loved to walk. The wiry fifty-six-year-old's morning constitutional was the delight of those visitors to Chicago who refused to leave the city until they had caught a glimpse of the internationally famous detective, and the bane of those subordinates who preferred to meet with the chief in the library of a gentlemen's club downtown, in leather chairs with snifters at their elbows. He conducted these conferences on the trot, swinging his stick and covering several miles of park and macadam without loss of breath. Nine years hence, that walk would end his life, when he would trip, bite through his tongue, and owing to careless treatment develop a fatal infection, making his the only documented case in history of a man having bitten himself to death.

But in the late spring of 1875, the rugged Scot was in the glory of good health, and Philip Rittenhouse, who had balked at neither the misery of three days aboard the stage aptly christened the Bozeman Bonebreaker nor a week of dysentery brought on by the chicken and dumplings served at Ma Smalley's boardinghouse in Omaha, found himself hard-pressed to keep up with his superior. The trek lacked the adventure of life on the border, with a subtext of sadism on the part of its instigator; for the man who coined the phrase "We never sleep" secretly loved to torture those in his employ, including the two who shared his blood. His sons, William and Robert, longed for his decline and their opportunity to remake the agency in their image, with due public obeisance to the old-world individualism of its illustrious founder.

Rittenhouse lifted his bowler to mop his bald head with a scarlet handkerchief, his only ostentation, and new since his Western sojourn—a sort of personal Order of the Garter for services rendered unto the goddess Justice. Those who called him the Reptile would gawk at the spectacle of his perspiring under any circumstances, including the old man's dreaded constitutional.

"I fail to see why you called me out of the office," said he, "unless the prospect of deadly apoplexy looks better to you than paying my pension."

"I ought to dismiss you for that. No one speaks to me so, including my sons. I sometimes wish they would."

"They're in a precarious position. You might decide to leave the agency to the boy who cleans the water closets, and they'll have to go to work."

"That is unjust. William at least is a top-notch detective. I know you've had your problems with him, but for my sake you might try to be insincere. I called you out here because I don't want to embar-r-rass you in the hearing of your colleagues. Jim Hume has been after me over Sioux Falls. That was your assignment."

"It still is, unless you've decided to take it out of my hands. Some cases take time to resolve, in spite of the lesson of those dime novels you write."

"Those are case histories. There is a great deal more to the detective business than apprehending criminals. The good will of the public is an invaluable source of unpaid information, and fear of retribution is a deter-r-rent to crime."

"Forgive me if I speak outside my station, but if we deter crime, do we not risk putting ourselves out to pasture?"

"I'm not hosting a debate," Pinkerton snarled. "Where does the investigation stand at present?"

"All over. I know from newspaper advertisements that Evelyn and Elizabeth Mort-Davies are performing in California, but if they're breaking the law, it's in too small a way to appear in the news columns. Cornelius Ragland seems to have fallen off the face of the earth, but then he was barely here to begin with. John Vermillion and April Clay have vanished also. I suspect they're in South America, or abroad. They attract attention wherever they go, but the effect is delayed here by the separation of culture and distance. It's possible the Prairie Rose has disbanded permanently."

"If that's the case, I advise you to swear out a complaint with the authorities in California against the Davieses and have them taken into custody. A rigid fare of bread and water ought to loosen the Major's tongue at least, if he's as fat as you say."

"He may know nothing of the others' whereabouts; in which case the publicity of the arrest will drive the rest deeper underground. I said it's possible they've split up for good. Such a move upon our part would make it a certainty."

"Suggest an alternative."

"The theatrical season begins again in the fall. We have crimes enough to occupy us until then. Ace-in-the-Hole and Turkey Creek struck within a few miles of each other in Wyoming Territory just last month."

"Each sustained a casualty, our confidential informants told me. Their luck has turned."

Rittenhouse was surprised. "I wasn't aware we had informants there."

"If I reported them to everyone in the agency, they wouldn't be confidential for long. We'll have ever-ry last man rounded up in a matter of weeks. Meanwhile the

Davieses may slip through our fingers. Swear out that complaint."

They'd stopped to let a streetcar pass. Rittenhouse wiped off his scalp again and used the handkerchief on the sweat-band inside the crown of his hat. Then he put it back on, reveling in the cool touch of the leather against his skin.

"Suppose we leave the authorities out of it for now and I investigate them in person," he said.

"Your last foray into the field was not a resounding success."

"I disagree. Before I made it, we thought a lone bandit had stuck up the Wells, Fargo office in Sioux Falls. Now we know the names of all the accomplices and have connected them with at least five other robberies, including one we didn't know about in St. Louis, which I suspect was their first. Thanks to reviews and advertising and my interviews, we know a good deal more about them than we do about Ace and Turkey Creek, not counting what you've heard from your phantom informants. Theirs may be the first criminal enterprise in history to employ the techniques of a press agent."

The streetcar had moved on, but the strollers had not. Pinkerton turned to study him. "What could you learn from the Davieses that sworn law enforcement could not?"

"Nothing, perhaps. Everything, possibly; but only if I went inside."

"Undercover?" The old man made an explosive noise, which for him was laughter. "Will you juggle, or sing opera, or teach a bear to dance?"

"Now would be an opportune time to inform you that my father was a theatrical booking agent on the vaudeville circuit. He represented people who did all those things and more, and I ran his errands until age fifteen. If you'll stake me to an office in Portsmouth Square and a couple of hundred for advertising and promotion, I'll manage the rest."

* * *

The voyage home was gentler than the one out. The sun was strong on the top deck, the motion of the waves soporific. In adjoining deck chairs, April half dozed over a book while Johnny sipped gin and bitters, a taste he'd acquired in London. A gull perched on the railing looking for crumbs and, detecting none, took its leave, flapping indignantly. The sound awakened April, who sighed and found her place on the page. Johnny peeped at the title stamped in gold leaf on the spine: *La Vie de Jeanne d'Arc.* "Research?"

She started a little and looked at him as if she'd forgotten he was aboard. "Mm-hm." She resumed reading.

"If the ship's library has Shakespeare, you might want to give Anne Page a look. Remember, we're opening with *The Merry Wives.*"

"Mm-hm." She turned a page.

"The Major will quite enjoy playing Falstaff, don't you agree?"

"Mm-hm."

He drained his glass and caught the eye of a steward, who came over for it. Johnny ordered another. The steward asked Mrs. McNear if she cared for anything.

"No, thank you."

When they were alone again, Johnny turned onto his hip. "If you're disappointed about Rome, I'll make it up to you in New York: a suite at the Astor, dinner at Delmonico's. I understand Verdi has a new opera opening on Broadway. That's at least a taste of Italy."

She said nothing, reading.

He reached over and tipped her book forward. "Your French isn't that good, dear. You've said more to the steward than you have to me. Is it Rome?"

She placed the attached ribbon between the pages and

closed the book. "I don't give two snaps for Rome. That was your idea. Johnny, have you never thought of retiring?"

"From the theater? I'm only thirty-one."

"You're barely *in* the theater, but you could be in it a great deal more. Denver is not so snobbish as St. Louis. If we played there three weeks, we could make as much as we took from any safe, and we'd not have to worry about arrest, or such horrible creatures as that fellow who assaulted Lizzie and ran us out of the country."

"Perhaps. And where then? Someplace like Tannery, at fifty cents a head and all the hump steak we can stomach? You're letting a few complimentary notices turn your head. We're far more successful desperadoes than thespians."

"We could be better if we kept to it. If we spent as much time rehearsing Corny's plays as we do preparing to commit felonies, we could put the Booths to shame. As it is we have some talent and only adequate skill."

"Bravado, certainly, and most of that onstage. You mustn't be discouraged by a couple of minor setbacks. Look at those guerrillas the Jameses and Youngers, hunted in every corner of the land. The Pinkertons and the railroad detectives don't even know we exist. Anyway, you knew the risks when you threw in with me."

She turned upon him the full force of her eyes. "We could be Mr. and Mrs. John McNear in truth. That's your real name, after all. You must have realized by now how fond I am of you."

"My father had a buggy horse he was fond of. That didn't stop him from having it shot when it broke a leg."

"Why must you bring your father into every serious conversation? He's dead, dead, dead!"

It was only the second time in their acquaintance he'd known her to display so much emotion without an audience looking on.

"Well?" she demanded.

"I wish—" He broke off.

"What do you wish?" she whispered, touching his arm. He felt an electric crackle: St. Elmo's Fire, not uncommon in open seas.

"I wish I were actor enough to know when you were performing."

Her expression did not change so much as congeal into something he could not hope to penetrate. She withdrew her hand.

"Well, we don't dock for a week. We'll discuss this again." She opened her book and returned to Joan of Arc.

The steward cleared his throat. It was Johnny's first intimation he'd returned from the bar. He turned back and accepted his drink.

"Lifeboat drill in fifteen minutes, sir. Will you be participating?"

Johnny squinted up at him. The sun was at his back. "Do they actually lower the boats into the water during the drill?"

"No, sir."

"In that case, the answer is no."

"Very good, sir." The steward bowed and left.

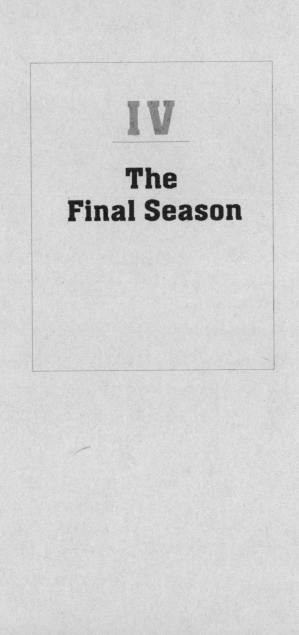

IV

The
Final Season

15

In June 1875, the nation—or at least that part of it not engrossed by the scandals of the Grant Administration, or preparations for the American Centennial celebration to take place in Philadelphia a year later, or the surrender to U.S. forces by the Comanches at Fort Sill, or in converting to Christian Science after reading Mary Baker Eddy's *Science and Health,* or following *The Adventures of Tom Sawyer*—thrilled to sensational accounts in the press of the destruction of one of the West's most notorious outlaw bands in the sleepy hamlet of Spanish Trot, Colorado Territory.

The James and Younger brothers were still at large, and would continue to commit depredations to the entertainment of Eastern readers weary of the dismantlement of the Tweed Ring in New York City for another year, when a similarly spectacular end awaited them in Minnesota. It was not them, then, who completed their bloody cycle in Spanish Trot, nor the Ace-in-the-Hole Gang; but the Turkey Creek Outfit, who would fade from history in the shade of Northfield, Little Big Horn, and the assassination of Wild Bill Hickok, all in 1876. ("I see no mystery in that," Bernard DeVoto would comment, two generations later. "Spanish Ridge, yes; perhaps even Spanish Fly. But Spanish *Trot*? I think I had a touch of it in Juarez.") There is no accounting for the choices made by posterity, as witness the inexplicably enduring legend of Billy the Kid, who in his only surviving photograph looks like the offspring of an incestuous relationship in the Appalachians, wearing a silly hat.

For a season, however, Turkey Creek in extremis offered all the active ingredients necessary to create an American myth: a daring daylight raid on a bank, the murder of an employee who in confusion transposed two digits in the combination of the vault, and a headlong plunge by the gang out the front door into a maelstrom of lead supplied by a determined citizens' committee that had been anticipating the visit for weeks. Interestingly, the information had come courtesy of the same gang member who had lost three fingers to a premature explosion of dynamite during the assault on the Santa Fe Railroad near Bitter Creek, Wyoming Territory, one month before, and who at the time of the bank disaster was recovering from his injury in Cheyenne. George Adam Cedarcrest, normally a fair hand with a powder charge, was an operative in the employ of the Pinkerton National Detective Agency. According to conventional wisdom, his conflict of interest had played an important part in his carelessness on that occasion. It also spared him his life, as Allan Pinkerton had turned over his intelligence to the local authorities to avoid tying up his agents for an indefinite period, and citizens' committees were not known to discriminate between friend and felon in the heat of fire.

Cedarcrest, whose maimed hand, together with his brief fame, had rendered him unsuitable for undercover work, was assigned to the file room in the San Francisco office, where he stayed until his retirement in 1891. Twenty-five years later, he died in the midst of negotiations with Famous Players-Lasky to adapt his self-published memoirs to the screen. The film was never made, and thousands of unsold copies of the book went back to the pulp mill. The rest of Turkey Creek found longer lasting recognition of a sort in 1974, when Time-Life Books published a picture of their corpses, arranged on planks for purposes of identification in Chicago, in its series on the Old West. The caption referred to them merely as a "bandit gang, ambushed by vigilantes in Colorado." (Black Jack Brixton, who saw the shot displayed in the window of a photographer's studio in New Mexico sometime after the disaster, noted a dirty toe poking out of a torn stocking, and laid in a supply of socks. He determined never to embark on another robbery without putting on a fresh pair.)

The other big story of that quarter, although it failed to inspire exclamatory headlines in the first column, proved more nourishing over the long run, in the form of journalistic speculation on slow news days. The disappearance of the Ace-in-the-Hole Gang, after a busy decade, puzzled authorities and was said to have created tension between Allan Pinkerton and the heads of all his Western field offices, who reported with palms spread that none of the sporadic episodes of rapacity that had taken place since the removal of one of their members from the jail in Table Rock bore their signature, and that nothing useful had been heard from any of the confidential informants they depended upon to keep track of itinerant marauders. A staple of frontier outlawry seemed simply to have floated off into outer space; a most unsatisfying end to an investigation that had claimed years and dollars far in excess of the amount Brixton and his followers had removed from banks, railroads, and express companies going back to the sack of Yale, Kansas, on April 10, 1865, twenty-four hours after the surrender of the Confederacy.

Pinkerton ordered a relentless search of all the gang's known haunts, beginning with Denver. An army of grim-faced men in bowlers invaded Nell Dugan's Wood Palace with mauls and axes, punching holes in suspicious-looking walls, splintering locked doors, and demolishing a pump organ large enough to conceal a man behind its front panels, which it did not. Nell and her ladies of easy reputation followed the agents from room to room, slashing at their cigar smoke with Chinese fans, derogating their efforts in language colorful and cutting, and energetically attempting to seduce them away from their mission, with some success; three of the searchers did not report back to the Denver office until the next day, when they were summarily suspended for a month without pay.

Eventually the trapdoor in the back parlor was discovered, and laying down their tools in favor of pistols, the Pinkertons descended into the basement quarters, where they found all of the beds stripped except one, their mattresses rolled, and no one in residence except a vagrant known and loved by the citizens of Denver, all of whom were aware of his sad story of impoverishment after the vein of gold he'd been mining had thinned to nothing and his first flush of prosperity had been squandered at the Palace and its competitors. He explained, at gunpoint, that Nell had employed him to conduct odd repairs and given him shelter. In the six weeks of his stay, he insisted, none but he had appeared below ground except the Negro maid who came to change the sheets once a week. After some difficulty over a heavy chest of drawers that had been inadvertently pushed over the trapdoor, sealing them in the basement, the agents departed empty-handed except for the tools they'd brought with them.

Altogether the damage to private property came to fifteen hundred dollars and change, which a judge of the First District Court of Denver County ordered the Pinkerton National Detective Agency to reimburse to Nell Dugan. The *Colorado Rocky Mountain News* denounced the decision in a fiery editorial that quoted liberally from Revelation and the Reverend Doctor Eccles Monsoon's multiple-volume history of the white slave trade in North America. The *Denver Post,* with whom Nell advertised the more wholesome entertainments of her establishment, celebrated it in half a column, pointing out that the Pinkertons had spent more money in the Wood Palace in one day than all its other customers combined spent in a week. The wires acquired this item and enlivened the telegraph columns of the Eastern press for weeks.

"Do we not do business with the *Post?*" demanded Allan Pinkerton, crumpling the copy of the Denver paper that had come by rail under Philip Rittenhouse's subscription.

William Pinkerton, seated in his father's office, re-crossed his legs and tugged down the points of his waistcoat. Unlike the old man, he was inclined to be stout, as was his younger brother Robert, and to bring dignity to his jowls wore coarse whiskers that twisted like rusted wire. "We have a standing order of two columns, three days a week. The Wood Palace buys half a page every Saturday. Miss Dugan may have the edge."

"Cancel the order. What in thunder has become of Ace-in-the-Hole?"

"Possibly they were frightened by what happened at Spanish Trot. Were I in their place, I'd consider it an object lesson."

"You're making the mistake of thinking like a detective and not like a criminal. Lessons are lost on them. They'll see it as a blow to the competition, and redouble their efforts to fill the vacancy."

"Evidently not, or we'd have heard from them before this. Outlaws have been known to return to the straight and true in the past."

"Not these outlaws. In Brixton's case, it would be no return. He killed his first man at the age of twelve."

"Ten, according to Ned Buntline. If this keeps up, he'll have been too young to stand up to the recoil."

"This isn't a subject for jest. If you spent more time studying case files and less time reading rubbish, you'd be a greater asset to this agency."

William pressed his lips tight.

"It's a conclusion with no payoff," said the old man. "If it *is* a conclusion, which I choose to doubt. They must be planning something hor-r-rendous."

"Perhaps your confidential informant has gone over to the other side."

"His silence explains nothing. These fellows have a way of calling attention to themselves." He picked his cigar out of the tray on his desk and puffed, apparently unaware it had gone cold. "I'm tempted to call in Rittenhouse from San Francisco. He knows more about what's afoot in the Gr-reat Desert without stepping outside his office than all the men we have on the spot. Certainly his talents are wasted in the field. I should not have let him talk me into letting him go."

"You indulge him. One would think he was your own blood."

In this, William echoed the whispers of all who hated and feared the Reptile, a society which included the heir apparent. It was a transparent canard. While it is possible to father a bastard at thirteen, at that age the old man was still in Glasgow, working day and night to support his mother and younger brother; he had not had time for a liaison of that kind. In any case, there was nothing of the Scot about Rittenhouse, who was Prussian in his meticulous method and disconcertingly American in the way he spoke out. But William never missed an opportunity to undermine his authority with Allan.

For his part, the old man gave no indication that he knew anything of the rumors. He was the world's foremost detective when it came to crime and the densest of men when it came to the office intrigue all about him. "If that were the case," he said, "I'd never have given him leave. I treat you and Robert no differ-rent from anyone else in my employ."

"Excluding the Rep—Rittenhouse," William corrected himself. He lit a cigarette to conceal his agitation.

Alerted by this gesture to the status of his cigar, the old man struck a match and reignited it, drawing smoke deep into his lungs. He blew a ring without thinking, and scowled at it. He disliked ostentation. "Who do we have in Mexico?"

"On the payroll, or under the vest?"

"Both."

"Well, Horton's the field man in Mexico City. We've a *federale* captain in Nogales and some informants masquerading as bandits or vice versa in Chihuahua. I can get their names."

"When you do, wire them descriptions of Brixton and his men, and have Denver and San Francisco send photographs and sketches. It's been my observation that whenever a band of brigands vanishes, it's to Mexico they've gone."

"Not Canada? It's a closer ride to where they were reported last."

"They're smart, or they'd not have lasted this long. They won't flee the Eye to risk the Mounties. I dislike dealing with the arrogant redcoats myself, but there's no denying they're effective. Perhaps if we had a queen in this country we'd have the same free hand."

"We're too close to Independence Day for that kind of talk." William scowled. "While I'm about it, do you want me to recall Rittenhouse?"

The old man smoked, shook his head. "No. We'll let him have the bit a while longer. I've a hunch the apprehension of the Prairie Rose would make a fine subject for a case history. It may even tell better than Ace-in-the-Hole."

16

Philip Rittenhouse, who unlike most detectives never laid claim to any sense beyond the five God had given him at birth, was oblivious to the discussion of his subject in Chicago. As it was taking place, he sat in the squeaky captain's chair in his furnished office above a Chinese laundry on Washington Street, with a view through the streaked windows of three of San Francisco's best-known shops of iniquity: Gilbert's Melodeon, Bert's New Idea, and the Adelphi. The Bella Union, more famous than all the rest, stood on the side of Portsmouth Square to which he had no window, only a patchwork quilt of playbills advertising extinct entertainments pasted over cracks in the yellow plaster.

He was conscious of it nevertheless, as a farmer in Nebraska was conscious of the Department of Agriculture in Washington and an architect in Buffalo was conscious of the Taj Mahal at Agra. But then they hadn't the thud of brass instruments in the soles of their feet to remind them, nor the *baroom* of a remote kettledrum in their ears whenever a dancer in pink tights executed a split. As Peter Ruskin, proprietor of the Ruskin Dramatic Arts Agency (est. 1875), he thrilled to the proximity of that splendid showcase of theatrical talent, and as Philip Rittenhouse, an operative with the Pinkerton National Detective Agency, he had the comfortable sensation of knowing that as long as places like the Bella Union existed, his work would always be in demand; for it drew thieves and murderers the way an abandoned carcass drew vermin, and the prices it charged for admission, as well as for the diversions inside, discouraged its clientele from honest occupations and the spare living most of them offered.

He'd been there, of course, as he had to its competitors. For three weeks he'd divided the rest of his time between the wormy cylinder desk, its pigeonholes stuffed with decaying programmes, telegraphic pleas for money from stranded artists, and bottles of whiskey that smelled like the sinister brown wax women used to remove unwanted hair—items left by the previous tenant—and his sweaty little quarters next to the coal furnace in a rooming house on Kearney Street built of old packing cases and green timber. For authenticity's sake, he'd traded his usual nondescript dress for a flowered waistcoat, green glass stickpin, tan bowler, and yellow garters, and chewed licorice to cover the scent of alcohol on his breath, of which actually there was none; he was a confirmed teetotaler, and there were only so many things a man would do to support his disguise. All these things he kept track of in his expense book in his personal code, as well as the cost of the advertisement that ran twice weekly on an inside page of the *San Francisco Call*, which we here insert, in its proscenium-arch border:

THE RUSKIN DRAMATIC ARTS AGENCY
Peter Ruskin, *Esq.*
Representing Artists
Specialising in
All Acts of Elocution,
Spiritual Uplift,
Poetical Recitation,
Melodrama,
Tragedy and Farce
No fees charged except for services rendered
Single rates for husband-and-wife acts
Inquire at
504B Washington Street
(Across from the Bella Union)

He was particularly pleased with the European spelling of "specialising," which he thought would appeal to the tastes of his intended target, and the bit about husband-and-wife teams sharing a single rate. The list of specialties had been selected with that same purpose in mind. Originally, he'd included acrobatic acts, but the parade of tumblers, high-wire artists, and human pyramids that had tramped through his office the first week had wearied him and he'd had the line removed. In any case, Mme. Elizabeth Mort-Davies, who his research told him had been no mean physical performer in her younger days, was past the age where limbs and sinew began to rebel at anything more ambitious than a short sprint (or a bicycle ride), and Major Evelyn Davies was too fat. The stream of applicants slowed to a trickle, and Peter Ruskin, *Esq.* (a real name from among his father's contemporaries, which happened to contain his own initials), turned them all down with professional brusqueness while possessing his soul in patience.

With one exception: He promised himself that if he heard "O, Captain! My Captain!" one more time, he'd strike *Poetical Recitation* from the list.

Saturday nights, he bought drinks for the bartenders in all four major houses of pleasure and left stacks of his business cards, with instructions as to the kind of husband-and-wife act he sought, promising a finder's fee for every one he booked. He refrained from asking for the Davieses by name. No agent in the show business did that, as the whole point of the enterprise was to discover obscure talent and exploit it. Bartenders were suspicious by nature, and the history of vigilante activity in Barbary kept the proprietor of every den of dissipation on his guard; one false step, and Allan Pinkerton would never know what had become of his most reliable man in Chicago.

On his way back to his room each evening, he stopped to purchase an armload of local newspapers, and sat up on his cornshuck mattress scanning the reviews and theatrical advertisements in the *Bulletin, Call, Chronicle,* and *Star* for some sign that the Davieses were playing locally. The fact that their names did not appear failed to deter him, as he thought it possible they sometimes worked pseudonymously, either to obfuscate their identities or in response to an old thespial superstition about changing one's luck with one's billing. He circled promising acts in pencil, turned out his lamp at ten o'clock in obedience to his landlord's curfew, and spent part of the next day visiting matinees, but so far had not spotted a performing couple who matched the descriptions he'd memorized.

At the end of these three weeks, his emotions were tangled. Pinkerton was impatient and a skinflint, and could not be expected to subsidize his subordinate's experiment in theater indefinitely. At the same time, the old man had caught the best-selling author's bug, and could not fail to grasp the entertainment potential in the apprehension of a company of actors who supplemented their box-office receipts with armed robbery. He might be contented with a looser grip on the reins this one time. The newspaper trail—Rittenhouse's answer to the great Chisholm—led solidly toward a Davies appearance in San Francisco, the pleasure capital of the American frontier. On the other hand, stage players were not often creatures of logic, and the Major and the Madame might have detoured into the interior after Eureka, for no other reason than that their train had struck and killed a white heifer, souring their luck. Artists were far less predictable than the common run of road agent. That was how John Vermillion's troupe had survived this long without having to flee a single posse.

There was also the possibility that he had waited too long to set his trap. He'd never questioned his assumption that the company would reconvene, and he did not do so now. He'd based his timetable on the conventional theatrical season, which began during the first frost of autumn and ended before the hammering heat of summer turned auditoriums into ovens, but upon reflection there was no defensible reason to expect this particular association to behave according to convention. Perhaps *The Diplomat Deposes* had returned to its trunk and its champions were even then steaming east to meet the others for a brand-new season of stirring oratory, thrilling swordplay, and thievery on the grand scale.

Such were the doubts and ruminations that befell the man who staked himself out as a goat in lion country.

There was one more: the likelihood, if his quarry did not surface soon, that Peter Ruskin would be forced to sign one of the acts that passed through his office. Agents, while discriminating, had to live, and if word got around that the representative was refusing to represent anyone, he stood the risk of discovery, or what passed for it in lieu of evidence to the contrary. There was no more certain route to a death sentence on the part of the shadowy hordes than to be exposed as a "crusher" working undercover for established law and order, no matter who was the object. Merely to be suspected invited tarring and feathering at the least. Rittenhouse made up his mind to offer his services to the next glimmer of talent that crossed his threshold.

Fortunately—for he was far less confident of his abilities as a booker of exhibitions than as a detective—that glimmer happened to belong to a middle-aged woman of preposterous height and her companion, who was as fat as a rolled armadillo and dressed like the Prince of Wales. He had made contact with the Prairie Rose at last.

The fogs of San Francisco harbor vanish, burned off as by a magnesium flash by a Panavision shot directly into the sun, with its chain of reflective circles: Welcome to the Chihuahua desert, where it's always 105 in the shade, and the nearest shade is in El Paso. The state bird is dead. Even the gila monsters have migrated north to the relative comfort of Caliente Infierno, which translates roughly as Hot as Hell.

But heat is of small consequence in the little village of San Diablo, where a fiesta is always in progress. Careering down from the Sierra Madres, we hear first the drunken tinny blatting of trumpets and the out-of-sync crash of tambourines, then swerve around a pie-faced peasant in a tattered sombrero fancy-stitching his way down the broad main street with a bottle in one hand, and pause with a pleasant sigh to regard the girl dancing barefoot on a plane table in the middle of the square. She is all flying black ringlets, bare brown shoulders, whirling skirts, slender feet, and the regulation dagger strapped by a garter to one thigh, to the accompaniment of guttural cheers from the guitar players and that climbing, tongue-fluttering squeal ending in a high-pitched cackle that no *Norteamericano* can imitate. In six years, the girl will resemble the gourd-shaped women in weeds grinding corn in stoneware bowls on the front porch of the mayor's hacienda nearby, slit-eyed, contagiously vilipendent, but just now she is a welcome sight after all those rocks and cactus. Her name is Fiona, but it may as well be Dolores, Conchita, Rosario, or Mirabelle. There is one in every community of its size in old Mexico; but one only.

Our pause is regrettably brief, as we are not here to take in the local fauna. From there we move on to a small pavilion constructed of four cypress trunks supporting a roof of woven fronds topped with black Spanish moss. Beneath its screen, Jack Brixton, Tom Riddle, Mysterious Bob Craidlaw, Breed, and the Kettlemans sit on cane chairs in a semicircle facing a man who is fat even by the standards of a generation that would elect Grover Cleveland to the presidency; the yards of white cotton in his simple shirt and trousers alone would furnish dust covers for a parlor full of furniture, and his hips are stuck fast between the arms of his fan-backed chair. Bandoliers of large-caliber shells cross his ringed torso. With one hand he fans his huge streaming moustachioed face while the other cups a convenient breast belonging to the fat *señorita* seated astraddle his enormous left thigh. His name is Matagordo.

Mexico's blood-flecked history has not been kind to Matagordo; even his first name has been lost. He was a general in the revolutionary army of Benito Juarez, which he joined after the government of Maximilian refused to promote him beyond the rank of lieutenant colonel. Had he accepted a peacetime post in Mexico City and helped to oversee the return of the country to its citizens, his fame might have survived that of his successors, Francisco Villa and Emiliano Zapata, but he chose instead to return to rural banditry. In June 1875, he'd settled into semiretirement in San Diablo, where the mayor was his creature, and Ace-in-the-Hole his guest.

"My friends, your stubborn sobriety pains me. In this pueblo, we nurse our children with tequila and wean them from their virginity after Communion. We produce bastards the way other pueblos produce apricots; therefore we depend upon visiting seed to prevent our women from bearing idiots. *Por favor,* help yourself to our hospitality. Business without pleasure violates our charter." His English was impeccable, if somewhat prosy, as he'd learned it from crumpled pages torn from American dime novels used as packing material for the weapons he ordered from New Mexico and Texas. Owing to the fragmented nature of his reading, he thought Buffalo Bill was a figure of mythology, part animal and part man.

"There'll be time later," Brixton said. "Will you loan us the men we need?"

This brought a grunt from Charlie Kettleman, who'd

risen to comply with Matagordo's appeal. He slumped back into his chair and crossed his arms. The general's *señorita* wore no underthings, and the occasional glimpse he received when she shifted her weight on the fat man's thigh made him restless. Since his encounter with Dr. Ruddock's dictionary in Table Rock, the only time his brains weren't snarled with medical Latin was when he was in a woman's arms. Brother Ed gave his knee a sympathetic pat.

Their host fanned himself, looking troubled. "You have not yet confided the purpose of your appeal. A train, yes; but you do not say *which* train, nor why you cannot manage to rob it with your own fearsome band. I must know the risks."

"What's it to you?" Breed cut in. "No horse could carry you across the Rio Grande."

"I would not ask it to, as I am kind to animals and small children. However, my men trust me not to send them into danger I would not myself face. There is also the matter of an enterprise I have planned in Hermosillo at the end of summer, which will be quite impossible if they do not return to me in the condition in which they left."

Brixton said, "It's a military operation, right up their alley. That's all I'll say if you don't give me your word it don't go beyond this here tent."

"You have it, as a gentleman and a soldier of fortune."

"That and a squirt of mercury'd cure a dose of clap."

The general aimed a scowl at Charlie Kettleman, saw where his gaze was fixed, and put on his sombrero to free his hand to adjust the fat girl's skirt. "The details, please, *Señor* Brixton. I won't ask again, and you may put aside any thought you have about trading me for my men. A dozen guns are trained upon you at this moment."

"Only a dozen?" But Brixton's face was gray beneath the sunburn.

"I took El Paso del Norte with less. All of those are present."

Brixton shrugged. "Custer and Terry's fixing to give the injuns what-for in the High Plains next year. Army train's on its way to Fort Abraham Lincoln with the payroll for the whole campaign. Fort Dodge is the first stop, up in Kansas; we'll hit it on its way there. Right around seventy thousand in greenbacks and double eagles, and under armed guard from the caboose to the cowcatcher."

Matagordo fondled the girl's breast, meditating. "What is your source?"

"I got friends. Just because they turned coat and swore to the Stars and Stripes don't mean it stuck."

"Seventy thousand?"

"Maybe more, maybe less. That's seven thousand to you, and you don't need to get up out of that there chair to earn it."

"He couldn't if it was ten," Tom Riddle said. "I knew a man fat as you died in a Pullman outside Sacramento. He was so stiff they couldn't get him out the door. They cut a hole through the roof and pulled him up with ropes and pulleys. You ought to go for a walk once in a while."

Brixton said, "Shut up, Tom. What about them men, General? That there dozen ought to do it."

Matagordo summoned over a little barefoot boy, possibly an illegitimate grandson, and spoke to him in rapid Spanish. The boy sprinted away. "In San Diablo, we seal all our transactions with tequila." The host looked at Tom. "We shall see which of us can walk at the end of the day."

The celebration stretched into three, at the close of which even Charlie Kettleman was content. It was time to go. Breed, who insisted it was his white half that couldn't tolerate liquor, slumped over his horse's neck, Tom was too drunk to prattle, and Ed dismounted often to vomit on the way out of town. Bob showed no effect, but then no one knew how much or how little he had drunk. They all avoided conversation with Brixton, who was exactly three times as mean when hung over as when he hadn't had a drop. The twelve men Matagordo had lent them for reinforcement, each a traveling arsenal with bandoliers, two Colt revolvers, and a Mexican carbine, were still drinking, and singing all the old songs of the glorious revolution at once. They had no idea where they were headed or what they were expected to do when they got there, but they loved and venerated Matagordo, and were sorry only that *El Tigre del Norte* had grown too fat in his retirement to accompany them. There wasn't a full set of natural teeth in the entire band, but they had enough gold in their mouths to charter a train to Kansas instead of riding their gaunt, grass-fed mongrel mounts.

When they had left, the general prised himself out of his chair and waddled to his spare soldier's quarters on the side of the square opposite the mayor's residence. With difficulty he pulled himself up the stout ladder to the stuffy attic, where twenty or thirty pigeons in wooden cages cooed and plucked lice from their feathers. He dipped a pen in the ink pot on a little writing table, scribbled on a sheet he tore off a tiny block, removed a fat bird from one of the cages—Benito, his favorite—and clipped the rolled sheet securely to one of its thin legs. It had made the trip to the El Paso office of the Pinkerton National Detective Agency twice as many times as any of the others and knew the way even in the dark.

Matagordo tugged on the rope that lifted the hatch away from the square opening in the roof, tied it off, kissed Benito on the head, and released him with an underhand scoop to help him in his flight. The bird took to the air, flapping furiously.

A shot crashed. Benito dropped straight to the ground and lay as still as if staked to the spot. The general stared, openmouthed, at the little carcass, then slid his gaze to the man seated on horseback in the square with the Winchester still raised to his shoulder. Mysterious Bob levered in another round and kneed his sorrel in a half circle to throw down on Matagordo.

17

"D o not mistake professional curiosity for desperation, Mr. Ruskin," announced Mme. Mort-Davies, stirring her chilled cucumber soup, a specialty of the Parker House dining room. "As a matter of fact, we've done quite well representing ourselves. However, one always wishes to know whether someone else might improve upon the status quo."

Rittenhouse touched his linen napkin to his lips. He was enjoying himself thoroughly, both with the company and with the superb fare at the hotel and gambling hall so convenient to his office, and whose prices he could not afford out of his day-to-day expenses. The old man would grumble, but he understood better than anyone that confidences came more quickly over good wine served in crystal than over a cup of rotgut with silverfish floating on top. Rittenhouse had lost no time in changing the venue after the initial introductions.

"No one would argue the regularity of your appearance on the middle of the bill," he said, with just a touch of Yiddish throat in his *r*'s. "But you were right to come to me. You should be nearer the top."

Major Davies stopped slurping his soup. "Not *at* the top?" He'd tucked his napkin under his guillotine collar and hung his silk hat and opera cloak on a hook on the pillar near their table. The hour was two o'clock, and ridiculously early for evening wear. His wife was attired more appropriately, but the ruffles in her shirtwaist accentuated her pigeon breast; even in jaded San Francisco, the couple attracted attention like a brass band that had turned down the wrong street.

Rittenhouse shook his head, smiling sadly. "I won't delude you with the impossible. That spot belongs to the empty-headed ingenue and her pompous beau: people who have outward beauty, but no character and, let us be frank, undetectable talent. Much has changed since the war. Theatergoers want their nosegays to look at and sniff."

"The war." The Madame's nod was grim. "Politicians speak of the loss of men, and poets write of it, but who will stand up and announce the death of culture?"

"It is not dead so long as such as the Davieses continue to perform."

"You've seen us? I say, waiter, this soup is cold."

The waiter who'd appeared regarded the Major. "It's intended to be served that way, sir."

"Then it's pudding, isn't it? Bring me chicken broth, and have the chef test it with his elbow."

The waiter bowed and departed with his bowl, which was nearly empty.

"I had the good fortune to admire you twice in St. Louis last fall," Rittenhouse said. "Once in *The Diplomat Deposes,* and again in *Twelfth Night.* I scarcely knew I was watching the same couple. You contain many parts."

He pretended interest in his salad, but watched their expressions closely from under half-lowered lids. His oblique reference to the Prairie Rose did not seem to have placed them on their guard.

The Major belched into a pudgy fist. "That was a lark. Not real Shakespeare, of course; you need a full-scale production to do the Bard justice. But a respectable sampler, if Bowdler's your cup of tea. Personally I prefer my Elizabethans full-bodied and bawdy."

"And your soup warm," said the Madame, not without amusement. Rittenhouse suspected she was fond of her husband. He would make no progress pitting them against each other.

"An admirably shaded performance nonetheless," he said. "The reviewers overlooked the nuances."

"Frogs, the lot of them! Had we done Molière, they'd have hailed us as Lafayette. I nearly called one of them out. Lizzie restrained me."

"For his sake, Evie, not yours." She touched his wrist. "If you admired us, why did you not speak with us there?"

"I felt I'd missed my opportunity. Actors are inclined to be contented just after they've joined a troupe. The time to approach you would have been after you left the company you were with and before you signed with another. In any case, I was with a large agency then, and was in town to persuade a Swedish soprano to let us represent her. She declined, straining my relationship with my superiors. It was after that I decided to open my own agency here in California. You cannot imagine how pleased I was to see you of all people enter my office."

The Madame said, "The bartender at the Adelphi gave Evelyn your card. He said you were looking for a married act."

"I began my search with you in mind. Not you, precisely; I'd hardly hoped that opportunity would come my way again. I thought I might perhaps find a pair of potential Davieses—in the bud, as it were—and bring them along. Have you left that company you were with? What was the name?" He sensed a stiffening in her attitude, if not that of the Major, who was watching the waiter setting his broth before him, and backed off. "Well, the name doesn't matter, if you're free of all ties. Waiter, if the chef hasn't started on my crepes, I believe I'll ask for a bowl of that broth instead. It looks quite hearty."

"It is," said the Major, using the corner of his napkin to mop off his moustaches.

"Very good, sir." The waiter collected his salad and the Madame's cucumber soup and left.

"The Prairie Rose Repertory Company," furnished the Madame. "We expect to rejoin them this fall. They have no ties upon us. We are free to leave whenever we wish, although of course we'd not leave them shorthanded once we're in rehearsal. What are you proposing?"

Rittenhouse rearranged his silver just so. He was walking on hen's eggs now.

"My agency is new, as I said, but my experience is not. At the moment, I'm a trainer with many contacts, but no stable. You have a history with this Prairie Rose, and if I'm any judge of human nature, it appears to be a happy one. I'd betray my principles if I tried to steal you out from under them and leave bad feelings all around. If you would grant me permission to speak to the head of the company—"

"Out of the question." The Major blew on his broth; steam rolled off it in a visible manifestation of chef's pique. "You could not speak for us on a contingency basis. Only an agent of record could undertake such a conversation."

The detective sipped water from his goblet. He hadn't expected integrity, particularly on the part of this elderly voluptuary, his face flushed on 1845 Bordeaux. He abandoned the flank for a frontal assault.

"Certainly not. I was hoping for an understanding before I made so bold. Jim Nixon, the proprietor of Nixon's Amphitheater in Chicago, is a personal friend, and he's in a bind. He requires a Ferdinand and Isabella for a grand pageant about the discovery of America this fall and his leads have separated. He'll pay one hundred dollars apiece per performance, six nights a week with a matinee on Saturday, and he'll guarantee seven months out of his own pocket. The only condition is that no legal complications are involved. It seems he had problems with Ned Buntline over *Scouts of the Plains*—an old felony warrant—and he wants assurance his profits won't go toward some lawyer, and possibly a fine, in case of litigation. In order to provide that assurance, I'll need to meet with the head of your company and obtain his signature on a release. It would be convenient if your intended reunion took place here, but if it's to be somewhere else, I must have time to adjust my schedule to include travel."

Again he watched them closely, this time without pretending disinterest; but they were actors, and he found their expressions unenlightening. They *were* actors, however, and therefore theatrical creatures. He decided to risk overplaying his hand.

"It's the opportunity of a lifetime."

"One lifetime, perhaps," said the Major. "Artists have so many."

"Shut up, Evie."

The Major shrugged and returned to his broth. Rittenhouse was alert. Without straining visibly, the woman seated across from him seemed to have grown taller, until she was peering down at him from a great height. She was a bigger talent than he'd realized.

"Your Mr. Nixon will have to be satisfied with your assurances based upon ours," she said. "We are not, as you made clear, headline performers. What you earned representing us the first month would not pay for the distance you'd have to travel to speak with the head of our company. It wouldn't be sound business."

"That would depend upon the distance."

She gazed at him with a considering eye. He felt like a small rodent trapped in the open by an owl, and thought he'd been seen through. She parted her lips; but it was her husband who spoke, confining himself for once to a single word.

* * *

"Wichita!" bellowed the conductor, crimson-faced with an accurate chart of the Kansas Pacific's route traced in purple on his nose. He carried his announcement to the next car, walking on shattered arches.

"They certainly named the place well." April spoke through a scented handkerchief. "Macbeth's crones never brewed anything that smelled more foul."

"Tut-tut, dear. The Major would have your tongue if he heard you mention the Scottish tragedy at the very start of the season. Think of the curse." Johnny watched the parade of clapboard slow to a crawl as they slid into the station. Lanky boys dressed in flannel shirts and faded dungarees leaned against porch posts, rolling cigarettes, and a face painted like a ship's figurehead peered between lace curtains in an upstairs window. Over everything lay the stench of cattle, rich and brown and shot through with sweaty greenbacks.

"What curse could be worse than this? Look, the undertaker's sign is shaped like a coffin. I shudder to think what's above the door of the bustle shop."

He hopped up to haul down their bags, as light of heart as he was on his feet. At last, April was complaining of old familiar things, assaults on her comforts and proprieties, and not their domestic situation. Women went through the most frightening phases, only to revert to normal once they were past. He'd vexed himself over nothing less transient than a case of sniffles.

"Is there a church, I wonder?" She took one last sniff at the crumpled linen and returned it to her reticule.

"Most of the Christian denominations seem to be represented, judging by the steeples I saw. Has the Continent converted you?"

"Only to the extent that I require a minister to sanctify

our union. Don't forget my train case, darling. You nearly left it behind in New York."

He reached for it, feeling clammy cold at the center.

By the time they stepped down onto the platform, he'd recovered sufficiently to clasp the hand of Tim Saunders, who stepped up to introduce himself as the proprietor of the local variety theater. He was a spare fellow with a sly face and untenable black whiskers in an Eastern-style suit. Johnny thought instantly of the ward bosses who'd lined up outside Scipio Africanus McNear's office in Chicago with their hats off and their hands out. Saunders bowed deeply to April.

"I withheld your arrival from the newspapers, as you requested," he told Johnny. "I hope they don't take it badly. They've run out of novel ways to announce the comings and goings of Texas herds."

Johnny said, "We'll make it up to them at the reception. At the moment, the Prairie Rose is spread across five states. We shan't steal the thunder from our other players."

"I think you'll find your accommodations at the Occidental Hotel quite comfortable. The rooms at the Texas House are larger, but they're undergoing renovation. Shanghai Pierce chased a stray through the front window last month and roped it in the pantry."

"Johnny! It's worse than Tannery."

"Patience, dear. I'm sure the good people of Wichita pass weeks at a time without a cow in the kitchen."

"We're young, miss, and I don't argue some of our transients couldn't do with a good spanking. But we value our entertainers. The night we opened, Eddie Foy took eight curtain calls and scooped ninety dollars in double eagles and silver off the stage floor."

"I'd prefer it if you'd hand us a bank draught," she said. "I left my shovel in Kansas City when we changed trains."

"Haw-haw! I heard you'd a hand for light comedy. The

ninety was in the way of appreciation from the house, over and above Mr. Foy's percentage of the box office. You'll break his record, or I'm a horse thief. When do you expect the rest of your company?"

"Mr. Ragland is on his way," said Johnny, "with the costumes and properties we stored in Denver at the end of last season. I expect to hear from Major and Madame Mort-Davies any day."

Before leaving New York City, Johnny had placed the following notice in the classified sections of the *St. Louis Enquirer,* the *Denver Post,* and the *San Francisco Call:*

SIR JOHN, DR. CAIUS, MRS. FORD:
Come home. All is forgiven. Wire
Fenton, Breevort Hotel, NYC.

The names addressed belonged to three of the principal characters in *The Merry Wives of Windsor*; Fenton was the leading man. Johnny selected the three major newspapers as those most likely to be obtained wherever the cast had scattered.

"Why so formal?" April had asked, when he showed her the text. "One would think you met them in a drawing room. What could they possibly have done that would require your forgiveness?"

"The gentleman from Avon saw fit to give only one of them a Christian name. I told them to expect something on this order. If they're smart enough to rob banks, they're smart enough to respond."

"Peace officers read Shakespeare, too. Some of them must. You could be arrested the first time you inquired for a message for Mr. Fenton at the desk."

"Am I to stand trial for placing a counterfeit notice? I rather think three wars were fought to preserve that right."

"Two, perhaps. Mr. Frederick Douglass might present you with an argument as to the third."

"I thought you were reading about Joan of Arc. When did you switch to Harriett Beecher Stowe?"

"You're always throwing up your education to me. One would think you studied at Oxford instead of the trash bin behind the city library." She returned to *La Vie de Jeanne d'Arc,* in which she'd made scant progress.

Johnny had then wired out the notices with payment.

Lizzie saw the advertisement in the *Call* and pointed it out to the Major, who'd seen the paper first but seldom ventured beyond the theatrical columns. They dispatched a telegram to New York saying they were under way, sent a message round to Peter Ruskin to inform him they would be unavailable to meet with him again in the foreseeable future, and set about packing their bags and trunk with the tent-show efficiency of experienced troupers. For once they settled their hotel bill; the guarantee of another successful season had made them expansive.

"Falstaff, by thunder!" said the Major on their way out of the lobby. "I've always wanted to play the old rogue."

"You do, Evie; you do."

After reading their message, Philip Rittenhouse lost no time. He closed his office, wired Chicago that he was on the move, hurried to the station with his bag, and upon learning that no couple of the Davieses' description had bought tickets that day, waited in an unobtrusive corner of the depot for them to arrive. He'd traded his bowler and loud waistcoat for a soft hat and linen duster and now looked very little like either a booking agent or a detective. When the Madame and the Major swept in with all the furor and feathers of comic-opera royalty, he waited until they'd checked their trunk and boarded before buying his ticket. They rode in separate coaches. He knew their destination, thanks to the loquacity of the Major, and that there was small danger of losing them at some stop along the route. He avoided the dining car and the possibility of a chance meeting there; it had been important to convince them Wichita was too far for him to travel just to ensure their availability.

"Pleasure trip, sir?" The conductor handed back his punched ticket.

Rittenhouse smiled. "Yes. As a matter of fact, I suppose it is."

"One can always tell." He turned toward the next passenger.

Cornelius Ragland, who in keeping with a lifelong habit of caution had formed the custom of purchasing all three of the above-named newspapers daily, as well as the *Kansas City Times,* the *New Mexican* of Santa Fe, and the *Portland Oregonian* (although he admitted to himself he took the last mainly for the variety of patent medicines whose manufacturers advertised in its inside pages), read the notice in the *Denver Post* and sent his immediate reply, volunteering to make arrangements to transport their costumes and stage equipment from Denver to Wichita. Johnny's response came by return wire:

BREAK A LEG
FENTON

The young man treated himself to one last, luxurious soak in steaming sulphur water, returned to his room, read and made corrections on the last pages of *The Tragedy of Joan of Arc,* and put the draft in his old leather portfolio along with a copy of *The Merry Wives of Windsor* bound

in scuffed green boards and his notes for the adaptation.
He'd intended to polish his original play first, then orga-
nize his notes on the comedy into a script, but now he
would have to embrace Shakespeare on the train. He packed
his valise, paid his bill, and took the hotel carriage to the
station. He didn't regret saying good-bye to Hot Springs.
His stay there had been rewarding personally and professionally; his health was stronger than it had ever been, and
he had written the best thing of his young career, which he
did not delude himself would ever be an old one. But it was
a deadly dull place, and his adventures with the Prairie
Rose had spoiled him for the life prosaic. Thus, his patience
was strained when the conductor announced that the train's
departure had been delayed to make room for an express
train headed West; he had no details to add.

Five minutes later, Cornelius spotted the conductor on
the platform outside his window, in conversation with the
clerk who'd sold him his ticket. He lowered the window and
strained to overhear what they were saying.

". . . make it up on the other end if they'll just come on
ahead," said the conductor, frowning at his turnip watch.

The clerk set fire to a stubby pipe, broke the match, and
ground it underfoot. "When's the last time you ever knew
the army to hurry up and do anything?"

"Well, it ain't like Fort Dodge has needed 'em since the
injuns went west."

18

hen Tom Riddle was lying on his saddle blanket in a
dank cave half a day's ride from Table Rock, burning with fever on one side, shivering with cold on the other
(a living campfire steak), he changed.

He wasn't proud of it, never spoke of it, but a fact was a fact; color of one kind meant you'd tapped into the mother lode and color of another meant you'd tapped out, and no matter how hard or soft you swung your pick, you couldn't change it. If he could, he'd be soaking his saddle sores in champagne up on Nob Hill right now and not contributing to them on the board seat of a day coach rattling its way north to Kansas.

Normally he liked to talk, and if it had been anyone else who'd survived a .44 slug fired into his chest at close range and Breed's indifferent efforts to carve it out with his big Bowie, he'd have gone on about it in all its detail until Ace-in-the-Hole's voices rose in chorus telling him to shut up. Instead he'd contented himself with a stretcher he'd concocted during his convalescence on his sister's pig farm about teaching a hog to do sums. Tom saw himself as a pioneer on the road less traveled, both in his choices of professions—prospecting, then robbery—and in his ability to tell tall stories he made up as he went along. But being a changed man was a commonplace on the frontier, where every third man had fled to escape illness, creditors, and past mistakes, and where every third one of that third had changed his name in a ceremony of self-baptismal gratification. If he'd *wanted* change, goddamn it, he'd have gone through it when he pulled himself out of that badger hole in California where his friends had left him to starve. He hadn't (although he'd lost his enthusiasm for digging in any kind of dirt), and *that* had been something to brag on. It was a rare man who was satisfied with himself no matter what; but the business in Wyoming had put paid to that.

Whiskey tasted better, for one thing, and the glow lasted longer. His first time with a whore after his recovery had been as good as anything he'd conjured up lying on his back under the stars thinking of the pen-and-ink sketches of the corset models in Sears &Roebuck, and a bowl of beans and a slice of cornbread in Guacho's Cantina in San Diablo after the long hungry ride down had nearly taken off the top of his head. He slept longer and deeper, his dreams were drenched in rich color, and he awoke as alert and ready for the new day as a child. It was a pain in the ass.

The core problem was he had to keep it all from his companions. Life on the scout was just a little bit better than hell, if you listened to the padres and believed what they said about the contorted chains of mortal souls and the lake of fire. You got piles from riding day and night, you entered every town through the asshole-ugly back section to avoid passing the post office and jail where your description was posted for all to see and compare, you shelled out money like Vanderbilt to live in rooms a dog wouldn't shit in just to keep your name off the registration, and when you were flush you couldn't spend a nickel because you were hiding out in a cave or a cornrick or the hole under an outhouse because of the way you got it and how many people were looking for you to get it back. Bitching about the life was your badge of brotherhood, and if for some jackass reason—say, you're alive when you should be dead—you found yourself whistling in the saddle for the pure joy of hearing the notes, you were just asking the fellow riding next to you to blow your skull through the back of your hat.

"Tom, you look like you just pissed a porcupine. What're you so mad about?" Ed Kettleman plunked himself down into the seat beside him.

Tom straightened his spine. He hadn't heard him coming up the aisle. "I never did take to trains. Somebody else is in charge and you never know when you're going to get robbed."

Ed hooted. "That'd be a sight to see. I'd admire to know how Jack would take to it."

"I reckon he wouldn't, if Salt Lake City means anything." That whole episode made him think of Ed's brother. "How's Charlie?"

"Nutty as pecan pie. Now he's talking about hanging out his shingle. He says getting hit with that doctor's book ought to qualify him for a country practice. I sure hope he snaps out of it."

"Maybe if you clobbered him with a Jesse James dime novel."

"It'd take a stack. That book left a dent big as Fort Worth. What you fixing to do with your part of that seventy thousand?"

The car was half empty, and no one was seated near them. Still, Tom lowered his voice a notch. "Go to Venezuela, I reckon."

"What's in Africa?"

"Venezuela's in South America, you dumb Texican. They just got through fighting a civil war; now they're building railroads, just like it was here ten years ago. I could start all over again with my own crew, and there ain't a Pinkerton in a thousand miles."

This was the first he'd let anyone in on the idea that had been teasing and plaguing him since before he left Nebraska. In order to occupy his mind while he was healing, his sister had handed him a stereoscope and a box of glass plates, among which was a series about Venezuela: the Andes, as tall and jagged as the Rockies; the *llanos,* indistinguishable from the Great Plains; and Lake Maracaibo, which made the one in Utah Territory look like a glass of tequila with salt floating on the surface. There stood Caracas, the capital, which was San Francisco and Denver and St. Louis all rolled into one huge sprawl, with mansions on the hills and (he'd bet his cut of the payroll train job) cute little mud huts down on the flat where a man could have fun for a fraction of what it would cost him in any of those other places.

When he was strong enough to drive a buckboard, he'd gone into Lincoln on the pretext of bringing back supplies and spent a couple of hours in the county library reading up on South America. Venezuela had gold and copper mines and tobacco plantations to rival the vast cattle ranches in Texas, and the only law worthy of the name rode on the backs of mules in the persons of loose bands of federal officers, which if they were anything like the ones in Mexico could be bought with a sack of gold dust. Tom Riddle had decided that if there was a heaven for highwaymen, Venezuela was that place.

"What do they talk down there?" Ed asked.

"Mexican, I reckon."

"I didn't hear you talk much Mexican when we was in Mexico."

"What do I got to know except 'Stick 'em up?' "

"Well, you can have your South America, and I'll raise you China. Me 'n' Charlie are taking our cut and opening a saloon in Tijuana. Even the greasers there talk American, and we can have prizefights every Saturday night, and take a cut off the top of every bet for the house. It's legal down there."

"When did anything not being legal ever stop you and Charlie?"

"We been running from one kind of law or another since we was kids. It'll be good to find out what it's like sleeping on the right side of the sheet. Also Charlie can jabber all he wants and no one'll pay him any more attention than a burro with a bellyful of loco weed."

"You can always put a burro down."

Ed rubbed his slack unshaven jaw. "I'll warrant you don't have any brothers."

"I got a brother-in-law on that pig farm I wouldn't mind putting down. He'd of charged me rent for that ticky bed if Aggie'd let him."

"It ain't the same thing. I'd take it a favor if you didn't bring it up again."

Tom was enjoying the conversation, that was the hell of it. He wondered just how long it took being happy to be still alive to wear off. It was worse than mescal, which made you drunk all over again every time you took a drink of water for a week. He changed the subject. "Where's the Mexicans?"

"Boxcar. The conductor didn't like their look, even without their bandoleros on. I expect they think it's a Pullman. They ain't rid inside since before the revolution." Ed produced a plug and offered it to him.

Tom shook his head, and looked out the window while the other cut himself a cud and went to work on it. For some reason, chaw was one thing Tom had lost his taste for; just watching someone chewing revolted him, and the smell made him ill. "What are the others fixing to do, you reckon?"

"I figure Jack to bury his part and go on sticking up banks and trains and shooting folks till they put a slug in him or string him up. I don't figure he got into this for the money as much as raising the devil. Breed, he'll just keep getting worse and worse till they elect him governor of hell. I don't calculate Old Scratch will put up much of a contest."

"What about Mysterious Bob?"

"Shit, I know better how that locomotive up front thinks than I do Bob. I seen him reading a book once written in Greek."

"How'd you know it was Greek?"

"I asked him what that book was he was reading. He said it was Greek."

"You believe him?"

"I don't see why not. It was just about the longest conversation we had since I knew him."

"What was the book about?"

"I didn't ask. I figured why push my luck. Anyway, the print looked like a mess of squashed bugs."

"Huh."

Ed nodded. "That about sums up Bob."

"When's the next stop?"

"About an hour. I asked the porter. We change to the Kansas Pacific in Wichita."

Johnny Vermillion had smoked a cigar on a balcony overlooking the Champs Elysées, with the gas lamps glowing saffron at twilight and stately coaches rumbling along the broad avenue with the Arc de Triomphe at their backs; drunk fifty-year-old port on a barge gliding down the Thames past Big Ben, the Albert, and the Houses of Parliament; wagered the last of his father's allowance on a single hand of poker in the bridal suite of the Palmer House, hung with cloth-of-gold and decorated further with Chicago's most beautiful ladies of the evening clad in nothing but their beauty patches; attended a reception for Lillie Langtry at the Academy of Music in New York City, where she'd sung selections from *Faust*; yet none of these places had granted him so fine a view as the window of his room in the Occidental Hotel in Wichita, Kansas, looking out on Douglas Avenue and the homely two stories of the Longhorn Bank.

He knew its history, as he was a serious student of his profession who learned all his lines as well as those of the other members of his cast, and was moreover a quick study. Open only two years, and christened strategically to attract both the cattle barons of Texas and the meatpacking moguls from Chicago, the institution advertised more than a million in assets, and at the height of the season (which it was approaching) stored as much as fifty thousand in its vault; in gold and silver, since neither the unlettered ranch-

ers nor the swollen-bellied businessmen who had survived the Panic of '73 trusted securities or greenbacks. He
wondered just how much that came to in pounds and
ounces, and whether he might have to make arrangements
involving some form of transportation other than Lizzie's
bicycle.

He knew the bank's present as well, or as much of it as
five days of casual observation could provide. At half-past
nine every weekday the guard, middle-aged and limping
slightly in a tight blue uniform and forage cap from which
all the military insignia had been removed, arrived and let
himself in the front door with a key attached to a ring the
size of a duck's egg; he wore what appeared to be a big
Navy revolver in a scabbard on his left hip. ("Left-handed,"
the observer noted.) The manager, a comfortable-looking
fat man in a clawhammer coat, appeared fifteen minutes
later, followed in close order by three cashiers, young men
dressed respectably but more simply—a diplomatic decision, no doubt. Almost invariably, customers were waiting
when the CLOSED sign on the door was reversed and the
door opened to the public. The routine never varied more
than a minute either way, and traffic coming and going was
steady until nearly closing, when it increased noticeably as
the hands crept around the clock toward four.

Johnny pondered briefly the wisdom of liberating the
early-bird customers of their parcels, but rejected that plan
on the theory that they would contain no more than one
day's receipts on the part of Wichita's other businesses, or
possibly documents of no value to the Prairie Rose. It would
be like leaving a laden banquet table with only crumbs
from the floor. In addition, he had developed a keen interest in the fat manager.

The spring roundups and brandings were over. The
drives had begun. Very soon, thirsty cowboys would de-
scend upon Wichita at the heads and flanks of thousands

of bawling beeves. The street would become a river of swaying horns and twitching tails, and the Longhorn vault would fill with Eastern money to buy them and the profits from the saloons and bawdy houses, stuffed to bursting with the drovers' wages. Johnny threw up the sash and breathed in the stench of herds past; that which offended April's delicate nostrils smelled to him like early retirement, and after only two seasons in the theater.

Then something happened that caused the image of money on the hoof and gold in his pockets to evaporate.

It started as a shudder, as of a thunderhead forming far out on the plain, or coal sliding down a chute on Michigan Boulevard. Then the sound separated into a rhythmic tramping. It was too regular for cattle, and too measured for hoofbeats. Then the first column of infantry rounded the corner from Second Street onto Douglas: blouses buttoned, caps tilted forward, a Springfield rifle on every shoulder. A master sergeant marched alongside them, chevrons blazing, bellowing cadence. Pedestrians and loafers gathered on the corner to watch them pass, merchants stood in the doorways of their shops, hands in their pockets. Two minutes passed, and half a hundred soldiers, before Johnny realized that his own heart was thumping in rhythm with their booted feet. A great deal more time seemed to have gone by before the end of the column passed beyond his view. A dog trotted behind, pausing to sniff for promising jetsam, then lost interest and scampered down the alley next to the bank to lift a leg next to a rain barrel. The pedestrians resumed walking, the loafers loafing. The merchants retreated behind their counters.

"Shut the window, Johnny. Isn't it bad enough the whole town smells like a stockyard, without the reek getting into the linens?"

He slid down the sash and turned from the window. He hadn't heard April entering. She wore one of the plainer outfits she'd bought in Paris, a blue cotton suit with gray suede patches on the shoulders and a hat of the same blue material. The inevitable parasol hung from one wrist by a thong.

"Knocking is a sound idea here in the provinces," he said. "You forget we're no longer Mr. and Mrs. McNear."

"Not at present. Anyway, I'm an actress. My morals are already in question. You must know everything there is to know about that bank from the outside by now. Isn't it time you paid a visit in person?"

"That time may have eluded us. Did you not encounter the Grand Army of the Republic on your way back to the hotel?"

"I've been back for an hour. I saw them through the café window: Boys. I doubt the entire company would offer a razor much challenge." She unpinned her hat and gave her hair a push.

"It's closer to a regiment. Do you suppose Corny or the Davieses got careless and tipped their mitts?"

"Don't talk like a Spitalfields ruffian. You never got closer to the East End then Waterloo Station. The army doesn't care what we're about. How conceited you are!"

"Who have you been lunching with, Phil Sheridan?"

"I had tea downstairs with the mayor. The dear old fellow manages DeMoose's Saloon, where I suspect he learns more from gossip than he does in his official capacity. The troops are here to reinforce an express coming through tomorrow. They're departing for the territories and some sort of campaign."

"Indian fight?"

"Oh, I suppose. We're not at war with anyone else, are we? It's so hard to keep up."

"I wonder if there's anything valuable aboard."

"Now, don't go off chasing butterflies. The mayor says the Longhorn does more business in Kansas than Wells,

Fargo. He was trying to impress me, poor dear. He's a stockholder."

"Well, *I'm* impressed. Why have I been wasting time standing at this window with you in my arsenal?"

"Why, indeed?" She smiled. "Oh, Johnny, we're such a good team. Can't you see we must seal the partnership?"

But he was facing the window again, and the path of the infantry. "Still, a train would be a refreshing change of pace."

19

Don't just stand around like a bunch of Denver whores. Get your goddamn horses before the train pulls out."

Tom Riddle, who'd paused on the busy platform with Ed and Charlie Kettleman waiting for the crowd to thin out, watched Jack Brixton's retreating back, headed toward the livestock car where they'd loaded their mounts in Texas. "Who the hell stepped on his tail?"

"Jack don't sit still good," Ed said. "It puts him off his general sociability."

Charlie muttered something that may or may not have been a medical term.

Brixton and Mysterious Bob had their horses off the car when the three got there. The Mexicans they'd borrowed from Matagorda, looking more rumpled than usual after their trip in the freight car, stood in a knot waiting their turn. They conversed in volleys of bastard Spanish broken by high-pitched cackles and kept passing around the same hand-rolled cigarette. Tom wondered if tobacco was so hard to come by down there. Breed had some trouble with his gelding, but a swipe alongside its head with the bridle crossed its eyes and brought it into line. The bridle in place, it fixed a baleful brown eye on its master as it came down the ramp. It had never really come to terms with its surgery.

Nobody at the station seemed to pay much attention to this strange new band that had come to town. Cowboys black and white had gathered to see who was arriving and departing, harlots dressed in all the bright colors of tonics and restoratives in a barbershop patrolled the yard scouting up business, drummers in tight waistcoats and dandies in piped lapels bustled about swinging their sample cases and sticks. A tame Indian in a plug hat and a dirty blanket wandered around asking strangers for tobacco until the station agent came out from behind his window and sent him on his way with a kick in the seat. Tom guessed the man would have his hands full of derelict savages in a year or so; for a Yankee, Custer could fight.

While Ace-in-the-Hole was leading its horses off the right-of-way, the train blew its whistle and backed onto a siding to make way for another coming in from the West under a distant plume of smoke. Half the Mexican mounts, runty and earth-colored and scrawny as coyotes, had no saddles, just blankets, and hackamores instead of proper bits and bridles. They all looked like biters to Tom, who had not failed to note that most of the men who led them had pronounced limps. He bet they'd each left a piece of a haunch somewhere in the Chihuahua desert. They were the sorriest-looking bunch of road agents he'd ever seen: sallow-skinned, underweight, and bowlegged, dressed as beggars with holes in their sombreros you could pitch a jackrabbit through without touching the sides. It was no wonder the *federales* hadn't been able to run them to ground in ten years of trying; they'd galloped right past them, looking for guerrillas.

He had to ask himself how they spent the gold they'd

stolen in the past. He doubted cute little Fiona could handle them all, and none of the other women he'd seen in San Diablo seemed to be worth it.

While he was pondering, a hesitation in his bay mare's gait distracted him. He knelt to examine a hoof and discovered the shoe missing. Ed agreed to take the reins, and Tom went back to see if he could find it on the cinderbed. He carried a hammer and a sack of nails in a saddlepouch for such emergencies, but spare shoes added too much weight. Black Jack would call him sixteen kinds of a son of a bitch if he had to go into town to find a farrier.

He was about to give up the search when he spotted one iron leg sticking out from under the railroad platform. Bending to pick it up, he found his eyes on a level with a slim ankle in a black patent-leather pump. Tom was a connoisseur of ankles. He steered away from thick ones, no matter how pretty the face or narrow the waist that went with it; they always meant a coarse temper, and if you forgot yourself and put the band on, a fat middle age. It was as if God had provided them with a foundation firm enough to build on later.

From there, his gaze went up a tall frame, past a bosom that reminded him of a prairie hen, to a disappointingly mannish profile, just before its owner turned away to instruct a porter who approached pushing a big trunk stood up on end on a handcart. Tom stood, forgetting the horseshoe. He'd recognized the face.

He watched her step inside the station on the arm of a fat old goat in cinderproof clothing, wearing yellow gaiters and carrying a stick with a gold knob the size of a cue ball. She didn't seem to have seen Tom, but if she had he was pretty sure she wouldn't place him. During their one encounter in Denver, she'd been more interested in Charlie Kettleman, who'd knocked her off her bicycle just outside

Salt Lake City and stolen back the money she and her companions had stolen from the Overland office there.

Philip Rittenhouse, who seldom missed anything, did not notice the reaction of the man who rose suddenly from a crouch off the edge of the platform just as Major and Mme. Mort-Davies were leaving it; nor did he connect the wizened features with the spare description that appeared on circulars offering a reward for his capture or death, although he'd read it often. He did note in passing that the fellow was an experienced horseman, more comfortable in the saddle than on the ground, and was gratified, when at length the man turned toward the open prairie, to see him turn back and stoop to pick up a horseshoe lying loose beside the track. A drifter, from his clothes and sunburn, but not a cowboy. One of those tramps he'd seen so often during his two visits to the frontier, living on odd jobs and handouts and whatever he could steal.

Such was the train of his thoughts, and had he been able to follow it down its track he might have come very close to the truth—indeed he would have, if Ace-in-the-Hole were his responsibility and all his instincts pointed in that direction. But his concern was the Davieses and the man they had come all the way from San Francisco to meet, and whom he had crossed the country three times to see in the flesh. Tugging down his soft hat to conceal his bald head, and flipping up the collar of his duster to dissemble his reptilian features, Pinkerton's man in Wichita turned away from the worst gang in the West and toward the Prairie Rose.

Within five minutes of his arrival, he got that first look and nearly destroyed his mission in the process.

Stepping into the dimness of the depot from the dazzling sunshine on the platform, he was blinded momentarily and banged shoulders with a man striding in the opposite direction. The man was tall and well built and his momentum spun Rittenhouse halfway around, almost toppling him. Instantly the stranger caught his upper arms in two strong hands and steadied his balance.

"I beg your pardon, sir. I didn't intend to derail you."

When Rittenhouse's pupils adjusted to the light, he found his face six inches from the regular features of a young man with fair moustaches and a well-trimmed triangle of beard in the hollow of his chin. He wore a black hat with a dramatic brim, almost Restoration in its width, and a caped overcoat too heavy for late spring, but which contributed to the dash of his appearance as naturally as the fine stick he had tucked beneath one arm. His reassuring smile was even and white. The detective, familiar only with descriptions in theatrical reviews and a crude engraving in the *Deseret News* of the actor who had portrayed Brom Bones in *The Legend of Sleepy Hollow,* knew nevertheless that he was in the presence of John Vermillion.

He muttered that it was his own fault and turned quickly away out of the young man's grasp; but he knew his face had been committed to memory and that his undercover status had been compromised.

Alarm flashed through him. He darted a glance around the inside of the narrow building and was relieved to find neither of the Davieses among the pilgrims and greeters trickling toward the street and the waiting carriages. He'd managed to make a spectacle of himself at the very outset, and had they witnessed it, they'd undoubtedly have recognized him. Even the Major was not so self-besotted as to accept an explanation that Peter Ruskin had traveled all this way merely to secure their release from the company. They would report their suspicions to Vermillion, who would abandon whatever was planned for Wichita, and possibly dissolve the association. As the old man himself was fond of saying, it was not the responsibility of the Pinkerton National Detective Agency to prevent crime or put an end to it, but to apprehend the criminals and bring them to justice, preferably in full view of an admiring press. They were in business to attract clients, and whatever personal satisfaction they might derive from running a band of brigands to cover could hardly be recorded on the black side of the ledger.

Hanging back from the street door, which stood open to give egress to those assembled inside, he spotted the Major smoking a cigar on the boardwalk, and next to him his wife, brushing nervously at creases in her costume. Plainly they awaited the return of their companion, who passed Rittenhouse a moment later carrying a carpetbag that one of them evidently had left behind on the platform. In a moment they had all boarded a handsome phaeton with the couple's oversize trunk strapped to the back and rattled off.

Rittenhouse waited a beat, then stepped outside and caught the attention of a cabman, who stepped down from his seat to take his valise.

"Never mind that. My friends left before I could find out where they were stopping. Please follow them until they alight." He described the phaeton.

When that vehicle turned down Second Street and drew up before a hotel on the corner, he directed his driver toward a plain-faced structure that faced it at an angle, identified by a sign as the Douglas Avenue Hotel. He did not fail to note, as he paid the fare and turned toward the entrance, that his hotel stood next to a bank, and that that institution stood directly across from the other hotel and a few doors down from the elaborate facade of a variety theater. The Prairie Rose was a most transparent enterprise—an important factor in its success so far. It was a veritable Purloined Letter, boldly concealed in plain sight.

He asked for a room facing the street, and was given one on the second floor. After unpacking and placing his things in a maple bureau, the revolver tucked between two folded shirts, he went to the window, drew down the shade, and slid it aside an inch to study the side of the Occidental Hotel across the way. He'd hardly hoped to catch Vermillion or any of his crew at a window, but instinct and experience told him the room occupied by the head of the company would face the bank.

He did not, in fact, see anyone standing at a window, nor any shades drawn with no bright sunlight striking that side to justify it, but he was contented his theory was correct. He'd been in town barely half an hour, and had spotted both his quarry and its target, leaping far ahead of where he'd been in six months of hard work. It nearly made up for his blunder at the station and the likelihood that he would have to wire Chicago and request a replacement unknown to the repertory players.

Rittenhouse sighed. Unpacking had been a waste of time as well as an exercise in foolish optimism. Common sense—and Pinkerton policy—required him to turn over his information to another agent, and with it the opportunity to trip the snare personally. He would not even get to see it happen, as the old man would undoubtedly recall him rather than take the chance of his being spotted. He'd already risked a great deal in trailing the Davieses halfway across the continent and failing to report the action to headquarters, knowing what steps the old man would take if he knew. Now the choice had been taken out of his hands.

He was about to let the shade slip back when his eyes were drawn toward a movement in a doorway, where a common loafer—that fixture in every frontier settlement—removed his shoulder from the frame to touch his hat to a woman passing his perch along the boardwalk that ran past the Occidental.

Instantly the loafer was forgotten. Notwithstanding the fact that the detective was a confirmed bachelor, and an ugly man who had surrendered all thought of unrecompensed feminine companionship late in his adolescence, he appreciated a small waist and a dainty profile as well as any male creature. The appearance of both in a comely pearl-pink dress and clever hat under a matching parasol was compensation enough for hundreds of hours spent watching buildings and strangers and conveyances passing to and fro. His angle gave him a view of the front of the hotel as well, on Second Street, and when the apparition stepped briskly around the corner and lifted an abundance of skirts and petticoats to climb the steps to the entrance, he was certain he'd identified the member of the company who'd commanded more column inches on the part of masculine journalists than all the rest combined.

He found himself (he was loath to use a word that connoted personal weakness, but no other signified) enchanted. In the romance of newspaper work, every victorious general was handsome and distinguished, every visiting dignitary a gentleman, every actress older than twelve and younger than forty a vision, virginal and touched with stardust; the facts, that Custer looked like a basset hound, Grand Duke Alexis was a drunk, and Sarah Bernhardt had the morals of an alley cat and rather resembled one, were things the mature subscriber assigned to harsh reality. But no hyperbole did justice to April Clay in the flesh. Even from a distance, Philip Rittenhouse understood immediately that it didn't matter how well or poorly the young lady acted as long as one could say that he had seen her. And he knew then that no other employee of the Pinkerton National Detective Agency would be the one to put her in shackles.

20

As long as he could remember, Jack Brixton loved to blow things up.

He'd conducted his first experiment in detonation at the age of five, removing a tablespoonful of black powder from the keg his father used to charge his squirrel rifle and mixing it with the tobacco in his pouch. When that rugged old farmer touched a match to his tightly packed corncob pipe, the powder went up with a sharp crack and a blue flash, singeing his whiskers and eyebrows and puncturing his right eardrum, leaving him deaf on that side for life. It was all very satisfying, and worth the razor-strop beating that followed, even though it made thick welts on his backside that many a woman of lewd reputation would remark upon in later years.

From there he'd gone on to blasting outhouses, rain barrels, and a bobcat that had scratched him something fierce as he held it down and slipped a collar over its spitting head attached to a snuff tin filled with powder, touched off a fuse made from packing cord soaked in coal oil, and let it go. It was his bad luck that the cat had doubled back his way.

He recovered more quickly from the burns than from the scratches, which became infected, contributing to his general disagreeability; but the memory of the close call led him to the decision to leave such technical things as timing fuses to someone more qualified like Tom Riddle, who'd blasted holes through solid rock in California looking for color. But Brixton never lost his fascination with the destructive power of a well-placed charge. He'd been known to blow up railroad tracks that could just as well have been barricaded by chopping down a convenient lodgepole pine, and to burst open safes in spite of the presence of a cooperative bank manager with the combination, just for the pleasure of the spectacle. When dynamite came to the frontier in the late 1860s, he'd celebrated by having Tom dump three tons of Rocky Mountain onto a train carrying nothing more valuable than what was in the passengers' pockets. The account of the atrocity that ran in the *Territorial Enterprise* marked the first appearance in print of the nickname Black Jack.

Train robberies were his favorite, because of the amount of explosives required to bring a charging locomotive to a halt and open the doors of strongcars with guards forted up inside. A satisfying blast, with boards and bodies and lengths of tangled rail flying and reverberations that shattered windows in towns a mile away, was often all the compensation that was needed for a disappointing haul. Breed, alone among the members of Ace-in-the-Hole when it came to speaking his mind, had once told Brixton he'd have blown up General Jackson just to see if he was really made of stone. (Brixton, in a mellow mood at the time with bits of brakeman on his shirt, had merely smiled in response.)

Now, three days' ride from Wichita, Brixton clung to the timbers of a tall trestle spanning the Arkansas River outside Fort Dodge, watching enviously as Tom bound a bundle of dynamite to a diagonal support and smeared the twine with tar to prevent it from soaking up water in the event of a sudden rainstorm and coming loose. Tom unwound several yards of cord from a spool hitched to his belt and threw the spool underhand to Ed Kettleman, standing atop the trestle where it rested on the high bank. He waited until Ed caught it, then wet the end of the cord between his lips like a bit of sewing thread and tied it to a blasting cap. He then inserted the cap in the bundle with the delicate touch of a surgeon. Tom had fine hands for a former pick-and-shovel man, slender and spatulated at the ends like a piano player's.

"Whyn't you just tie it off and pay it out yourself when you climb back up?" Brixton asked. "If Ed missed, you'd have to climb all the way down to the river to fetch it back."

Tom drew a sleeve across his glistening forehead. "You know much about blasting caps?"

"Not a thing. I got out of the blowing-up business myself before dynamite."

"I used to prospect with a fellow name of Spangler. He came up with the same plan. He retired all over northern California."

Brixton scowled at the bundle of sticks. "It don't look like it would blow up much more than a man. You reckon it's enough?"

"It ain't how much you use, it's where you put it. You could tie it to that there strut and just impress the fish, but if you put it in the right place you can blow up Ulysses S. Grant and most of the Republican Party."

"I'd admire to do that. I would for a fact."

"That's where you and me choose up sides. I'm a common thief, not no anarchist."

Brixton narrowed his eyes, which never much opened wider than bullet creases to begin with. "What's got in you, Tom, apart from that Yankee banker's slug? Sometimes I think you got your brains all scrambled like Charlie's."

Tom thought, not for the first time, of telling him about the woman he'd seen at the Wichita station. But Brixton was unreasonable when it came to that Prairie Rose crowd. His fixation seemed to run counter to Ace-in-the-Hole's best interests. Once again Tom censored himself. Above all he had to keep secret the euphoria he felt each time he drew a breath. Black Jack wouldn't understand it, and what he didn't understand he extinguished.

"War's over, Jack. General Lee's writing his memoirs and the niggers got the vote. We got to stick with what we know best: robbing folks and blowing things up."

Brixton grinned, surprising him almost off his perch into the river thirty feet below. Black Jack just never showed his teeth except when he was gnawing on a chicken leg. "You ever blow up a bobcat?"

"You mean on purpose?"

"Well, sure."

"No, Jack, I can't say I ever did. I blew up a cinnamon bear once, but it just happened to come along when the fuse ran out."

"Bobcat's a mangy critter, sucks eggs and licks its privates right out there in front of God and Jefferson Davis."

"That may be so, but I don't see the percentage in blowing one up."

"You might try it once, I mean when you're testing a cap or somesuch. But you want to make sure and jump clear when you let go of it. You never know which way a bobcat's going to run once you got your charge in place."

Tom chewed on that. For the first time since he was shot he wished he had a plug between his teeth, just to cover up how much thinking he was doing. There weren't any rules at Ace-in-the-Hole about thinking as such, but there wasn't any evidence of it either, beyond the engineering. Weasels put their intellectual activity on hold once they'd found a hole in the henhouse.

"Well, Jack, I consider that smart advice. If I ever do take it into my head to blow up a bobcat, I'll be sure and jump clear."

But Brixton didn't appear to be listening. He was watching the Arkansas gurgling far below, carrying away twigs and muskrat huts and clumps of Kansas. "You ever blow up a building?"

"You mean like a bank? All you got to blow up's the vault or safe. You can pop open a Smith and Waddell with half a stick if you know where to put it, but a Foreman Choirmaster's made mostly of iron. Half a stick would just bend it out of shape. Two'd blow off the door and turn all the greenbacks into rat's nests. I wouldn't go beyond a stick and a half with no Choirmaster."

"I don't mean like a bank. I mean like a theater."

Something about the way Brixton drew out the word— "thee-ay-ter"—filled Tom with icy dread. The drawl had a drooling quality. The whole conversation had been a bubble off true, but this was hydrophobic.

He decided to play it out. "Six sticks might do it, if there's a second story. Maybe one more for luck. Depends on whether it's board or brick."

"Tell you when I know."

Brixton seemed ready to continue, but Breed's harsh twang cut across the noise of the river. He stood on the bank with his fists on his hips.

"If you two hens are through squawking, that train's due in ten minutes. Don't you figure we ought to mount up and make like we're fixing to rob the U.S. Army?"

Tom climbed up after Brixton. He'd never thought he'd welcome an interruption from Breed.

"Goodness me, what has become of our poor frail moth? He's grown into an eagle."

Cornelius Ragland, so hailed, stepped down from the vestibule into the embrace of Little Nell, Lady Macbeth, and Joan of Arc, distilled into one intoxicating beverage. One sip of April Clay and he felt himself floating above the train platform.

"Ponce de León was misled," he said, when he managed to land. "The fountain of youth was in the Old World all along; and you have come fresh from it."

"Such a pretty compliment."

"And uncannily specific," said Johnny, placing his stick on his shoulder. "How did you know she was in Europe?"

"I sent him a postcard from Paris. Don't be cross; I didn't write anything on it. What's the point of going abroad if no one envies you?"

"The culture, perhaps. The history, the museums, Queen Victoria, the crème brûlée at Le Grand Véfour. If envy was your aim, you could have bought a French postcard in Kansas City and posted it from there."

"With a Kansas City postmark? The effect would suffer, don't you think?"

"But how would you know where to send it? We all took special care not to tell the others where we were staying." He took the stick off his shoulder and tapped Cornelius on his.

"You needn't try to beat information out of Corny with your silly club. Where else would he spend his holiday, if not Hot Springs? He talked for months of taking the cure. Honestly, Johnny, you'll never make a successful criminal if you don't learn to think like a detective." She lowered her voice to a husky whisper on the last point, although the crowd had thinned out from around them.

"It was the coastal circuit for us." Major Davies, attired eccentrically in a deerstalker cap and travel-worn Inverness, wrung Cornelius' hand. "We were forced to steal out of Eureka in disguise to avoid a horde of well-wishers."

"Steal we did. They were quite eager to detain us. Welcome to the wilderness, young man. You indeed look fit." Mme. Mort-Davies leaned forward for a kiss on the cheek, a service he performed with some discomfort. The cheek was leathery and cold.

A porter appeared and asked him if he had any luggage to be unloaded. He shook his head, holding up his valise and fat leather portfolio. When the railroad employee withdrew, touching his visor, Cornelius asked Johnny if the costumes and properties had arrived from Denver.

"I had them placed in storage in the theater basement.

We'll go through it all for damage later. You look to have nothing less than the complete works of Shakespeare stuffed in that case."

"The complete works of Ragland, at any rate. I finished mutilating the merry wives on the train. Directly I'm settled in I'll begin transcribing copies."

April pouted. "What of St. Joan? Don't tell me you've given her up."

He smiled and drummed his fingers on the portfolio. "I wouldn't do that, so soon after the French. She's *en deshabille* at present, I'm afraid; not fit for your eyes."

"You're overestimating her exposure to the language," Johnny said. "All she managed to pick up in Paris were a few phrases and forty-four boxes of hats and parasols. She's been stuck on page ten of a biography of Joan for a month. He means to dress her in ribbons, dear, so you'll know her for a saint and not a scrubwoman."

"Oh, please don't torment me. I shall make allowances. I must read it right away or perish."

Johnny nodded. "I'd comply. She's pigheaded enough to do what she says, and then we'll be out our Anne Page."

Cornelius set down his valise, untied the portfolio, and handed her a thick sheaf of paper bound with faded ribbon. She seized it in both gloved hands and read the title page. "Oh! It's in English."

"I thought it best," he said. "In this country you can sing opera in any language but English. The reverse is true in drama."

They turned and drifted toward the station. Johnny placed a hand on Cornelius' shoulder. "I'm happy to see you. The Prairie Rose is back in bloom."

The Mexicans, who agreed without exception that Matagordo was a general of uncommon brilliance, had to confess that for a gringo, *Señor* Brixton was no slouch when it came to tactics and strategy.

First, he had set them to work with their machetes, hacking away undergrowth in the tall stand of trees north of the Arkansas River, leaving only a shallow fringe at the edge visible from the Kansas Pacific tracks so that it would appear not to have been tampered with. Then he had stationed them a dozen abreast on horseback among the trees where they would not be seen, far enough apart so that as the train approached the trestle they could slide through the spaces between as smoothly as water. When *Señor* Tomás, the man with all the words and an understanding of dynamite, touched off his two charges, destroying the trestle before the train and the tracks behind it, sealing it between, they would emerge, galloping and shooting and pinning the gringo soldiers in the crossfire from their guns and those of *El Jefe* Brixton's men on the other side of the tracks. When enough of the soldiers had been slain, and a number of single sticks of dynamite flung at the train from horseback in order to complete the confusion, both forces would converge, kill or stay the hands of the remaining defenders, and remove the payroll, to be divided among them when they assembled later at a place called Cimarron, in the panhandle of the Indian Nations across the Kansas border. It was a plan worthy of Juárez, only this time with gold rather than glory awaiting them at the end. A man could not eat glory after all, nor use it to bind his bare feet against rattlesnakes and cactus. These *Norteamericanos* were not so dull and slow-witted as they appeared when they came to the border towns to drink tequila and catch the clap.

Now the sons of Mexico sat on their tough, grass-fed mounts with carbines unshipped, listening to the clarinet whistle of the train and waiting for the first explosion, which was the signal to put the spurs to their flanks. Even

the horses were wound tight as watches, snorting and toss-
ing their manes and pawing the ground; but horses were
stupid and carried no memory of previous injuries. They
were in it for the oats.

"If just one of you greaser bastards twitches his thumb,
we'll scoop you all up with tortillas."

They turned their heads to a man. Not more than two or
three understood English, but the flat smack of the Middle
Western voice from behind them was gringo to the core. It
belonged to a red-whiskered cavalry sergeant seated in the
center of twenty men astride fat horses, and every one of
them had a Springfield rifle trained on a Mexican back.

21

It's a comedy of manners," Johnny explained.

The gentleman representing the *Wichita City Eagle,* a
wiry fifty with a tuft of white beard at the end of his
chin—the living embodiment of the character the political cartoonists of a later day would christen Uncle Sam—
smiled over his glass of wine. So far he'd shown no sign of
carrying a notebook on his person. "Most of our readers
know the meaning of comedy," he said. "You might have
to define manners."

Tim Saunders, proprietor of the variety theater, refilled
the man's glass from one of a half-dozen bottles standing
uncorked on the table. "You mustn't pay much heed to anything Mr. Cyrus has to say," he told Johnny. "He's determined to send the few subscribers he has left over to Mr.
Dockerty."

Dockerty, publisher of the *Wichita Beacon,* took his nose
out of his glass. It was a long nose, and a drop of wine quiv-

ered on the tip. "I'm not sure what good they'd do us. Most of them can't read."

Johnny laughed. "Give me a community whose newspapers are out to let each other's blood and I'll give you a well-informed populace. Briefly put, *The Merry Wives of Windsor* is the story of a scheming thief and the wondrous variety of ways he receives his comeuppance."

"I'd pay to see that."

This statement, and the voice that delivered it with a mild Irish lilt, drew Johnny's attention to a balding fellow with sleek handlebars. He wore a starched white shirt buttoned to the throat under a town coat and was the only man in the room not holding a glass. Johnny switched hands on his own glass and offered his right. "I don't think we've been introduced."

"Mike Meagher." The Irishman grasped it firmly and let go. His pale eyes held on to Johnny's afterward.

"Meagher's our city marshal," Saunders said. "His brother John is sheriff in this county. We pay them a king's ransom to keep the peace, and they earn it."

Cyrus of the *City Eagle* helped himself to the bottle. "Fortunately, we pay them a straight salary rather than a commission based on the number of men they kill in the performance of their duty. We'd be bankrupt otherwise."

An unhealthy silence followed, broken by Dockerty of the *Beacon.*

"That's the editorial policy that's shrunken the *Eagle*'s circulation and swollen ours: alienation and exaggeration. Without the brothers Meagher, we'd be burying innocent citizens by the day. We approve of cowboys, we do; they work hard, and they spend money like water, to our great benefit. But once they come out from under the harsh conditions of a long trail drive—well, a stampede would be hard put to compare with the damage to life and property.

Mike and John remind them of those manners Mr. Cyrus finds so scarce among his readers."

"Yes, a corpse behaves well under most circumstances." Cyrus drank.

"Mr. Cyrus prefers to keep his collar clean without the unpleasantness of a laundry bill," Meagher said, "and so I must pay it myself. As a dramatic actor, Mr. Vermillion, how many bows do you take when your villains go unpunished?"

"None, I'm bound to say. Our audiences will have justice or nothing. However, I'm happy to add that theater is not life." Johnny took a swift sip from his glass and beckoned to April, standing next to Cornelius and the Davieses with an affectionate hand resting upon the arm of her saloonkeeper mayor. The reception was taking place in a hospitality suite at the Occidental Hotel, with the press and leaders of the community invited. April drifted over, a glittering vision in a ruby-colored Paris gown she wore off the shoulders and a crown of white feathers in her hair. Her smile radiated when Johnny introduced her to the marshal.

"Such a strong hand." She squeezed Meagher's. "I haven't felt so safe since I left Park Avenue."

Meagher held her gaze as he had Johnny's. "I'm looking forward to the play. I'm told you catch a thief in it."

"And without a shot fired. Primitive, those Elizabethans." Cyrus stumbled over the last word. He was drunk.

"We don't catch him so much as teach him a lesson," April said. Johnny couldn't tell if she was fascinated with Meagher or transfixed by him, as a hen by a snake.

"Lessons are lost on outlaws. The only way to get them to change their habits is to change them for them."

"Perhaps that's why people enjoy our little fantasies," she said. "The world is so much less—forgiving."

"That's just what I was saying," said Johnny. "Look, there is Mr. Munn. I met him when I went to the Longhorn

Bank to make change. Please excuse us, gentlemen, while we mingle."

The men inclined their heads; all except Cyrus, who was draining a bottle into his glass. Johnny entwined his arm with April's and they moved away. "Munn's the manager," he murmured.

"Gracious, he's as big as a barn!"

"Not so solid as that. He has the lecher's eye. Let it rest on you a moment and he'll tell you the combination of the vault and how much he has in his wallet."

"It hardly seems possible he and that splendid marshal belong to the same gender."

"Steer clear of Meagher. I swear he suspects us of something."

They were nearing the fat bank manager, who turned toward them and away from a member of the city commission, tugging down the corners of his swollen vest. She giggled and fluttered a fan in front of her mouth; Johnny would have thought it over-the-top if she'd suggested it, but in practice it seemed to work. "Actors are always suspect," she whispered. "You've a touch of stage fright, that's all. You haven't trod the boards in months."

"You're right, I suppose. I just wish his brother weren't sheriff. They're both killers, Cyrus says. That stacks the odds a bit."

She laughed gaily and lifted her voice. "Oh, Johnny, don't be ridiculous! I'm sure Mr. Munn is much too important to offer investment advice to someone of my small means."

"Good girl," he whispered, and made the introductions. When the pair were deep in conversation he wandered over to join the rest of the troupe, where the Major insisted on addressing the mayor as "m' lord."

* * *

Philip Rittenhouse, sitting up in bed chuckling over Allan Pinkerton's *The Expressman and the Detective,* looked up at a knock on the door of his room and set aside the elaborately bound volume. He slid his revolver from under the adjoining pillow and padded over in his stocking feet. He put his ear to the panel.

"It's Meagher." The voice was muffled, but he recognized the slight brogue. He twisted back the latch and opened the door.

"I've just come from the reception," said the marshal when they were locked in. His gaze swept the room and alighted on the open book lying face down on the bed. "I hope you haven't been reading too much of that. If you hadn't told me what you have, I'd take them all for jackanapes; though the girl's a dash of ginger, I'll say that. They might pinch a watch or a poke, but as to desperadoes I'd be laughed out of town if I said that to a soul."

"That's good news. I asked you not to take anyone into your confidence, especially the bank manager. He'd tip his hand the first time he laid eyes on them, and we'd be back where we were last fall."

"I'm not so sure you shouldn't be. They seem harmless enough. I couldn't rattle them."

"These are actors. They're trained to stay in character. It isn't like buffaloing a drunken cowboy or chasing guerrillas. According to our calculations, they've stolen close to forty thousand dollars from seven places, probably with the same Colt revolver, without busting a cap. We don't even know if it's ever been loaded."

"I hope yours isn't. You're waving it around like an umbrella."

Rittenhouse returned the weapon to its hiding place. He'd forgotten he was holding it.

"They're not your usual marauding gang," he said. "Unless they've changed their method, which based upon its success so far I doubt they will, they'll send one of their actors into the bank while the rest are performing onstage, cleverly switching costumes back and forth so that no one in the audience realizes any of the cast is missing. The robber could be any one of them, even the women; both are experienced at portraying male characters."

"Not April Clay. Not even a bank cashier is that stupid."

"Pioneers are hard to deceive, yet she's managed to convince several hundred of them she's a boy. It's even easier for Elizabeth Mort-Davies; she needs her corsets and ruffles just to convince people she's a woman. She has a bosom, but it's easier to conceal than you might think. It's just flesh, after all."

"I was married, Mr. Rittenhouse. It's more than that."

"Only if the woman chooses to make it so. Clearly you don't know much about the theater."

"I've never attended a performance. When that curtain goes up I'm too busy rattling doors."

"Assign a deputy to that duty Friday night. I suspect you're in for a treat, no matter how you feel about Shakespeare." As he spoke, the Pinkerton indicated that day's number of the *Wichita Beacon* on the nightstand, open to a quarter-page advertisement announcing the opening of *The Merry Wives of Windsor (An Abridgment)* at Saunders' variety theater three nights hence.

Meagher shook his head. "If what you say is true, or even if it ain't, I'll be inside the Longhorn Bank that night. They've got a coat closet just big enough for a man and a Stephens ten-gauge. I hope you're right about that Colt not being loaded, or it's one of them three men sticking the place up. I never busted a cap on a woman. It don't mean I won't, if it comes to that; but I'll lose some sleep."

"They'll choose the matinee Saturday," Rittenhouse said.

Meagher made no comment, no matter what he thought of the bald statement. The Pinkerton admired that. Some of these frontier lawmen were more than guerrillas with badges. He went on.

"The Longhorn closes at four o'clock, same as every other day of the week, and all the employees including Manager Munn go home at half past the hour. At two o'clock Saturday afternoon, Munn and Edgar English, his head cashier, lock themselves in with the week's transactions and the ledger and make sure everything balances before the bank reopens on Monday. That gives them all day Sunday to clear up any discrepancies. The guard isn't present, and no customers are flowing in and out. They're never less than two hours adding up the columns and double-checking the figures. The curtain goes up on the matinee of *The Merry Wives of Windsor* at one-thirty Saturday. If I were the Prairie Rose Repertory Theater, I'd give my audience one act to become absorbed in the genius of the Bard, then rob the Longhorn Bank shortly after intermission; say, between a quarter past two and three o'clock, when Falstaff is making his escape from the clothes basket. I'd choose Major Davies for the actual stickup, as he's invisible from the audience for most of that scene. I could be wrong on that detail."

Marshal Meagher smoothed the corner of one of his moustaches. "You wouldn't mind showing me those credentials of yours once again, Mr. Rittenhouse?"

Rittenhouse laughed and produced them from beneath the Bible in the drawer of the nightstand. "Detective work is worlds away from merely keeping the peace," he said. "You find yourself thinking more often like a criminal than like a defender of justice."

Meagher returned the badge and business card. "All the same, I hope you won't take it hard if I skip Saunders' theater and try the door of the Longhorn Friday night."

"Certainly not. I'll be in the doorway of the Occidental, just across the street."

Cornelius Ragland looked up from his pocket-size translation of Molière, realized the horse-faced waiter standing there had asked him a question, and pushed forward his glass for a refill of mineral water. The waiter carried away the empty vessel with an air as if it weighed ten pounds. Cornelius considered withholding his gratuity, or perhaps leaving one of preposterous size to teach the fellow humility, but knew that in either case he would have lost the battle of the classes. Johnny, he felt sure, would have sent the fellow after some impossible vintage of French wine, and regardless of whether the waiter was successful, reduced him to his station by leaving a banknote of an unconscionably large denomination. Instead, he sighed, fished out a quarter, and slid it under his linen napkin, to be discovered after he'd drunk his water and retired upstairs. He would never be Johnny Vermillion no matter how hard he tried.

"Thank goodness I found you, Corny. I knocked and knocked at your door. I thought you'd taken a sleeping draught."

Molière was better than his press, and his press was exquisite. He'd lost himself once again in those lines, so deceptively featherweight in their grasp of the gravity of the absurd, and had missed the descent of an angel (devil?) into his world. April, still clad in the exquisite jewel-colored dress she'd worn to the reception upstairs, stood before his table with a beautifully embroidered shawl drawn over her shoulders. She cradled the hefty manuscript of *The Tragedy of Joan of Arc* in one arm.

Quickly he closed his book and rose, nearly upsetting his glass. "I wasn't sleepy. Will you join me? May I order for you?"

But the horse-faced waiter was already there, genuflecting. April never had to wait more than a few seconds for service. She smiled. "Tea, I think. Charge it to two-oh-eight; and the gentleman's order as well."

"The gentleman is having water."

"The gentleman will have tea as well," said Cornelius; and for that one moment knew what it was like to be Johnny. "Charge both to two-sixteen. I insist," he told April firmly.

He managed to beat the waiter to her chair and held it for her, then returned to his own. She placed the stack of pages on the table in front of her and pushed her shawl back off her shoulders, seemingly oblivious to the male heads that turned her way from nearby tables. She spent some moments turning back sheets. Their tea came. She paid no attention as waiter and tray withdrew. Finally she paused with her finger on a line of neat cursive, then slid a gold lorgnette from between her breasts and peered through the small egg-shaped lenses. Cornelius smiled. This was a new affectation.

She lifted her eyes to his. " 'Seraphic'?"

"Angelic," he said. "Isaiah had a vision of seraphim hovering above God's eternal throne. In this case I used it as a substitute for 'pious.' It's difficult not to overemploy the term when one is writing about St. Joan." He stirred his tea. "Shouldn't you be reading *Merry Wives*? We open in three days."

" 'The dinner is on the table; my father desires your worships' company.' I know it backwards and forwards. For the leading lady, it isn't a very big part. Not like Joan."

"It's much smaller in the original. I borrowed some of Mrs. Page's best lines for you; I'm afraid it altered the character. Somehow I doubt Shakespeare would object if he ever saw you in performance."

"That's charming, and quite sweet. People are always

presuming to speak for Shakespeare, but I have an idea he was a tyrant in rehearsal. Look at Johnny."

"He has a lot on his mind. It's more important to him that we all behave like actors than it is to the head of the average company."

"You needn't apologize for him. I know him better than anyone. That's why I proposed marriage."

A lance went through his heart. He had to clear his throat of the butt end before he spoke. "Does that mean congratulations are in order?"

"Not just yet. He said no. I'm wearing him down, however." She shuffled pages, and remembered the lorgnette. "Joan's frocks are very simple. The scenes in armor will be stunning, but the rest of the time I might as well be one of Lizzie's nuns. This huge cross, for instance; it says here I'm to hang it around my neck. Can I not wear it a bit off the hip?"

"I'll have to consult my sources, but offhand I'd say no. It was the Dark Ages, not *La Belle Epoch*."

"I'm concerned about the waistline. There isn't one."

"We can do something about that, I suppose. Do you like the part?"

"It's fascinating. She's a bit less humble than I'd expected."

"I wrote her with you in mind. You're more interesting than Nilsson."

"You're a dear." She sprang up before he could rise and leaned down to kiss his cheek. She gathered up the pages. Her teacup was untouched. "A bit of gold braid, perhaps, around the waist; with a tassle. I almost forgot." Her voice dropped. "Johnny said to make sure the revolver's in working order."

She said good night and left, her skirts rustling like pages of gold leaf falling.

Cornelius drained his cup of a beverage for which he had

no liking, then drank water to rinse the brown taste from his tongue. His face felt hot, but he didn't think it had anything to do with his old malady. He knew then that it was possible to burn with jealousy. He had no doubt April would wear Johnny down. They would marry, and she would take him away.

22

Ed Kettleman said, "Is that train slowing down?"

From the Kansas Pacific tracks, the land sloped down gently toward a patch of scrub oak almost directly across from the stand of trees where General Matagordo's Mexicans waited on horseback for the first of Tom Riddle's two charges to go off. Ace-in-the-Hole lay on their bellies among the stubbly growth, their horses down beside them, each with a hand on its neck to comfort it while in such an unaccustomed position. From there, every man could see the sputtering sparks and coxcombs of smoke belonging to the two fuses, the one to the left burning faster; Tom had allowed a gap of ten seconds to give them time to mount up during the confusion caused by the collapsing trestle. The frontal assault would commence simultaneously with the second explosion behind the train.

There were only five cars, counting the tender and caboose: a day coach where the officers rode, the strong-car containing the payroll for the Indian campaign, and a flatcar behind that, bristling with armed troops, made up the rest. With the troops exposed in the crossfire from the Mexicans and Brixton's men, and Tom hurling more dynamite from horseback as they charged, the cargo would be theirs for the taking. But Ed had been right. The train was definitely throttling down as it approached the trestle, and the brakes were being applied; the wheels screeched, spouting geysers of orange sparks from the friction. The chugging slowed.

"Maybe the engineer don't trust the bridge," Ed Kettleman said.

Tom chuckled. "He don't know the half of it."

"Pipe down and get ready." Brixton's voice was tight.

The trestle went up in a huge blossom of smoke and fire and dirt and sawdust and twisted girders; they felt the rumble beneath their sternums and rose as one, scrambling into their saddles even as the horses struggled upright, galvanized by their training under battlefield conditions. The troopers aboard the flatcar, well trained also, assumed combat positions, some kneeling, the rest standing to clear their field of fire. When the second explosion came, erupting in a dome of earth and steel like an elephant-size mole bursting through the surface, Ace-in-the-Hole was galloping full speed up the slope, spreading out and firing their pistols with rebel yells. Tom, carrying a coil of unattached fuse burning at the end, used it to light a stick of dynamite, whirled it over his head by a loop of fuse like a lasso, and flung it toward the flatcar, then lit another and threw that after the first. They discharged short of their target, but threw up a screen of dirt and smoke, through which the gang rode, shrieking and shooting, like demons through brimstone.

The returning fire, however, was heavy. Ed Kettleman yelled and fell off his horse. Breed's mount went down with a squeal of pain; the rider got his feet out of the stirrups in time to land running, caught Ed's riderless horse, and swung a leg over without losing momentum or his grip on his revolver. A bullet split the air next to Brixton's right ear with a crack.

"*Where in hell's the Mexicans?*" he shouted.

Just then he broke through the smoke into the open—and

hauled back on the reins hard enough to throw it onto its haunches had not that splendid animal the instinct and experience to adjust to the abrupt change. As it was, it reared and clawed the air, twisting for balance and nearly unseating its rider. Mysterious Bob, reacting even faster, spun his sorrel into a wide circle to slow it down and take himself out of the main path.

The rest saw the danger too late. Charlie Kettleman, Tom Riddle, and Breed were still charging hard when the big side door on the strongcar finished sliding open. When the sun struck the brass-bound barrels of the Gatling gun mounted inside, they tried to change course, but the chattering lead found them all and flung Ace-in-the-Hole in every direction like so many bloody cards.

It's not for nothing that professional thespians are so often referred to as players. When the trunks were brought up from the basement of the variety theater and the Prairie Rose dove inside to retrieve costumes and properties they hadn't laid eyes on in months, they laughed and jostled one another like children opening a chest filled with toys.

Major Davies, who was as fast as any of them once he got his bulk into motion, clawed out Falstaff's sword belt and doublet (these had served as well for *Twelfth Night*'s Sir Toby Belch, and would in fact suffice for all of the Bard's older gentlemen of gravity and healthy appetite, except perhaps the Romans), and had them fastened in place while Cornelius was still looking for Dr. Caius among the jumble and April and Lizzie were each tugging at a sleeve of the same ornate frock. Johnny, aloof to the scavenger hunt, waited until the congestion had cleared, then stepped forward and claimed his prize: a fencing foil with an elegantly rounded guard, fashioned from tin but painted to resemble gold.

Holding it at shoulder level, he peered down its length, frowned, exerted pressure with both hands to straighten a bend in the blade, then went into fighting stance and described a swift figure eight with the blunted point. At the swish, Cornelius looked up from the bit of lint he was removing from the plumed crown of the French physician's hat. He read the eager expression on Johnny's face, then shrugged, clapped the hat onto his head, and drew another foil from the same trunk compartment. They squared off.

Two minutes later, Cornelius stood pinned against a stack of leaning canvas flats with his foil lying on the floor six feet away and the button tip of Johnny's weapon pressing against his throat. The cast, distracted from their bright scraps of cloth, applauded.

The loser swallowed against the pressure. "Where did you learn that?"

"In Paris; where else? From the finest swordsman in France; who else? Also the one with the least pleasant personality. Which says a great deal when one is speaking of the French." Johnny withdrew his foil, described a bright whizzing pattern in the air, and slung the blade into an imaginary scabbard on his hip. It seemed to have left a thin blue phosphorescence in its wake.

Cornelius enjoyed once again the unobstructed motion of his Adam's apple. "You realize there is no swordplay in *Merry Wives*."

"I thought I might persuade you to write some in. I need the practice, and I don't think dear Will would object."

"With whom will you fight?"

"With you, of course. We represent two sides of a love triangle, do we not?"

The other hesitated. Of course Johnny was speaking of their characters in the play. "I won't be able to offer you much contest. All the fencing masters in Hot Springs left their hardware at home."

"You'll have lessons from the finest swordsman in Wichita. We'll work them into rehearsals."

"But, who will, er—"

Johnny smiled. "You'll make love to the fair Anne in Act Three, Scene Four. I'd thought of sending forth the Major after the clothes-basket business, but he's on probation for Salt Lake City. You've filled out, Corny; my costume will fit you this time without padding. Just wear your hat low and mind your moustaches are stuck on tight. Where is the revolver?"

Cornelius got the bundle from the chair where he'd hung his street coat, unwound the cloth, and handed him the Forehand & Wadsworth that Lizzie had found on the ground after she was assaulted outside Salt Lake City.

"I forgot we'd lost the Colt," Johnny said. "I hope we didn't make a poor trade. What did you do with the cartridges?"

"I took them out to clean it. Do you want it loaded?"

"God, no. Why change our luck now? April can tell you what kind of sharpshooter I am. I just wanted to make sure you didn't leave the shells lying around for the chambermaid to find."

"I threw them out the window into the alley."

"You aren't usually so foolish, Corny." April, who'd won the tug-of-war with Lizzie, held the frock against the front of her person, looking at herself in a dusty cheval glass with a crack down its center. "What if someone stumbles upon them?"

"This is Wichita, dear," Johnny reminded her. "The duellists don't allow each other much time to reload. There is bound to be spillage."

"I should take out my bicycle once or twice before Saturday," said Lizzie, fingering a loose paste diamond on a tiara. "I haven't ridden all year."

"That won't be necessary. I've made other arrangements to recover the money."

April looked up. "Without consulting us?"

"The details would only distract you. Our blocking needs work." Johnny tossed up the revolver, caught its trigger guard on the end of his foil, and extended it toward Cornelius. "Put away this fowling piece, good sir, and take up your weapon from the ground. This is an affair between gentlemen."

Cornelius returned the Forehand & Wadsworth to its cloth and bent to retrieve his foil. As he did so, a projectile the size and shape of a percussion ball grazed the back of his neck and struck the wall backstage with a sharp *ping*.

"Oh, damn!" said the Major. "I've popped a button off my doublet."

The best of it was Tom Riddle had found a cure for his euphoria. The worst of it was he was dying.

He'd been struck, he reckoned, three times by the Gatling. The hunk of meat he'd lost from his left upper arm could be patched up, and he'd done that after a fashion by tearing off his sleeve and knotting it in place with his teeth as he rode away. The broken collarbone was more serious, but the bullet had passed straight through, and Mysterious Bob, who knew a thing or two about stopping up wounds from the fighting in Missouri, had stuffed more rags into the holes that would keep Tom from bleeding out until he could get to a doctor. But there was nothing anyone could do about the slug in his belly. That was the payoff.

It hurt plenty bad, but not as much as he'd always heard. Mostly he was cold. The fire they'd built in the kitchen hearth belonging to the first farmhouse they'd come to couldn't reach as far as his insides, and that was the source of the chill. He lay on his back on the plank table where the farmer and his wife took their meals with his legs dangling off the end, staring up at a squirrel hole in the ceiling and trying not to move. He didn't know what Bob and Black Jack had done with the couple. Shot them, he supposed, or gagged and hog-tied them and put them in the barn.

Something gurgled. Tom didn't turn his head to see what it was. Brixton had probably found a jug. He and Bob stood guard at the windows near the opposite end of the house facing the road, in case the troopers came trailing them. It was a long open building, with no interior walls to divide it up into separate rooms. So far as Tom knew, they three were what was left of Ace-in-the-Hole.

"They knew we was coming," Brixton said. "You sure you took care of that greaser general?"

"I took care of him."

"Maybe it was his men. They never came out of them trees."

"They stood to profit better if the job came off. Somebody got the drop on them."

"Well, it sure wasn't Breed or Charlie or Tom, there; he's gone as the Confederacy. What about Ed?"

"Ed got it first. If he wasn't dead when he hit the ground, he was by the time we finished riding over him on the way out."

"It was that woman."

There was a little silence. Tom wasn't sure they'd heard him; it had come out in a croak.

"What woman's that, Tom?" Brixton's voice was so close it made him jerk. A fresh wave of cold swept through him, followed by a pain like a toothache in the pit of his belly. Sweat pricked his forehead like fire ants. He gathered up spit to take out the croak.

"That Prairie Rose woman. The tall one Charlie jumped in Salt Lake. I seen her that time in Denver and again in

Wichita just before we rode out. At the train station it was. I was as close to her as I am to you."

He saw Brixton's face then, looking down at him from up near the ceiling, and knew he'd miscalculated the distance between them. Black Jack seemed to be peeping through the squirrel hole. The hole was too small and his face too far away to see what was on it. But then Black Jack always looked sore.

"You seen her at the station?"

"She was with a fat jasper, probably the one stuck up the freight office. I didn't say nothing, 'cause you got a mad on against that there Prairie Rose, and we had us a train to rob. I was fixing to tell you about it after."

He breathed in and out a couple of times. He never thought talking would ever take so much out of him. That was one thing he'd always been able to do, even when he was stuck underground and drawing in a peck of dirt with every breath. "I reckon she must of saw me too, though I didn't think she'd know me," he said.

"You reckon?" Something squeaked; metal against leather, or maybe the squirrel was back.

"She must of went to the law for the bounty, and they told the army, and the army figured out the rest," Tom said. "That's how I see it. Thing is—"

"Shut up, Tom." The muzzle of Brixton's big American was as big as the squirrel hole. It swallowed Tom up.

The Wichita Variety Theater provided only a single dressing room for its visiting artists, but it was large enough to accommodate a company larger than the Prairie Rose, with a cheerful buffalo-plaid blanket suspended from a rope tied across the middle for the modesty of the female players. Tim Saunders had added a second entrance for the ladies and planned to construct a permanent partition by next season. Cornelius, who shared space with Johnny and Major Davies, entered that side without knocking and found the head of the company filling two crystal glasses from a stout black bottle, using the top of an upright trunk for a table. The Major plucked one up and sniffed at the contents. Sir John Falstaff's cotton burnsides still adhered to his scarlet face, and nineteenth-century galluses held up Johnny's puffed Elizabethan pantaloons, the straps resting on shoulders clad in a white linen undervest.

The newcomer bore the Saturday editions of both the *City Eagle* and the *Beacon,* containing excellent reviews of the Friday-night opening; but as he was sure the others had seen neither, he drew the obvious conclusion.

"I take it things went smoothly at the bank."

For answer, Johnny tilted the neck of the bottle in the direction of the oilcloth sack slumped heavily on the chair of the dressing table; it was the twin of the one that had been taken from Lizzie in Utah, along with the money the Major had robbed from the Overland office there. Johnny filled a third glass and held it out.

"You brought it *here*? What if there's a search?" Cornelius took the offering and swallowed half. His face flushed as from fever.

"Easy, old man; that port slumbered a quarter-century below ground before I woke it up and carried it across the sea. It's a bit touchy. As for the sack, I told you I'd made other arrangements."

"What sort of—"

"Goodness, what's the fight about? I should have thought you lads had spent all your energies playing at swords." April emerged from behind the blanket, brushing her hair. She wore a green silk dressing gown with matching slippers and her face glistened with residue from the cream she used to remove her makeup. Without paint and powder she looked as fresh as a child.

"Corny thinks we're about to be pinched. I say, this is capital stuff." The Major took another drink.

Lizzie emerged in a faded-pink terry robe, veteran of a dozen tours, took the glass from his hand, and helped herself to a healthy sip. "Evie, this is far too rich for you. You'll be down with gout before dark."

Johnny poured another and handed it to April. "I was just explaining that a new season calls for a new system. Especially since it's our last. As of today, the Prairie Rose Repertory Company has taken its final curtain call."

Eyebrows shot up all around. Cornelius was first to find his voice. "Did we do so well, then?"

"I hadn't time to count, of course, but I've gotten to be a fair judge of weight since we opened in St. Louis. It seems an excellent year for the United States beef industry. We should clearly sixty thousand after expenses."

The members of the company began chattering all at once. April threw her arms around Johnny's neck, spilling port down his back. He disengaged himself and called for quiet. "Come, come. The reviews can't be *that* good; drowning out the cowboys will only lead to suspicion."

Cornelius said, "It's a bit late for caution, isn't it? We haven't even begun packing, and that blasted sack's a prison sentence for us all."

"Dear old fellow." Johnny set down his glass. "What exactly do you think is in it?"

"Empty ink bottles, or I've misjudged my source."

This was a new voice, coming from the opposite end of the room. The company turned in a body to look at the stranger who'd appeared from behind the hanging blanket. He was an ugly toad of a man with a polished bald head, wearing a suit that needed a press and a brush.

"Good Lord, it's Ruskin! What are you doing so far from—Barbary?"

The Major's voice trailed off on the last word. Lizzie had placed a hand on his arm, silencing him.

"Philip Rittenhouse. I represent the Pinkerton National Detective Agency." With the air of a man somewhat ashamed of its gaudiness, the stranger opened a leather folder to which was pinned a golden orb engraved on a shield.

No one moved. Rittenhouse pocketed the badge and stepped forward to seize Johnny's hand. "I can't tell you what a pleasure it is to meet you. I've followed your career with keen interest ever since Nebraska. I'm sorry I missed both performances here. Last night I was busy, but I did manage to catch a piece of your act this afternoon; from the back row, as it were. You were in and out of the bank so fast I almost missed you."

When he let go of Johnny's hand, it fell to his side like an empty sleeve. Rittenhouse walked around the silent half circle as if it were a reception line, shaking masculine hands and bowing crisply over feminine ones. "Miss Clay: Brava. Major Davies: I apologize for misrepresenting myself in San Francisco, but thank you for the splendid review. I'd hardly hoped to impress so experienced a pair of thespians as you and Madame Mort-Davies. Madame. Mr. Ragland: Perhaps when Mr. Pinkerton publishes his account of his investigation you'll consent to look at the galley proof and provide comment. The reading public responds favorably to endorsements by other famous writers."

Johnny cleared his throat. The Pinkerton looked at him. There was something beyond amusement in the reptilian face. It was almost the proprietary pride of a sincere admirer watching him step back into character after a profound shock.

"Mr. Rusthouse—"

"Rittenhouse; but I think you knew that. You've a reputation for committing pages of dialogue to memory swiftly. Floor plans as well."

"Rittenhouse. You've made an honest blunder. You overheard us rehearsing Mr. Ragland's new play and drawn the obvious conclusion."

"Please pardon the interruption." Rittenhouse raised his voice. "Come in, Marshal. You have the key."

No one but the Pinkerton appeared to have noticed the knock at the door. It opened and Marshal Meager entered, carrying a short-barreled shotgun.

"I doubt you'll need that." Rittenhouse took a step past the chair where the oilcloth sack rested, lifted the Forehand & Wadsworth from the table, and inspected the chambers. "Empty. Stage pistols usually are, unless the script requires blanks to be fired. But then there are no revolvers in Shakespeare." He slid it into his right side pocket. From the left he drew April's Remington derringer, balanced it on his palm a moment, then returned it. "Two rounds there, but a lady needs protection. All the more reason not to leave her reticule lying around."

April stepped up to Rittenhouse and slapped his cheek. Meagher said, "Hey!" and palmed back the shotgun's hammers.

The Pinkerton raised a hand to calm him, then used it to rub the red patch on his sallow skin. "I'll cherish that, Miss Clay. No woman's even kissed me, let alone struck me for a cad."

"You're worse than a cad. You're a detective."

"Haw-haw!" barked the Major. "If I had my stick, I'd give him another memory to press between his pages."

Rittenhouse picked up the sack suddenly and shook out its contents. They clattered to the floor with a noise that rattled eardrums, but none of the hundred or so squat ink bottles shattered. They were made of thick glass, and although many had no stoppers, no ink spilled out.

"LaVern Munn, the Longhorn manager, is a frugal man," he said. "The bank goes through a lot of ink in six months' time, but he saves the bottles and returns them to a man who comes through twice a year to collect them for the ink company to refill. The company pays him ten cents a pound for the service." He looked around. "I can tell by your expressions that Mr. Vermillion didn't take you into his confidence. He seems to enjoy surprising people."

"Who told *you*?" demanded Cornelius.

"Mr. Munn, when I confronted him with what I'd learned about him from my colleagues in Chicago. Before he emigrated West, our banker friend ran odd jobs there for the late Scipio Africanus McNear, principally delivering graft to the heads of various city departments. He failed to deliver some of it, and fled here to invest his new fortune. Would you care to provide the rest, Mr. McNear?"

"Vermillion," Johnny corrected. "There's no law against being a politician's son. What's the penalty for stealing fifty dollars' worth of empty bottles?"

"I think we can persuade Marshal Meagher to waive that charge. That is, if his people caught the shipment?" Rittenhouse looked at the lawman.

"I just got the wire. Dodge City's got its hands full with a train robbery, but they took it off the nine-fifteen from Wichita. They're holding it."

Johnny seemed to remember then he was still holding his glass of port. He drained it, but the color barely stained his pale cheeks before receding. It was the first time the company had seen him other than saturated with his own confidence. Cornelius turned his head away.

"Munn's agreed to testify in return for a shorter sentence," Rittenhouse went on. "Vermillion threatened to expose his past if he didn't agree to turn over all the gold and silver in the vault. He was reluctant to bring up the five percent fee Vermillion allowed him for the service, but when I suggested searching the bank and his home, he volunteered that information as well. Once all the figures are tabulated, the examiners will find that Munn has embezzled no small amount on his own from his depositors. That's why Vermillion staged the robbery, so the sum could be rolled into the loss.

"The ink bottles were supplied merely to weight the sack and convince any chance eyewitnesses that a robbery had taken place. Munn gave Vermillion the money before the bank opened this morning, and Vermillion put it on the first train, addressed to the Coronet Hotel in Denver, to be held for the Prairie Rose Repertory Company. I got that much from the station agent, who saw to it personally that the large parcel was placed aboard."

"You're all under arrest," Meagher said.

Major Davies said, "I fail to see why. I knew nothing about any stolen money being placed aboard a train. My wife did not, and you've given me no reason to suspect either Miss Clay or Mr. Ragland. Actions taken by Mr. Vermillion without the knowledge of the rest of us reflect only upon himself. We are actors, not thieves."

"Oh, Evelyn," said Lizzie. "You really are the most contemptible creature."

Rittenhouse smiled at the Major. "I wasn't being untruthful when I told you in San Francisco I admired your talent. You'll have the opportunity to play before an appreciative audience when your case comes to trial; you all will. Just in case the witnesses I've established fail to identify each of you positively as a bandit in a series of robberies from Missouri to Utah, I have a preponderance of evidence that the Prairie Rose was performing in each of those places at the time of the outrage and a stack of glowing reviews testifying to your ability to assume disparate roles at the drop of a hat. It shouldn't be hard for a competent prosecutor to prove the possibility of so talented a crew to appear in two places at once."

"That won't be necessary in my case," April said. "I helped plan the robbery of the Longhorn Bank."

Johnny laughed his old laugh; once again he was back in character. "If you believe that, Rittenhouse, you belong to a legion. Miss Clay is a gifted actress."

"I helped as well," Cornelius said.

Lizzie said, "We all did. Stop spluttering, Evie. You know perfectly well you can't survive without me."

"Oh, blast." The Major dropped onto the dressing-table chair and emptied his glass. "I suppose I'll play Sidney Carton if I must. I despise Dickens."

Rittenhouse rubbed his hands. "Since you're all so willing, I'll ask the marshal to manacle Vermillion only. I doubt he brought enough for the entire troupe."

Meagher grunted and fell to the floor, sprawled facedown on top of his shotgun. Every eye in the room rose from the bloodied back of his head to the man standing in the open doorway behind him, holding a large yellow-handled revolver by its barrel. He spun it on his finger, palming the butt with a smack and thumbing back the hammer. His long granite face was burned as dark as his hat and his worn and faded clothes were streaked with lather. He stank of horse and spent powder. "Everybody stay put!" he barked. "This here's a snake that bites from both ends."

"Who the devil are you?" said the Major.

"Black Jack Brixton."

The newcomer swung his gaze on Rittenhouse. "Last man called me that wound up right where your friend is. Put them hands high. I heard enough to know you're heeled."

The Pinkerton raised his hands.

"You're Brixton?" Johnny said. "I thought you'd be taller."

"I'll look plenty tall when you're all bleeding out on the floor. This is the second time this herd of yours cost me a payroll train."

"What train?" April stepped in front of Johnny, who grasped her shoulders to hold her back.

Brixton lunged and took her wrist in his free hand, tearing her out of Johnny's grip. Johnny stepped forward. A harsh metallic clack stopped him. Heads turned toward a tall man standing in front of the blanket that divided the room, holding a Winchester against his hip with the barrel level and a fresh round racked into the chamber. He was burned as deeply as Brixton, his clothes stained from the same hard ride.

"That there's Mysterious Bob." Brixton spun April to face the others, twisting her arm behind her back. She cried out. "We call him that on account of nobody knows just when he'll cut loose with that repeater."

"What do you want?" Rittenhouse asked.

"I want you to wire Dodge City and get me that bank money I heard you squawking about," Brixton said. "But that can wait till we settle with these five."

"Why do you want to kill us?" Lizzie sounded as calm as the chambermaid in *The Diplomat Deposes*. "You got back all the money from the safe in Salt Lake City."

"That's spent. We had to quit Denver when you spotted Charlie Kettleman there. We was all fixed to hit the army train headed for the mint. Then we got ourselves shot to hell out by Fort Dodge on account of you seen Tom Riddle here and told the army. I think maybe I'll shoot that fat husband of yours first so you know what's coming."

"I don't know what you mean," she said. "I don't know any Tom Riddle."

Brixton made a movement that drew a gasp from April

and rested the barrel of his revolver on her shoulder, pointing it at the Major, who sat holding up his empty glass as if waiting for a refill.

Johnny made a long stride to his right. As the revolver pivoted that way, he swept up a fencing foil leaning in the corner and swirled the blade in a lazy *S*. On the upstroke, the button point snagged the inside of the muzzle and tore the weapon from Brixton's grasp. It made a slow arc and struck the floor near the outside wall, jarring loose the hammer. The report rang like a huge iron bell. A piece of gilded wood jumped off the frame of the dressing table mirror.

"Bob!" Brixton's shout was muffled in the echo of the shot.

Mysterious Bob placed the muzzle of his carbine against the back of Johnny's head. The foil dropped to the floor with a clank.

Rittenhouse had his hand in the pocket where he'd put April's derringer.

Brixton gave April's arm a yank. She screamed. "Take it out and drop it or I'll snap her arm clean off."

"Let her go first."

She screamed again. The Pinkerton drew the pistol out slowly and let it fall.

"You, sir, are a knave," said the Major.

Brixton let go of April's arm and shoved. She stumbled forward. Johnny caught her in his arms. Brixton went over and picked up his revolver. "I got five more in the cylinder. That's one for each of you and I'll let Bob finish this one." He kicked Meagher in the temple. The fallen marshal, who had begun to stir, groaned again and fell silent.

"What about me?" Rittenhouse said.

"I ain't got that far in my figuring. If you do a good job getting me that bank money maybe I'll let you see Chicago again."

Johnny said, "Someone must have heard that shot. The sheriff is the marshal's brother. He's probably on his way here with deputies."

Brixton grinned. "Well, then, I reckon I better get to it. Stand up, you." He turned his barrel on the Major.

"No!" Lizzie took a step. The Major flung out an arm, stopping her. He placed his glass carefully on the dressing table and heaved himself to his feet with a grunt.

"Tomorrow, and tomorrow, and tomorrow," he said. "I should have died hereafter."

Brixton thumbed back the hammer and took aim at the Major's broad middle.

An explosion shuddered the room. The Major winced and fell back against the dressing table. He groped at himself, opened his eyes.

The impact of the bullet had slammed Black Jack Brixton into the wall behind him, jarring the revolver from his grasp. This time it struck the floor without discharging. He slid down the wall with a look of wonder on his face. Then his chin fell to his chest and his hat tilted forward over his eyes.

Mysterious Bob lowered his smoking carbine. His unreadable face turned toward Rittenhouse's. "You'll have to take my word on it," he said. "I threw my badge away in sixty-five. You can't ride and camp with the same men for ten years and keep a thing like that hid."

V

The Comeback

24

Allan Pinkerton made three attempts to write *The Prairie Rose and the Detectives* and gave up after fifty pages. Although General Matagordo, a paid Pinkerton informant of years' standing, was alive and well and mourning the death of his favorite carrier pigeon in San Diablo, Robert Jules "Mysterious Bob" Craidlaw had committed many questionable acts in his efforts to win the trust of Black Jack Brixton and the Ace-in-the-Hole Gang, and no amount of literary license could guarantee that the attention would not blacken the all-seeing eye of the Pinkerton National Detective Agency. His publishers, G. W. Carleton & Co., agreed to accept a substitute case history, and *The Spiritualists and the Detectives* appeared in 1877.

For this reason, and the fact that numerous legal maneuvers delayed the trial of the members of the Prairie Rose until June 1876, when news of the massacre of George Armstrong Custer and the Seventh Cavalry at the Little Big Horn crowded every other story out of the lead columns, the larcenous adventures of Johnny Vermillion and his company of artists occupy no more than a line in the few histories of the West that take notice of them. Yellowing documents of court proceedings report the following:

* * *

Evelyn Beverly Davies, referred to variously as "the Major," "Old Porky," and, in England, "Sir Rot Rotter of Rotting Lane," was released by the State of Kansas for lack of evidence connecting him to the embezzlement of the Longhorn Bank in Wichita, but ordered to stand trial in Salt Lake City for the lone robbery of the Holladay Overland Mail & Express Company office. Daniel Oberlin, the Overland manager, identified him positively—mostly by his "plummy" voice—as the masked fat man who had commanded him to "hand over the swag." He was convicted and sentenced to serve three years at hard labor, which the judge reduced to probation because of the defendant's age and physical condition and the fact that it was his first offense.

Elizabeth Jane Mort-Davies, his wife, née Janey Timble, formerly of the Ten Tumbling Timbles, withdrew her confession to complicity in the Longhorn case on the grounds that it was made under duress. The charge was dropped against her as well, and although the Pinkerton National Detective Agency attempted to have her held pending the result of its investigation of the other robberies in which the Prairie Rose was suspected, none of the eyewitnesses who were questioned would submit that the "tall bandit wearing a bandanna" was a woman. She was released.

April Clay, alias Emma April Klauswidcsz, did not retract her confession, but her tearful appearance in the witness box, dressed fetchingly in widow's black lace, convinced the twelve men of the jury in Wichita that she was innocent. They acquitted her.

(No records exist to indicate that any attempt was made to try April Clay elsewhere. It's believed all such plans were abandoned after the case collapsed against Mme. Mort-Davies.)

Cornelius Ragland was convicted on the evidence of his

confession in the presence of Marshal Mike Meagher and Agent Philip Rittenhouse. The judge rejected the defense team's plea for clemency on the grounds of his delicate health, but suspended his two-year sentence because it was his first offense. He was immediately extradited to Wyoming Territory, where he was convicted of the robbery of the Cattleman's Bank in Cheyenne. He served eight months at hard labor in the territorial penitentiary and was released four months early for good behavior; guards told parole authorities he was an industrious worker "for a skinny feller," who gave them each a sample of the poetry he wrote in his cell.

LaVern Munn, charged with embezzlement and conspiracy to embezzle funds from depositors' accounts in the Longhorn Bank of Wichita, did not stand trial. He pleaded guilty to the lesser charge of conspiracy and received a sentence of six months. The sentence was suspended, with a warning never again to seek employment with a financial institution.

Johnny Vermillion, alias John Tyler McNear, spent nearly two years on trial in Kansas, Missouri, Nebraska, and the territories of Idaho, Wyoming, and Utah. He was convicted of all charges and sentenced to serve a total of forty years at hard labor, beginning in Kansas.

Topeka Daily Capital, Tuesday, March 8, 1878:

Authorities throughout the state have joined the hunt for five convicts who escaped last night from the Kansas State Penitentiary while Warden Lawler, many of his guards, and the majority of the convict population were gathered in the prison cafeteria to watch a theatrical presentation of *The Count of Monte Cristo,* performed by members of the incarcerated community. All of the men who are reported missing belonged to the cast.

Staff and penal servers alike appeared to be entertained by the play, adapted from the novel by M. Alexandre Dumas the Elder (ironically, about an escape from prison) by one John T. McNear—known also by the name Johnny Vermillion—who was also its director and lead player. So engrossed were the spectators that they sat for several moments staring at the crudely painted set after the makeshift curtain rose on the last act before realizing that the dramatis personae had fled.

Subsequent investigation revealed that each of the players had practiced assuming one another's role, and that by changing costumes created the illusion that no member of the cast was out of sight of the hundreds assembled for longer than two or three minutes. By this ruse they managed to take their leave of the prison piecemeal by means of a homemade rope ladder slung over a section of wall rendered invisible to the guards in the corner towers by deep shadow. Those still remaining took advantage of the brief interval between the second and third acts to follow in their path. The trusty who pulled the rope to raise the curtain has been isolated for questioning, but as of this writing continues to maintain his ignorance either of the plan or of the whereabouts of its practitioners.

All of the escapees are characterized as dangerous felons sentenced to periods of long servitude. McNear, who is believed to be the ringleader, is a convicted bank robber, described as . . .

Philip Rittenhouse, seated comfortably in his spartan office in Chicago, scanned the item quickly when it took its due place on top of his stack; then read it again slowly and with the pleasure of a man enjoying a good book. Then he picked up his shears and began to cut.

Forge

Award-winning authors
Compelling stories

. . . .

Please join us at the website
below for more information
about this author and other great
Forge selections, and to sign up for
our monthly newsletter!

. . . . www.tor-forge.com . . . .